DEATH OF A DREAM

Martin Luther King, Jr. broke down the rifle like an expert. He oiled it and rubbed it with a soft rag, even though it didn't need it. It had only had a single box of ammunition run through it to check the sights and the scope. He was amazed at how easy and natural it all seemed. . . .

He had no illusions. In the morning he would die. But he would take the President of the United States with him.

ALTERNATE WARRIORS

Edited by Mike Resnick

TOR®

A TOM DOHERTY ASSOCIATES BOOK
NEW YORK

This is a work of fiction. All the characters and events portrayed in this book are fictitious, and any resemblance to real people or events is purely coincidental.

ALTERNATE WARRIORS

Copyright © 1993 by Mike Resnick and Martin H. Greenberg

Cover art by Barclay Shaw

A Tor Book
Published by Tom Doherty Associates, Inc.
175 Fifth Avenue
New York, N.Y. 10010

Tor ® is a registered trademark of Tom Doherty Associates, Inc.

ISBN: 0-812-52346-6

First edition: September 1993

Printed in the United States of America

0 9 8 7 6 5 4 3 2 1

COPYRIGHT ACKNOWLEDGMENTS

To Carol, as always,

And to Gardner Dozois, Susan Casper, and Pat Cadigan, who really ought to be writing for this book rather than reading it.

NOTE TO THE READER

This collection of short stories is a work of fiction. Although some of the characters are real, they are used fictitiously; their thoughts, actions, and words, and the events surrounding them, are entirely imaginary.

Contents

Introduction

The late Isaac Asimov was very proud of having coined the phrase, "Violence is the last resort of the incompetent," which appears throughout his famed Foundation series.

I believe that it was another science fiction writer, Jerry Pournelle, who responded, "Right; the competent don't wait that long."

For this third in my series of Alternate anthologies for Tor Books, I decided to see which of those two men was right. It has been said that history is written by the winners—and the winners are usually on the side with the most guns and the best generals.

And yet, over the centuries, there have been a few men and women who have taught us to take that other route, the path of reason and pacifism. Some went down to utter defeat, but some triumphed over the longest odds: a quarter of the world's population believes in Jesus, who taught us to turn the other cheek; India, a nation of more than half a billion people, cast off the yoke of British colonialism by adhering to the philosophy of Mohandas Gandhi, the prophet of passive resistance; Nobel Prizes go not to generals and admirals, but to men and women of peace like Dr. Martin Luther King and Mother Teresa.

And yet it has also been men of peace and goodwill who have gotten us into situations from which it required supreme military efforts to extricate ourselves: Neville Chamberlain's "Peace in our time" speech from Munich springs instantly to mind.

How might history have changed had Chamberlain been willing to go to war, had Gandhi taken up arms, had Martin Luther King's dream included violence?

To answer that question, I sought out some of the finest science fiction writers around and posed the question to them. Each was invited to write a story about an historical figure, with the stipulation that in *this* alternate history those figures would fight for their beliefs rather than die for them, a subtle but very meaningful distinction.

As always, the remarkable men and women who ask *What if?* for a livelihood proved more than equal to the task.

—Mike Resnick

Julius Nyerere, the first president of Tanzania, is acknowledged to be one of the great socialist philosophers of this century. He was also the only African leader to stand up to Idi Amin, and eventually went to war with him.

Shortly after the war began, Amin offered Nyerere a challenge of a type that hadn't been issued in centuries: he and Amin would meet in physical combat, and the victor would be declared not only the winner of the fight but of the war.

Nyerere rejected the offer and won the war anyway, though it bankrupted his already-impoverished country. One of the nice things about science fiction is that it allows you to examine alternatives.

Mwalimu in the Squared Circle
by Mike Resnick

While this effort was being made, Amin postured: "I challenge President Nyerere in the boxing ring to fight it out there rather than that soldiers lose their lives on the field of battle . . . Mohammad Ali would be an ideal referee for the bout."

—George Ivan Smith
Ghosts of Kampala (1980)

As the Tanzanians began to counterattack, Amin suggested a crazy solution to the dispute. He declared that the matter should be settled in the boxing ring. "I am keeping fit so that I can challenge President Nyerere in the boxing ring and fight it out there, rather than having the soldiers lose their lives on the field of battle." Amin added that Mohammed Ali would be an ideal referee for the bout, and that he, Amin, as the former Uganda heavyweight champ, would give the small, white-haired Nyerere a sporting chance by fighting with one arm tied behind his back, and his legs shackled with weights.

—Dan Wooding and Ray Barnett
Uganda Holocaust (1980)

Nyerere looks up through the haze of blood masking his vision and sees the huge man standing over him, laughing. He looks into the man's eyes and seems to see the dark heart of Africa, savage and untamed.

He cannot remember quite what he is doing here. Nothing hurts, but as he tried to move, nothing works, either. A black man in a white shirt, a man with a familiar face, seems to be pushing the huge man away, maneuvering him into a corner. Chuckling and posturing to people that Nyerere cannot see, the huge man backs away, and now the man in the white shirt returns and begins shouting.

"Four!"

Nyerere blinks and tries to clear his mind. Who is he, and why is he on his back, half-naked, and who are these other two men?

"Five!"

"Stay down, Mwalimu!" yells a voice from behind him, and now it begins to come back to him. *He* is Mwalimu.

"Six!"

He blinks again and sees the huge electronic clock above him. It is one minute and fifty-eight seconds into the first round. He is Mwalimu, and if he doesn't get up, his bankrupt country has lost the war.

"Seven!"

He cannot recall the last minute and fifty-eight seconds. In fact, he cannot recall anything since he entered the ring. He can taste his blood, can feel it running down over his eyes and cheeks, but he cannot remember how he came to be bleeding, or lying on his back. It is a mystery.

"Eight!"

Finally his legs are working again, and he gathers them beneath him. He does not know if they will bear his weight, but they must be doing so, for Mohammed Ali—that is his name! Ali—is cleaning his gloves off and staring into his eyes.

"You should have stayed down," whispers Ali.

Nyerere grunts an answer. He is glad that the mouthpiece is impeding his speech, for he has no idea what he is trying to say.

"I can stop it if you want," says Ali.

Nyerere grunts again, and Ali shrugs and stands aside as the huge man shuffles across the ring toward him, still chuckling.

It began as a joke. Nobody ever took anything Amin said seriously, except for his victims.

He had launched a surprise bombing raid in the north of Tanzania. No one knew why, for despite what they did in their own countries, despite what genocide they might commit, the one thing all African leaders had adhered to since Independence was the sanctity of national borders.

So Julius Nyerere, the Mwalimu, the Teacher, the President of Tanzania, had mobilized his forces and pushed Amin's army back into Uganda. Not a single African nation had offered military assistance; not a single Western nation had offered to underwrite so much as the cost of a bullet. Amin had expediently converted to Islam, and now Libya's crazed but opportunistic Qaddafi was pouring money and weapons into Uganda.

Still, Nyerere's soldiers, with their tattered uniforms and ancient rifles, were marching toward Kampala, and it seemed only a matter of time before Amin was overthrown and the war would be ended, and Milton Obote would be restored to the presidency of Uganda. It was a moral crusade, and Nyerere was convinced that Amin's soldiers were throwing down their weapons and fleeing because they, too, knew that Right was on Tanzania's side.

But while Right may have favored Nyerere, Time did not. He knew what the Western press and even the Tanzanian army did not know: that within three weeks, not only could his bankrupt nation no longer supply its men with weapons, it could not even afford to bring them back out of Uganda.

"I challenge President Nyerere in the boxing ring to fight it out there rather than that soldiers lose their lives on the field of battle. . . ."

The challenge made every newspaper in the Western world, as columnist after columnist laughed over the image of the 330-pound Amin, former heavyweight champion of the Kenyan army, stepping into the ring to duke it out with the five-foot-one-inch, 112-pound, fifty-seven-year-old Nyerere.

Only one man did not laugh: Mwalimu.

"You're crazy, you know that?"

Nyerere stares calmly at the tall, well-built man standing before his desk. It is a hot, humid day, typical of Dar es Salaam, and the man is already sweating profusely.

"I did not ask you here to judge my sanity," answers Nyerere. "But to tell me how to defeat him."

"It can't be done. You're spotting him two hundred pounds and twenty years. My job as referee is to keep him from out-and-out killing you."

"You frequently defeated men who were bigger and

stronger than you," notes Nyerere gently. "And, in the latter portion of your career, younger than you as well."

"You float like a butterfly and sting like a bee," answers Ali. "But fifty-seven-year-old presidents don't float, and little bitty guys don't sting. I've been a boxer all my life. Have you ever fought anyone?"

"When I was younger," says Nyerere.

"How much younger?"

Nyerere thinks back to the sunlit day, some forty-eight years ago, when he pummeled his brother, though he can no longer remember the reason for it. In his mind's eye, both of them are small and thin and ill-nourished, and the beating amounted to two punches, delivered with barely enough force to stun a fly. The next week he acquired the gift of literacy, and he has never raised a hand in anger again. Words are far more powerful.

Nyerere sighs. "*Much* younger," he admits.

"Ain't no way," says Ali, and then repeats, "Ain't no way. This guy is not just a boxer, he's crazy, and crazy people don't feel no pain."

"How would *you* fight him?" asks Nyerere.

"Me?" says Ali. He starts jabbing the air with his left fist. "Stick and run, stick and run. Take him dancing till he drops. Man's got a lot of blubber on that frame." He holds his arms up before his face. "He catches up with me, I go into the rope-a-dope. I lean back, I take his punches on my forearms, I let him wear himself out." Suddenly he straightens up and turns back to Nyerere. "But it won't work for you. He'll break your arms if you try to protect yourself with them."

"He'll only have one arm free," Nyerere points out.

"That's all he'll need," answers Ali. "Your only shot is to keep moving, to tire him out." He frowns. "But . . ."

"But?"

"But I ain't never seen a fifty-seven-year-old man that could tire out a man in his thirties."

"Well," says Nyerere with an unhappy shrug, "I'll have to think of something."

"Think of letting your soldiers beat the shit out of *his* soldiers," says Ali.

"That is impossible."

"I thought they were winning," said Ali.

"In fourteen days they will be out of ammunition and gasoline," answers Nyerere. "They will be unable to defend themselves and unable to retreat."

"Then give them what they need."

Nyerere shakes his head. "You do not understand. My nation is bankrupt. There is no money to pay for ammunition."

"Hell, I'll loan it to you myself," says Ali. "This Amin is a crazy man. He's giving blacks all over the world a bad name."

"That is out of the question," says Nyerere.

"You think I ain't got it?" says Ali pugnaciously.

"I am sure you are a very wealthy man, and that your offer is sincere," answers Nyerere. "But even if you gave us the money, by the time we converted it and purchased what we needed it would be too late. This is the only way to save my army."

"By letting a crazy man tear you apart?"

"By defeating him in the ring before he realizes that he can defeat my men in the field."

"I've seen a lot of things go down in the squared circle," says Ali, shaking his head in disbelief, "but this is the strangest."

"You cannot do this," says Maria when she finally finds out.

"It is done," answers Nyerere.

They are in their bedroom, and he is staring out at the reflection of the moon on the Indian Ocean. As the light dances on the water, he tries to forget the darkness to the west.

"You are not a prizefighter," she says. "You are Mwalimu. No one expects you to meet this madman. The press treats it as a joke."

"I would be happy to exchange doctoral theses with him, but he insists on exchanging blows," says Nyerere wryly.

"He is illiterate," said Maria. "And the people will not allow it. You are the man who brought us independence and who has led us ever since. The people look to you for wisdom, not pugilism."

"I have never sought to live any life but that of the intellect," he admits. "And what has it brought us? While Kenyatta and Mobutu and even Kaunda have stolen hundreds of millions of dollars, we are as poor now as the day we were wed." He shakes his head sadly. "I stand up to oppose Amin, and only Sir Seretse Khama of Botswana, secure in his British knighthood, stands with me." He pauses again, trying to sort it out. "Perhaps the old *Mzee* of Kenya was right. Grab what you can while you can. Could our army be any more ill-equipped if I had funneled aid into a Swiss account? Could I be any worse off than now, as I prepare to face this madman in"—he cannot hide his distaste—"a boxing ring?"

"You must *not* face him," insists Maria.

"I must, or the army will perish."

"Do you think he will let the army live after he has beaten you?" she asks.

Nyerere has not thought that far ahead, and now a troubled frown crosses his face.

He had come to the office with such high hopes, such dreams and ambitions. Let Kenyatta play lackey to the capitalist West. Let Machel sell his country to the Russians. Tanzania would be different, a proving ground for African socialism.

It was a dry, barren country without much to offer. There were the great game parks, the Serengeti and the Ngorongoro Crater in the north, but four-fifths of the land was infested with the tsetse fly, there were no minerals beneath the surface, Nairobi was already the capital city of East Africa and no amount of modernization to Dar es

Salaam could make it competitive. There was precious little grazing land and even less water. None of this fazed Nyerere; they were just more challenges to overcome, and he had no doubt that he could shape them to his vision.

But before industrialization, before prosperity, before anything else, came education. He had gone from the brush to the presidency in a single lifetime, had translated the entire body of Shakespeare's work into Swahili, had given form and structure to his country's constitution, and he knew that before everything came literacy. While his people lived in grass huts, other men had harnessed the atom, had reached the moon, had obliterated hundreds of diseases, all because of the written word. And so while Kenyatta became the *Mzee*, the Wise Old Man, he himself became *Mwalimu*. Not the President, not the Leader, not the Chief of Chiefs, but the Teacher.

He would teach them to turn away from the dark heart and reach for the sunlight. He created the *ujamaa* villages, based on the Israeli *kibbutzim*, and issued the Arusha Declaration, and channeled more than half his country's aid money into the schools. His people's bellies might not be filled, their bodies might not be covered, but they could read, and everything would follow from that.

But what followed was drought, and famine, and disease, and more drought, and more famine, and more disease. He went abroad and described his vision and pleaded for money; what he got were ten thousand students who arrived overflowing with idealism but devoid of funds. They meant well and they worked hard, but they had to be fed, and housed, and medicated, and when they could not mold the country into his utopia in the space of a year or two, they departed.

And then came the madman, the final nail in Tanzania's financial coffin. Nyerere labeled him for what he was, and found himself conspicuously alone on the continent. African leaders simply didn't criticize one another, and suddenly it was the Mwalimu who was the pariah, not the bloodthirsty butcher of Uganda. The East African

Union, a fragile thing at best, fell apart, and while Nyerere was trying to save it, Kenyatta, the true capitalist, appropriated all three countries' funds and began printing his own money. Tanzania, already near bankruptcy, was left with money that was not honored anywhere beyond its borders.

Still, he struggled to meet the challenge. If that was the way the *Mzee* wanted to play the game, that was fine with him. He closed the border to Kenya. If tourists wanted to see his game parks, they would have to stay in *his* country; there would be no more round trips from Nairobi. If Amin wanted to slaughter his people, so be it; he would cut off all diplomatic relations, and to hell with what his neighbors thought. Perhaps it was better this way; now, with no outside influences, he could concentrate entirely on creating his utopia. It would be a little more difficult, it would take a little longer, but in the end, the accomplishment would be that much more satisfying.

And then Amin's air force dropped its bombs on Tanzania.

The insanity of it.

Nyerere ducks a roundhouse right, Amin guffaws and winks to the crowd, Ali stands back and wishes he were somewhere else.

Nyerere's vision has cleared, but blood keeps running into his left eye. The fight is barely two minutes old, and already he is gasping for breath. He can feel every beat of his heart, as if a tiny man with a hammer and chisel is imprisoned inside his chest, trying to get out.

The weights attached to Amin's ankles should be slowing him down, but somehow Nyerere finds that he is cornered against the ropes. Amin fakes a punch, Nyerere ducks, then straightens up just in time to feel the full power of the madman's fist as it smashes into his face.

He is down on one knee again, fifty-seven years old and gasping for breath. Suddenly he realizes that no air is coming in, that he is suffocating, and he thinks his

heart has stopped . . . but no, he can feel it, still pounding.
Then he understands: his nose is broken, and he is trying
to breathe through his mouth and the mouthpiece is pre-
venting it. He spits the mouthpiece out, and is mildly
surprised to see that it is not covered with blood.

"*Three!*"

Amin, who has been standing at the far side of the ring,
approaches, laughing uproariously, and Ali stops the
count and slowly escorts him back to the neutral corner.

The pen is mightier than the sword. The words come,
unbidden, into Nyerere's mind, and he wants to laugh. A
horrible, retching sound escapes his lips, a sound so alien
that he cannot believe it came from him.

Ali slowly returns to him and resumes the count.

"*Four!*" Stay down, you old fool, Ali's eyes seem to say.

Nyerere grabs a rope and tries to pull himself up.

"*Five!*" I bought you all the time I could, say the eyes,
but I can't protect you if you get up again.

Nyerere gathers himself for the most difficult physical
effort of his life.

"*Six!*" You're as crazy as *he* is.

Nyerere stands up. He hopes Maria will be proud of
him, but somehow he knows that she won't.

Amin, mugging to the crowd in a grotesque imitation
of Ali, moves in for the kill.

When he was a young man, the president of his class
at Uganda's Makerere University, already tabbed as a future leader by his teachers and his classmates, his fraternity entered a track meet, and he was chosen to run the
400-meter race.

I am no athlete, he said; I am a student. I have exams
to worry about, a scholarship to obtain. I have no time
for such foolishness. But they entered his name anyway,
and the race was the final event of the day, and just before
it began his brothers came up to him and told him that
if he did not beat at least one of his five rivals, his frater-

nity, which held a narrow lead after all the other events, would lose.

Then you will lose, said Nyerere with a shrug.

If we do, it will be your fault, they told him.

It is just a race, he said.

But it is important to *us*, they said.

So he allowed himself to be led to the starting line, and the pistol was fired, and all six young men began running, and he found himself trailing the field, and he remained in last place all the way around the track, and when he crossed the finish wire, he found that his brothers had turned away from him.

But it was only a game, he protested later. What difference does it make who is the faster? We are here to study laws and vectors and constitutions, not to run in circles.

It is not that you came in last, answered one of them, but that you represented us and you did not try.

It was many days before they spoke to him again. He took to running a mile every morning and every evening, and when the next track meet took place, he volunteered for the 400-meter race again. He was beaten by almost 30 meters, but he came in fourth, and collapsed of exhaustion 10 meters past the finish line, and the following morning he was reelected president of his fraternity by acclamation.

There are forty-three seconds left in the first round, and his arms are too heavy to lift. Amin swings a round-house that he ducks, but it catches him on the shoulder and knocks him halfway across the ring. The shoulder goes numb, but it has bought him another ten seconds, for the madman cannot move fast with the weights on his ankles, probably could not move fast even without them. Besides, he is enjoying himself, joking with the crowd, talking to Ali, mugging for all the cameras at ringside.

Ali finds himself between the two men, takes an extra few seconds awkwardly extricating himself—Ali, who has

never taken a false or awkward step in his life—and buys
Nyerere almost five more seconds. Nyerere looks up at
the clock and sees there is just under half a minute remaining.

Amin bellows and swings a blow that will crush his
skull if it lands, but it doesn't; the huge Ugandan cannot
balance properly with one hand tied behind his back, and
he misses and almost falls through the ropes.

"Hit him now!" come the yells from Nyerere's corner.

"Kill him, Mwalimu!"

But Nyerere can barely catch his breath, can no longer
lift his arms. He blinks to clear the blood from his eyes,
then staggers to the far side of the ring. Maybe it will take
Amin twelve or thirteen seconds to get up, spot him, reach
him. If he goes down again then, he can be saved by the
bell. He will have survived the round. He will have run
the race.

Vectors. Angles. The square of the hypotenuse. It's all
very intriguing, but it won't help him become a leader.
He opts for law, for history, for philosophy.

How was he to know that in the long run they were
the same?

He sits in his corner, his nostrils propped open, his cut
man working on his eye. Ali comes over and peers intently at him.

"He knocks you down once more, I gotta stop it," he
says.

Nyerere tries to answer through battered lips. It is un-
intelligible. Just as well; for all he knows, he was trying
to say, "Please do."

Ali leans closer and lowers his voice.

"It's not just a sport, you know. It's a science, too."

Nyerere utters a questioning croak.

"You run, he's gonna catch you," continues Ali. "A ring
ain't a big enough place to hide in."

Nyerere stares at him dully. What is the man trying to say?

"You gotta close with him, grab him. Don't give him room to swing. You do that, maybe I won't have to go to your funeral tomorrow."

Vectors, angles, philosophy, all the same when you're the Mwalimu and you're fighting for your life.

The lion, some 400 pounds of tawny fury, pulls down the one-ton buffalo.

The 100-pound hyena runs him off his kill.

The 20-pound jackal winds up eating it.

And Nyerere clinches with the madman, hangs on for dear life, feels the heavy blows raining down on his back and shoulders, grabs tighter. Ali separates them, positions himself near Amin's right hand so that he can't release the roundhouse, and Nyerere grabs the giant again.

His head is finally clear. The fourth round is coming up, and he hasn't been down since the first. He still can't catch his breath, his legs will barely carry him to the center of the ring, and the blood is once again trickling into his eye. He looks at the madman, who is screaming imprecations to his seconds, his chest and belly rising and falling.

Is Amin tiring? Does it matter? Nyerere still hasn't landed a single blow. Could even a hundred blows bring the Ugandan to his knees? He doubts it.

Perhaps he should have bet on the fight. The odds were thousands to one that he wouldn't make it this far. He could have supplied his army with the winnings, and died honorably.

It is not the same, he decides, as they rub his shoulders, grease his cheeks, apply ice to the swelling beneath his eye. He has survived the fourth round, has done his best, but it is not the same. He could finish fourth out of six in a foot race and be reelected, but if he finishes second tonight, he will not have a country left to reelect him. This is the real world, and surviving, it seems, is not as important as winning.

Ali tells him to hold on, his corner tells him to retreat, the cut man tells him to protect his eye, but no one tells him how to *win*, and he realizes that he will have to find out on his own.

Goliath fell to a child. Even Achilles had his weakness. What must he do to bring the madman down?

He is crazy, this Amin. He revels in torture. He murders his wives. Rumor has it that he has even killed and eaten his infant son. How do you find weakness in a barbarian like that?

And suddenly, Nyerere understands: you do it by realizing that he *is* a barbarian—ignorant, illiterate, superstitious.

There is no time now, but he will hold that thought, he will survive one more round of clinching and grabbing, of stifling closeness to the giant whose very presence he finds degrading.

Three more minutes of the sword, and then he will apply the pen.

He almost doesn't make it. Halfway through the round Amin shakes him off like a fly, then lands a right to the head as he tries to clinch again.

Consciousness begins to ebb from him, but by sheer force of will he refuses to relinquish it. He shakes his head, spits blood on the floor of the ring, and stands up once more. Amin lunges at him, and once again he wraps his small, spindly arms around the giant.

"A snake," he mumbles, barely able to make himself understood.

"A snake?" asks the cornerman.

"Draw it on my glove," he says, forcing the words out with an excruciating effort.

"Now?"

"Now," mutters Nyerere.

He comes out for the sixth round, his face a mask of raw, bleeding tissue. As Amin approaches him, he spits out his mouthpiece.

"As I strike, so strikes this snake," he whispers. "Protect your heart, madman." He repeats it in his native Zanake dialect, which the giant thinks is a curse.

Amin's eyes go wide with terror, and he hits the giant on the left breast.

It is the first punch he has thrown in the entire fight, and Amin drops to his knees, screaming.

"One!"

Amin looks down at his unblemished chest and pendulous belly, and seems surprised to find himself still alive and breathing.

"Two!"

Amin blinks once, then chuckles.

"Three!"

The giant gets to his feet, and approaches Nyerere.

"Try again," he says, loud enough for ringside to hear. "Your snake has no fangs."

He puts his hand on his hips, braces his legs, and waits.

Nyerere stares at him for an instant. So the pen is *not* mightier than the sword. Shakespeare might have told him so.

"I'm waiting!" bellows the giant, mugging once more for the crowd.

Nyerere realizes that it is over, that he will die in the ring this night, that he can no more save his army with his fists than with his depleted treasury. He has fought the good fight, has fought it longer than anyone thought he could. At least, before it is over, he will have one small satisfaction. He feints with his left shoulder, then puts all of his strength into one final effort, and delivers a right to the madman's groin.

The air rushes out of Amin's mouth with a *whoosh*! and he doubles over, then drops to his knees.

Ali pushes Nyerere into a neutral corner, then instructs the judges to take away a point from him on their scorecards.

They can take away a point, Nyerere thinks, but they can't take away the fact that I met him on the field of battle, that I lasted more than five rounds, that the giant went down twice. Once before the pen, once before the sword.

And both were ineffective.

Even a Mwalimu can learn one last lesson, he decides, and it is that sometimes even vectors and philosophy aren't enough. We must find another way to conquer Africa's dark heart, the madness that pervades this troubled land. I have shown those who will follow me the first step; I have stood up to it, faced it without flinching. It will be up to someone else, a wiser Mwalimu than myself, to learn how to overcome it. I have done my best, I have given my all, I have made the first dent in its armor. Rationality cannot always triumph over madness, but it must stand up and be counted, as I have stood up. They cannot ask any more of me.

Finally at peace with himself, he prepares for the giant's final assault.

After a while, certain science fiction writers go back to particular themes and characters so often that they virtually lay claim to them within the field. Barry Malzberg, for example, practically owns November 22, 1963; Lucius Shepard is the master of the jungles of South America; Maureen McHugh is currently erecting a literary fence around China; and Esther Friesner, author of such outstanding works as *Hooray for Hellywood* and *Gnome Man's Land,* has written so often and so well about Jane Austen that no one else would dare to invade her territory.

In this alternate history, Jane and an American backwoodsman have a confrontation with Napoleon Bonaparte that the history books have somehow overlooked.

Jane's Fighting Ships
by Esther Friesner

"I will not go to the Pump Room," said Jane, tucking in her small, round chin in a manner that always indicated that a subject was beyond any hope of discussion. "I am astonished that you would so much as suggest such a thing, Cassandra, knowing as you must my aversion to the place."

Cassandra Austen looked at her stubborn younger sister and sighed. Sunlight streamed in through the high windows of the Austens' modest abode in the ancient city of Bath and threw a mantle of golden light over the delicately made little woman. With her gray eyes flashing defiance and the light striking sparks of auburn flame from her light brown hair, she made quite a different picture from her country-mouse rector's-daughter reputation. Charming as Jane could be, delightful penwoman that she unarguably was, the child (thirty-six, yet still to Cassandra a child) could become quite extraordinarily tiresome at times.

"I do not understand this sudden antipathy on your part, Jane dear," Cassandra said. "For as long I care to recall, Bath has been your special Sangreal. What is more, the Pump Room itself was once to you a veritable Mecca of the Turks, the lodestar which forever drew your eyes and heart. You could scarcely bear to endure the waiting between the time some friend or relation extended you an invitation to the spa and the actual moment of your departure from home. Yet now that Father has at last moved the family here from the country, you avoid the very prize you ere this so earnestly desired."

Jane's chin tucked itself in a further notch and she folded her arms across the bosom of her white lawn gown. "These past years, Cassandra, have done much to teach me that the world is full of more important matters than the vain pursuit of pleasure and the idle social round."

"Oh, not *that* again!" Cassandra rolled her eyes to the ceiling.

"I will not go to the Pump Room," Jane maintained. "*They* will be there. You know they will, Cassandra! I cannot in good conscience as a true daughter of Britain allow myself to venture into a situation where circumstance might conspire to force me to meet one of *them* socially."

Cassandra folded her own arms and took her stand opposite her sister. There was a generous streak of obstinancy in the Austen blood, and by no means had all of it devolved to Jane. "I am as great a patriot as you, I dare say. Will you brand me traitor for taking the waters

simply because I might happen to have need of addressing a Frenchman or woman while there? I have seen you
return Lieutenant Dubuque's morning salutation many a
time on our promenades. True, they are our conquerors,
but I have heard that the Emperor himself is in Bath this
week, come down on purpose from London, so it is quite
safe to assume that all of his fellow-countrymen will be
on their best behav—"

"Oh, Cassandra, how foolish you can be!" Jane burst
out, springing to her slippered feet. "To think it is the
French I dread meeting?" She gave a short, bitter laugh.
"What are the French barbarians compared to the American savages?"

"But Jane—"

"But me no buts, Cassandra! I am resolved. I cannot
bear the thought of coming face-to-face with one of them
in a public place. Oh, the exasperating *condescension* of
the race! The blatant contempt with which they regard
us! Have you no ears, no eyes? Tell me in all honesty that
you know a single English soul who had encountered an
American and has not been treated by the same in a
shamefully humiliating manner! Yes, tell me that and I
shall accompany you to the Pump Room without further
demur."

Cassandra's arms unfolded to hang limp by her sides.
Cassandra's head drooped until she was the very embodi-
ment of Britannia Victa, that eyesore of a quasi-Egyptian
monument which the Emperor had ordered erected in the
heart of London. "You know that I cannot say that, Jane,"
she said. "Not if I would speak the truth. Very well, I shall
abide by your decision. Since you do not wish to accompany me to the Pump Room and since there is no other
suitable companion for me today, I shall remain at ho—at
ho—ho—" A series of dainty hiccups siezed possession of
Cassandra's throat and swiftly blossomed into the heart-
rending sobs which they in reality were.

Jane's stern countenance immediately melted into one
of the most sororal tenderness. She rushed forward to

fling her arms around Cassandra's heaving shoulders and to press her cheek to her own dearest sister's tear-wet face. "Sweet heavens, Cassandra, what is this passion of weeping?"

"I cannot say," Cassandra moaned. "Oh, do not ask me to say!"

Although the younger by several years, Jane was possessed of a finely honed insight which ladies many decades her senior might have envied and done well to emulate. "It is a matter of the heart, is it not." There was no need for her to inflect it as a question, for she knew. (Although she fancied herself well past the age of susceptibility to such fond vapors, she did not discount the possibility that the gentle delusion might yet affect her elders.) Rather needlessly, Cassandra nodded her head to confirm her sister's already unassailable certainty.

"Jane, darling Jane, whatever am I to do? I did not *mean* to fall in love with him."

"How seldom do we *mean* to do such a thing," Jane murmured, stroking her sister's dark curls. "Yet how often do we do it." She compelled Cassandra to look up and meet her Olympian gaze. "You may correct me if I err, Cassandra, but I assume the gentleman is not one whose suit Pappa and Mamma would approve."

Cassandra bobbed her head miserably. "The vein of patriotic feelings throbs as strongly in their bosoms as it does in yours, I fear."

Jane was aghast. "Mercy, Cassandra! You cannot mean to tell me that you have given your heart to an *American*?"

"What?" Cassandra was momentarily startled out of her tears. "Goodness, Jane, what a chimerical fancy! Do you think no better of me? No, no, the chosen of my soul is most certainly not *that*." She sniffed prettily. "I believe his face and name are in fact not unfamiliar to you."

"Lieutenant Dubuque!" Jane exclaimed so loudly that Cassandra had to place a hushing finger to her little sister's lips.

"Not so loud, I implore you! You will bring the whole

house down upon us. Yes, it is Lieutenant Dubuque ...
Jean-Marc. The Emperor himself has taken note of his
sterling qualities. Though young and gently bred, he took
an active part in the Invasion of 1798 and acquitted himself heroically."

"Can you call it heroism?" Jane demanded, her tone
ice. "Can you, when your lover's valor was measured out
in precious drops of English blood?"

Cassandra broke from her sister's suddenly cold embrace. Burying her face in her hands, she whirled towards
the windows. "God help me, you are right! And yet, I am
incapable of helping myself do aught save love him. The
gap of years which separates us is as nothing. What are
earthly measures of temporality to kindred souls which
by their own innate, imperdurable nature transcend all
question of age? He feels as I do, else why would a man
of his undoubted merits of person, breeding, and expec-
tation regard a woman of my age as a suitable *pari* when
there is not even the dream of a grand dowry to lure
Avarice whither Eros might not elsewise tread?"

"Is it so?" Jane wondered aloud. She knew Lieutenant
Dubuque tolerably well, and could not place his age above
thirty. As to the truth of the paltry—nay, nonexistent—
hopes the unwed Austen daughters had of being richly
dowered brides, it was a grim phantom which had
haunted Jane's life and work relentlessly. "Does he truly
love you, as ol—as penniless as you are?"

Her wretched sister affirmed this with a gesture. "He
has told me as much, and by the grace of his own family's
holdings in France is willing to take me for his bride
barefoot in my shift. As if that happy instant might ever
be! The only place that he and I may exchange more than
a curt good day is in the bustle of the public rooms at
the spa. Jane, did you but know how I hunger for merely
the sound of his voice! To have that, I would use every
stratagem and wile of which I am capable to beguile you
from your chosen moral stance. I have sunk beneath contempt. For Jean-Marc's sake, I would even condemn you

to encounter *Americans* socially." She shuddered. "Oh, I am lost, lost, dead to shame! In the autumn of my life, I have given my heart willingly into the hands of our conquerors. Now despise me."

Jane came up softly behind her sister and gently made Cassandra turn around. "You must not cry, Cassandra," she said. "Otherwise your nose will turn quite red and everyone will comment upon it when we enter the Pump Room."

Jane stood as far removed from the swirl and chatter of the madding crowd as the Pump Room walls permitted. A cup of the ill-smelling waters—upon which noisome liquid foundation Bath had raised its reputation as a spa since Roman times—remained untasted in her hand. It was as much a stage property as she felt herself to be, mere dressing for the sentimental drama presently unfolding between Cassandra and her lieutenant.

An impish smile curved Jane's lips, displaying to the world the rare flash of two extremely appealing dimples. She could not help but do so. Poor Cassandra, who desired nothing more than the opportunity to exchange some few whispered words of affection with Jean-Marc, would have to bellow them aloud if she wanted to be heard. The Pump Room was a tumult of noise, a fearsome press of people. Small wonder: the Emperor himself was taking the waters.

Jane was well content to observe His Imperial Majesty from a distance. That was all to the good, since she had in fact no other choice. Courtiers of every bright feather fluttered in fawning attendance upon the person of the jumped-up Corsican who had laid his boot upon the white neck of England thirteen short years ago. With a chronicler's disppassionate eye, Jane took the measure of the man before whom all Europe bowed and trembled. Although she knew that the sight of Bonaparte should by rights rouse feelings of unmitigated loathing in her bosom, she was forced to admit that her only thoughts were of how she could best include this splendid scene of pomp and grandeur in one of her novels.

"Little feller sure does make a purty picture, now don't he?"

Jane gave a small leap, startled by the deep voice which sounded so unexpectedly at her back. She turned to see a tall young man, fashionably if not exquisitely dressed, whose luminous brown eyes and dark good looks stirred unfamiliar emotions within her. As swiftly as these arose, Jane mastered and subjected them. If her initial glimpse of the speaker was disquieting, the enduring voice of plain common sense did not fail to make her see at once that he was too much her junior for such feelings on her part to have aught but a farcical denouement.

"Were you addressing me, young man?" she replied coldly.

His smile was as engaging as his person. "Yes'm. That is, if you don't mind my taking the liberty."

"It is indeed a liberty, seeing as we have not been formally introduced." She turned her shoulder to him, as if searching the crowd for a friend, and hoped that he would understand that their interview was over.

She was not to be so fortunate. "Well now, I do apologize, ma'am. And if my ma were here, I just know she'd thump me a good one for talking out of turn to a fine lady like yourself. But you see, ma'am, back where I come from, we don't hold with such formalities. Truth is, life's a hard row to hoe down Tennessee way, and we don't always have the time for parlor manners. Life's a chancy thing at best; all the more when you've got redskin neighbors who might take a fatal dislike to you all of a sudden. When a man's eye lights on another soul who looks like maybe he'd make a good, solid friend—he *or* she, I should say—well, you just step right up and say howd'y'do."

A creeping horror of realization inched its way from the soles of Jane's feet to her heart's core as the young man spoke. Social instinct demanded that she cut him dead and remove herself without delay from his vicinity.

Alas, the same perverse demon that rode the tip of her pen now kept her rooted to the spot and caused her to inquire, "You are then . . . an American?"

His grin was at the same time fascinating and hideous to her sight. "Yes, ma'am, I have that honor. Though to gauge by the look on your face, you'd like it better was I to say I was an honest murderer." His eyes twinkled. "When I was a boy back home, I had sight keen enough to pick a 'coon out of a canebrake at fifty yards and an ear that could hear the moss growing on a turtle's belly. I've still got senses sharp enough now I've reached the ripe old age of twenty-five to tell that when a lovely lady like yourself says *American* that way, it's just 'cause she was raised too polite to say— Well, I guess I was raised too polite to use that kind of language neither."

Jane felt the color mantling her cheeks. "I assure you, sir, I bear you no personal antipathy."

"Mighty kind of you, ma'am," he replied, making a short, graceful bow. "Mighty generous of you not to hate me personally, now we've met, while you're so busy hating a slew of folks you don't even know, just on the principle of the thing." His grin never wavered. It was commencing to get on Jane's nerves.

"*Must* you show your teeth at me in that manner?" she huffed. "It puts me in mind of legends regarding the anthropophagi."

"Oh, there's legends aplenty back where I come from, if you like such truck," he responded. "No better soil than Tennessee earth for growing 'em. Why, some folks even hand 'round a few 'bout me, if you can believe it. Talk 'bout my grin, they say that one time I saw me a 'coon up a tree stump a-grinnin' like he owned Glory. So I grinned back, just to teach ol' Mister Coon some manners. We stood there, a-grinnin' and a-grinnin' at each other for three solid days and nights 'til finally that varmint tumbles off'n that stump, deader'n Pharaoh's dog."

"Really," said Jane. She tried to maintain a voice of frost, yet the longer she listened to this American person's bizarre tale, the more unwillingly spellbound she became with his fictions.

"Yes'm, and that's not all. When I went to skin me that critter, I saw that not only had I grinned the 'coon dead, I'd also grinned all the bark clean off the stump he was roosting on, and that's a fact."

She could not help it; she burst into laughter. The young man smiled.

"That's the purtiest sound I've heard from an English-woman's lips since I came over here with Mr. Clay. Pretty lips, too, if you'll forgive the liberty." He extended one large, sun-browned hand. "David Crockett, at your service."

Jane's own hand slipped into his before her mind could formulate a sensible objection. "I am Miss Jane Austen and I am very pleased to meet you, Mr. Crockett."

"Call me Davy," he said, giving her hand a warm squeeze. "That is, if it's not another liberty."

"I shall continue to call you Mr. Crockett, sir, if you do not find that entirely disagreeable. The proprieties supersede all question of liberty in this country." Jane laughed again. It sounded far less brittle than the first. "Liberty is a great concern of your Americans, is it not? You are all confirmed fanatics on the subject, I believe."

For a wonder, the legendary grin vanished, leaving its master looking every inch the sober, philosophical gentleman. "If you mean us wanting free of your rule back in '75, I won't deny it. Though I will say I'm surprised to hear you talk of us winning our liberty like it was a joke. I reckon that to your eyes, we Americans do look like a passel of rowdy children, kicking up a fuss when we don't like something. The grown-up way's to stay calm and talk, not bawl our fool heads off and throw things, ain't it?"

Jane's dimples showed even deeper. "So I would say. And rather vengeful little urchins you've become, gloating over the present unfortunate state of your former rulers."

"Gloating, ma'am?"

"That is the best word I can summon to describe the

attitude of every American—yourself excepted—I have ever seen on English soil. Your fellow-countrymen comport themselves with a swaggering smugness I find decidedly unsympathetic. I grant you, the support your rebel forces received from France was instrumental in the eventual attainment of independence, but I would hope that there remained some spark of affection—however dimly flickering—for the land which gave your forefathers birth."

"Oh, I see." Mr. Crockett stroked his smooth, strong chin. "You mean America's like a scrawny kid who's always getting licked by his big brother 'til he gets grown enough to put a stop to it. Then along comes this other bully—and my hide's not worth a flea's tallow if the Emperor hears me call him *that*!—and whomps the tar out'n the big brother proper. Does it right under the scrawny sprat's eyes, too. How's he to act then? I reckon he's got a choice 'tween being glad to see his old nemesis getting a taste of his own physic or sorrowful 'counta they're still of the same blood, and let history go hang. *You're* saying we shouldn't dance for joy when our kinfolks've been laid low, no matter if they did treat us poorly in time past."

"Er—yes. I suppose that is what I mean." The American's straightforward rustic turn of speech was eloquent, in its own way, and wonderfully perplexing to Jane. She felt an earnest desire to hear him speak at greater length.

Her wish was granted, albeit in a way she had never anticipated. "Miz Austen," he said, "I ha'n't been dealing honest with you, and it shames me. Just now, when I come up and commenced talking, 'twasn't by chance. I asked a friend to point out special Miz Jane Austen, the famous writer."

"Indeed." Jane felt the old ice creeping back into her bosom. "Then I assume I was under a misapprehension in thinking that you had dared breach the societal conventions for the sake of my personal attractions alone?" Her tone was so dry, it made the noise-laden air of the Pump Room crackle.

"Personal—?" Mr. Crockett was taken aback. "Why,

mercy love us, ma'am, I can tell you straight and true that if I wasn't who I was and didn't have this burden on my shoulders, I'd still have done my level best to have a word with a woman as pert and purty-looking as you—and get my face slapped for it, likely." He grinned.

Jane was provoked to find herself no less able to resist that grin than the late " 'coon" of Mr. Crockett's tall tale. "You should not be slapped," she replied amiably.

"No?" He raised one brow in delighted speculation. "That's a mighty great encouragement to give a lonely American far from home."

"There is no encouragement intended," Jane replied. "The proprieties which you so readily scorn look askance on the creation of any scene in a public place."

His handsome face fell, a visible sign of disappointment so plainly made manifest that Jane experienced an unsettling revelation that this incredible young man did find her society agreeable and her appearance attractive.

"Then let's respect the proprieties, by all means," he said rather heavily. "Ma'am, I'd like to have some plain speech with you, privately. Is there any way for a man and a woman to do the same without stirring up one of them *scenes* you dread so much?"

Jane's sharp eyes scanned the Pump Room. Cassandra and Lieutenant Dubuque had both been drawn into the Emperor's orbit. The penwoman in her found it fascinating to observe how a single being's force of personality could be the linchpin of an empire. If Napoleon's presence were the sun around which the great planets of subjected nations turned and lesser stars danced attendance, at least this Copernican model allowed for all manner of smaller cosmic events to transpire with no notice being paid them whatsoever.

Which was why Jane felt she could say without fear of giving rise to gossip, "I will walk out with you, Mr. Crockett, and hear what you have to say."

* * *

On the way home that evening, Jane's face burned so hotly that she was certain her sister must note it and at the very least inquire whether she was feverish. But Cassandra's thoughts were fixed upon Lieutenant Dubuque, to the exclusion of all else. Despite the fact that Jane's extended absence in the company of Mr. Crockett had granted Cassandra more than ample time to delight in the young Frenchman's company, she was quite crestfallen when they left the Pump Room. Jane, owning a sensitivity that rose above her own concerns, could not help but ask what had happened.

"He is being sent away," Cassandra replied, the portrait of wretchedness. "The Emperor returns to France within the week, there to remain for an indefinite period of time. He shall sail from the port of London aboard the *Belle Créole*, and wishes Jean-Marc to become attached to his regular suite. Jean-Marc does not wish to go, but he sees no way to avoid it. It is" —her voice caught— "a signal honor."

Jane laid an unusually warm hand over her sister's chilly one. With Mr. Crockett's fiery oratory yet ringing in her ears, how could she help but feel some measure of that volcanic zeal imbuing her extremities? The nebulous sentiments which had so long permeated her bosom decrying England's present servitude beneath the French yoke were at last galvanized into solid form by the backwoodsman's impassioned views on liberty. He had spoken at length, and with rising ardor, of the vast territories which the Emperor's government held in the New World. In specific, he had railed against the French control, unto a stranglehold, over the Mississippi River and the port of New Orleans.

"I'm telling you all this, ma'am, because of who you are," he said. "Your books have got bite and backbone, and I only wish I had the words to say how much I admire you for the fine way you manage a pen. That's why I asked to have you pointed out to me, back there in the Pump Room. I figgered to myself, 'Davy, Tom Paine proved that one good writer can influence more people than a gunnysack full of politicians, and this lady's a sight purtier than old Tom.' "

"And whom might you require me to influence, sir?" Jane asked, flattered in spite of herself.

"Oh, no one much." His grin was a trifle sheepish. "Just the Emperor."

"Your faith overwhelms me." Jane attempted to preserve a façade of indifference. "His Imperial Majesty is more open to the influence of cannon than of compositions."

"Well, we all do what we can, ma'am, with our own gifts," Mr. Crockett countered. "I think I can trust your discretion enough to say that there's some of us ready to try more . . . direct means of persuasion on old Boney."

"Persuasion . . ." Jane echoed.

"We've got no choice, when it comes to the fate of the West. Time was, the Spaniards held those lands. They gave us leave to use the river and even have right of deposit at the port scot-free. When the Emperor took Spain, he let arrangements go on like they'd been, and got the thanks of good folk in the western states for his kindness. There was even a time it looked like he'd be willing to let the whole passel of land go to us for a song." His mobile mouth twisted in an ironic *moue*. "Too bad he changed his tune."

Alone with Cassandra, Jane could still hear young Mr. Crockett discourse upon the Emperor's new plans for the Louisiana territories. He spoke of ruinous fees for right of deposit and commercial river traffic permitted solely aboard vessels of proven French origin, also at prices meant to break the purse of the simple farmers and traders of the United States frontier. She could still see his eyes grow cold as he spoke of the Americans' known penchant for resisting the dictates of crowned tyrants, especially when these flung a noose around their mercantile endeavors. Likewise she could see those same eyes soften and grow warm once more as she—in defiance of all proper breeding—could not help but voice her passionate agreement with the opinions he so fluently expressed.

"Where there is tyranny," she said, "there can be no thought of past animosities or alliances. Although our nations are old foes, sir, the Corsican's high-handed manner with both our peoples can not leave us other than firm friends, united in the just cause of liberty!"

That was when he took the liberty of kissing her.

Jane's face flamed anew at the memory. A perturbing thrill of nerves racked her slender body with slightly less vehemence than she had experienced during Mr. Crockett's original presumption. The guilty recollection that she had not offered the dashing young American any resistance nor, in fact, meted out any chastisement for his insolence, caused her cheek to color even higher.

The further thought of that unwonted service which she subsequently had volunteered to render him in freedom's name dyed her face a uniform scarlet so bright that even a distracted and heartsick Cassandra could not help but observe and remark, "Jane, dear, have you taken a chill?"

"Perhaps I have," Jane replied. "I feel somewhat flushed."

"And here am I, feeling sorry for myself when your health is imperilled! Oh, my dear sister, what matters my sorry state beside your fragile constitution!"

"A constitution is a thing to be guarded," Jane commented with a cryptic air which eluded her sister completely. Abruptly she posed a most peculiar question: "Cassandra, are you certain that Father is implacable concerning a match between yourself and Lieutenant Dubuque?"

"I do not *think* he is so immutable." Cassandra's brow furrowed. "He has on occasion spoken not unfavorably of the gentleman, having encountered him as we have, in the course of a neighborhood promenade. Were he but to think of Jean-Marc as an individual and not merely as just another Frenchman in service to the Emperor, all might be well." She sighed. "But these are gossamer hopes. How shall Father ever have the opportunity to truly know my darling's character now? When the *Belle Créole* sails—"

"Or if," said Jane softly.

"What?"

"We all do what we can, Cassandra, with our own gifts."

"Ah, Mademoiselle Austen." The Emperor inclined his head slightly to acknowledge the Englishwoman's deep curtsey. "You are welcome aboard this vessel. Please rise." He offered her his hand and smiled as she complied. Looking her in the eye, he said in lightly accented English, "The books which you so generously sent me proclaimed your talent, but said nothing of your beauty."

Jane returned the imperial smile, although her heart remained as stone and her thoughts cynical in the extreme. *So you say, milord Emperor,* she mused. *But how much of my beauty do you assign to the fact that I am one of the few Englishwomen who do not overtop you?*

Aloud she replied, "Your Imperial Majesty does me too much honor." She permitted him to escort her to the large plush banquette, backed by a grand window which overlooked the stern of the *Belle Creole*. Sunset's mantle of purple and gold, more splendid than any in the Emperor's possession, unfurled itself over the port of London. A few small ships lay at anchor within sight, all save one flying the tricolor of France.

"It is you who do me the honor, Mademoiselle Austen," Napoleon gallantly replied. "The note accompanying your novels said that you wished my permission to make mention of me in your next work, and to dedicate me the same." He poured them both wine with his own hands. "I am not so vain as to believe my empire is eternal. Even great Caesar's conquests devolved to dust. But literature—! Ah, *ça vive toujours!*"

Jane smiled demurely at Napoleon's enthusiasm, which caused him to lapse into French sporadically. "Then I may assume you will most graciously permit me the liberty?"

"The liberty? Ha! *Bien sûr*. Take as many such liberties as you desire, mademoiselle. Perhaps you know that our Empress is quite the devotee of *belles-lettres*? She keeps her own private coterie of tame authors at Malmaison, you know. My place in the scroll of history is secure, but to know that I shall also live in other volumes— Ah, to see Josephine's face when I tell her of this! It is a conquest that will impress her more than any other." He lifted his glass. "And what shall be the title of this great work, mademoiselle?"

"Persuasion," Jane replied. She sipped her wine, then said, "Your Imperial Majesty, I should deem it a great favor if you would deign to accept a small gift on my part, in thanks for your indulgence."

Napoleon was taken aback. "A gift? But your novels— No, no, it is unnecessary," he said, yet his eyes glittered with greed.

"I insist," Jane replied. "I have taken the liberty of leaving it in the charge of your attendant, Lieutenant Dubuque. If you would be good enough to summon him?"

The Emperor did so with a haste that belied his stated reluctance to receive any further gifts from his guest. The handsome young lieutenant entered, bearing a large box. Jane indicated by a gesture that His Imperial Majesty might open it at once, which was likewise accomplished with dispatch.

"Mon Dieu! Qu'est-ce que c'est?" Napoleon's face was colorless as he lifted the *objet* from its pasteboard nest.

"Do you like it?" Jane asked innocently.

"But of course, mademoiselle." The Emperor turned the gift this way and that. "What is it?"

"It is a clock," Jane replied, taking it from Napoleon's hands. "A most clever design, based upon the habits of a creature native to the Americas. Do you see? The clock face is set into a gilded stump and when the hour strikes, the raccoon atop the stump opens its mouth in time with the chimes. All in all, a gift as unique as its recipient."

The Emperor continued to regard the clock askance. "The beast is *grinning* at me," he said, half in protest.

"It is, I believe, an expression natural to the raccoon." An impish look made Jane's face piquant. "Your Majesty could always essay grinning back." Before Napoleon could say another word she added, "With your permission, I shall set the mechanism in motion." The Emperor, transfixed by the leer on the face of the clockwork raccoon, was powerless to stop her.

It was some time later that Lieutenant Dubuque escorted Jane from the *Belle Créole*. The young Frenchman seemed ill-at-ease as well as loath to relinquish Jane's company even after she was safely on the dock. She noted a folded paper in his hand, added this to his bashful, hesitant mien, and understood.

"It is a *billet-doux* for my sister, is it not?" She spoke gently, but the poor young man still jumped, then nodded. "I presume that your attentions toward Cassandra are honorable?" Jane went on. Again the lovelorn youth nodded. "Then be so good, Lieutenant, as to accompany me only a little farther."

Wordlessly and without comprehension, Lieutenant Dubuque allowed himself to be led whither Jane willed. The guards of the *Belle Créole* saw nothing amiss in this, privy as they were to the Emperor's instructions that the English authoress be given safe conduct under Dubuque's aegis. She guided him along the London docks until they reached the sole ship that flew a three-colored banner that did not pertain to France. He had scarcely set foot on board—bestowing *en passant* a rather dubious salute to a saturnine gentleman in ragged captain's finery who observed him from the otherwise deserted poopdeck—when Cassandra burst from hiding and flung herself into his embrace.

"Jean-Marc, Jean-Marc, oh, it is wonderful! We are to be wed at once!" she exclaimed. "The captain of this vessel will himself perform the ceremony." This intelligence caused the lieutenant to be first dumbstruck, then to jabber a scandalous number of questions in his native tongue.

"Your sister's gallant is, of course, delighted, but would like to know what accounts for this sudden happiness," the dark man translated. "He asks whether he has your influence with the Emperor to thank for it."

"Thank you, Captain Lafitte," Jane said drily. "I have sufficient knowledge of French. However, it might be best if a man of your delicacy and sophistication were to inform him that the same circumstances which shall permit his marriage to Cassandra shall also perforce soon relieve him of all further occupation in the Emperor's service, beginning approximately"—she cocked her head to catch a peal of church bells tolling the hour—"now."

Half the great stern window of the *Belle Créole* blew outward in an explosion of tinkling glass.

"That will be our signal for departure," Captain Lafitte said in his lazy, feline manner. He set a silver whistle to his lips and blew. Immediately the deserted decks swarmed with a ragtag crew of disreputable-looking seamen. With swift, silent efficiency they had the ship away from the dock and well downriver while the hubbub surrounding the *Belle Créole* was yet in its infancy.

Jane leaned against the rail and observed the swarming French soldiers as Captain Lafitte's ship glided past. "I wonder whether he is dead," she murmured.

"I doubt that's so," said a sweet, familiar voice beside her. "There's just so much gunpowder a raccoon'll hold. But we sure did get the old boy's attention."

"An attention you may come to regret," Jane pointed out to Mr. Crockett, who had exchanged the tailored garments suitable to Bath society for a simple tunic and trousers of fringed buckskin.

He merely shook his head, causing the tail of his coonskin cap to swing back and forth as if the creature were alive. "An empire run from one country lacks the manpower to be everywhere at once. Old Boney's got too big for his britches. If he sends troops against us in the States, it'll be a costly business. He'll have to withdraw them from somewhere in Europe, and then the folks who see 'em go will take their chance. But let him try to quash their bid for freedom, and we'll r'ar up at his back, more ornery than a bear with a sore paw."

"A bear that shall also stand ready to scoop up the Louisiana territory in its paws," Jane remarked.

"We're just giving him a little hint about it, is all." Mr. Crockett gave her a fond wink. In the flickering light from the burning imperial flagship, the 'coon head adorning the front of his cap appeared to do the same. "And if he lets this hint go by, we'll send him another and another, 'til his blasted Gallic pride won't let him rest without he tries teaching us Americans some manners."

Jane's dimples showed. "As I recall, we British learned the hard way that you Americans are devilish difficult to teach anything."

He doffed his cap. "That all depends on what you're trying to teach us, ma'am," he said, and swept her into his arms. "Do you fancy Cap'n Lafitte might find it in his heart to marry off two sisters for the price of one?"

Jane's grin was the equal of any trueborn Tennessee 'coon's. "I reckon so, Mr. Crockett," she replied. "I reckon so."

Lawrence Schimel is probably the youngest member of the Science Fiction Writers of America, but though still a student at Yale, he is far from the least accomplished, with over a dozen sales in the past year.

For his alternate warrior, Lawrence chose Dr. Martin Luther King, who may well have dreamed *this* dream.

Taking Action
by Lawrence Schimel

Precognition is a curse, yet many yearn to be so afflicted, hoping to use their "talent" to look into the future and see: which stocks to buy, which horses to bet on at the races; hoping to become filthy rich, usually with a bit of fame thrown in as a sideline: guest appearances, celebrity fortune-tellings, that sort of thing. They do not realize you have no control over when you saw: sometimes it is tomorrow, and sometimes decades, or even centuries, into the future; sometimes the visions come in hard succession—three within a single hour, say—and sometimes there is a dry spell of years between them; they come of their own accord.

Martin Luther King was one of the unfortunates plagued by this curse. When he had The Dreams they came to him as a montage of silent images, like old-time black-and-white films, or watching the news on television with the sound turned off.

One dream King had, on the first of December 1955, was as follows:

INT.—COURTROOM—DAY

A black woman sits on the witness stand. As if a caption, a newspaper is superimposed over the scene. Only the headline is readable.

FLASH: **Millions of viewers transfixed by sexually explicit duel for the truth.**

Another angle. Her lips move, but no sound is heard. Beyond her, the courtroom is full.

FLASH: **Anita Hill—another victim to blame.**

A black man is now on the stand. He is well dressed, and seems articulate. Her witness?

FLASH: **Harassment controversy highlights political, cultural, class divisions.**

Another angle. Hill is visible in the lower left corner. [SFX: a telephone ringing]

FLASH: **White House role in Thomas defense.**

CUT TO REALITY:

The telephone rang again. King answered it, still trying to figure out the vision. It was Ralph Abernathy.

As he hung up the phone, Coretta asked, "Martin, what is it?"

He could not look at her. "Rosa Parks was just arrested for refusing to give up her seat to a white man."

* * *

The weeks which followed were gratefully free of further visions. King did not have time for them with: the bus boycott to deal with, being elected president of the newly formed Montgomery Improvement Association, Mrs. Park's trial, his parish to tend, and his own family.

But driving home from a Montgomery Improvement Association meeting on the twenty-sixth of January he had another Dream:

EXT.—LOS ANGELES HIGHWAY—NIGHT

A black man lies on the ground outside his car. He is surrounded by a group of policemen, who are beating him with nightsticks, kicking him, whatever strikes their fancy.

Again, a series of headlines is superimposed over the scene like captions, changing rapidly.

FLASH: **Beating-case jury hears laughter on tape.**

FLASH: **Officer testifies King beating was 'violent . . . brutal' and justified.**

FLASH: **L.A. beating victim arrested after alleged assault on officer.**

FLASH: **Jury picked for King trial; no blacks chosen.**

CUT TO REALITY:

King eased his foot off the gas pedal. The visions came like that, without warning; he was lucky he was still alive. Behind him a siren blared. Mechanically, King braked and pulled over to the side of the road, still caught in the afterimages of the Dream. Who was this other King? Or was that supposed to be him? He rolled down the window as the police officer stepped up to it.

"Please step out of the car, you are under arrest."

"On what charges?"

"You were going thirty in a twenty-five zone."

King began to open the door.

(FLASH: **U.S. seen as unlikely to charge LAPD bystanders.**)

There was a flashlight under the front seat for emergencies. This was an emergency; he would not let himself become the man in the vision. His fingers closed around the flashlight and he flung the door open, knocking the officer against the car. As the officer recovered and moved to pull his gun, King, leaning over the top of the car door, knocked the officer's nose to the back of his head. The officer crumbled against the car. King turned him around and hit him in the face with the flashlight. The officer fell to the ground. When King stopped, the officer's features were no longer recognizable. At last he managed to open his fingers, and the flashlight dropped to the ground next to the corpse. King got back into the car. He got out, took the officer's gun and the now-bloodied flashlight, and got in the car again.

An arm crunched as King drove away.

The next Dream came during dinner that Wednesday:

EXT.—HOWARD BEACH—NIGHT

Again a car, this one broken-down by the side of the road. It is winter. A black man lies on the ground, his head split open like an overripe melon. A group of white teenagers with baseball bats and tree limbs chases another black man, herding him toward the Belt Parkway.

CUT TO REALITY:

There was an explosion in the front room. Yoki began to cry. Coretta looked at Martin, but did not get up from the table. Mrs. Williams tried to comfort the baby.

"Please pass the salt," Martin asked. He poured salt on his corn, and continued eating without commenting on the bomb which had been thrown onto his front porch. The images of the vision haunted his sight. On his plate was a black man's head, split open by a baseball bat. And now this bomb. There comes a time when people get tired of being trampled over by the iron feet of oppression; they must take action now. But he said nothing, for it was not right to involve the women in these actions. They gave each other nervous looks as he thought and ate, but eventually, once Yoki had stopped crying, they too returned to dinner.

Later in the evening, with the help of Roscoe Williams and a handful of men from the Montgomery Improvement Association, King fought fire with fire. Crosses were burned at Montgomery bus stops. Important Ku Klux Klan and White Citizens Council members were pulled from their houses late that night and taken out on distant roads from which they did not return.

In the years to follow, King is too busy for Dreams, but they came when they would, although infrequently. He advocated civil rights through demonstrations and court actions. Racial segregation on city bus lines is ruled unconstitutional. Montgomery buses are integrated.

(DREAM: MALCOLM X MURDERED BY BLACKS IN NEW YORK CITY)

King is elected president of the Southern Christian Leadership Conference. *Time* magazine puts Dr. King on its cover as the leader of the black civil rights movement in the United States. King meets with Vice President Richard M. Nixon. President Eisenhower mobilizes Arkansas National Guard to escort nine Negro students to an all-white high school in Little Rock. Martin Luther King III is born. King meets with presidential candidate John F.

Kennedy. Dexter Scott King is born. King leads the Freedom Riders.

(DREAM: WILDING IN CENTRAL PARK)

King plans the Birmingham student riots. Bernice Albertine King is born. Birmingham Director of Public Safety Eugene "Bull" Connor orders the use of police dogs and fire hoses upon the student protesters.

(DREAM: THE ASSASSINATION IN DALLAS)

Connor is killed by a bomb hidden in his car.

Governor George Wallace swallowed hard as he saw the angry mob of Negroes approach the school, but he held his ground, backed as he was with a dozen armed police officers.

King stepped forward and approached the door to the University of Alabama, where Wallace blocked entrance to the group of waiting black students. "I suggest you move and allow these students to enter. You're breaking the law. This university was ordered integrated by the Supreme Court of the United States of America."

Wallace spat on the ground between them. "Ain't no niggers coming in this schoolhouse."

"I'm sure we can come to some sort of agreement."

"I'm not bargaining."

"I think you should reconsider. As you can no doubt see, if there is a fight, you are going to be overwhelmed, and inevitably killed. However, many of us are likely to be killed as well. Which we are willing to do for the satisfaction of seeing you dead. However, there is an alternative."

Wallace eyed the size of the mob of Negroes in front of him. "What is it you propose?"

"I'm offering you a chance. A chance at life."

Wallace waited to hear what it was. King did not say anything. Wallace did not want to admit the upper hand to a nigger, but at last he demanded, "Well, what the hell is it?"

King smiled. "A duel. Drawn pistols at ten paces. I want the satisfaction of killing you myself."

Wallace considered King for a moment, looking the nigger up and down. He would love to blow him away, after all the trouble he'd caused him. "Agreed."

They stood back-to-back on the lawn in front of the schoolhouse. The Reverend Ralph Abernathy began to count slowly: one . . . two . . . three . . .

They moved in slow motion, a step with each number. King: dark and inevitable, like molasses, confident; Wallace: tense with nervousness as the pair drew apart from each other: four . . . five . . . six . . . seven . . .

King began to pivot. Eight. He extended his arm and shot Wallace in the back. Wallace's gun flew from his hands as he landed in the grass.

Nine. Abernathy did not stop counting. Wallace rolled himself over, gasping as the numbness turned to pain. He could not move his legs at all. He raised an arm to point at King, as if the hand still held a gun.

Ten.

"You—" Wallace tried to take in a deeper breath of air, but could not. "You cheatin' nigger."

Letter from Birmingham Jail

April 16, 1963
Birmingham, Alabama

My Dear Fellow Clergymen:

While confined here in the Birmingham city jail, I came across your statement calling my recent activities "unwise and untimely." Seldom do I pause to answer criticism of my work and ideas. If I sought to answer all the criticisms that cross my desk, my secretaries would have little time for anything other than such correspondence in the course of the day, and I would have no time for constructive work. But since I feel that you are men of genuine goodwill and that your criticisms are sincerely set forth, I want to try to answer your statement in what I hope will be patient and reasonable terms.

Contrary to Wallace's allegations of my cheating, I wish to draw your attention to a principle I call "affirmative action," which has underlain my activities here in Birmingham. It consists of preferential concessions to compensate for past injustices ...

Michael P. Kube-McDowell has made his reputation with "hard science" novels such as *Alternities* and *The Quiet Pools* and *Exile* . . . and yet this is his third appearance in the series of Alternate anthologies I have edited for Tor, and I am not convinced that his greatest strength isn't his ability to create truly memorable characters possessed of truly memorable passions.

Such as Mohandas Gandhi, this century's first great practitioner of passive resistance.

Because Thou Lovest the Burning-Ground
by Michael P. Kube-McDowell

The new arrival at the *choultrie* on the Rajkot road wore the heavy Kathiawar turban, a man's turban, but his face was that of a boy. His long dark coat was dusted with the miles behind him, his countenance darkened by the miles ahead.

There were other travelers at the wayside grove west of Lathi—two merchants and their families around a cook fire, a sepoy messenger and his horse, an old man sitting cross-legged before the shrine, a Brahmin and his servant with a camel cart.

But the youth did not acknowledge them. Avoiding their eyes and pretending deafness at a called greeting, he hung back until there was no one by the well. Only then did he move forward to wash the salt and sweat-streaks from his face, and drink deeply of the cool, metallic water.

After a brief, private obeisance at the shrine, he found himself a place safely away from the others, in the shade of a lime tree. Overhead, green parakeets chattered and small monkeys screeched, but they did not expect Mohandas Gandhi to answer them, and so he could tolerate their presence.

He watched the monkeys cavort for a time, then stretched his slender, narrow-shouldered frame full length on the ground, hugged his small pack to his chest, and closed his eyes. His body ached with fatigue, but he could not sleep. Hunger made his stomach cry out, and misery gnawed at his heart.

"Look you, there, a scorpion," a voice said sharply, close by. Mohandas sat up with a start, then flinched when he found the old man standing over him, a heavy walking stick in his hand.

As Mohandas flinched, the old man stabbed at the ground beyond Mohandas's feet with his walking stick and flicked something into the air and out into the grass a dozen paces away. "There, the creature has moved on," the old man said with a yellow-toothed grin.

"Thank you," said Mohandas with an effort, still puzzled. He did not think he had been dozing, but he had not heard the man's approach.

"Scorpions are everywhere this season," he said. The man's warning had been in Hindi, but now he spoke in Gujarati. "The merchant's son was stung while playing here, not an hour ago. I saw you come this way and came to warn you. My name is Jafir."

"Mohandas Gandhi," said the youth, offering *Namaskar*, the salute with folded hands. "I am in your debt."

Without invitation, Jafir settled cross-legged on the ground beside Mohandas. "I cannot remember when they have been this plentiful," he went on.

Have I been rescued from the scorpion by a leech? Mo-

handas wondered anxiously. "Perhaps I should find another place to rest."

The old man ignored the polite cue. "Gandhi—was it a
kinsman of yours, then, who was *dewan* of Rajkot?"

Mohandas swallowed. "My father, Karamchand. Yes, of
Porbandar and then Rajkot, until his death."

"A fine man, I have heard. You are the head of the
household now, then."

Shaking his head, Mohandas said, "No—my eldest
brother, Laxmidas, has that duty."

"Still better, since no son ever took his father's place
without bringing a family strife. Better that you should
marry and be master of your own house. Are you married?"

Mohandas nodded, his face brightening. "My wife, Kasturbhai, bore me a son while I was at school in Bhavnagar.
His name is Harilal. I have not yet seen him."

Stroking the coarse hairs of his flowing white mous-
tache with his fingertips, Jafir said, "A son—you are
blessed. Did you say Bhavnagar? You are at the new college, then?"

"Yes," Mohandas said, squirming.

"You are fortunate. I have heard that the teachers at
Samaldas are excellent. It is a splendid opportunity for a
young man."

In an instant, Mohandas's misery spilled out to paint
his face. He jumped to his feet and turned away to hide
his distress, but it was too late. "I must find a place where
I can rest," he said curtly, and hastened away.

Jafir made no move to follow. "Sleep deeply, young
Mohandas," he called gently after him. "Sleep well."

Sleep being a refuge, Mohandas slept deeply, and late
into the next morning. By the time he arose, the merchants, the sepoy, and the Brahmin were all gone from
the *choultrie.*

But the old man was waiting—clearly waiting, sitting by
the side of the road with his walking stick laid across his

knees. Mohandas's shoulders dropped with resignation when he saw him.

"The road is longer when walked alone," Jafir said, rising to his feet as the young man approached. "You do not mind if I speed my journey with your company, do you?"

"Not if you can keep my pace," said Mohandas, thinking quickly. "I am eager to see my son."

"As I can well understand," said Jafir with a smile. "Let us see how I manage."

Mohandas thought he could quickly leave the old man behind, wobble-legged and gasping, and regain the solitude he preferred. But it proved a vain hope, as Jafir matched—without sign of distress—any pace that Mohandas himself could sustain. Nor did a brisk stride silence him with breathlessness. And eventually, his rambling conversation wandered back to the subject to which Mohandas had shown such an allergy the night before.

"I was a teacher when I was younger," Jafir was saying. "Did I tell you that? I had many devoted students—yes, and a few disappointments. They are all gone now, though, good and bad alike. All gone. What did you say was your interest?"

"The bachelor of arts," Mohandas said uncomfortably. "I went to Samaldas to study for the bachelor of arts."

"Ah, very prudent. A B.A. will certainly assure you of a sixty-rupee post in the government service. There is much security in the minor posts. Here, you did not eat this morning—share my rice."

After a moment's hesitation, Mohandas stopped and accepted the old man's generosity. He said nothing, but when he turned and resumed walking, it was at his normal pace. Jafir said nothing as he fell in on Mohandas's right. They went on in silence together as Mohandas ate, an old man and a young man walking a dusty road as strangers and companions.

"The truth burns my heart every time I refuse to speak it," Mohandas said at last, with bitterness. "You have been kind to me, Jafir, and I will not lie to you out of pride.

Your innocent curiosity stabs into my wounds. The truth is that I am not eager to reach Rajkot."

Jafir pursed his lips. "I thought there was a weight on your shoulders when I first saw you. I thought to myself, 'Those frowns will give his face lines like old Jafir's if he is not careful.'"

Despite himself, Mohandas smiled.

"Do you carry bad news, or fear it?" Jafir asked, peering back over his shoulder at the road behind them.

"It comes with me and through me," Mohandas said. "I have humiliated myself and shamed my family."

"How is that so?"

"Because the truth is I have left school, and I will not return."

"It was not to your liking? Did you squander your scholarship on pleasures?"

"No, no—I was careful with my money, despite the temptations of Bhavnagar." He hesitated, then plunged on. "I have completely failed to give a good account of myself. The son of Karamchand, and no better scores than eighteen of one hundred in history, thirteen of one hundred in Euclid? I am the laughing stock of Samaldas."

"You seem a bright enough young man. How can this be?"

Mohandas threw up his hands. "From the first moment of class, I am lost. I cannot understand the professors—everything is taught in English, and much too quickly. Geometry, astronomy, history, even Sanskrit and Persian."

"Then you are unready, not unfit."

Mohandas shook his head. "I am incompetent—yes, and unwilling. Tell me, what is the sense of it, for an Indian boy to memorize a hundred lines of Milton? Why should teacher and student alike struggle with a foreign tongue when they could speak to each other as easily as we do, in Gujarati? Why are there no translations? I did not have to learn Bengali to read the poetry of Rabindranath Tagore."

"That is easily explained," said Jafir, a sudden sharpness in his voice. "If you speak English you will think English, and take on English manners, and begin to forget that you are Indian. The gun is not a conqueror's only weapon."

"Should I tell my family, then, 'Be proud—I am unconquered. I have escaped the obligation of government service. Rejoice—the English will not buy me for sixty rupees a month.'" His voice was scalded with self-hate. "How am I to provide for my wife and son?"

"There are other ways," said Jafir, "to feed one's family than service to the viceroy."

His words passed Mohandas's ears unheard. "I cannot bear to think of telling Laxmidas," he said near tears. "I would almost rather die than carry this shame home."

"Does this failure exhaust your every ambition? I pity you, then, for a life so empty."

"Don't ridicule me!" Mohandas said with an unexpected flash of anger, his dark eyes flashing warning.

Shrugging, Jafir stabbed the ground with his walking stick, leaving an angled gouge. "Is it ridicule to turn your own words back at you? Young men—why do you so love the dramatic? As though your entire life turned on this moment." He laughed. "You have no notion how much more life there is ahead of you, or what it turns on. Come, I ask you again—have you no other passions, no secret ambitions? Is sixty rupees a month all you ever hoped for?"

Mohandas hung his head sullenly, saying nothing for another score of strides.

"If I had my wish, I should like to study to become a doctor," he said finally. "It is what I have wanted since my father took ill, and I watched and listened to the English doctors who tended to him. The knowledge to heal, and the burden to comfort—that is a high and privileged service, it seems to me. Yes, I should like to be a doctor, an English doctor, for they are the most learned of all."

"Then do."

"I can't," Mohandas said, shaking his head. "It is impossible."

"Why?" demanded Jafir.

"The Vaisnava forbid the dissection of the dead. My father was devout—in respect to him, Laxmidas would never approve of my choice. And my mother takes her counsel from a Jainist monk, a man who wears a mask lest he inhale an insect and harm it, who will not walk in the dark for fear he may tread on a worm." Mohandas shook his head again. "No, it is impossible."

"You surrender yourself to their disapproval?"

"I have no choice. A medical education would cost ten thousand rupees, and no one in the family will help me without their consent."

"Ten thousand?" said Jafir, again glancing back the way they had come. "That is not so much. I have acquired and spent a hundred times that amount in my lifetime."

"You? You boast. Or you are even older than you look."

"It is not how long I have lived—it is how far I have fallen," Jafir said. "Do not think that we all wear our fortunes on our faces."

Mohandas kicked a stone angrily, and it skittered ahead of them. "It does not matter, unless you propose to make a gift to me of ten thousand rupees."

"Alas, I cannot."

"Then what good is my ambition?" Mohandas demanded. "Good only for imagining, and proclaiming my impotence to strangers. 'Why, yes, I, too, have a foolish dream—' "

Jafir clucked disapprovingly. "Look there," said the old man, pointing into the sky ahead. "My eyes are frail—is that kite or crow on the wing?"

Lifting his gaze, Mohandas squinted against the brightness. As he did, a noose of fabric settled around his throat from behind with a whisper, and a massive blow to the middle of his back knocked him forward and drove him to the ground. The noose snapped tight, choking off his cries.

He clawed at it desperately, struck wildly at the air seeking the hands that held it, fought the weight that pinned him in the dust, but all to no avail. In seconds, only Mohandas's lungs were still fighting. The rest of his body was bound into a single great spasm of panic and pain, frozen rigid by the screams of knotted muscles. Death was agony. Dying was an eternity.

Then, unexpectedly, the weight on Mohandas's back vanished. The cloth noose whipped free, burning his throat, and was gone. Between retches and coarse, racking gasps, Mohandas raised himself weakly to forearms and knees, his head touching the ground as though he were praying.

"I have killed the boy who was in such misery," Jafir said commandingly. "But I have spared the boy who cared enough to fight me. He is free now. Allow him to pursue what he wants."

With a great effort, Mohandas raised his head and turned toward the voice. He saw Jafir standing a few strides away, calmly knotting his sash around his waist— the yellow sash that moments before he had wielded as a weapon.

"Who are you?" Mohandas asked hoarsely. His throat burned when he spoke. "Madman? Bandit?"

Jafir made a scoffing sound, and drew himself up taller. "I am *Thag*, a deceiver. I am *bhurtote*, a strangler. I am Jafir, the last *subahdar* in Gujarat. I alone keep the secrets of the noose, the sacrifice of the sugar, and the consecration of the pickax.

"You have failed because your mother's gods are too soft and weak. Your father's heroes are cowards. The true power comes from Mother Kali, to those whom she has blessed as her own.

"I could have had your life and your poor purse, Mohandas Gandhi. But Kali has called me to teach once more. She has sent me to be your *ustad*, your tutor, in the ways of Thuggee. I will not let you fail. You will learn

the way and the art, and they will make you strong. You
will have your ten thousand rupees, and more.

"Now get up, and begin your life over."

Slowly, Mohandas gathered his shaking legs beneath
him and rose from the dust. He beheld Jafir with reverent
awe.

"*Ustad,*" he said, tears streaming from his eyes. "Guru.
Father. I am ready to learn."

*I met Jafir on the bleakest, emptiest day of my life. I was
consumed by depression and self-loathing, enslaved by the
expectations of my family and the obligations of my new
child, defeated by my failure at school.*

*Jafir was strength where I was timidity, certainty where I
was insecurity, power where I was impotence, fire where I
was as colorless as air. He was everything that I hungered
to be. It was impossible to doubt that his appearance was a
portent, that Kali had sent him to claim me.*

*I asked for death, and Jafir showed me its face. I craved
direction, and he filled my emptiness with purpose. I was
without prospects, and he offered me the wealth that meant
freedom. I was drawn to him as I had been to Sheikh Mehtab,
who taught me guile, at whose prodding I first ate meat, and
entered a brothel, and stole from Ba.*

*But Sheikh Mehtab was a schoolboy, lazy, selfish, careless
of his friends, shallow. He deserved neither respect nor the
compliant followers he had.*

*My father had taught me to respect age, and wisdom, and
authority, and Jafir embodied all these. He had seen into my
heart as through a glass—I could not help but accept him as
my teacher.*

*That his teacher had been bloody Kali did not trouble me,
for I was full of anger, and ready to fall into her worship.
Nor was I troubled that the cult was banned, the Thug clans
crushed by Captain Sleeman when my father was still a boy.
There was still power in the very name, and I was certain
Jafir knew all of the secrets of those days. I could not refuse
the honor he had offered me.*

* * *

To explain his long absences from home, Mohandas told his family that he had taken a job as a messenger for a Bhavnagar merchant. Knowing his fondness for long solitary walks, Laxmidas and his mother accepted the deception, along with the honest promise that he would find a tutor in English and someday return to his studies.

Until then, there was far more to learn than Mohandas had dreamed—the taking of auspices, the omens through which Kali made her will known, bird, wolf, jackal, and hare—the secret language Ramasee, the wordless signs and road markings, the signals for murder.

"It troubles me," said Jafir one day, watching Mohandas clumsily dig a *gobba*, the round grave, "that I must hasten your initiation. Thuggee is a discipline, and each step a test, from the young scouts to the sextons who dig the graves, to the *shumseeas* who hold the victim's hands and feet, the *bhurtotes* who wield the nooses of Khaddar cloth.

"Nor is that the final initiation, for beyond lies *beylha* and *sotha*, *hilla* and *jemadar*, *subahdar* and *burka*. At any step a man may falter, showing sympathy or fear, or otherwise betraying his unfitness.

"Kali is testing me, to see if I am worthy of being called *burka*, one thoroughly instructed in the art. The measure of the *burka* is that, alone, anywhere in India, he can form a gang of Thugs from the rude materials he finds around him.

"Yet to teach you the lore and art, I must go against what I was taught. No Thug kills alone, by Kali's instruction, and I will not defy her. But that means I cannot bring you into the clan by measures, as I would a young boy, as I was myself. On your first expedition, you must be prepared to join me in Kali's work. Your first test will be a stern one."

"I will not falter," Mohandas vowed.

"You dare not. You were chosen by Kali, and she does not forgive weakness."

"When will I be ready? Let me prove myself."

"You will never be ready, no matter how long your test is delayed," Jafir said. "So it does not matter. But I have made a pact with Kali to give half of the life I have left to your training." He smiled. "And I am not in a hurry to die."

So it was another year before Mohandas first tasted *goor*.

The flames of the dung fire flared up, filling the air with the aromatic scents of sandalwood, butter, incense, and herbs. Jafir sat on a carpet before the fire pit, the curved iron blade of his pickax resting on a brass dish at his knees. Mohandas perched silent and motionless on his haunches nearby, watching.

"Once, the world was ruled by the demon Rukt Bij-dana, who devoured men as fast as they were created," pronounced Jafir. "Kali went forth with her sword to slay the demon, but from every drop of its blood there sprang a new monster. She did not falter, but went on destroying the blood-brood, until they multiplied so quickly that she grew weary, and paused to rest.

"From the sweat brushed from her own arm, she created two men, and gave to one a *rumal* torn from the hem of her garment, and commanded them to strangle the demons. This they did, returning to her when all had been slain. For her labors and service, she presented them with one of her teeth for a pickax. She bade them pass the *rumal* and the pickax to their sons, and to destroy all men who were not their kin, for the stranglers alone are her favored children."

Jafir took the pickax blade and passed it seven times through the fire, once for each blood spot he had marked along its length. Then he turned, placed a shelled coconut on the brass dish, and shouted to Mohandas and the empty grove, "Shall I strike?"

Mohandas leapt to his feet and cried his approval.

"All hail mighty Kali, great Mother of us all!" Jafir shouted. He raised the pickax blade over his head and brought it crashing down on the coconut, shattering it to pieces.

Mohandas Karamchand Gandhi took a step forward, his heart racing, his black eyes glowing with eagerness. "All hail mighty Kali—and prosper the Thugs!"

The auspices being favorable, they traveled five days to the northeast, to the vicinity of Surendranagar. Burying the pickax each night and taking their direction from its point each morning, they made their way along the busy road without attracting undue attention.

On the sixth day, they heard the croak of a mountain crow from high in a tree in a roadside grove, and settled there to wait for the rich traveler that sign promised.

They passed over a potmaker from Ahmadabad, because he was of the Camala cast, which Jafir explained was under Kali's protection. A trader traveling to a wedding—who was plainly *bunij*, one worth murdering—was spared because he was in the company of his wife.

"A Thug may not kill a woman, nor leave a witness alive," Jafir reminded Mohandas. "When my clan numbered fifty, with a dozen stranglers in that number, we thought nothing of falling on a party of as many as ten. But you and I must choose more carefully."

Finally Jafir settled on a trader in indigo, traveling alone and driving a horse-drawn *tonga*. The cart was empty, which told Jafir that the trader's purse should be full.

The trader was talkative and generous, and they made his acquaintance easily. They traveled a whole day in his company, with Jafir riding in the back of the *tonga*—a courtesy from the trader, on account of Jafir's age—while Mohandas walked alongside.

They were often alone on the road, and it seemed an excellent opportunity for an ambush, with Jafir perched behind the trader and Mohandas ready to seize the harness and control the horse. But Jafir never gave the sign. For much of the day, Mohandas wondered if he had missed a cautionary omen—the braying of an ass, or a wolf crossing the road from left to right, or the crying of owls to each other.

Finally, Mohandas realized that Jafir was simply savoring the trader's innocence that these were his last hours, and watching with curiosity to see how he lived them.

It was then that Mohandas understood the liberating power of the inevitable. Kali had chosen their victim and delivered him into their hands, and he would die swiftly when the moment came. But haste was not part of the strangler's way, and there was an unexpected pleasure in the waiting.

The thrill of foreknowledge drove out Mohandas's guilt, until he could laugh as easily as Jafir at the joke the trader had not yet been told, and relish the taste of death to come.

Death came in the night. At Jafir's whisper, "*Bajeed*—it is safe," Mohandas shook the trader to waken him. When the man sat bolt upright in confusion, Mohandas seized his hands, and Jafir whipped the yellow *rumal* around his throat. It was done soundlessly, and with scarcely a struggle. In the darkness, Mohandas found it dreamlike and unreal, even as they carried the body away to the *baras* where they would bury it.

Jafir allowed Mohandas the honor of digging the grave in the sand. Then Jafir drew his knife and mangled the corpse in the prescribed manner, spilling the trader's blood only in the grave itself. When the grave had been filled, Jafir sprinkled fleawort seeds over the ground, to discourage the curiosity of dogs and jackals.

Of the trader's possessions, they kept only his horse, which they later sold in Mahesana for seventy rupees, and his heavy purse, which contained more than a hundred silver rupees and a delicate gold ring. The rest they burned, even the *tonga*, so that there would be no sign that a man had vanished in the night, or that Thuggee had returned to west India.

* * *

Jafir conducted the ritual of *tuponee*, the sacrifice of the sugar, in the privacy of a clearing in the jungle well away from any road. When the offering had been buried, Jafir divided the consecrated sugar that remained and presented half to Mohandas, who looked at him in surprise.

"It is true that only those who have strangled with their own hands are thought worthy of the consecrated sugar," said Jafir. "It is also true that for generations, teachers of the art secretly gave *goor* to their favored disciples, in the belief that it would speed their advance. So I do now."

Mohandas's heart soared with gratitude, and his hands trembled as he held the sacred crystals, waiting.

"Kali, accept our offering, and fulfill your servants' desires," Jafir prayed solemnly. Then, sharply, he gave the command to strike. *"Bajeed. Ki jai."*

He raised his palm to his mouth, and closed his eyes in rapture.

Mohandas found the power of the *goor* dizzying. His heart raced and his throat burned, until he had to lie back in the grass. The stars shimmered before his eyes.

"Mohandas," Jafir said, his voice sounding far away, "there were long years when I thought that I would never taste the *goor* again. This is a gift you have given me.

"It is the *goor* which changes us, which drives out pity, which gives us our strength. Let any man once taste the *goor* and he will be a Thug, though he know all the trades and have all the wealth in the world.

"Long years," he repeated. "You cannot imagine."

Puzzled, Mohandas asked, "How is this my gift?"

Jafir nodded slowly. "I have kept this from you until now. But it is time for you to know—how it is I am here, and why I was alone.

"I have let you believe that I escaped the great hunt, those black years when the *nujeebs* of the British demon smashed even the strongest of the clans. Thousands of young Thugs did escape, it is true—I knew many who went into hiding, or joined the armies of the princes of the Indian states, who would protect them.

"But there was no Thug clan, no family, which did not have friends or kin in the jail at Saugor, awaiting trial and execution. No matter what our numbers or where we fled, we were not safe, not even in the Indian states, so long as we lived as Thugs, and did Kali's work. The Company's soldiers were relentless.

"Mohandas, my clan never strangled a single white man—no Thug of my acquaintance ever did. But they hunted us to extinction all the same.

"It was not that there were so many of them. The *nujeebs* were led by Thug informers, the approvers—men who had broken the sacred oath to save their own lives—" His voice trailed off as he stared into the darkness.

"You were arrested," said Mohandas.

"Yes," Jafir said with a sorrowful nod. "More than twenty of my clan were captured in the spring of 1832, after a pursuit of hundreds of miles. It was an approver, Noor Khan, who led the *nujeebs* to our hiding place. Other Thugs who had been known to us denounced us before the judge, and we were sent to a crowded prison to join our brothers waiting to die.

"I was a young *bhurtote* then. I had seen nine expeditions, strangled no more than a dozen men. But I was facing the British noose as surely as someone like Buhram, who had confessed to nearly a thousand murders.

"No one doubted that all of Thuggee was to be destroyed—there was much talk in jail that this was Kali's verdict on us. It was known that many women had been strangled, along with holy men, and those of the Camala caste. We had brought this misfortune on ourselves. It could even be believed that it was the approvers who did Kali's work—

"I was young, and frightened. I did not wish to die, and Thuggee could not save me. I lost the faith. I made a full confession, and offered myself as an approver.

"They tested my truthfulness, and in the end accepted me, commuting my sentence. I served them for the next year. Sixteen Thugs were hanged on my words, and a score more branded and transported for life.

"Mohandas, I am a betrayer."

Mohandas would not hear it. "No—no, it was the British—"

Jafir shook his head. "No, the blame is mine. But I hate them, Mohandas," he said in a cold whisper. "I hate them for making me weak. I hate them for the way they have taken what was ours. I hate them for destroying my life and my people.

"I have been a shadow since those days. I spent thirty years in the approvers' compound at Saugor, until they decided at last that I was harmless. Since then, I have been alone—ostracized, denied the way of my father and his father, denied the blessings of Kali."

For the first time in long minutes, Jafir looked directly at Mohandas, and his gaze was soft with gratitude. "Tonight, I live again. That is the gift you have given me."

We strangled six other travelers, no two on the same road or the same day, before returning to Rajkot. The profit was divided in the traditional manner, two shares to Jafir as the leader, and one and a half shares to me for my part, less the offering held for Kali's priests.

That division left me with 521 rupees in silver and gold, and jewelry worth an equal amount, or more. I gave 50 rupees to Laxmidas for his support of my household, which greatly pleased and surprised him. The rest I concealed in my house, save for the cost of several measures of fine Khadi cloth, a gift to Kasturbhai.

We made three more expeditions before the rains came. On the last of these, Jafir began my instruction in the making and use of the rumal, and before we returned home, I at last became one of those privileged to murder for Kali. I felt no remorse, only delight. There is a sweetness, unexpected, exhilarating.

The rains meant the end of our first season. Jafir did not stay in Rajkot, choosing to return to Indore. But he returned in October with two horses, and we set off on what would be our longest journey together—a pilgrimage to Kali's temple of Vindhyachal, on the Ganges.

There we offered our thanks, and Kali's share of our booty from the previous year, in the manner which Jafir prescribed.

Whether the priests knew us for Thugs, we could not say. But the temple had once been such a focus for Thuggee that it was there that Sleeman's spies and approvers began the terrible campaign against us. To return to Vindhyachal was to reclaim it as ours.

Kali showed her pleasure by favoring us during our return. It is unlucky for a Thug to kill on the way to the temple, but Kali placed seven travelers in our hands on the roads back to Rajkot, and the booty was richer than any we had yet taken.

Jafir had decided that I should know all of the sacred places of the brotherhood, for our next expedition was to the ancient tomb of Nizam Oddeen Ouleea, near Delhi. On the way, he instructed me further in Thuggee lore, and told me tales of Ouleea and other celebrated stranglers. And again, our trip home was most profitable, which only confirmed Jafir in his determination.

So we then set out for Ellora and the temple of Kailasa, carved out of a mountain by Krsna himself, where the strangler's art is depicted in stone carvings a thousand years old. The journey to that great shrine would take us halfway across India, so Jafir bought a mule to carry back the riches he was certain we would gather.

But on the road west of Dhule, Jafir fell asleep while riding in the midday sun. He slipped from the saddle before I could notice, and fell heavily to the hard-packed ground. Jafir's horse avoided trampling him, but the mule did not. One hoof grazed Jafir's temple, and another came down squarely on his ribs—I heard the bones crack.

He died there in the road, cradled in my arms, while the mule grazed nearby, innocent of what it had done.

That was the second time I had watched, helpless, as a man who was everything to me slowly and painfully surrendered his life. It seemed to me that there must be something

*that could be done, if I only had the knowledge—but I did
not have the knowledge. I could not help Jafir, as I could not
help my father.*

*I took it into my heart as a rebuke. I had only learned
Kali's way—life was still a mystery.*

*I bought sandalwood for Jafir's cremation, and carried his
bones to the sacred river myself. Then I went home to Ba,
counted my money, and found a tutor in English. Two months
later, I took up my studies to be a doctor—an Indian doctor,
from an Indian school.*

*Kali had freed me by taking Jafir. My days as a Thug
were over.*

"Father, you must come at once!"

Dr. Mohandas Gandhi looked up from the desk in his
small examination room to the anxious face of his son,
Harilal. "What has happened?" he asked, rising from his
chair even as he asked. "Is it Ba?"

"There has been shooting in the Jallianwalla Bagh. Bring
your bag—hurry!"

They hastened together through the narrow streets of
Amritsar toward the garden. Harilal could tell his father
little more, for he had only caught the rumor as it rippled
outward through the city: there had been a gathering for
a Sikh festival in the Bagh, which was often used as a
meeting place.

"The man who told me to fetch you lives in a house
near the garden. He said that he had heard rifle shots, so
many that he could not count, and screaming. The gunfire and the screaming went on for so long that he grew
afraid and ran away."

"What reason could there be for such a thing?" Mohandas asked. "I cannot believe it."

But as they neared the Bagh, it became clear that something terrible had, indeed, happened. There was a strange
wildness in the streets outside the garden—the buzz of
angry voices and wailing, the acrid smell of gunpowder
hanging in the hot, still late afternoon air.

A woman saw that Gandhi was a doctor and rushed out from a doorway, her face anguished, to seize his elbow and hurry him along. "Come, please help, so many are hurt—"

"What has happened?" Mohandas demanded.

"Soldiers—British soldiers, Gurkhas, and Baluchis. They marched in, fired at the crowd until their weapons were empty, and then marched out again."

"Was there a riot?"

"No! Everything was peaceful."

"Madness," Mohandas muttered. "I cannot believe it." But he allowed her to guide him down one of the narrow entrances to the garden.

Once inside, he found himself on a gentle rise overlooking the vast open courtyard that was the Bagh. At his first clear glimpse of what awaited him, he tore himself free from the woman's grip and stood rooted by the entrance, struck, wordless by what he saw.

The Bagh, spread out below him, was a wasteland, littered with the bodies of a thousand Sikhs, many still, many more writhing in agony. Their moaning assaulted him, overwhelmed him, and he averted his eyes with an abrupt jerk of his head.

Mohandas saw then that empty brass cartridges were everywhere on the ground around his feet. The British soldiers had stood where he was standing, calmly firing down into the hollow while the garden blossomed with blood flowers—the realization sent a poisoned chill through his body, and his legs weakened.

"Come!" the woman said, grabbing his arm again, almost angry in her impatience with him. "Do something!"

The agony of the wounded was palpable even from the rise. Mohandas could not go down among them, but somehow he did. Numbly, he moved from victim to victim, doing what little he could to staunch bleeding and banish pain, until he could go no farther. It seemed that all of India was dying in his arms, and still he was helpless. He drew himself into a ball on the ground near the speaker's platform and wept until he could weep no more.

But then anger began to creep into the hollow left by the exhaustion of his despair, replacing his weakness with the strength of a cold resolution for revenge. Mohandas regained his feet, mounted the platform, and surveyed the carnage about him—slowly, deliberately, unblinking, determined to burn the images into his memory.

He attracted no attention, for he was not an imposing figure—a slender, thick-lipped man in a dusty, bloody suit, with big ears and bristly hair that was rapidly turning white. But the vision he was nurturing in that moment gave him a power that no one who saw him could have guessed. The circle of his life had closed—the massacre of the stranglers and the massacre of the Sikhs were the same act, flowing from the same evil. And he knew what power could destroy that evil.

The wind came up, and it was fragrant with death. "In all your years as a *bhurtote*, Jafir, you took no prize of value, ever," Mohandas Gandhi said to the wind. "But before I am done, I will."

Mohandas, *jemadar* of Thuggee, surveyed the faces of the twenty men in the circle surrounding the fire. They were as different from each other as could be—Sikh and Hindu, Kshatriya and Brahmin, man and boy. But they were one in their purpose, and their belief in the promise.

"Once," said Mohandas, "the world was ruled by the white demon, Rukt Bij-dana, who devoured men as fast as they were created. Kali went forth with her sword to slay the demon, but from every drop of its blood there sprang a new monster. She did not falter, but went on destroying the blood-children, until they multiplied so quickly that she grew weary, and paused to rest.

"From the sweat brushed from her own arm, she created two men, and gave to one a *rumal* torn from the hem of her garment, and commanded them to strangle the demons. This they did, returning to her when all had been slain. She bade them pass the *rumal* to their sons, and to use it to destroy all who were not their kin, for the sons of India alone are her favored children.

"Now the white demon has returned to the land Kali gave to us. The British are the spawn of the devourer, whom Kali sent us to destroy. Because we have forgotten our devotions, and abandoned the worship of the Black Mother, we have become weak, and the demons rule over us.

"It is our task, and our honor, to teach what has been forgotten, and restore what has been neglected, and so make India strong again."

He took up the pickax and passed it through the fire, then placed the white coconut on the brass plate. "Shall I strike?" he asked.

The gang cried their approval, in a voice that shook the trees of the grove.

"All hail mighty Kali, great Mother of us all!" Mohandas shouted. He raised the pickax over his head and brought it crashing down on the coconut, shattering it to pieces.

They cheered, and answered as Mohandas had taught them: "All hail mighty Kali—and prosper the sons of India!"

Then they sang together, the melody haunting, their voices strong in the dark grove:

> "Because thou lovest the Burning-ground
> I have made a burning ground of my heart—
> Naught else is in my heart, O Mother
> Day and night blazes the funeral pyre . . ."

There are five hundred million of us, and not five hundred thousand of them. We are their servants, their sepoy soldiers, the farmers who grow their indigo and tea. They cannot rule without us.

The brotherhood of Thuggee must grow, until we are everywhere, invisible, until the demons do not know which of us they can trust, and so they can dare trust none of us. They will fear the night, and the light, and the shadows, until fear is all they know.

I do not fear death, because if I die in the service of Kali, I know that she will deliver me to sadhu, ecstasy. The demons will fight us, but they cannot defeat us. Wherever they resist us, we will strike and kill.

The demons will leave this land, or they will die. This I have promised Kali. This, Kali has promised me.

Kathe Koja has written so many brilliant stories and novels that it's hard to remember that the author of *The Cipher* is still a relative newcomer to the field. That she writes with a skill and maturity that belies her experience was never more evident than in this story about the great Spanish poet Federico García Lorca.

Ballad of the Spanish Civil Guard
by Kathe Koja

The poet has beautiful fingers, long fingers, fingers like a girl. Paintbrush hands, his father called them, his father being a man of some humor; his mother said no, they were the hands of a musician. Had not the boy loved music early?—before he could talk he was humming the folk songs, songs of nature, the fields, the terrible strange light of the virgin moon; he knew all the words, he could sing them like an expert. He will be a musician one day, said his mother, stroking his hair with her fingers, pulling fondly the strands like raveled string, dark and lank; and he looking up at her through that string, cat's cradle, bridge: hair like cords to bind the soul, that was what the gypsies said. Hair, blood, semen, all of it useful, all of it rich with secrets and with needs.

* * *

The moon is not in evidence; there is nothing here but walls, four stone squares in dark abutment, one to the other to the next; his arms ache, his back, the backs of his weary legs. Across the room, there, is a man with a gun; he is smoking a cigarette and eating an orange, spitting the seeds on the floor.

"You want a cigarette?" the guard says.

The poet shakes his head, mouth open a little, and tries to talk; there is blood on his lower lip, itself split almost down the middle; blood on his pale shirt and loose tie, the kind artists wear. The guards had noted that, one to the other, with derision. An artist; a queer, some of them said, *maricas, apios* they called them in Seville; it was understood that many artists were queer.

Orange seeds on the floor; the sound of men laughing, dark and quiet in the corridor. The poet clears his throat as best he can, prefatory to speech; he has had nothing to drink for almost eight hours, since they came to the home of his friends, his protectors. The black squad: silent eyes and hands beneath his damp elbows, to take him away. "Water?" he says to the guard.

The guard has not understood; the poet must speak again, ask, request: "Water?" Words are his *métier*, his life's blood; he uses them now with caution, with pity, with terror; it is after all his words which have brought him here, to this room with four walls and no moon, cigarette smoke dense and acrid as arsenic, the guard with his orange and his gun. "May I have water, here?"

The guard surveys him, eyes half-closed and in one motion slips the peel denuded between his lips: his whole mouth now one grotesque and pebbled grin, a pumpkin's toothless smile: spits it into his hand and laughs, a little joke on and for himself. "Water?" he says. "Let us see."

The poet's hands twist warm and nervously; there are rings of dried sweat beneath his shirt. They have handled him roughly, true, true also that they have split his lip; but no one has said anything about murder, no one has mentioned the road, the olive groves; the work to be done

there. He has heard about the olive groves, about the men
come to dig the graves, spade in one hand, bottle in the
other and finding, what? The dead uncle, the dead
brother; the dead son. These are times not so much per-
ilous as beyond peril; walking through fire, one forgets to
fear the singeing of the sleeve. One will be consumed,
devoured dry as that orange, there, its poor peel bent
awkward and backward and wrong; or one will live. It is
really very simple after all.

The guard returns; no, water is not permitted. No. "Cigarette?" in the proffering hand, reiteration of the one solace
available. Take it, *el poeta*, it is all you are going to get.

It is very hard to smoke with a mouth so sore but he
manages; he fears—without shame; this room is too small
and too dark for shame, it would be a luxury, a decadence
almost into which he must not fall; what room for decadence when panic is at the door?—and fears to say no to
the guard's offer; it may do nothing for him in any case
but oh, *el poeta*, it is truly all you are going to get. It is a
cheap brand of cigarette; on its paper, now, see the bright
new stain.

Somewhere down the corridor, a man screams. The
poet thinks he can smell olives, their oil crushed colorless like blood upon his hands.

No more talk from the guard: he sits, legs crossed, so
still he might passably be in sleep if it were not for those
eyes, never closed, barely shifted. He is not a man, the
poet thinks, for much rumination, the habit of thought is
simply not there. Open up his head (still whimsy; still
desperate; some habits simply will not die) and what
would you find? Bullets, their empty lolling roll? A piece
of meat, a warm pudenda, what? Remnants of a speech,
fragments on one side gold and red, the colors of tym-
pani, martial colors—but on the other side, ah, the cheap-
est newsprint, foolscap apropos for the task. If he
remembered that much, beyond the imprecations, the
shouting and the noise; if he even listened to words of
the speeches his leaders made.

He had listened, the poet, nervous hands jammed together like little animals crawling one over another, seeking frantic the burrow that is no longer there, destroyed by a foot, a hand, a motion: forward motion, marching to the future. Death is the future, is it not? Everyone's future, reached at different times, by different ends; as inevitable as birth itself, as suffering, as love. Was it not the gypsies who talked of Death as the lover? Death, the beautiful boy unsmiling, in one hand the mace and scepter, in the other his own wet flesh, tumescent, hard with blood; was it then so hard to understand?

No, finally; but acceptance was another matter, he can accept nothing now, the poet, but the hard floor, the scattered scraps of rind like callused flesh torn by Furies not in rage but indifference: one must eat, after all. After all. He smokes the cigarette down to a burn on his trembling finger; the guard's gaze never leaves him once.

He is a Red, they said, a Russian spy; he has done more damage with his pen than others with their guns. *El poeta*, they said, you are a dangerous man; there in the light, they bring their own light with them, they do not fear for him to see their faces; how confident, after all, they all are. Especially the man in the middle, the one with the long slim eyes, long sleepy lids like a cat's, a lizard's in the sun. Very dangerous, he says.

It is not pride that makes him shrug; there is no room for pride here, either, barely room enough for truth but it is truth that moves his trembling shoulders; he is trembling all over, now. "Not dangerous," he says, trying for clarity, trying to move his swollen lips so he will be understood. "The truth is dangerous."

"The truth," says the man in the middle, "is often what you make it. Is that not so?"—not, note, to the men beside him, to the guard now in the doorway who seems almost to have fallen asleep where he stands: it is very late after all. No, this man, this leader speaks to the poet himself, addresses him as cleanly and directly as a pistol shot.

"The truth is what is believed to be true. You should know that, Federico."

The use of his name unnerves him; but already he trembles, he is a glass brimful of fear: what more can be done to frighten him, but death? Torture? He thinks of the gypsies again, the music of *cante jondo*, the deep song that cries in black sounds of pain, loss, the sorrow everlasting of love; and yet hearing it, immersed by it, who can sorrow? be sad? It is the music of the blood in the body; or thus it was explained to him. What wild cantos, now, sing his blood, driven by fear, the animal terror of the body confronted by the idea of the end, no more? The gypsies know what death is.

"Is it not so, Federico?" says the narrow-eyed man, and the poet realizes the man has been speaking, all this time, speaking to him and expecting now perhaps an answer. His throat is so dry it clicks when he swallows, a painful click that makes the men smile, grin at him for what they perceive as another manifestation of his fear; but he is not ashamed: why should he not be afraid? Only a fool does not fear. He tries to clear his throat for speech and finds instead it is simply too dry.

Mouth open like a fish, he gestures—earnestly, earnestly; communication is important, even now; especially now. The guard at the door is dispatched for water, returns with a cup full of something wet and warm: for a moment the poet fears his thirst will overcome his judgment, that he will swallow urine, or blood, or whatever foulness is contained in evil joke inside the cup: but it is water, after all, if somewhat warm and none too clear. He drinks it all, forcing himself to go slowly, while the narrow-eyed man watches, arms crossed like a schoolmaster awaiting a pupil's response.

"Now," he says, when the poet has drunk the cup down. "You will give us your decision, Federico."

The poet is silent; the most important question, or at least the most crucial, of his life; and he does not know what to say. There are no windows here in the room; if

only he could see the moon, he might know better, might
have some idea what he must do. Under his armpits he
smells his own sour sweat; perhaps they will kill him
now.

But the narrow-eyed man is not displeased by his silence, or does not seem to be so. Arms crossed, he un-
crosses them, scratches himself through the warm brown
fabric of his trousers. "We must have an answer," he says.
"Danger, like truth, is what you make of it. As is opportunity. You must realize, Federico, it is opportunity we
offer to you now." And he smiles, this man, a smile of
impatience and vast simplicity, it is all very simple in the
end, so simple the poet need not even hear the words
again to know them: from the smile itself he knows them,
from the word, *dangerous*, spoken so formally before.

"It is not a consideration offered to many," the narrow-
eyed man says; his smile has gone. "It is a chance to
participate in history, have you thought of that? Your beloved gypsies, Federico, what will become of them in history's waters? Will they swim? Will they drown? Your
answer cannot save them—I am sure you know this already, I give nothing away—but it may save you, to im-
mortalize them, perhaps? in poetry? All wars end,
Federico, all wars and insurrections. And conversations;
this one is ending now. What will you?" and all the men
in the room save the poet seem to stand a little taller,
holding themselves as if in the wind of history itself.

"What you offer is monstrous," says the poet. "Even
you must know that."

"Mother of God," the narrow-eyed man says; finally he
is angry, or at least profoundly annoyed. "Monstrous, not-
monstrous, why do you play this game with me now?
Either you will do as is suggested or we will kill you, so.
You are done writing poems in any case."

Mother of God, Mother of Sorrows, only two days ago—
three?—he had stood praying, hands clasped before an
image of the Sacred Heart. On the piano, the image benevolent, crying inside and praying, praying without

words: asking for: what? What do you want, *el poeta*? You
are done writing poems in any case.

The narrow-eyed man does not even shake his head;
gestureless, he gestures to the door. "Coffee," he says.
"Give him plenty of coffee." The code for an execution,
why such coyness now, such brutal tact? do they think
he does not know these things? can they imagine for one
moment he does not *know*? For one wild instant he
dreams a window, a moon, hands bright with weapons in
its light: *we have come to save you, Federico, we have come
to get you out*.

There is no window; there is no moon. If he could have
been saved it would have been accomplished before now;
nothing will happen now but the inevitable, as relentless
as the last act of a play. He is handcuffed to another man,
a teacher with a wooden leg, and together in lockstep
both are forced into the waiting car, in the sorrow of the
cricketless night.

He will die, he thinks, like a matador, like Ignacio Sán-
chez Mejias: *I remember a sad breeze through the olive
trees*. Like a matador, like Christ, dying with his hands
open in the shadeless midnight of the olive grove. He is
not trembling any longer, nor shivering, he barely feels
the manacles about his wrists. The teacher is shot dead;
his wooden leg is particularly pitiful.

You next, *el poeta*.

What will the gypsies make of his blood, his sweet
white bones? He has heard the body voids itself, in death,
leaks urine and nightsoil, semen and sweat. All of it has
power, all; even his hair against the ground like roots
asearch for purchase, dark and hungry motion on the
pebbles and the stones; does not the *cante jondo* tell us
so? Perhaps they will fashion another poet from his leav-
ings, a stronger man than he. Or perhaps it will be a
different species entirely; a warrior, say. He would not be
displeased; surely they will know this, divine it in silence

and that deepest understanding, swirling twinned to marrow in the bones.

The eager splash of the Fuente Grande, that famous spring there at the killing ground; perhaps the gypsies are watching, now, and waiting, patient only for the bullet to begin their work; O remember me! he cries in his heart, as behind him a man curses, the leaves of the olive trees move. Already his fingers lie open like a lotus, long fingers like a flower to mark the spot where they must begin.

Laura Resnick, an award-winning romance writer and a Campbell nominee in the science fiction field (and your editor's daughter), spent a number of years living in Sicily, the birthplace of the Mafia, and in New York, where the Mafia is just another high-powered business organization. She draws upon both experiences for this story about Pope John Paul I, who died—quite possibly from unnatural causes—a month after ascending to the papacy.

The Vatican Outfit
by Laura Resnick

In September of 1978, Pope John Paul I died only thirty-three days after his election to the papacy. At the time of his death, he had already decided on startling changes which would affect the doctrine, hierarchy, and finances of the Church. Too many powerful and ruthless men (including certain underworld figures) had a great deal to lose under the papacy of John Paul I, and it is widely believed that he was murdered.

Everyone needs friends. Hey, it's the way God made the world. A man without friends had better start digging a six-foot hole in a peaceful spot, if you catch my drift. And not just *any* friends, either. *Special* friends. When I was a boy in Sicily, we called such friends men of respect, or men of honor. Or, if we was being real careful, we called them the friends of the friends—*gli amici degli amici*.

When Albino Luciani, His Holiness Pope John Paul I, took his place in the Apostolic Palace in Vatican City in August of 1978, it didn't take no genius to realize that he lacked the one thing that any man needs to survive past sundown: the right kind of friends. Unfortunately, being a naive polenta-eating priest from Venice, he just didn't understand these things. I mean no disrespect to the Holy Father; it's just the way those northerners are.

Well, we—my associates and I—watched the situation very closely for about a month. Everyone we talked to had only kind things to say about Papa Luciani. He was soft-spoken, intelligent, educated, modest, and even celibate. But, everyone admitted, he possessed two unfortunate character traits that were sure to get him into serious trouble, particularly in a place like the Vatican; he was honest and principled.

All right, all right, so maybe that's not *such* a terrible thing. Sure, you wonder how a guy like that becomes the Pope, the *capo di tutti capi*, and you have doubts about his ability to run a big outfit like the Church; but, in the end, you take the material you're given to work with, and you do the best you can. Am I right? Okay, so he was a strange choice for the job, and who the hell knows what those boys in the conclave were thinking of when they made him boss, but I've seen crazier things. Just take a good look at the boss we got in the White House right now.

Anyhow, the real problem with Papa Luciani, you see, was that the guy didn't know how to keep his opinions to himself. I mean he just could not keep his trap shut. It was like he thought that being Pope made him untouchable, or like he believed that a few Swiss pansies in silly suits could really protect him from the hit he was just begging for. I gotta tell you, by late September, we was pretty worried. The poor *schlameil* (that's a Jewish word I learned from Meyer Lansky, may he rest in peace) was going after *everybody*: Licio Gelli, Michele Sindona,

Roberto Calvi, cardinals, bishops, P2, the Vatican Bank . . .
Well, it was starting to look like Paul VI, may he rest in
peace, was the only Vatican guy who wasn't gonna be ex-
communicated by the time the smoke cleared.

My esteemed employer, Mr. Corvino—who, I'm pleased
to say, beat that white slavery rap and isn't gonna be
deported after all—has always had a keen eye for business
opportunities. After a couple of stressful years of doing
business with certain Colombian families, Mr. Corvino
felt a strong desire to return to his roots (figuratively
speaking, of course, since no person in his right mind
would want to move back to Corleone) and do business
only with Italians. If the Pope wanted to sever certain
business connections, it only made sense that he'd also
be interested in establishing new ones. And, since some
business connections are a little more difficult to sever
than others, Mr. Corvino figured that Papa Luciani could
probably use the help of an experienced businessman like
myself.

That's how I wound up in Vatican City on September 28,
1978.

Mr. Corvino pulled a few strings, and of course, we had
help on the inside. My sister's youngest son, Angelo Cos-
tello, was working for Papa Luciani's outfit. Yeah, right
there in the Vatican. The kid got his button about five
years before Luciani became Pope. No, no, not *that* kind
of button. Angelo was—whaddya call it—*ordained*, right
here in New York City. I can't say I was completely in
favor of it at the time, because I had a real good job lined
up for the kid. But he wasn't interested in my perfectly
legitimate business concerns, and so he became a priest.
What are you gonna do with the younger generation?

Anyhow, maybe Angie made the right choice. I was
worried at first, because the Church isn't family; hell, they
ain't even all Italians. But I could see after a while that
they wasn't so different from us after all, and that made
me feel better. Angie was working his way up through the
ranks almost as fast as he would have if he'd stayed in

the Corvino family. He was a real stand-up guy, and his bosses could see that. So, when the opportunity came, they sent him off to Rome. I guess *his* people wanted someone on the inside, too, huh?

"Uncle Vito, you look well," Angelo said, greeting me in my guest room at the Vatican just a few minutes after I arrived.

"Can't say the same about you, kid. Your face is all green. Did you eat some bad fish?"

He looked over his shoulder, like he was expecting to see someone watching us from the doorway. "Please don't call me 'kid,' Uncle Vito."

"What—I'm gonna call my own nephew 'Father'?" I slapped him on the back and pinched his cheek. "Get outta here."

"What are you doing here?"

"Why are you whispering?"

A priest walked past the doorway, and I thought Angie was gonna jump out of his skin. "What are you doing here?" he whispered again.

I caught on. The kid was obviously afraid we were being watched, maybe even bugged. But whispering wasn't gonna help. I was glad I'd arrived in time to teach him a few things. "This room's a little stuffy, don't you think?" I said real casually. "Let's take a walk."

"In public? Where people can see us *together*?" He looked like he was gonna faint.

"Hey, that's the best place to be right now." I put on my coat and hat, took him by the elbow, and led him down the hallway and out of the building. We took a little stroll in St. Peter's Square. "You afraid of being whacked out, kid? Is that why you're sweating like a bride on her wedding night?"

"Whacked out?" he bleated.

"Hey, relax. We're as safe out here as we'll ever be. Look at all these tourists. No one's gonna clip us in front of all these people, trust me. Whenever you know someone's gunning for you, it's those private, isolated places that you want to avoid. Stay out of your room, the confessional, and dark restaurants. Speaking as an expert, if I was gonna whack someone, that's where I'd do it," I told him.

"Jesus, Mary, and Joseph!"

"Yeah, brightly lit public places, lotsa people, plenty of witnesses. That's the kind of background you need to make you feel safe. And, if someone is dumb enough to try to clip you in public, chances are that they'll clip a perfect stranger by accident and you'll get away without a scratch."

"*What?*"

"So you just listen to your Uncle Vito, and everything's gonna be all right."

"What are you—"

"Another thing—and this is very important: don't ever talk inside, and don't ever talk on the phone. You got that? You wanna talk, go outside. And don't go anywhere without me." I patted his cheek. "I'm gonna take good care of you and your boss, kid."

"My boss?"

"Yeah. Because *my* boss is very worried." I looked around, because you can never be too careful. Sure enough, some blond broad was standing a little too close to us. "Beat it, sister!"

Angie turned red. "Uncle Vito, you can't—"

"Listen, kid. This is serious. Are you paying attention?" He nodded. "We're pretty sure there's a hit out on your boss, and we think it may go down tonight."

"A *hit*? On my *boss*?" He was talking real slow, like English was a problem for him or something. "Whoa, hang on a minute, Uncle Vito. I think you're confusing me with my brother."

"Well, not that you asked, but Joey's doing fine. In fact, he's up for parole next month. And your mother would like to know why you don't call her more often."

"The FBI wiretap just sort of took all the joy out of family phone calls." He sounded a little pissed-off.

"Here," I said, remembering the wad in my pocket. "Your father asked me to give you this." I stuck a few grand in his hand.

"Vito! I can't accept this!"

"Go on, kid, take it. Your old man had a good year, and he knows that this outfit don't pay you much."

"The Roman Catholic Church is not an out—"

"And may the Blessed Virgin forgive me, but that's all the time I got for family business. I need to see your boss right away."

"The Pope? You expect me to introduce *you* to the Holy Father?"

"Hey, I know this goes against protocol. If I want to offer a temporary alliance to help stop a takeover, I should approach his *consigliere* first. Problem is, Angie, I think the *consigliere's* in on it."

"The *consigliere* . . ." Angie's jaw dropped. "Are you trying to tell me that Carmine Corvino sent you here because he believes that the Vatican Secretary of State is involved in a plot to assassinate the Pope?"

"We ain't pointing no fingers at nobody. All I'm saying is that there's gonna be a hit on the Pope, and except for you and me, nobody in this outfit is above suspicion."

"That's impossible!"

"Yeah, and I'll bet that's just what Joe Bonnano said before the Banana War started and he had to go into hiding."

Angelo's forehead got all wrinkly while he thought it over. He was always a quick kid; one hour later we was having a sit-down with the Pope.

"Your Holiness," Angelo said, as we walked around some fancy little garden, "I would never presume to interrupt your busy schedule like this if I didn't believe this were truly a life-and-death emergency."

I was looking around, kind of nervous about being in such an isolated spot. Frankie (the Noodle) Barone bought it in a place just like that garden.

"Carmine Corvino may be a racketeer, an extortionist,

a narcotics dealer, and a murderer, but he's no fool," Angie went on.

"Mr. Corvino is a perfectly legitimate businessman," I corrected. Vicious rumors start so easily.

"If Corvino says there's going to be an attempt on your life, Your Holiness, then I believe that there will be. If anyone could be considered an unimpeachable source of underworld information, it's my Uncle Vito's, um, associate."

"So, Albino," I said. "I can call you Albino, can't I? This is the situation. It's not just that we've gotta avoid the hit; we've also gotta take out the boys who are involved in it. All of them, Al, even if that means whacking your *consigliere*."

"Whacking?" the Pope said.

"Assassinating, Holy Father," Angie said. These college boys!

Well, Luciani looked pretty shocked. I could see it was time to lay out the deal for him.

"Al, come on, we're all men of the world here. Let's be frank," I said. "This is a very big outfit you got here, and you've had some very tough boys working for you over the centuries. But now, times have changed, and you've all grown a little soft. Your income is good, you hardly got any trouble with the feds, you got pretty good public relations, and you got soldiers like my nephew here joining up almost every day. You got a good thing here. But let's be honest, Al." I looked him right in the eye. "When war comes, and it *is* coming, it's usually the good who die young."

Luciani thought it over. "If I accept your assertion that I'm in danger of being assassinated—"

"*If?*" I said. "Al, you'd better not wait too long to start believing it, or you're gonna find yourself with a bullet between your eyes and a quick trip to the Pearly Gates. And then I'm gonna have to tell Mr. Corvino that Angie and I failed here. And Mr. Corvino don't like it when his boys fail."

"Wait a minute!" Angelo said. "I'm not—"

"Quiet, kid," I ordered.

Well, Luciani was hard to convince, but the fear of death has a way of making any man reasonable. Particularly since that night, I figured out how they was planning to ice him.

Angie convinced him to let the two of us hide in his suite of rooms to protect him. Luciani had been pretty grumpy ever since our little conversation, but I had the feeling that he secretly liked me, so I was patient with him. After all, no boss likes to hear from a *capo* from some other outfit that he's gone soft.

So there we were, late at night, prowling around the Pope's bedroom, when I remembered something Mr. Corvino said after Crazy Vinny Vitelli's body was found decomposing in a perfume shop on West 56th Street: "If you want to whack someone without getting caught, learn his habits." You see, Vinny used to slip behind the counter at this shop to pinch the sales girls, and the Matera family, whose turf Vinny had violated, knew about this. I bet Vinny never even knew that the last ass he pinched before croaking belonged to a transvestite hit man from the West Coast who the Materas brought in special for that job.

When I saw the glass of medicine on the Pope's bedside table, I knew. "Al! Wait!" I hollered, just as he was lifting it to his lips. He paused long enough for me to grab it from him. "You take this stuff every night?" I asked.

"Yes. It was prescribed by my—"

"This is how they planned to do it," I said, absolutely sure.

"Poison?" Angie asked.

"Sure. I should have thought of it before. It's so clean and simple. There wouldn't be any bullet holes to explain away." I nodded. Just to be sure, we gave a little of the medicine to the Pope's cat. The poor thing was dead within seconds. I locked eyes with the Pope. "These guys ain't no dummies, Al."

"Which guys?" Luciani asked.

I wish you could've seen his face. He believed me now, all right. A near brush with death can change a man's whole outlook on life. I told him to get some sleep, since they wouldn't try twice in one night, and then we could talk about it in the morning.

"Sleep?" Angie howled. "Uncle Vito, how can you talk about sleep at a time like this?"

"Hey! This is wartime now, kid. We're going to the mattresses." I was a little tough with him. He had to grow up fast, like it or not. "You gotta look after your health, which means you gotta eat and sleep whenever you got the chance. You gotta be ready to move at a moment's notice. And you gotta keep the other side guessing. You understand what I'm saying?"

Well, I slept pretty good that night on a couch near the Pope's bed. Luciani tossed and turned all night, and Angie was still pacing when I woke up the next morning.

"You were pacing when I went to sleep," I said to him. "Didn't you even sit down once? Didn't you sleep at all?"

"Of *course* I didn't sleep!"

"What did I say to you last night, huh? We're going to the matt—"

"Excuse me, Vito. Perhaps we should eschew needless recriminations for the time being and decide upon our immediate course of action," Luciani interrupted.

"Yeah, maybe you're right," I admitted.

"While I appreciate your saving my life, I can't help feeling apprehensive about Mr. Corvino's interest in my well-being. I mean . . . He does have a certain reputation."

"Al, please, you're embarrassing me. Mr. Corvino is a good Catholic, and *your* enemies are *his* enemies. Of course, he sees that you're gonna have to do some serious housecleaning here. You got some boys placed pretty high up who can't be trusted no more, and your outfit has got its fingers in some pretty sticky pies."

"And once our house is clean and our fingers are un-stuck?" Angie asked.

I smiled. "Well, you're gonna have a pretty big gap to fill. And Mr. Corvino is a pretty big guy who is prepared to fill that gap with his perfectly legitimate business interests, so that you and your boys can concentrate on ... whatever it is that you like to concentrate on."

"But we would have to clean house Corvino's way, right?" said Angie.

"That's part of the deal. You wanna shake on it, Al?"

"I'm afraid that that's completely out of the question, Vito. I'm a priest. I am now the spiritual leader of the entire Roman Catholic world. I can't go around ordering assassinations of the Church's enemies. I must deal with these evil men and their institutions in a legal and Christian fashion."

"Al, that's gotta be just about the dumbest thing I ever heard in my whole life."

"Nevertheless, it is my decision."

Well, Mr. Corvino had figured on something like this happening, just like he figured that Luciani's enemies weren't gonna give up so easily. So I hung out at the Vatican for another couple of weeks, keeping Angelo's boss alive. He was one stubborn guy, let me tell you, and it wasn't until his private toilet was rigged with plastic explosives that he finally realized that we was gonna have to do things the old-fashioned way, like it or not.

"That's the fifth attempt on your life since I got here, Al," I said. "Are you ready to let Mr. Corvino help you?"

The poor guy had been dividing all his time between trying to waste his enemies in a "legal and Christian fashion" and trying not to get killed. It kept him so busy that he hadn't had any time left over to comfort the poor, give a mass, or baptize any babies. And as for running his legitimate business concerns—forget it! I could see the time was right to bring him into the fold.

"What do I have to do?" Luciani asked.

We started by placing a phone call to Chicago, where a certain cardinal was giving Luciani a hard time. When the guy answered the phone, I reminded Luciani, "Just say exactly what I told you to say."

He nodded and said into the receiver, "This is Big Al Luciani." He frowned a second later and said, "You know—the Pope . . . Yes, *that* Pope."

"He's stalling you, Al. Get on with it," I said.

Luciani cleared his throat. "So here's the scam, Johnny. I don't like the way you've been handling your branch of the outfit . . . The outfit . . . You know, the Holy Roman Church." He took a deep breath and got tough. "You ain't been following orders, Johnny, and that makes me mad. What's more, you've been ignoring all my messages, and that makes me hurt. I don't think you want me to be mad and hurt, Johnny, 'cause then I get mean. And do you know what happens when the boss of this outfit gets mean? People get whacked. I ain't saying it's gonna be you, Johnny, but then, I also ain't saying it ain't."

Well, that guy in Chicago was one stubborn idiot— what is it about priests?—but he finally saw reason. A perfectly legitimate associate of Mr. Corvino's, who's based in Chicago, reported that the cardinal took a small suitcase and five grand in cash and disappeared that very afternoon. Last I heard, he was flipping burgers at some roadside joint in Oklahoma.

Now, personally, I don't like violence. But, under certain circumstances, I'm all in favor of whacking. It's over quickly, and, more importantly, you don't have to worry about a guy squealing to the feds after he's been whacked. But Big Al didn't want anyone to be clipped, and so we had a little disagreement when Roberto Calvi was found dead in London.

"Al, what are you so upset about? The cops called it suicide!"

"You were supposed to *talk* to him, Vito."

"And I did."

"What did you say that convinced him to jump off Blackfriars Bridge with a rope around his neck?" Luciani snapped.

However, these little disagreements aside, we got along very well. By the time Luciani called a sit-down with his *consigliere* and the head of the Vatican Bank, he hardly needed my help at all.

"Boys," he said, "my friends—my *real* friends—think I should have you whacked out."

"*Whacked out?*" said the American one.

"Don't interrupt Mr. Luciani," I said.

"Now," Luciani continued, "I'm a perfectly legitimate priest, and I don't like violence. But, when I found a cobra in my bed last week, boys, I felt violent. Isn't that the truth, Vito? You remember how violent I felt?"

"Pretty violent, Mr. Luciani."

"Holy Father, surely you don't think—"

"Don't interrupt His Holiness," Angie said.

"So I tell you what I'm gonna do," Luciani said. Angie and I pulled out our pieces. The priests started to look like they might wet their pants. Luciani placed some documents in front of each of them. "I'm gonna give you both a chance to resign from office and enter lifelong service at a Catholic mission in rural Uruguay. You'll only miss electricity and plumbing for the first year or two. What do you boys say?"

"Holy, Father, how could we possibly—"

"Or," Luciani said, "I could leave you alone with Vito for twenty minutes and send your remains to the zoo. I gotta tell you, the second way would be easier for me, but I'm trying to be a nice guy here."

For a second there, I thought they might call his bluff. But then they must have remembered Calvi's suicide, and they caved in. When it came to wise guys like Sindona and Gelli, it was so easy I almost felt embarrassed. Mr. Corvino knew where the bodies were buried, and so Mr. Luciani was able to hand them over to the cops on a silver platter.

We was so busy that time just flew by. Finally, it was a week before Christmas, and as far as I could tell, the war was over.

"Big Al," I said, "it's time for me to go home. I got grandchildren, I got a wife. You know how it is."

"A man should be with his family at Christmas," Luciani agreed. "We'll be fine here. The worst is over. I had no idea that a dirty operation could be cleaned up so quickly."

"It's something to keep in mind for the next time you have trouble with your boys," I said.

"Yes," he said. "I'll certainly keep all this in mind."

Well, I should have paid more attention to the look in his eyes that night, because here we are, all these years later, going to the mattresses again. Angie became Luciani's *consigliere*, and then the two of them finally turned around and bit the hand that fed them. Four days ago, Mr. Corvino's oldest son, who's been running the Vatican Bank for over a dozen years, was plugged by a priest. Luciani's got some pretty tough boys in his outfit these days, and I don't kid myself that this is gonna be an easy war. Mr. Corvino says we both made the same mistake with Big Al Luciani; we taught him everything we know, and now he don't need us no more.

It's too bad, too, 'cause I kind of liked the guy. And it's gonna break my heart to clip my sister's only son. But business is business. Those boys in the Church got greedy. They just don't wanna share no piece of their operation no more with perfectly legitimate businessmen like myself and Mr. Corvino.

Maureen McHugh, author of the excellent *China Mountain Zhang*, went further back in history than any of our other writers to choose her alternate warrior . . . and came up with a woman from almost four thousand years ago in this powerful little saga of King Tut's wife.

Tut's Wife
Maureen F. McHugh

(Ribadda the Lesser, servant to the Queen)

Outside the sunlight is hot, but inside the red ocher floor is cool enough to feel through my sandals. General Horemheb is sweating even here, his pleated linen sticking to the small of his back. He is looking at the Queen, who is looking at the floor, or maybe nothing at all. Only in this debased time could a general talk to the daughter of a pharaoh the way he talks to her, but that could be laid at her father's feet. The General had been at the court in Tel el Amarna, he had seen the Pharaoh open the doors of his life. But where Akhenaten had wanted us all to see the mixture of divine and mortal, some had only seen mortal.

"So read it, then," someone says. I think it's Neferuben-ef. Horemheb has already told us what is in the letter.

What was she thinking, to write such a letter to the Hittite King? Even the High Priest, Ay, can't protect her at this moment.

Horemheb reads from the letter in his hand, "Why do

you say, 'Are they attempting to deceive me?' If I had a son, would I write to a foreign country and so humiliate me and my country? You do not believe me and you even write this to me!" Horemheb looks up, but the Queen sits with her eyes down, so it is hard to tell if she is listening or not.

The General goes back to reading. "He who was my husband is dead and I have no son. Should I then perhaps take one of my servants and make of him my husband? I have written to no other country, only you. People say you have many sons. Give me one of your sons and he will be my husband and Lord of the Land of Egypt."

A Hittite prince, and she was offering to make him Lord of the Land of Egypt. Someone hisses through their teeth, a strange, pleasant kind of sound in this place. Horemheb is stern, controlled, the man of iron. For a moment I think she's going to say something, and then Horemheb will kill her, without rancor but without remorse, spill her blood all over the floor. I close my eyes because I've seen her family's blood on the floor and I'm an old man. Writing to a foreign king and promising to make him a god. Sometimes I think that her father is too much in her. Sometimes I think she's crazy the way he was at the end. I used to think that he went crazy because he was not strong enough in these debased times to be the vessel of Aten, but now I think that whether or not he was Aten on earth he was also human and he was just crazy.

He would have been crazy here, in this place where all the old gods look down on us; Amen-Ra, Nut, Horus, Thoth, stork-headed, falcon-headed, like the cousins at a family dinner whose presence you dread, but who always insist on their right to wine. There she sits, the princess we used to call Small Bird, silent under the eyes of the old gods. I am waiting for Horemheb to kill her for her treachery.

But she doesn't look up.

"Your prince is dead," Horemheb says. "His party was

caught as they crossed over from Lebanon. Do you want to hear about how he died?"

She doesn't move, just studies the floor. It crosses my mind that she is having a fit. Her dead sister's fits weren't always the gibbering, thrashing kind, sometimes she would go still that way. Ankhesenpaaten had never had fits before, but maybe now, under the strain, her health has broken and her soul is wandering the west while her body sits among us. Maybe she is already among the dead. It saddens me, even though it doesn't matter, because Horemheb is going to kill her, just the way they killed her father and her husband.

But she finally looks up, looks at Horemheb. "How excellent are your designs, O Lord of Eternity," she says. The prayer to the one true god, Aten. Her voice is so quiet that most of the people standing back near me can't make out what she said. They wouldn't know what she is saying anyway, she is surrounded by her enemies, these people are all Thebans. But Horemheb knows what she said, and All-Father Ay, the high priest and her only protection, and I know what she said. The figures on the walls should climb down—hawk-headed, jackal-headed, cow-headed—they should confront her. She has spoken anathema, she has brought the one true god into this place, this room full of the other gods.

Horemheb is furious, his composure broken. He will kill you now, I think, you are the daughter of the divine son of Aten, but you are human.

But the old gods are powerless, and quiver in their places on the walls. Even here, where the light of Aten can't penetrate, nothing moves against her. Horemheb shakes with something, I thought it was anger but maybe it was something else. Civil war shakes the length of the Nile, civil war shakes the General.

He commands that they take her to her suite.

I shake, too, but I'm an old man. I shake all the time.

* * *

(Horemheb, General of the Armies)

When you breed horses for chariot, sometimes you get a throwback, a horse that's scrawny and coarse and tough and nearly untrainable. Something that can survive in the desert. Sometimes I think I'm like one of those horses, hammer-headed and long-eared. I am fifty-two years old, I know I'm not young and handsome. I sit up when I hear the door open—it's not my wife, my wife hasn't come to my bed in twelve years, an arrangement that suits us both.

It is the Queen, in a transparent linen shift in fine pleats thin as slivers of reed. But startling, she is wigless. She looks sweet and vulnerable, her scalp barely covered by dark soft hair, her eyes unnaturally big in her face. If I am a throwback, she is all breeding, with her long skull and tiny hands and feet.

I laugh. "Who let you in?" I ask.

She doesn't answer, but I know who had to let her in—the little girl who takes care of this room.

"Lady of Two Lands," I say, "I am too old to be corrupted by anything but power, and you have no power." Not quite true, she is a solar princess, and the right to rule is in her veins. The man who marries her is pharaoh.

She is trembling visibly. Of course I feel for her, I held her on my lap when she was a toddler; in some ways the princesses were more like my children than my own. But this country has been torn in two by her father, and if I have to sacrifice the daughter to bring it back together, I will. She's not the only way to the double crown; there is her aunt, who is old, but who is also a solar princess.

She slips out of the shift, the fine linen rustling to the floor. Tiny breasts and smooth hips; she is only twenty-five. She looks younger, looks like a girl. In the light she carries I can see the marks on her belly from childbirth, faint silver lines. She was a child herself when she gave birth. The little princess Tasheray is (I have to think for a moment) eleven? Where have the years gone? My own children are grown and have children of their own.

If she would cry I would remain unmoved, but she

simply stands there, trembling and hopeless. The lamp cast flickering shadows on the walls and the figures in the paintings blink and shift. Priests in leopard skins.

She puts down the lamp and crawls into my bed. I don't do anything.

She reaches to stroke me and I pull her hand away. "It didn't work with your father," I say.

Cruel thing to say. I wonder at my own tongue. I've said things to her in the last weeks that I would have believed no one could say to a pharaoh's daughter and survive.

"My father," she repeats, leaning on one arm. "Sometimes I think you were more a father than he ever was."

"That would explain what you are doing here," I say, sardonic.

She shakes her head, but simply lies down, no longer reaching for me with those elegant hands. The air is strong with her perfume. I know what she is doing here. She is the dead pharaoh's wife, but she is powerless. I am General of all the Armies, Guardian of Egypt, and there is talk of making me pharaoh. I am her only hope to hold on. And what else has she got except quick wits and her sex?

I don't want her, she is too much like a child to me. I'm healthy as a donkey but I'm old enough that lust is no longer the overpowering force it was. And I'm not her father, the pharaoh with six daughters and no sons, who took each of his three eldest daughters to his bed to try and make himself a prince.

She curls up on the bed, keeping a space the width of my hand between her knees and my side. She is really not suited for seduction, this small bird.

I am so tired my bones ache. The kingdom is in civil war, my days are too long for me to spend my nights throwing young women out of my bed, not matter how royal. So I turn my back on her. I lie there, listening to her breath, watching the lamplight steady on the wall. She doesn't go to sleep. Not that I expected her to. I make my own breathing as even as possible, feigning. I keep waiting for her to touch me, and when she does I will throw her out. Lying there so still. My knees ache, I'd like to shift, but I keep myself still.

I feel her move and I tense, but she's only trying to make herself more comfortable. I imagine I can feel the heat off her skin. I imagine she is reaching out, her fingers almost brushing my back.

But nothing touches me and I don't know if I'm really feeling her body heat or if I'm just imagining.

And eventually I do go to sleep.

I wake once, and she's curled against the small of my back, a warm comforting feel.

And sensibly, somewhere near dawn I feel her stir and slip out of the bed. I can hear the rustle of linen as she picks her shift up off the floor, and the door opens and then grates shut.

(Ribadda the Lesser, servant to the Queen)

The Queen is closed in upon herself. She is not under arrest, not exactly. She doesn't go anywhere, she doesn't much eat. She has dark shadows under her kohled eyes.

She asks me to bring her things from Tel el Amarna, the city where she grew up. "Things are gone from there," I tell her. The people have all left. I do not tell her that it has all but gone back to sand, her father's city to Aten. I'm not sure she would believe me, or even understand. I am not sure of her mind, and we watch her, all of us, afraid that she'll harm herself.

"I had a blue necklace," she says wistfully, "tiny flowers."

A child's necklace. She is still small, it's no trouble to find such a necklace and bring it to her and it's worth it to see her animated for a few moments. She sits on her stool, knees together, and Bet, her maid, carefully clasps the necklace for her. She has even taken to dressing casually, childishly, wearing a linen skirt and leaving her small breasts bare. She is thin and her collarbones stand out in arches and the blue glass necklace falls to the hollow of her throat. She is smiling though.

"Lady," I say, "have a sweet." Maybe when she's distracted we can get her to eat.

But when I make the request her face clouds over. She turns away from me.

"Small Bird," I say, not comfortable with the informality, but it is the way we talked to the princesses at Tel el Amarna and it seems to me her mind is there. She doesn't rebuke me, but she will not eat, as willful as she ever was as a child.

(Horemheb, General of the Armies)

She comes again at night, and again she doesn't touch me. She comes in, drops her shift to the floor and stands shivering in the cold dry night air until I move over. I don't say anything, because I'm waiting for her to say something. Women cannot bear silence.

But she doesn't, she simply climbs on and curls up like a little cat, her back to me.

"What are you doing?" I ask.

"Are you going to make me leave?" She says this to the air, I am talking to the march of her vertebrae.

"You are the Lady of Two Lands," I say, amused. "I am only your servant."

She can have a sharp tongue, but she doesn't respond. She is wearing nothing but a little necklace, blue glass beads. She has had it since she was a girl, I remember the three older girls all had them.

So I wait for whatever curious path she has set for herself, wait for her to say what she is going to say. I have the blanket, and she has to be cold. If I wait I'll find out.

She sighs, and her ribs rise and fall. Little animal. Even a princess, even a queen, and she is just as much an animal as any of the rest of us. And yet the divine spark is there, isn't it? She is a mixture of animal and god, child of a god.

Goose bumps rise on that brown skin. Her mother,

Nefertiti, had blue eyes. And her grandmother, Ty, had red hair. But she is brown-haired, black-eyed, like her father.

And she is asleep, curled up and cold. Why does she come here? What does she want? Maybe she cannot sleep by herself anymore; because she is afraid, because she knows her life hangs on a whim. The High Priest, All-Father Ay, he wants to marry her. He controls the temples, I control the armies; until one of us can gain the upper hand she hangs between my sword and Ay's marriage bed. So why come to me? Why not go to Ay? Ay would protect her. Ay is her uncle.

Because Ay is as devious as a cobra, and with me she knows where she stands even if that means that she knows I will kill her eventually. Because in some strange way, she trusts me.

I cover her with part of the blanket, and sighing myself, turn my back on her and try to go to sleep. Sleep is a long time coming. Finally, she shifts a little, still breathing evenly, and tucks in against my back. I feel her young warmth. It seeps into my old back that has slept on stones in too many campaigns. And so I sleep, too.

(Horemheb, General of the Armies)

I have grown accustomed to her. I expect her each night, wait for her. It's always the same; she comes in, climbs up and curls up and goes to sleep without a word. There is only that sigh, the sound of her dropping everything the way she drops her shift to the floor.

But this evening she's different. She climbs up and I wait for her to lie down so I can cover her with the blanket. I can't go to sleep until she gets here, I wait for her. But she sits.

"What is it?" I ask. With some trepidation, because I am afraid that she's going to try something—I have all but convinced myself that she is not going to seduce me.

She sits, her chin propped on her drawn-up knees.

I don't want her to attempt to seduce me because that will ruin everything.

But she doesn't do anything or say anything. Just sits, her knees drawn up, her toes curled under her feet because of the chill. I can roll over and attempt to go to sleep or I can wait for her to tell me what is bothering her. And I have discovered that she feels no compunction to talk.

"Small Bird," I say, using her old pet name, "what is it?"

"Solstice is coming," she says.

And it is. For a moment it is just a statement, a fact, and then the ramifications hit me. Solstice is the high holy day of Aten.

She lies down, curls up on her side.

"You have been following Amen-Ra for years," I say. It's true. Akhenaten is dead and those of us who are still alive have given up the belief that there is only one god, and that all the rest are merely debased versions of the one pure god.

"Only when people were watching," she says. "He and I used to still pray in private."

At first I think she means her father but then I realize it is Tutankhaten, her husband, she is referring to. Tutankhamen. They changed their names, Ankhesenpaaten to Ankhesenpaamen, to show that they had turned their backs on her father's madness. But most of us never learned to think of them that way. The boy, her husband, murdered while she watched. As her mother was murdered while she watched. She doesn't usually speak about the dead.

How long since I had prayed, except at public occasions? I stand in the temple and invoke Amen-Ra and Nut, Osiris and Horus and Thoth but it's just obligation. But then, for the last years of her father's reign I had stood in the blasting sun in Tel el Amarna listening to the pharaoh invoke the one true god, Aten, and that was only obligation. It's a long time since I felt the presence of something holy.

So it touches me, to think of these two young people praying in private to the one god, Aten. And when she died, when I had her killed, then would anyone still pray to Aten? Or would his name disappear? Not that it should really matter, the seer of her grandfather's court, Amen-hotep, son of Hapu, told me when I was a boy.

It isn't that the gods aren't real, he had said, it's that they are imperfectly understood. They are this aspect and that aspect of what the one true god is. The godhead is wise, but we break that part off and call it Thoth. The godhead started the world as a potter starts his wheel, but we call the divine creator Ptah. It is all Aten. Aten is the divinity. And the name doesn't matter. It's just that by worshipping all the rest, you are ignoring the truth.

I was profoundly affected by that. It told me that the truth was simple, and clean and pure. And that made sense.

Nothing makes much sense anymore. Truth doesn't seem simple, clean and pure. Honor involves murdering a young woman because she is the tool of the enemy. And in the end, Akhenaten wasn't joyous in his worship of Aten, in the end we stood baking in the sun while he harangued us and waited for someone to have the courage and anger necessary to strike him down. And finally someone did.

But this young woman and her husband, who had every reason not to believe that things were ever pure and clean; they worshipped truth. I ache thinking of that.

"I have to be in temple that day," I said. "But I'll come to your rooms at sunset."

I wait for something from her, but not surprisingly, she doesn't speak.

(Ribadda the Lesser)

The morning of the Solstice she wakes in a state. She has had a nightmare. We are roused in the predawn be-

cause there is a scorpion in her bed, but I know there is
no scorpion. She has seen it, crawling into the things on
her bed, looking for warmth. When she was a girl she
would see things at night, soldiers in the nursery, dogs
running across the floor, she would hear the click of their
toenails on the tiles. She stands, shivering and naked,
while a sleep-stupid girl checks the blankets. Night ter-
rors. "Get the princess a wrap," I command. They bring
her a robe and some warm milk and honey. "It is early,"
I say. "Sleep a little longer. Mu will sleep with you."

Usually she can be soothed back to sleep; she's not
really awake when she has these dreams. But this morning she will not. "I have to be clear-headed," she says,
mostly to herself.

She sits by the window, waiting for the sun.

Ay will be coming to collect her, to stand her next to
him in the temple. She's afraid of him. I have known Ay
all his life, I knew him when he was young and cruel,
and now he is old and cruel. In the rare moments when
he is preoccupied, when he is not watching everything
around him, I can see in him his sister, Nefertiti, Ankhesenpaaten's mother. But Nefertiti was pliant and beautiful, and Ay is cold.

But Ay wants to be pharaoh, and if he marries the
Queen, he can be. Right now the only thing that stops
him is the year of mourning for the late pharaoh and the
fact that the General has control of the army.

Ankhesenpaaten dresses early in fine yellow linen, and
then suddenly she clasps my hands. Her hands are cold.
"Ribadda," she says, "Have you seen Fish?" The Mitannian girl is called "Fish" because she has an outlandish
foreign name that sounds like we are all calling her "carp."
She is a favorite.

No, I haven't seen Fish.

The Queen seems afraid that Fish won't come. I ask
where Fish has been, but the Queen's answer is vague.
She has been with her mother, maybe. Or maybe it's her
uncle, Ankhesenpaaten doesn't know.

Why would the girl go to visit her family and come back on the holy day? I am afraid. Small Bird seems desperate.

I wait in the outer room, watching for the Mitannian girl, and finally she comes. She is red-haired, a pretty girl, like the late Queen Mother, Ty. She has a packet and as she tries to brush by me to go into the Queen I take her arm. "Girl, what have you got?"

She is afraid. "It is for the Queen," she says.

"Show me," I say. The packet is small, linen folded into a little square. I take it from her, open it carefully. It is full of pale brown powder. Poison? The Queen has asked for poison? I look at the girl. Oh, Small Bird.

"Ribadda," says the Queen from the door.

"Lady," I say.

"It's not for me," she ways. "It is for the General. It is a tonic. Fish told me about it, and I mentioned it to him. He asked me if I would get him some." She walks up to me.

I don't believe her. I smell the powder and for a brief moment the room swirls. The light seems brighter, the colors sharper.

The Queen laughs, "Be careful, Ribadda." She takes the packet from my hands and folds it carefully. Then she calls to one of the other girls and hands it to her. "Deliver this to the General, in precisely the manner we discussed." I stand, mazed and aware. It is not that I cannot clear my head, it is that my head is so clear, and the world is so sharp. I can see the intricate braids of Fish's hair. I can see the creases and dust in her linen and the tiny downy hairs around her nipples and the way the black of her pupils spills a little onto her iris.

The world is only this way for a few moments, and then it dulls again. I sit down heavily on the stool and watch the Queen. She is at the window again, watching outside, her chin in her hand.

"What is it?" I ask.

"It's a tonic," she says.

It doesn't seem to be poison. I'm too old. I can't figure this out.

When Ay comes she is strangely light. "Uncle," she calls him. He is dressed in leopard skins for the temple. She is sitting on a stool and he is a tall man, so he bends and she holds his face cupped in her hands. She says something to him I cannot hear but I hear "Horemheb" and "sunset." Ay pulls back from her, surprised. She sits all expectant, her narrow feet together.

"Come," he says to her. And she rises obediently, and walks out with him, trailing the heavy sweet scent of her perfume. When she is gone, her perfume hangs in the air like a ghost.

She is going to surrender to Ay. That's good. He will marry her, he needs to marry the solar princess in order to be pharaoh. When he marries her then she'll be protected. She'll be the pharaoh's wife again.

I'm an old man and I shouldn't be afraid to die, but I am. I want her to marry Ay.

(Horemheb, General of the Armies)

Ay, Ankhesenpaaten and I stand in front of the alter. We the triumvirate that represents power in this land.

In this day spent in temples my mind is not on the shadow spirits around me; the hawk-headed god, the god in the galley rowing across the heavens. Mostly I'm thirsty. This morning there was juice in my room, I suppose in honor of the holy day, because I didn't ask for it. Lemon and honey, with a strange sweet-tart taste. I'm so thirsty now it's all I can think of. I drank some but not too much. Anymore, if I drink before a public function my bladder is full too quickly.

This Theban temple is dark and full of ghosts. I can see up into the shadows, and it seems as if I can hear high strange sounds, sounds that I could hear before but never noticed. Ghosts move, little *kas*, tiny winged souls, whispering in the smoke above us like owl's wings. Like bats. The boy, Tutankhaten, is here. And his brother, An-

khesenpaaten's father. And the sage who taught us both
that there was only one god, one absolute principle. Fan-
ciful thoughts run in my head this morning.

The Queen is standing between Ay and myself. We are
a strange triumvirate. She is the pivot, a solar princess,
carrier of the royal line. No man can be pharaoh unless
he marries the daughter of a pharaoh. There are only two
solar princesses alive right now, and most people have
forgotten the other.

My future sickens me. For so long my goal has been to
reunite this land. The treasury is nearly empty, the campaign with Syria is a disaster. I will marry Mutnedjmet,
Nefertiti's strange sister, who is also a solar princess. Mutnedjmet who all these years has never married, with her
two dwarfs and her gambling and her sarcasm. I will be
a good pharaoh, make my prayers to these gods, these
shadows. Live a lie.

My life has become complicated with power. It seems
so far from the days when I just wanted to do right in all
things. Ankhesenpaaten's father and I used to argue about
the way a life should be led. He said there was a joy, an
ecstasy like a bell inside him that told him when the
spirit of Aten was in him and his path was right. Sometimes at dawn, watching him pray, I believed him. His
face was suffused with something that, throwback that I
am, I thought I could never feel.

I feel faint. It is the smoke from the offerings, perhaps,
and the fatigue of years of war, and age. I do not know
what it is. Perhaps they are poisoning me, and if so, at
the moment I don't care. Ay is watching me. The world
seems farther and farther away. It is all the smell of
charred meat, the smoke rising up to the gods, rising in
a pure stream for a while and then breaking into a curl,
a swirl, patterns returning in on themselves.

The world darkens around me, and I try to turn, to
walk outside, into the sun—

—and I'm outside in the sun, and people are talking to
me, but for a moment I can't respond. Fainted, I think, I

fainted. I'm ashamed. I've never fainted before. I can hear them but I can't say anything. The sun is so bright that the sky is white, a brilliant white light—

My head is filled with light. In the sudden clarity of that light, my destiny comes to me, as if Aten himself had reached down and laid his hand across my forehead. I understand the difference between the royal family and us. They have always lived with Aten. They are touched, and now I have been touched, too. When I marry the solar princess, it will not *make* me different, only Aten himself can do that. But it will show the world that Aten has taken me and placed me in this place that I would be his instrument.

(Ribadda the Lesser)

For so long there has been almost no sound in these apartments. We have spoken in whispers, afraid to be noticed. But this afternoon, when the heat of the sun should make us all still as lizards, there is noise. Voices, the sound of people in the halls, and then the Queen, and the General, and a retinue. Something has happened. In her old way, the Queen is ordering, "Something cool to drink, and a basin with water, and a stool. The General is ill." She claps her tiny hands and when the stool is brought she seats the General on it, gives him cold water and bathes his face. His kohl comes off on the cloth like black tears. He raises his face blindly to her.

I am old, but I'm not a fool. What has she done? She didn't poison him. He sits there, befuddled as I was, but he isn't really ill.

They eat roast fowl and fruit and drink wine. Although things are quiet again they don't feel quiet. We have been sleeping. Or waiting, suspended over the flood waters like the heron, waiting to see the water recede. Now something is happening, she is herself.

"Fish," she says. "Prepare juice, no, better, wine for the General, juice for me."

"Have you always felt him?" Horemheb asks her. Unlike the Queen, he is not himself. He is dazed and slow.

Fish comes with the jugs. Is there powder in the wine? I take the jug from her, uncork it. The General pays no attention to me, but the Queen is watching me from the corners of her kohled eyes.

"This has gone off," I say firmly. "It smells like vinegar. I'll bring better."

The Queen doesn't say anything when I bring a fresh jug. I'll shatter the old jug when they've left and throw the pieces in the river. I don't know what she's doing but she must understand that her only course of action is to marry Ay. Ay will protect her.

Horemheb doesn't leave. He sits at the table, sometimes talking, sometimes looking around the room as if the world were new to him, until the shadows lengthen. Finally, apropos of nothing he says, "I don't know the words."

The Queen understands. "I know the words," she says. Fish brings plates of offerings. We watch, all of us, while they stand at the window and the sun goes down.

> When you set in the western horizon of heaven
> The world is in darkness like the dead.
> They sleep in their chambers . . .

She stops, but Horemheb picks it up:

> They sleep in their chambers,
> Their heads are covered,
> Their nostrils stopped, and each is alone from the other.

His voice is hesitant; as he remembers each line it gives him the next, but he doesn't know if he'll remember it all. The Queen is unable to say the words, she can only cover her mouth and close her eyes. And all of us, who remember better times, stand there listening to him say the prayer of night. All of us are afraid.

A movement catches my eye and there is the High Priest, Ay, in the doorway. I open my mouth, but he gestures for me to be silent. Flat-eyed, a snake of a man, watching them incriminate themselves. I don't know what will happen. I only know that he sees treachery, his enemy and her, together. The General's voice gets stronger as he gains confidence, until he finishes as if he were on the parade ground.

> You make shadow and it is night,
> And in shadow the animals creep out.
> The young lions roar after their prey—
> They seek their meat from Aten.

He turns, and she turns, and there is Ay.

And the General laughs. "It's too late," he says. "She won't marry you."

(Horemheb, General of the Armies)

She stands in her chariot, looking like a boy in her war leathers. She's stood for hours, as we passed through villages abandoned ahead of our army. She is my queen, my own Small Bird. She reads maps with me in the evening, her small fingers pointing. There has never been a queen like her.

I knew, that day that I fainted in the temple, that Aten had touched me, had told me that I would bring him to all of Egypt. And soon, all of Egypt will worship one god. And the name Horemheb will go down through the ages. Thebes is under military law, we head north for Memphis and Heliopolis. The country is open from years of civil war and there is nothing to stop a man who will take anything, even from his own people, to feed his army. We are conquering our own kingdom.

I need her here beside me, her presence reminds me again and again what we are. We are divine. I felt in the temple what it is to be touched by Aten. She has known all her life. Sometimes, when I see the damage done to this land, I could weep. Hundreds die. I don't have enough money so we rape the land itself.

But it will be all right, because it is for Aten. And I must have faith that his plans will bear fruit.

(Ribadda the Lesser)

We camp, and the girls make her ready to go to him. I sit with her and take her correspondence. No more letters to Hittite princes. Fish takes her war sandals, brings her slippers.

"I feel so lonely," she says this night.

"It's hard," I say. "But you have the pharaoh."

"He's . . . it's not as if he's a companion. Not like," she sighs, and I think of the boy, Tutankhaten.

"Those were dark days," I say. "But you brought us through. You were more clever than any of us knew." It is the closest I have ever come to admitting that I know what she did. Or at least, some of what she did.

"I was just trying anything. When I gave him the powder," she says, "I thought would make him weak. Then I could take care of him, and maybe get him to marry me. But Ribadda, he's like my father, he's mad!"

He is not like her father, but he is like a horse that can't be turned. And sometimes I'm afraid of him, with the light of Aten in his eyes. Sometimes I think of the old pharaoh, her father.

"Ribadda," she says, "will we be all right?"

"Yes, Lady," I say, "Aten will watch over us."

"Don't say that to me," she whispers. "Say it to him, but not to me."

I am bemused, hasn't Aten brought us through when I was sure we would all die?

She looks at me, her face like Ay's, her kohl-rimmed eyes cold. "There are no gods," she says. "There is only us, using what we can find."

And outside, Egypt lies ruined.

Nicholas DiChario, one of our hottest new writers, author of "The Winterberry" and a handful of other gems, here presents a gripping portrait of Susan B. Anthony, the remarkable woman whose face was on the dollar coin that never quite caught on, and her participation in the heinous crime of Extreme Feminism.

Extreme Feminism
by Nicholas A. DiChario

For the love of me and the saving of the reputation of womankind ... load my gun, leaving me only to pull the trigger.

—Letter from Susan B. Anthony to
Elizabeth Cady Stanton, circa 1860

Susan B. Anthony cupped the Smith & Wesson revolver in her hands as if it were a fragile flower. The weapon frightened her—the evil beauty, the heaviness, the sleek power.

"Miss Anthony." Captain Mansfield extended his hand for the gun. "Allow me."

Elizabeth Cady Stanton nodded discreetly. Susan, feeling flushed, placed the gun in the captain's gloved palm. "It certainly is hot today," she said. Hot and humid. The tiny room that surrounded them made her feel as if she were imprisoned in a brick oven. The smell of tobacco and rum clung to the walls. Susan silently cursed her clothes. A boned bodice, a stiffened petticoat, a wire waistline that choked off her very breath as well as her blood circulation, a gingham bonnet. Was it any wonder women fainted dead away in the street? This costume, Susan had decided long ago, was part of the subtle male subterfuge that kept women subordinate. No wonder men hated bloomers. A woman comfortable and alert might be a woman dangerous.

Captain Mansfield looked as vexed in his dark blue flannel sack coat as Susan felt in her bodice. Sweat glistened in the short hairs of his long gray sideburns, and his round belly pushed at the buttons of his military coat. His discomfort gave her some satisfaction. Lizzy had investigated Mansfield thoroughly before approaching him with their offer. A surreptitious Copperhead, the captain had sat out the War Between the States behind a Federal desk, where he'd managed to divert troop supplies to eager merchants in Virginia and North Carolina. Susan doubted he'd ever drawn his saber from its leather scabbard other than to apply cloth-and-spit.

"This is the newest model Smith & Wesson pocket revolver." He clicked open the cylinder, making an exaggerated show of it. "As you can see, the chambers are bored all the way through so a man can take a metallic cartridge like this," he picked a bullet up off the table, "and load it from the back like this ..." He pushed the cartridge into an open chamber and spun the cylinder. "First of its kind, ladies. All a man has to do is load, cock the hammer, and pull the trigger. Much easier than the single-shot ball-and-powders, wouldn't you agree?"

Susan didn't know how to answer. She stepped to the oak door and thought about pushing through. Holding that gun in her hands had been a mistake. Enough is enough, she thought. Walk out; put an end to this madness now. From the very beginning, Victoria Woodhull had been excited about Lizzy's plan, but Victoria was young and impatient. What was Susan's excuse? What was Lizzy's?

From the other side of the door came the sounds of drunken men arguing over a poker game. Susan heard a cork pop. Glasses clinked. Someone who didn't know how to play the piano assaulted the keys. Thank God she and Lizzy had entered through the back door. How could Lizzy have agreed to meet his sly little military man in the back room of a tavern, after all their good work for temperance? Was it so long ago Susan had preached against the evils of alcohol? What would her father have said?—God rest his soul—a man of intelligence, a man of peace, a Quaker.

"Susan," Lizzy said, "the least we can do is thank the captain for getting us all these lovely guns. I'm sure it was no small feat."

"You can do more than thank me. I'm afraid it's going to cost a bit more than we agreed."

Susan glanced at Lizzy. Lizzy had warned her about this: *"We'd better dress like proper ladies, and act ignorant and suppliant. Give the captain what he wants, and we'll get what we want."* Lizzy had been right about everything so far, everything since Susan had known her.

They first me in 1851. Susan had been campaigning for temperance and women's rights and black emancipation. Lizzy convinced her that women's rights must become the primary issue because as willing as women were to aid everyone else's charitable causes, no one would be willing to aid suffrage. If women didn't have the right to their own property or money, the freedom of speech, the right to sue for divorce, and—her most radical proposal of all—the right to vote, women would never be able to precipitate any real change in these United States of America. Women would never be free.

The right to vote. That had always been Susan's goal, Susan's dream. Now, as then, it seemed it would never happen.

"Captain," said Susan, "I pray you can hold to our original agreement. We don't have any more money to spend."

Outside in the alley, Susan heard a horse clack a hoof on the cobblestone street. The horse was hitched to a wagon. The wagon held 112 Smith & Wesson .44-caliber pocket revolvers and two crates of ammunition. Lizzy had outdone herself this time.

Mansfield frowned. "The fact of the matter is, I've got to cover my expenses. These guns are—were—military property. I've got to make them all disappear without a trace. Some of the men involved in such an enterprise are—how can I phrase this delicately?—men of ill repute. I'll need to pay them well for their silence. I realize women don't have the sensible minds we men do, but think of it as an investment, the cost of financing an independent business venture."

Susan clutched her purse to her chest. She had been listening to men talk like this all her life. Why should women tolerate being treated like idiots? Why should women be ashamed of themselves? That's really what men wanted: to allow *their* interpretation of the Bible, the constraints of *their* traditional society, and the letter of *their* law to break the backs of women so they wouldn't have to work so hard at it themselves, although it was work they seemed to enjoy. Susan had been called an old maid and a shrew so many times she'd lost count. A writer from the Utica *Evening Standard* had once labeled her "personally repulsive." At a Sons of Temperance meeting in Syracuse, New York, a minister stood up and pointed his morally superior finger at her and accused her of being half man, half woman, belonging to neither sex.

Things had to change. Susan had been fighting for too long. Could it really be twenty years? She was forty-five years old now. She'd taken the lead in forming how many different organizations?—the Woman's National Loyal League, the American Equal Rights Association, the National Equal Rights Society, the Woman's Suffrage Alliance—and had gained nothing but the ridicule of lawmakers and the contempt of the very women for whom she fought. How had this happened? Why?

Susan let go a deep breath. It amazed her how Lizzy had upheld the cause all these years, with a husband and children to tend and a household to run. Lizzy even found time to write all of Susan's speeches. Susan, unmarried her entire life, seemed not to possess a fraction of Lizzy's boundless energy.

Lizzy stepped around the table. "Captain, all of our husbands have been so supportive and patient, allowing us to work on our projects and travel to conventions. I can't begin to tell you how often we've neglected our chores. We wanted so much to buy our men something special, to show them our appreciation, and we don't have another penny to spend. Not one."

Captain Mansfield grinned, perhaps sensing the upper hand. Hopefully the upper hand would be enough for him. It was true they had run out of money. The inn they'd rented and the expense of widely publicizing tomorrow's rally would cost them every last cent. With the assassination of President Abraham Lincoln three months ago at the hand of Mary E. Surratt, women had been prohibited from purchasing guns legally without a husband's written consent. Mansfield's ego and greed and lack of imagination hadn't even allowed him to consider the possibility the ladies might be wanting the guns for their own purposes.

"I thought Miss Anthony here was a spinster," he said, directing the comment toward Lizzy. "Why should she care about the men?"

Susan answered: "I sympathize with what the husbands have had to endure. In many respects I'm responsible for much of their inconvenience."

Mansfield paced the floor, with his hands held stiffly behind his back. "Admirable sentiment, ladies. I suppose this one time I could afford to take a bit of a loss. You suffragists should start treating men with more respect. Women have a place in the home. We men wish we had it so well. You are protected. Men coddle you. You wear the prettiest clothes. It's not like you have no responsibilities. You cook and clean and raise our children. That's important work. What more do you want? Myself, I'm a military man. I risk my life for you women every day. You should appreciate that." The captain straightened his coat, shifted his sword and scabbard to the rear of his hip, and sat at the table.

Susan removed a handkerchief from her reticule and dabbed the sweat from her nose. She felt her heart pounding. To hell with the gun. She could kill this man with her bare hands. Control, she told herself. Lately it had become so difficult to maintain control.

Lizzy dropped a burlap sack on the table in front of Captain Mansfield. It landed with a heavy thud. "Thank you so much, Captain. Our husbands will be so pleased." He did not see the firm set of Lizzy's jaw, the stiffness of her back. He opened the sack and began counting.

The hot air stood still under the setting sun. Susan fanned herself with her handkerchief. Lizzy held the reins tightly and kept the horse's pace slow and steady as their wagon clattered along the banks of the Erie Canal, following the towpath that led to the Seneca Valley Inn. The murky brown canal water, muddied with clay, had been low for almost a month. Exquisite pale sandstone lined the gorge. Finches, wrens, and bluebirds darted between gray and white birch trees. Dandelions, daisies, and Queen Ann's lace spotted the surrounding hillsides yellow and white. During the War Between the States, the Seneca Valley Inn had been used as an Underground relay station for runaway slaves.

Neither Susan nor Lizzy spoke. Over the past few days uncomfortable silences had fallen between them suddenly, like large black walnuts dropping from an ancient tree. If Lizzy's plan didn't work, didn't gain them some influence with legislators and an influx of new donations, their women's rights campaign would surely limp away, crippled beyond repair.

The abolitionist movement had taken its toll not only on the Union and the Confederacy but on women's suffrage as well. Just when it seemed they had been making some headway, seven Southern states seceded from the Union. The eyes of the nation turned to the more urgent matters of war, of death, of family upheaval and financial disaster. Women's suffrage lost its flame, cooled to ashes.

Susan understood the feeling of desperation that had inspired Lizzy's plan, but she couldn't help worrying that they might be acting rashly. They meant no harm, of course, no violence. At the culmination of Susan's speech tomorrow afternoon, each woman would raise her gun and fire off a single round straight up into the air. One hundred twelve guns and two crates of ammunition. A show of solidarity. Something to shock the men, to show they meant business. Susan and Lizzy hoped to be imprisoned for the shooting. The speech—although Susan and Lizzy had labored over the exact wording for months—consisted of only two sentences.

There would be a huge crowd gathered if the weather held, many supporters, many more who would come to jeer and taunt. There would most certainly be children present. Women did not know how to use guns. There was a possibility someone might get hurt. An accident. How would Susan feel then? Would she be able to live with herself?

The time had come to take some risks, Victoria Woodhull had urged them. Victoria Woodhull brought a certain glamour to the women's rights movement that Susan and Lizzy had never enjoyed. Her publication, *Woodhull Weekly*, ran stories about birth control, abortion, and prostitution. She advocated "free love" and extramarital affairs. The young woman had a flair for drama. Men listened to her simply because she was beautiful. She quickly gained popularity and converts. Most of Susan's supporters had fallen victim to Victoria Woodhull's brash enthusiasm. "Extreme feminists," they called themselves. Not Susan. Susan resisted. Perhaps her own movement had outgrown her.

Dusk shadowed the landscape by the time Lizzy guided their wagon to the rear of the Seneca Valley Inn. Victoria Woodhull met them with a dozen of her closest confidantes. Victoria wore a man's shirt and pants, and she had cut her hair so short it barely touched her neck.

"This is wonderful," Victoria said. "I never dreamed you'd succeed. Quickly everyone. Move quickly. Into the cellar."

They unloaded the wagon, dragging their guns and ammunition into the wine cellar. Susan and Lizzy followed, descending silently into the staunch odor of fermented berries. There were more women downstairs, in among the wine barrels and thick cobwebs and tall racks of bottles. The women began breaking open crates on the dirt floor with claw hammers. No one spoke. Victoria Woodhull ushered Susan and Lizzy into a corner where they sat awkwardly on a cedar storage chest that smelled faintly of Indian spices. The dank air came as a cool relief.

"I don't want you two to worry about the details," Victoria Woodhull said. She looked strange and silly and dangerous in her baggy shirt and pants. It was a look not altogether unbecoming. She reached inside her pocket and removed a painter's cap and pulled it over her head. "I've got everything under control. These are twenty-five of my best lieutenants. They all know how to handle guns. They've all fired derringers."

"Oh, my" said Susan. Mary E. Surratt had used a derringer to assassinate President Lincoln. "Captain Mansfield told us these were new-model guns—"

"Yes, Smith & Wesson pocket revolvers. Backloaders. My girls are going to load the guns and distribute them to the other women to conceal in their purses for tomorrow's speech. We've got enough ammunition to put a bullet in every gun. We'll explain to each woman how to use her weapon safely. You sit tight."

"How—" Susan began, but Victoria left them to go help her girls. Susan glanced at Lizzy but Lizzy avoided her eyes. Susan noticed something on the floor behind the wine barrels. Someone hiding in the shadows? No. Someone bound and gagged—a man! She leapt to her feet. "Victoria! What is the meaning of this?" She went over to the man. He lay motionless in his undergarments, a thin line of blood trickling down the back of his neck, a short iron pipe in the dirt beside him. Susan knelt in her cumbersome bodice and began to work at the knotted ropes around the man's wrists. Victoria Woodhull pulled her to her feet.

"I'm sorry, Susan, we had no choice. He found us in the cellar and he would have revealed our plan if we didn't tie him up."

"You've done more than tie him up. You've hurt him. You're wearing his clothes, Victoria."

A woman came up behind Victoria Woodhull and said, "We've got the guns loaded and packed and we're ready to move out. It's just about nightfall. We should probably get started."

"All right. Go on. Be careful."

"Wait," Susan said. "Everyone stop!" Her knees felt weak. She stepped over the splintered lumber strewn across the cellar floor. "Can't you see what's happening to us? We devise a plan, not exactly legal, something that will make a little noise and get us some attention. We buy guns. We learn how to use them. We violently strike down a man. We want our constitutional rights, yet we break laws right and left to get them. This is not the way. We're losing sight. We're becoming just like *them*." She pointed at the man curled on the floor behind the wine barrels. Her hands trembled. "Are women merely in training to become men? Power is everything to them. We must have higher ideals."

"He doesn't look so powerful to me," Victoria Woodhull said in a quiet, precise voice. The sentence made Susan feel foolish.

Lizzy stepped forward. "Susan, I know it all seems very bad right now, but tomorrow, after we've made our statement, things will look much different. You'll see."

For a brief moment their eyes met, and Susan felt as if she and Lizzy were the only two women in the room, just like the old days when it seemed no one else cared. Susan B. Anthony and Elizabeth Cady Stanton against the world Had Susan gotten comfortable in her fantasy? Was she resisting the change for which she had so passionately lobbied all these years? Perhaps she had replaced what was best for the cause, what was best for women, with what was best for Susan B. Anthony.

Lizzy looked tired. Not a spirited tired, like when they were exhausted after a meeting or a speech or a hard day of petitioning, but the hurtful kind of tired she used to watch her mother carry on her shoulders, the kind of tired that chiseled away the soul. Susan's mother, according to the women who knew her well, had been a spirited young Baptist girl who loved to sing and dance and wear the flashiest clothes. She gave it all up for the love of Susan's father, a Quaker, who introduced her to the world of spinning and weaving and sewing and quilting and cooking and ironing and childbirth—six children in all. Susan, the second oldest, grew up in the shadow of her mother, a woman who had become somber, withdrawn, as gray as the Quaker dresses she wore. Why did it have to be that way? Why did women have to give up everything for men? It didn't seem right. It didn't seem fair. It was a mistake Susan vowed never to repeat.

Women deserved better. But guns and bullets were not the answer. Lizzy knew that. "This wasn't your plan at all, was it, Lizzy? This was all Victoria Woodhull's idea."

No answer.

"It's slipping away from us. We're losing control. Surely you can see what's going on here."

Lizzy approached Susan and held her hands. "Yes, I can see what's going on. The same thing that's been going on for twenty years of campaigning. The same thing that's

been going on for centuries. Women trying; women failing. Tomorrow you will deliver the speech, two sentences, that's all, and we will carry out our plan. It's the
only way. Guns talk; men listen. It took a civil war to
free the slaves. A revolution. It's the only language men
understand. Now it's our turn to be heard. We've started
something and we have to finish." Lizzy kissed Susan
lightly on the lips, turned away, walked over to the storage chest, and sat down.

Everyone stood motionless. Susan couldn't believe what
she was hearing. Lizzy didn't even attempt to reassure her
no one would get hurt. Susan felt something oily between
her fingers. Blood. *His* blood. "Get me a washbasin," Susan said to no one in particular. "And a towel." She went
over to the man in the corner.

Victoria came up behind her. "We can't let him go."

Susan knelt down. The man was unconscious. She held
his head to her chest and brushed the hair back from his
wound.

Susan always felt jittery the night before a speech. On
this day she rose trembling and sweating before dawn.
She lit a candle and opened one of her favorite books, a
leather-bound edition of *The Letters of Abigail Adams*. She
read an excerpt from April of 1776, a message to husband
John concerning the Declaration of Independence:

> *I long to hear that you have declared an independ-*
> *ancy— In the new Code of Laws which I suppose it*
> *will be necessary for you to make I desire that you*
> *would remember the Ladies, and be more generous*
> *and favourable to them than your ancestors. Do not*
> *put such unlimited power into the hands of the Hus-*
> *bands. Remember all men would be tyrants if they*
> *could. If perticular care and attention is not paid to*
> *the Ladies we are determined to foment a Rebellion,*
> *and will not hold ourselves bound by any Laws in*
> *which we have no voice, or Representation.*

Another hot sunny morning sifted through the distant pine trees. Susan donned a loose-fitting calico dress that fell to her ankles, and a black jacket with long ruffled sleeves. She fastened her hair in a tight coil at the base of her neck.

In the center of town sat Lilac Park, just two blocks east of the Seneca Valley Inn. Susan and Lizzy walked over early to make sure the tent had been pitched and the chairs and podium had been properly arranged. They exchanged no more conversation than necessary. By mid-morning, the park overflowed with parasols; women perspiring in heavy clothing; men in black trousers and stovepipe hats; children running circles around wagons and horses, pleading for their parents to buy them peppermint sticks. The smell of horse dung and peanuts and lilac bushes filled the air. A string quartet that had traveled from Rochesterville plucked and tuned its instruments. Around noon a parade of local militiamen marched down the center of town, fronted by a fife and drum corps and a troop of Federal cavalrymen dressed in formal blues, led by Captain Mansfield. Susan's speech was scheduled for two o'clock. She wandered off into the crowd by herself.

Everywhere Susan looked she saw women with purses. Which ones held Smith & Wesson .44-caliber pocket revolvers? She thought she recognized a few of the women who had been in the wine cellar last night. She watched a group of little girls watching a collection of young boys throwing stones at a huge oak tree. She noticed Horace Greeley, the publisher of the New York *Tribune*, buying a candied apple. Once a staunch supporter of women's rights, Greeley had recently turned harsh critic, favoring black emancipation. Susan wondered how he would report this afternoon's activities.

By two o'clock the tent was filled with hundreds of people. The advertisements in the local gazette and the announcements posted in neighboring towns had proven overwhelmingly successful. There were a lot more men than usual. Most of them, Susan was certain, had come to catch a glimpse of the stunning Victoria Woodhull.

Susan walked under the shade of the tent, and it occurred to her that soon guns would be firing off inside this wobbly construction of lumber and cloth, where innocent people had come to listen to a peaceful speech supporting women's rights. She wondered how the innocent people would feel afterward, after she raised her gun above her head and blasted a hole in the roof of the tent. She thought about how the Smith & Wesson would feel, and tried to block out the memory of that first time, only yesterday, when she held the weapon in her hands. She thought about pulling the trigger, and decided she would close her eyes before she fired, and by the time she reopened them 112 holes would dot the canopy overhead and people would be fleeing in terror. And it would be over. Finally it would be over. There. She'd allowed herself to think it through. Nothing to fear. A speech and some noise and she would never again have to touch a gun.

"You're late," Lizzy whispered. Lizzy took Susan's hands and knotted a thick piece of rope loosely around her wrists, pulling Susan's ruffled sleeves down in front of her to hide the rope. "Loose enough?" Lizzy asked. Susan nodded. Lizzy pushed the reticule with her revolver between Susan's fingers.

This time it was Susan who avoided Lizzy's eyes. She clutched her purse and climbed the rostrum. The crowd fell silent. She set her purse on the podium and stepped forward so everyone could see her clearly. "Ladies and gentlemen," Susan began, "I stand before you . . . a slave." She raised her hands above her head and her sleeves slid down, revealing the ropes that bound her wrists.

The people in the audience remained stunned for only a moment. Hisses escaped the men. Shrieks and clapping from the women. Some people laughed. Susan heard bits and pieces of comments. *"Ridiculous display . . . how dare she . . . hens with nothing better to do than . . . somebody*

pull her off the stage ... children shouldn't be ... call her-
self a lady ... what did she expect ... an embarrassment
to ..."

Susan walked across the platform, hands held high
above her head. *Look at me,* she was saying. *Bondage is*
bondage. Every man is a slave-owner. Admit we are slaves
and free us. You have done it for the Negroes.

The jeering grew louder. Looks of indignation spread
throughout the men. Now she was supposed to walk over
to the podium, break her bonds, pull out her revolver,
and shout *"Free me!,"* firing a single bullet into the air.
The women would pull their triggers in support. Then
Susan need only await the fallout. Arrest, imprisonment,
public outrage perhaps. Still, a message delivered, national attention when they needed it desperately. Susan
approached the podium.

She had truly intended to raise her gun and pull the
trigger. That was the plan and she would do her part, as
always, for the cause. But Susan realized before she even
touched the gun she would not be able to follow through.
She lowered her arms and looked off to the side for Lizzy.
She hoped her friend would someday be able to forgive
her, but if a message like this was to be sent, someone
else would have to send it.

Susan saw Victoria Woodhull in her baggy shirt and
pants and painter's cap rise out of her seat in the front
row, the Smith & Wesson in her hand. She aimed at
Susan and fired. The bullet struck the podium. Wood
chips flew. Susan ducked, fell to her knees. Screams
erupted from the audience. The podium toppled beside
Susan and she grabbed her purse. Another shot sounded
out. Susan saw a man in the crowd clutch his bloodied
chest, cry in agony, fall to the ground.

"Lizzy!" Susan shouted.

Men in Federal uniforms sallied forth, surrounded the
tent, and closed in on the rostrum. Hundreds of panicked
people rushed to get past the incoming troops. Men and
women yelled. Children screeched. Horses stamped and

whinnied and snapped their tethers. Susan saw two, three, four women take aim with their revolvers and shoot. More men went down—soldiers this time—spitting blood. The smell of smoke and gunpowder spread throughout the tent. Susan spotted Lizzy off the platform to her left, kneeling behind a row of fallen chairs. They crawled toward each other.

Captain Mansfield marched straight down the aisle, his gaze fixed on Lizzy.

"Dear God, no!" Susan cried.

Captain Mansfield unsheathed his sword, stepped alongside Lizzy, and thrust. At first Susan thought he'd missed, but then she saw that the sword had passed so cleanly through Lizzy's ribs that her flesh and bones had offered no resistance. Only when Captain Mansfield withdrew the saber did Susan see streaks of wet crimson clinging to his blade. Lizzy tried to stand, and looked confused when her legs didn't work. Her mouth hung open and she reached out to Susan with one stiff arm. Susan felt the world spin out from under her knees. "Lizzy!" Her purse. The gun.

Someone yanked Susan to her feet. Victoria Woodhull. Another half dozen women carrying S&W .44s closed ranks around her. They forced Susan off the platform and out the back of the tent.

"Let me go!"

"Stop struggling," Victoria said. "We're trying to save your life!"

"You just tried to kill me!"

They ran. More gunfire blasted behind them. Susan couldn't even feel her legs moving. Were the women carrying her? She couldn't get a breath. Lizzy. Dear God. It seemed to take them only seconds to reach the Seneca Valley Inn. Victoria Woodhull and her lieutenants led Susan down into the wine cellar. She unfolded like a paper doll, collapsing on top of her reticule.

"I want two lookouts on the roof of the carriage house," Victoria Woodhull said, "and two guards at the wine cellar doors. If the cavalry comes we'll move her out through the Underground."

The other women marched up the steps, leaving Susan alone with Victoria Woodhull.

"What do you think you're doing?" Susan said. Tears filled her eyes and streamed down her cheeks. "What have you done?"

"What you should have done a long time ago. This is a revolution, Susan."

"No, this is *your* revolution, not mine."

"It's much bigger than the two of us. You're in the middle of it whether you like it or not."

"I won't cooperate."

"It doesn't matter."

"The hell it doesn't!" Susan pounded her fists on the hard-packed dirt beneath her knees. "People saw you try to kill me. No one will believe I'm involved in this."

"Don't be an idiot. If I wanted to kill you, you'd be dead. The world will believe a man took a shot at you and missed."

"But there were hundreds of witnesses—" Susan stopped. The clothes. Of course. Victoria Woodhull stood before her, dressed in her shirt and pants and painter's cap. Susan sat back against a wine barrel and took a deep breath. She dabbed at her eyes and nose with her ruffled sleeve.

Victoria said, "Women need to know you're still fighting. It will give them hope. Our revolution will gain strength every day you're alive. We will otherthrow this Republic and plant a government of righteousness in its stead. In time you will come to understand our action was necessary, unavoidable."

"And what about the next action, and the next, and the next? All necessary? All unavoidable?"

"Your problem, Susan, is that you were never willing to make sacrifices. You wanted change for yourself, in *your* lifetime. Nothing comes that easily. Still, it was a good start. You have a lot to be proud of. You will be remembered as the mother of feminism."

No, thought Susan. She would be remembered for turning a peaceful demonstration into a riot. She would be remembered for a bloody massacre in a lovely little park where families had gathered for a speech on a quiet Saturday afternoon. How many Federal officers had been killed? How many innocent people? Yet Susan had to admit there was more than a grain of truth in Victoria Woodhull's words. Susan and Lizzy had been selfish. They had entertained goals and dreams of their own. The sin of pride.

Susan felt the purse beneath her legs. Ah, Victoria, something you forgot about. She reached inside the reticule, withdrew her Smith & Wesson, and pointed it at Victoria Woodhull.

Victoria looked stunned for a moment, then she reached quickly into her own pocket, but her gun wasn't there. She stiffened. "Go ahead and kill me," she said in a defiant tone. "It won't matter. You'll regret it for the rest of your life and it won't make one bit of difference. You know I'm right about the revolution. You know it in your heart. You and Stanton always wanted it, you just didn't have the stomachs for it."

Was that true?

Lizzy, dead. Gutted by that cowardly Copperhead, Mansfield. Susan felt a horrible sense of loss and rage. She had dreamed of someday walking arm in arm with Lizzy into a schoolhouse and legally registering to vote. Now that dream was as dead as her friend. Why hadn't Lizzy used her gun to defend herself? Had she even thought of it? What would Susan have done if Mansfield had come for her? She would always remember Lizzy's last look of confusion. So unlike her not to have an answer, a solution.

Susan gripped the revolver and brushed the trigger with her fingertip, keeping her eyes trained on Victoria Woodhull. How easy it would be to kill Victoria. How easy it would be to kill herself. She had been right yesterday about the gun. Such evil beauty, such sleek power. She thought of Mary E. Surratt. She wondered what could have been going through her mind when she held the derringer with which she planned to assassinate the President. Did she crave the elusive power that belonged only to men? Did she want to kill so badly she could taste it? When the deed was done, when the hot gun burned in her hand, did she own that power? Once women were corrupted by the evil beauty, there would be no turning back. Even Susan could see that.

Susan heard a shuffling sound come from behind the wine barrels. A man stepped out of the shadows. He was wearing undergarments. He clutched an iron pipe in his fists. Susan noticed the set of ropes that had been binding him lying in a heap on the dirt floor, in the corner of the cellar. Victoria Woodhull saw the man and took a backward step. Her breath came hard and fast.

The man moved between Susan and Victoria. He was not a young man. Susan could read the fear in his eyes. He was probably still in shock from the blow he'd taken to the head. He must be wondering where he was, who had hit him and why, whether he should fight. Susan was feeling much the same way. The man reeked of sweat. His biceps bulged as he gripped the iron pipe.

No one moved. They waited for Susan. Susan held the gun, after all. What would Lizzy's solution have been to this predicament? One gun, one bullet, and something that no woman of Susan's generation had ever known: a choice.

WANTED
DEAD OR ALIVE
$1,000 REWARD

Anthony, Susan Brownell:
Age: 45
Height: 5'5" Weight: 123 lbs.
Hair: Brown
Eyes: Blue

Crimes against the United States of America:
Inciting Revolution;
Murder;
Extreme Feminism.

BEWARE
ARMED AND DANGEROUS

Who is perhaps the unlikeliest alternate warrior of this century, including Gandhi, including Martin Luther King, including Julius Nyerere? Why, Mother Teresa, of course.

Writing her story is Jack Nimersheim, author of more than twenty books outside the science fiction field, who has recently invaded our turf with more than a dozen stories in the past year.

The Battle of All Mothers
by Jack Nimersheim

They vaporized Kalighat in 1995. Few clues survive a nuclear holocaust. Based on radiation signatures and the size of the crater left smoldering in its wake, however, the experts surmised that this one must have been the result of a small, low-yield fission device. Probably hand-delivered. Possibly disguised as a suitcase or some equally familiar and innocuous object.

Whatever the cause, the effects were obvious. Twenty thousand people in the immediate vicinity of ground zero perished instantly. Fifty thousand others unfortunate enough to be caught on the perimeter of the blast, their bodies now ravaged by radiation poisoning, faced a slower and immeasurably more gruesome, but no less certain, death.

Like so much scientific jargon, low-yield is a relative concept.

The death and destruction may have been localized—

another relative term—but the shock waves from that violent explosion reverberated around the globe.

Arani Bhakti studied Mother's loving gaze. It was kind and caring and filled with compassion, staring out at her from the locket she clutched in her hands. For more than a decade, that locket and the photograph it contained had accompanied Arani everywhere. How she worshipped those gentle eyes, that wizened yet wise countenance.

"Mother, forgive me," she whispered. With these words, Arani discarded her most precious possession. She watched sadly as it dropped to the sidewalk. Arani then turned and entered the narrow alleyway indicated on the crumpled piece of paper that had guided her to this blasphemous place.

The world mourned Mother Teresa's passing. Nations and governments tripped over one another to praise the frail nun from Albania who dedicated her life to caring for the sick and the needy. They lamented the fact that, despite her eighty-five years on this earth, much of what Mother hoped to accomplish remained unfinished at the time of her untimely death.

Amidst the eulogies and epithets, a few isolated voices sounded alarms. They attempted to point out the dangers inherent in the political instability triggered by Kalighat's annihilation. As it so often does, a self-absorbed humanity turned a deaf ear.

"I realize how frightening all of this must be, Ms. Bhakti. Unfortunately, the current political climate in our country forces us to take such extreme precautions. I'm sure you understand. Try not to be afraid, please. We'll reach our destination shortly."

Arani recognized "Dewey's" voice. She had nicknamed her mysterious companions Huey, Dewey and Louie. For reasons Arani could not fully understand, their disembodied voices recalled the three fictitious characters of her youth. How easy life was, back then. Every day she'd run home from school, arriving just in time to catch her favorite cartoon show on the Disney Channel. The only satellite dish in Arani's village was one of the more welcome benefits that accompanied her father's appointment as governor of the local province.

She had no idea where they were, where they were going, or how long it was taking to get there. Arani had lost all sense of time and direction shortly after being blindfolded and bundled into some type of vehicle—she could not tell what—back in Calcutta. Her enigmatic escorts were not rude or unkind, to be sure, but neither did they provide much in the way of information or companionship. The long intervals of silence between their infrequent and largely unsuccessful attempts to allay her fears were especially difficult to endure.

Arani drew some solace from the fact that this discomfort seemed minor, compared to the alternative. Her current isolation, after all, was temporary, prompted by a need for stealth and secrecy. The permanent ostracism Arani faced, had she elected not to pursue her present course, would have been intolerable.

As the dust settled—both literally and figuratively—on what had once been Kalighat, the world saw reason for hope. It watched with optimism as previously hostile factions throughout the Indian subcontinent united in shared sorrow over Mother's death. The elation did not last long.

Three months after the holocaust, Nanak Singh declared himself President of Trans-India. Like the legendary Phoenix, Singh emerged from the ashes of catastrophe to become the first leader of this newly formed nationstate. Once in power, the former general of the Indian army combined equal parts of Mephisto, Machiavelli and the Messiah to create one of the most repressive regimes in modern history.

* * *

The sudden, unanticipated stop nearly threw Arani out of her seat. Without a word being spoken she sensed, somehow, that they had reached their final destination. Nothing happened for several seconds. It was "Huey" who finally broke the silence. "We've arrived, Ms. Bhakti. Watch your step, please. As you may recall, there's about a two-foot drop off the truck. We'll have to walk several hundred meters over some pretty rough terrain before your blindfold can be removed. Hold onto me and you should have no trouble."

A strong but gentle hand touched hers. The skin was soft and smooth, hardly a match for the image Arani had created of Huey in her mind's eye, based on the few times he'd spoken during the long ride.

A slight breeze greeted Arani as she felt herself being lifted down to the ground. The temperature was noticeably cooler than when they left Calcutta. As she walked, Arani no longer felt the warmth of sunlight on the exposed skin of her face and arms. Was it evening—or even night—already? she wondered. If so, the journey had lasted several hours at least, considerably longer than she had initially thought.

Only two sets of footsteps broke the silence. Arani wondered where Dewey and Louie had disappeared to. Did they stay behind in the truck? (Thanks to Huey's warning, at least Arani knew what kind of vehicle had transported her here.) The ground beneath her feet felt like fine gravel. Every once in a while, Huey alerted her to a large rock or some other obstacle barring their path. Each time he'd guide her around it, taking special care so she would not lose her footing. After walking for several minutes, they stopped.

"I must leave now. There's a building just ahead of you. Someone will be with you momentarily. Remain here and, please, Ms. Bhakti, try to relax. There's nothing to be afraid of, I assure you."

Try to relax? This was easier said than done. Anxiety had been Arani's constant companion for the better part of a month, ever since that afternoon the doctor recommended by a friend outlined the options available to her, given her current condition. This same friend later gave Arani the hastily scrawled map that ultimately led her here—wherever "here" might be.

"You may uncover your eyes now, my child." The words startled Arani. After listening to Huey's footsteps recede, she had sensed no one else's approach. Nevertheless, she felt reassured by this feeble voice. It was filled with kindness. It also sounded strangely familiar.

Reaching behind her head, Arani untied the blindfold and removed it. As she surmised, night had fallen. Her eyes, unused for so long, had difficulty focusing. The darkness only made matters worse. Arani did not need to see clearly, however, to recognize the delicate figure standing before her.

"Mother!" Arani cried, sinking to her knees in both shock and supplication.

She was young again. Young and innocent, running through the warmth of a tropical afternoon. Her home lay just around the next bend. As one with the wind, she flew down the narrow dirt road and up the porch steps, bursting through the front door.

"Father! I'm home!" Her voice echoed much more loudly than it should have. "Father?"

Arani did not remember the house being this large, this empty. Nor could she recall it ever being so dark. It sounded and felt as if she were in a huge cavern. The only light Arani saw was a flickering glow coming from the far end of the hall.

Of course, Arani realized. That would be the television in the parlor. Anticipating her arrival, her father or one of the servants must have already focused the monstrous dish in their back yard on a tiny satellite circling the earth, approximately 36,000 kilometers overhead. (How did she know this? Surely, a child of seven growing up during the mid-1980s in a small village in central India would not understand the concept of a geosynchronous orbit.) The theme music filtering down the hallway re-assured her. Slowly, she moved toward the familiar sound.

Everything was wrong. The room was empty, except for the television set and a single, straight-backed chair. Where were the tall, oaken bookshelves that contained her father's precious collection of law and history books? Where was the wicker furniture he'd had shipped from the apartment in Jubbulpore, shortly after settling into his new position? The wall that normally held several framed pictures—including Arani's favorite, a shot of the entire family taken on holiday in Sri Lanka, shortly before her mother's death—was bare.

Oh, well, thought Arani, with the acceptance and adaptability of youth, at least she could still watch her favorite TV show.

Here, also, however, nothing was as it should be. The adolescent characters she loved so much were now full grown—towering over even their rich uncle. Masks covered their faces, each one matching the color of the cap and shirt that provided the only clue to its wearer's identity. And they pursued their adventures, not with the mis-spent energy and misguided exuberance of youth, as she remembered, but with an undeniable streak of ruthless-ness.

At one point, Arani felt compelled to turn away from the screen, as her childhood icons played a particularly cruel and deadly practical joke on a playmate. Try as she might, however, she could not avert her eyes from the gruesome scenes playing out before her. Macabre turned to madness when the trio of transformed ducklings stepped out of the picture tube and advanced toward her, a strange mixture of lust and rage in their eyes—just like the three soldiers, that night in her village.

The Arani in the chair was an adult now. She was try-ing to flee. To get up. To run. To hide. Escape, however, proved impossible. She could not move. She was helpless. Again, just like that terrible night. Her attempts to scream also failed. A deathly silence permeated the room.

One of her cartoon captors—Arani could not identify him, his cap and mask having faded to a dull and dingy gray—reached out to touch her. His fingers, protruding forth from a grotesque combination of human hand and avian wing, brushed against her ...

Arani awoke with a start. Her mouth was dry, her body drenched in sweat. She was only dimly aware of the hand gently touching her shoulder.

"Do not be frightened. It was only a dream—though not a very pleasant one, I would imagine, judging from the way you were thrashing about."

Few would characterize the face gazing down at Arani as being beautiful. Mother had weathered too many summers in the hot, tropical sun to sustain this ephemeral quality. It was, however, beatific. The pictures Arani had seen of Mother throughout her life, including the one she'd carried so long in that now discarded locket, only portrayed Mother's image. They failed to capture her essence.

"Mother! You're alive! Or have I perished, only to be reunited with you in the afterlife?"

"Rest assured, my child, that you are still among the living, as am I."

"Where are we? Where have you been? How did you escape the destruction of Kalighat? Who ... oh ... I have so many questions, I don't know where to begin."

"And they all shall be answered, in due course. Do not trouble yourself with these matters just now, however.

"I apologize for interrupting your rest. Sleep should be calming, curative—an opportunity for the mind to commune directly with the spirit. Upon observing your agitation, I felt it best to awaken you. It did not seem charitable to permit turmoil to intrude upon your all too brief respite from harsh reality. Your soul faces enough challenges in the days ahead."

"Then, you know?"

"Your presence here provides all the information I need."

"Oh, Mother, can you ever forgive me?"

"It is not *my* forgiveness that should concern you. But let us not talk of these matters, just yet. There will be ample opportunity later for such discussions.

"There's a shower just across the hall. Feel free to use it. When you've finished, I'll accompany you to the cafeteria. You must be famished, following yesterday's journey. The morning meal has just begun. Let us take care of your immediate needs. Then you and I will speak of other matters."

Arani was convinced, beyond any shadow of a doubt, that the Lord held Mother in special favor. How else to interpret the fact that, only hours before disaster struck Kalighat, she was called away to welcome an unexpected member into her flock? One premature birth could not offset so many deaths, but it did prevent Mother from being counted among the casualties.

"And no one knew of your good fortune?"

"Sadly, no. Everyone who might have been aware of my being absent from Kalighat that night perished in the explosion, along with the others. All the dead, God rest their souls." Mother bowed her head as she touched the fingers of her right hand to forehead, breast and both shoulders. "Only the people in the village where I had gone to witness the baby's birth knew of my survival."

"Why didn't you try to contact anyone, to let them know you were still alive?"

"It was not that easy, my child. The electromagnetic pulse generated by the bomb disrupted communications in an area several hundred square kilometers surrounding Kalighat. Telephones were useless, as was the radio in my truck."

"But surely you could have found some way to get a message out?"

"Oh, I did. A young man offered to deliver word of my

fate to an army outpost located a short distance from the village. He must have succeeded. For not long after he departed, the soldiers arrived.

"Watching them approach, we assumed they were coming to provide assistance. We believed so right up until the moment they opened fire on the small group of children who ran out to greet them." Once again, Mother bowed her head and crossed herself. This time, when she looked back up, a single tear trickled down her cheek. It followed the deep lines in her aged face like a stream flowing through an ancient creek bed.

"Over three hundred men, women and children were massacred that night, including the infant I'd delivered just a few hours earlier. Only a handful of villagers escaped the slaughter. It was they who spirited me away to safety. I've been in hiding ever since."

"Then why stay here? There must be some way you can flee Trans-India. Once you reach the sanctuary of a neighboring country, you could safely reveal yourself to the rest of the world."

"You still have much to learn about us. And you shall. Before this process begins, however, you have concerns of a more personal nature to contend with."

It was the first time during the entire conversation that Mother mentioned her condition. Arani suddenly realized how little she'd thought about it herself, since their brief conversation before breakfast. Now that the topic had resurfaced, there was one question she felt compelled to ask.

"How is it that I ended up here? You must know what I was looking for, when I sought out your people in Calcutta."

"Of course I do. We make our services available to anyone we believe can benefit from them. To all others we remain quite hidden, I assure you. You would not have found us, had we not wished to be detected."

"But why, Mother? My decision makes a mockery of our faith."

"Do you want to see a true mockery, my child? Come with me."

Mother stood up from behind her desk and walked out of the small room in which they had been talking. As they moved down the hall, Arani could not help but notice the uncertainty in her gait. Not that this surprised her. Mother's physical condition had started to deteriorate almost a decade earlier, long before recent events undoubtedly exacerbated the situation.

Word of the heart attack in 1989 reached Arani's isolated village even before it appeared on CNN. To Arani's recollection, this was the only time she had been allowed to invite friends into the house to watch the satellite broadcasts. For almost a week, that September, she and several of her classmates crowded around the television set after school, waiting for the latest news from Calcutta. Arani did not even mind that this meant missing her favorite afternoon shows. Cheers filled the parlor when it was announced that the operation to implant a pacemaker had been successful.

Arani remembered how pale and vulnerable Mother looked, the day they wheeled her out of the hospital door and into the bright glare of the television lights. She recalled how weak Mother's voice sounded, as she offered polite responses to even the most inane questions from the gathered reporters. The woman now opening a door for Arani resembled that emaciated figure just recovering from major surgery.

It was the first time she had been outside the windowless building since her arrival the previous night. The sudden brightness temporarily blinded her. It must have been nearing or just after noon. The sun was almost directly overhead. A muggy wind blew in from Arani's left. In the absence of shadows, there was no way to determine the direction from which it originated.

Mother waited a moment for Arani's eyes to adjust to the light before she spoke. "You asked earlier why I do not flee Trans-India. There is the answer to that question."

As Arani's vision cleared, she found herself gazing at the crater that had once been Kalighat. Obviously, the tedious trip that consumed so much of the previous day had been a ruse, a ride considerably longer than the actual journey it represented.

"Oh, my God ... um ... pardon me, Mother. I did not mean to take His name in vain."

"No need to apologize, Arani. I admit to having a similar reaction, upon returning here for the first time."

The two women stood on the brink of nothingness. No other word seemed sweeping enough to describe the barren landscape spread out before them. The circle of destruction—nearly a half-kilometer in diameter, Arani recalled from news accounts at the time—reminded her of a photograph she had once seen of the American volcano, Mount St. Helens, taken shortly after it erupted. But on a much larger scale. A thick layer of fine gray dust blanketed the area. Except for an occasional bird gliding over the desolation, the crater appeared devoid of any signs of life.

"Do you see that dust?" Mother asked. Arani nodded in mute response. "It is partly composed of the remains of those caught in the blast. 'Remember, man, that thou art dust,' the Bible says, 'and unto dust thou shalt return.' This place stands in stark witness to those sacred words.

"I do not want to mislead you, Arani. Death and Kalighat were hardly strangers to one another. In truth, far fewer people perished in the explosion than had died previously on this same site, since we first opened our doors to the forgotten citizens of Calcutta many years earlier. Unlike the twenty thousands souls lost in that one, terrible instant, however, the faithful to whom we extended our care were permitted to die with dignity. By contrast, the people destroyed the night Kalighat disappeared were nothing more than victims, their lives forfeit as fodder in a struggle they neither initiated nor understood."

"Were you ever able to find out who did this, Mother?"

Mother solemnly surveyed the bleak panorama before her. Several seconds of silence separated Arani's question from the older woman's response.

"Tell me, Arani, do you truly belive that one person could have caused all of this?"

"It's possible, Mother. I remember the scientists saying at the time that Kalighat was probably destroyed by a single nuclear bomb, one that would have easily fit into something as small as a suitcase. Those people were experts. I have no reason to doubt their opinion."

"That's true, my child. Nor do we suffer a dearth of suspects. The most obvious, of course, is Singh. It was he, after all, who benefited most directly from what happened here. Many, however, question his ability to conceive and carry out such an elaborate scheme. They seek their scapegoats elsewhere, often in the strangest places. One person whose opinion I normally value went so far as to imply that our Holy Father in Rome may have been involved.

"In the end, such speculation accomplishes little. Identifying the individual responsible for the destruction that occurred here would permit retaliation, to be sure. This, however, is nothing more than a fancy word for revenge. And vengeance resolves nothing. Nor is it ours to dispense.

"In truth, it does not matter who delivered death to Kalighat that fateful night. He or she was but the agent of a more insidious evil. The true villain here is a humanity that values life far less than its own selfish desires and ambitions. That is the enemy we must confront, the adversary we must vanquish, if we ever hope to emerge victorious in a war as old as time itself.

"You asked earlier how you ended up here. You're here because you've met this enemy. It's with you now, whispering in your ear, tempting you to join its cause. You're here because I wanted you to see the potential conse-·quences of your decision. I thought you should view, first hand, the enemy's handiwork. Finally, you're here because I wanted you to realize that this is a battle you need not fight alone.

"Before us lie the ruins of the old Kalighat. Behind us, adjacent to this destruction, I've already started rebuilding the dream, laying the foundation of a second Kalighat. The people you met at breakfast, and thousands more like them throughout Trans-India, are but the beginning. Others will surely follow.

"You can, also, my child. Join us, if you wish. There is no reason to fight this battle alone.

"I'll leave you to ponder your decision. Before I go, however, I have something that I believe belongs to you." Mother reached into the folds of her habit, withdrew a small envelope, and handed it to the younger woman. "I took the liberty of having this retrieved and brought here. I trust you won't mind. I've always found the uncertainty of the future is easier to accept if we carry the lessons of the past close to our hearts."

Reaching into the envelope, Arani gently pulled out the locket and clutched it to her breast. As she looked up at Mother, tears filled her eyes. It was the first time Arani had cried in many months.

The long and lonely nightmare was over. The healing had begun.

When I asked Mercedes Lackey, a multiple best-seller whose books are omnipresent on the stands these days, to contribute a story to this anthology, she promptly chose T. E. Lawrence.

But Lawrence of Arabia is known far and wide as a warrior, I explained; I need *alternate* warriors.

Trust me, she said.

So I did. And, as it turned out, I was right to.

Jihad
by Mercedes Lackey

Pain was a curtain between Lawrence and the world; pain *was* his world, there was nothing else that mattered.

"Take him out of here, you fools! You've spoiled him!"

Lawrence heard Bey Nahi's exclamation of disgust dimly; and it took his pain-shattered mind a moment to translate it from Turkish to English.

Spoiled him; as if he was a piece of meat. Well, now he was something less than that.

He could not reply; he could only retch and sob for mercy. There was no part of him that was not in excruciating pain.

Pain. All his life, since he had been a boy, pain had been his secret terror and obsession. Now he was drugged with it, a too-great force against which he could not retain even a shred of dignity.

As he groveled and wept, conversation continued on above his head. There were remonstrations on the part of the soldiers, but the Bey was adamant—and angry. Most of the words were lost in the pain, but he caught the sense of a few. "Take him out—" and "Leave him for the jackals."

So, the Bey was not to keep him until he healed. Odd. After Nahi's pawing and fondling, and swearing of desire, Lawrence would have thought—

"You stay." That, petulantly, to the corporal, the youngest and best-looking of the lot. Coincidentally, he was the one who had been the most inventive of the torturers. He had certainly been the one that had enjoyed his role the most. "Take that out," the Bey told the others. Lawrence assumed that Nahi meant him.

If he had been capable of appreciating anything, he would have appreciated that—the man who had wrought the worst on his flesh should take his place in the Bey's bed.

The remaining two soldiers seized him by the arms. Waves of pain rolled up his spine and into his brain, where they crashed together, obliterating thought. He couldn't stand up; he couldn't even get his feet under him. His own limbs no longer obeyed him.

They dragged him outside; the cold air on his burning flesh made him cry out again, but this time no one laughed or struck him. Once outside, his captors were a little gentler with him; they draped his arms over their shoulders, and half carried him, letting him rest most of his weight on them. The nightmarish journey seemed to last a lifetime, yet it was only to the edge of the town.

Deraa. The edge of Deraa. The edge of the universe. He noted, foggily, that he did not recognize the street or the buildings as they passed; they must have brought him to the opposite side of the town. There was that much more distance now between himself and his friends and allies. Distance controlled and watched by the enemy.

Assuming he wanted to reach them. Assuming he wanted them to find him, see him—see what had been done to him, guess at the lacerations that were not visible.

No.

His captors let him down onto the muddy ground at the side of the road. Gently, which was surprising. One of them leaned over and muttered something—Lawrence lost the sense of it in the pain. He closed his eyes and snuggled down into the mud, panting for breath. Every breath was an agony, as something, probably a broken bone, made each movement of his ribs stab him sharply.

He heard footsteps retreating, quickly, as if his erstwhile captors could not leave his presence quickly enough.

Tears of despair, shameful, shamed tears, trickled down his cheeks. The unmoved stars burned down on him, and the taste of blood and bile was bitter in his mouth.

Slowly, as the pain ebbed to something he could think through, he itemized and cataloged his injuries to regain control of his mind, as he had tried to count the blows of the whip on his back. The bones in his foot, fractured during the chaos of the last sabotage-raid, had been shattered again. The broken rib made breathing a new torture. Somewhere in the background of everything, the dull pain of his head spoke of a concussion, which had probably happened when they kicked him to the head of the stairs. The lashes that had bit into his groin had left their own burning tracks behind.

His back was one shapeless weight of pain. He had thought to feel every separate, bleeding welt, but he could only feel the accumulated agony of all of them in a mass. But as he lay in the mud, the cold of the night numbed him, leaving only that final injury still as sharp and unbearable as ever, the one that was not visible. The laceration of his soul.

Now he knew how women felt; to be the helpless plaything of others, stronger or more powerful. To be forced to give of their bodies whether or not they willed or wanted it. To be handled and used—

Like a piece of meat—

And worst of all, at one level, the certainty that he had somehow deserved it all. That he had earned his punishment. That he had asked for his own violation. After all, wasn't that what they said of women, too?

It was this final blow that had cracked the shell of his will and brought down the walls of the citadel of his integrity.

How could he face them, his followers, now? They would watch him, stare at him, and murmur to one another—no matter how silent he kept, they would know, surely they would know. And knowing, how could they trust him?

They would not, of course. He no longer trusted himself. His nerve was broken, his will, his soul broken across that guardroom bench. There was nothing left but despair. He literally had nothing left to live for; the Revolt had become his life, and without it, he had no will to live. The best thing he could do for the Revolt would be to die. Perhaps Feisal would take it upon himself to avenge his strange English friend, Aurens; certainly Auda, that robber, would use Aurens' death as an excuse to further raid the Turks. And Ali, Ali ibn el Hussein; he would surely exact revenge. But could they hold the Revolt together?

Inshallah. As God wills it. Here, in his extremity, he had at last come to the fatalism of the Moslem. It was no longer his concern. Life was no longer his concern. Only death, and the best way to meet it, without further torment, to drown his shame in its dark waters where no one would guess what those waters hid.

This would not be the place to die. Not here, where his beaten and brutalized body would draw attention—where his anxious followers might even come upon it and guess the foulness into which he had fallen. Let him crawl away somewhere; let him disappear into the waste and die where he would not be found, and let his death become a mystery to be wondered at.

Then he would be a martyr, if the Revolt could have such a thing. It might even be thought that he vanished, like one of the old prophets, into the desert, to return at some vague future date. His death would become a clean and shining thing. They would remember him as the confident leader, not the battered, bloody rag of humanity he was now.

He lay in a sick stupor, his head and body aching and growing slowly numb with cold. Finally a raging thirst brought him to life—and spurred him to rise.

He struggled to his feet and rocked in place, moaning, his shaking hands gathering his torn clothing about him. He might have thought that this was a nightmare, save for the newly wakened pain. Somewhere he heard someone laughing, and the sound shocked him like cold water. Deraa felt inhuman with vice and cruelty; he could not die here.

The desert. The desert was clean. The desert would purge him, as it had so many times before.

He stopped at a trough by the wells; scooped a little water into his hands and rubbed it over his face, then drank. He looked up at the stars, which would not notice if there was one half-Arab Englishman less on the earth, and set off, one stumbling step at a time, for the clean waste beyond this vile pit of humanity.

He walked for a long time, he thought. The sounds of humanity faded, replaced by the howling of dogs or jackals, off in the middle distance. Tears of pain blurred his sight; he hoped he could find some hole to hide himself away before dawn, a grave that he might fall into, and falling, fall out of life.

He stumbled, jarring every injury into renewed agony, and a white light of pain blinded him. He thought he would die then, dropping in his tracks; then he thought that the blackness of unconsciousness would claim him.

But the light did not fade; it grew brighter. It burned away the pain, burned away thought, burned away everything but a vague sense of self. It engulfed him, conquered him, enveloped him. He floated in a sea of light, dazzled, sure that he had dropped dead on the road. But if that were true, where was he? And what was this?

Even as he wondered that, he became aware of a Presence within the light. Even as he recognized it, it spoke.

I AM I.

On the bank of the Palestine Railway above the huddle of Deraa they waited: Sherif Ali ibn el Hussein, together with the two men that Aurens had designated as his bodyguards, Halim and Faris, and the sheik of Tafas, Talal el Hareidhin. "Tell me again," Ali said fiercely. "Tell me what it was you did."

Faris, old and of peasant stock, did not hesitate, although this was the fifth time in as many hours that Ali had asked the question. Talal hissed through his teeth, but did not interrupt.

"We came into Deraa by the road, openly," Faris recounted, as patient as the sand. "There was wire, and trenches, some flying machines in the sheds; some men about, but they took no note of us. We walked on, into Deraa. A Syrian asked after our villages, and whether the Turks were there; I think he meant to desert. We left him and walked on again; someone called after us in Turkish, which we feigned not to understand. Then another man, in a better uniform, ran after us. He took Aurens by the arm, saying 'The Bey wants you.' He took Aurens away, through the tall fence, into their compound. This was when I saw him no more. I hung about, but there was no sign of him, although I watched until well after nightfall. The Turks became restless, and looked evilly at me, so I left before they could take me too."

Talal shook his head. "This is pointless," he said. "Aurens is either dead or a prisoner, and in neither case can we help him. If the former, it is the will of Allah; if the latter, we must think of how long he will deceive them, and where we must go when he does."

"Into the desert, whence we came," Ali said glumly. "The Revolt is finished. There is no man of us who can

do as he has done, for there is no man of us who has not
a feud with another tribe; there is not a one of us who
has no tribe to answer to. There is no one we may trust
to whom the English will listen, much less give gold and
guns to. We are finished."

Talal widened his eyes at that, but did not speak. Ali
took a last look at Deraa, and the death of their hopes,
and turned resolutely away.

"Where do we go, lord?" asked Faris, humbly, the peasant still.

"To Azrak," Ali replied. "We must collect ourselves,
and then scatter ourselves. If Aurens has been taken and
betrayed us, we must think to take ourselves where the
Turks cannot find us."

The others nodded at this gloomy wisdom, as the rains
began again, falling down impartially upon Turks and
Bedouin alike.

The ride to the old fortress of Azrak, which Aurens and
his followers had taken for the winter, was made longer
by their gloom. There was not one among them who
doubted the truth of Ali's words; and Ali thought perhaps
that there was not one among them who was not trying
to concoct some heroic scheme, either to rescue Aurens
or to avenge him. But a thousand unconnected raids of
vengeance would not have a quarter of the power of the
planned and coordinated raids Aurens had led them in.
And there was still the matter of gold and guns—gold, to
buy the loyalty of the wilder tribes, to make Suni fight
beside Shia, half-pagan desert tribesman beside devout
Meccan. Guns, because there were never enough guns,
never enough ammunition, and because there were those
who would fight for the promise of guns who would not
be moved for anything else. Swords would not prevail
against the Turkish guns, no matter how earnest the
wielder.

They must gather their people, each his own, and scatter. Ali would take it upon himself to bear the evil news

to Feisal, who would, doubtless, take it to his father and the English.

More ill thoughts; how long would King Hussein, ever jealous of his son's popularity and inclined to mistrust him, permit Feisal even so much as a bodyguard? Without Aurens to speak to the English, and the English to temper the father, the son could not rally the Revolt either.

It was truly the death of their hopes.

The fortress loomed in the distance, dark and dismal in the rain. Ali did not think he could bear to listen to the spectral wailings of the ghost-dogs of Beni Hillal about the walls tonight. He would gather his people and return to his tribe—

What was that noise?

He raised his eyes from contemplating the neck of his camel, just as a shaft of golden light, as bright as the words of the Koran, broke through the clouds. Where it struck the ground, on the road between them and the fortress, there was a stark white figure, that seemed to take in the golden light and transmute it to his own brightness.

Ali squinted against the light. Who was this? Was it mounted?

Yes, as it drew nearer, strangely bringing the beam of sunlight with it, he saw that it was mounted. Not upon a camel, but upon a horse of a whiteness surpassing anything Ali had ever seen. Not even the stud reft away from the Turks was of so noble a color—

Now he saw what the noise was; behind the rider came every man of the fortress, cheering and firing into the air—

Ali goaded his mount into a loping canter, his heart in his throat. It could not be, could it?

From the canter he urged the camel into a gallop. The size was right; the shape—but whence the robes, the headcloth, even the headropes, of such dazzling whiteness? They had been mired in mud for months, he had not thought ever to see white robes until spring.

It was. His heart leapt with joy. It was! The figure was near enough to see features now; and it was not to be mistaken for any other. Aurens!

He reined his camel in beside the white stallion, and the beast did not even shy, it simply halted, though Aurens made no move to stop it. He raised his hand, and the mob at his back fell respectfully silent.

Ali looked down at his friend; Aurens looked up, and there was a strange fire in those blue eyes, a burning that made Ali rein his camel back a pace. There was something there that Ali had never seen before, something that raised the hair on the back of his neck and left him trembling between the wish to flee and the wish to fall from his camel's back and grovel at the Englishman's feet.

"Lawrence?" Ali said, using the English name, rather than the one they all called him. As if by using that name he could drive that strangeness from Aurens' eyes. "Lawrence? How did you escape from the Turks?"

The blue eyes burned brighter, and the robes he wore seemed to glow. "Lawrence is dead," he said. "The Turks slew him. There is only Aurens. Aurens, and the will of Allah."

Ali's blood ran hot and cold by turns as he stared down into those strange, unhuman blue eyes. "And what," he whispered, as he would whisper in a mosque, "is the will of Allah?"

At last the eyes released him, leaving him shivering with reaction, and with the feeling that he had gazed into something he could not, and would never, understand.

"The will of Allah," said Aurens, gazing toward Deraa, toward Damascus, and beyond, "is this."

Silence, in which not even the camels stirred.

"There will be *jihad*."

General Allenby swore, losing the last of his composure.

"He's *where*?" the commander of the British forces in the Middle East shouted, as his aides winced and the messenger kept his upper lip appropriately stiff in the face of the general's anger.

"Outside of Damascus, sir," he repeated. "I caught up with him there." He paused for a moment, for if this much of the message had the general in a rage, the rest of it would send him through the roof. He was sweatingly grateful that it was no longer the custom to slay the bearer of bad news. "He sent me to tell you, sir, that if you wish to witness the taking of Damascus, you had best find yourself an aeroplane."

The general did, indeed, go through the roof. Fortunately, early on in the tirade, Allenby said something that the messenger could take as a dismissal, and he took himself out.

There was a mob lying in wait for him in the officers' mess.

"What did he say?" "What did he do?" "Is it true he's gone native?" "Is it—"

The messenger held up his hands. "Chaps! One at a time! Or else, let me tell it once, from the beginning."

The hubbub cooled then, and he was allowed to take a seat, a throne, rather, while the rest of them gathered around him, as attentive as students upon a Greek philosopher.

Or as Aurens' men upon his word. The similarity did not escape him. What he wondered now, was how he had escaped that powerful personality. Or had he been *permitted* to escape, because it suited Aurens' will to have him take those words back to Jerusalem?

First must come how he had found Aurens—he could no more think of the man as "T. E. Lawrence" than he could think of the Pope as "Binky." There was nothing of Britain in the man he had spoken to, save only the perfect English, and the clipped, precise accent. Not even the blue eyes—they had held something more alien than all the mysteries of the East.

"I was told he had last been seen at Deraa, so that was

where I went to look for him. He wasn't there; but his garrison was."

"His garrison! These wogs couldn't garrison a stable!" There was an avalanche of comments about that particular term; most disparaging. Kirkbride waited until the comments had subsided.

"I tell, you, it was a *garrison*." He shook his head. "I can't explain it. As wild as you like, tribesmen riding like devils in their games outside, the Turkish headquarters wrecked and looted—but everything outside that, untouched. The Turks, prisoners, housed and fed and clean—the guards on the town, as disciplined as—" He lacked words. The contrast had been so great, he could hardly believe it. But more than that, the town had been held by men from a dozen different tribes, or more—and yet there was no serious quarreling, no feuding. When he ventured to ask questions, it had been "Aurens said," and "Aurens commanded," as though Aurens spoke for Allah.

Aurens, it appeared, was on the road to Damascus, sweeping all before him.

"They gave me a guide, and sent me off camel-back, and what was the oddest, I would have sworn that they knew I was coming and were only waiting for me." That had been totally uncanny. The moment he had appeared, he had been escorted to the head of the garrison, some sheik or other, then sent immediately out to the waiting guide and saddled camel. And the only answer to his question of "Where are you taking me?" was "Aurens commands."

Deraa had been amazing. The situation outside Damascus was beyond imagination.

As he described it for his listeners, he could not fault them for their expressions of disbelief. He would not have believed it if he had not seen it. Massed before Damascus was the greatest Arab army the world had ever seen. Kirkbride had been an Oxford scholar in history, and he could not imagine that such a gathering had ever occurred even at the height of the Crusades. Tribe after feuding tribe was gathered there, together, in the full strength of fighters. Boys as young as their early teens, and scarred old graybeards. There was order; there was discipline. Not the "discipline" of the British regulars, of drill and salute, of uniforms and ranks—a discipline of a peculiarly Eastern kind, in which individual and tribal differences were forgotten, submerged in favor of a goal that engaged every mind gathered here in a kind of white-hot fervor. Kirkbride had recognized Bedouins that were known to be half-pagan alongside Druses, alongside King Hussein's own devout guard from Mecca—

That had brought him up short, and in answer to his stammered question, his guide had only smiled whitely. "You shall see," he said only. "When we reach Aurens."

Reach Aurens they did, and he was brought into the tent as though into the Presence. He was announced, and the figure in the spotlessly white robes turned his eyes on the messenger.

His listeners stilled, as some of his own awe communicated itself to them. He had no doubt, at that moment, that Aurens *was* a Presence. The blue eyes were unhuman; something burned in them that Kirkbride had never seen in all of his life. The face was as still as marble, but stronger than tempered steel. There was no weakness in this man, anywhere.

Aurens would have terrified him at that moment, except that he remembered the garrison holding Deraa. The Turks there were cared for, honorably. Their wounded were getting better treatment than their own commanders gave them. Somewhere, behind the burning eyes, there was mercy as well.

It took him a moment to realize that the men clustered about Aurens, as disciples about a master, included King Hussein, side by side, and apparently reconciled, with his son Feisal. King Hussein, pried out of Mecca at last—

Clearly taking a subservient role to Aurens, a foreigner, a Christian.

Kirkbride had meant to stammer out his errand then—

except that at that moment, there came the call to prayer. Wild and wailing, it rang out across the camp.

Someone had translated it for Kirkbride once, imperfectly, or so he said. *God alone is great; I testify that there are no Gods but God, and Mohammed is his Prophet. Come to prayer; come to security. God alone is great; there is no God but God.*

And Aurens, the Englishman, the Christian, unrolled his carpet, faced Mecca with the rest, and fell upon his face.

That kept Kirkbride open-mouthed and speechless until the moment of prayer was over, and all rose again, taking their former places.

"He did *what?*" The officers were as dumbfounded as he had been.

Once again, Kirkbride was back in that tent, under the burning, blue gaze of those eyes. "He said to tell Allenby that if he wanted to see the taking of Damascus, he should find an aeroplane, else it would happen before he got there." Kirkbride swallowed, as the mess erupted in a dozen shouted conversations at once.

Some of those involved other encounters with Aurens over the past few weeks. How he had been in a dozen places at once, always riding a white Arabian stallion or a pure white racing camel of incredible endurance. How he had rallied the men of every tribe. How he had emptied Mecca of its fighting men.

How he had appeared, impeccably uniformed, with apparently genuine requisition orders for guns, ammunition, explosives, supplies. How he had vanished into the desert with laden camels—and only later were the orders proved forgeries so perfect that even Allenby could not be completely sure he had not signed them.

How, incredibly, all those incidents had taken place in the same day, at supply depots spread miles apart.

It was possible—barely. Such a feat could have been performed by a man with access to a high-powered motorcar. No one could prove Aurens had such access—but

Hussein did; he owned several. And Hussein was now with Aurens—

It would still have taken incredible nerve and endurance. Kirkbride did not think *he* had the stamina to carry it off.

No one was paying any attention to him; he slipped out of the officers' mess with his own head spinning. There was only one thing of which he was certain now.

He wanted to be in at the kill. But to do that, he had to get himself attached to Allenby's staff within the next hour.

Impossible? Perhaps. But then again, had Aurens not said, as he took his leave, "We will meet again in Damascus"?

Kirkbride sat attentively at the general's side; they had not come by aeroplane after all, but by staff car, and so they had missed the battle.

All six hours of it.

Six hours! He could scarcely credit it. Even the Germans had fled in terror at the news of the army camped outside their strongholds; they had not even waited to destroy their own supplies. The general would not have believed it had not French observers confirmed it. Allenby had mustered all of the General Staff of the Allied forces, and a convoy of staff cars had pushed engines to the breaking point to convey them all to the city, but Kirkbride had the feeling that this was the mountain come to Mohammed, and not the other way around. He had been listening to the natives, and the word in their mouths, spoken cautiously but fervently, was that Aurens *was* Mohammed, or something very like him. The victories that Allah had granted were due entirely to his holiness, and not to his strategy. Strangest of all, this was agreed upon by Suni and Shiite, by Kurd and Afghani, by purest Circassian and darkest Egyptian, by Bedouin wanderer and Lebanese shopkeeper. There had been no such accord upon a prophet since the very days of Mohammed himself.

Allenby had convinced himself somehow that Aurens was going to simply, meekly, hand over his conquests to his rightful leader.

Kirkbride had the feeling that Allenby was not going to get what he expected.

Damascus was another Deraa, writ large. Only the Turkish holdings had been looted; the rest remained unmolested. There were no fires, no riots. High-spirited young warriors gamed and sported outside the city walls; inside, a stern and austere martial order prevailed. Even the hospital holding the wounded and sick Turkish prisoners was in as good order as might be expected, for a place that had been foul when the city was in Turkish hands. There was government; there was order. It was not an English order; organization was along tribal lines, rather than rank, to each tribe, a duty, and if they failed it, another was appointed to take it, to their eternal shame. But it was an order, and at the heart of it was the new Arab government.

Allenby had laughed to hear that, at the gates of the city. As they were ushered into that government's heart, he was no longer laughing. There were fire brigades, a police force; the destitute were being fed by the holy men from out of the looted German stores, and the sick tended by the Turkish doctors out of those same stores. There were scavenger gangs to clear away the dead, with rights to loot the bodies to make up for the noisome work. British gold became the new currency; there was a market already, with barter encouraged. Everywhere Kirkbride looked, there was strange, yet logical, order. And Allenby's face grew more and more grave.

Aurens permitted him, and the envoys of the other foreign powers, into his office, commandeered from the former governor. The aides remained behind. "My people will see to us, and to them," Aurens said, with quiet authority. A look about the room, at the men in a rainbow of robes, with hands on knife hilts, dissuaded arguments.

The door closed.

Kirkbride did not join with the others, drinking coffee and making sly comments about their guardians. He had the feeling, garnered from glances shared between dark faces, and the occasional tightening of a hand on a hilt, that all of these "barbarians" knew English quite well. Instead, he kept to himself, and simply watched and waited.

The hour of prayer came, and the call went up. All the men but one guarding them fell to praying; Kirkbride drew nearer to that one, a Circassian as blond as Aurens himself.

"You do not pray?" he asked, expecting that the man would understand.

And so he did. He shrugged. "I am Christian, for now." He cast his glance towards the closed door, and his eyes grew bright and thoughtful. "But—perhaps I shall convert."

Kirkbride blinked in surprise; not the least of the surprises of this day. "What was it that the caller added to the end of the chant?" he asked, for he had noted an extra sentence, called in a tone deeper than the rest.

The man's gaze returned to Kirkbride's face. "He said, 'God alone is good, God alone is great, and He is very good to us this day, O people of Damascus.'"

At that moment, the door opened, and a much subdued delegation filed out of the door. Allenby turned, as Aurens followed a little into the antechamber, and stopped. His white robes seemed to glow in the growing dusk, and Kirkbride was astonished to see a hint of a smile on the thin, ascetic lips.

"You can't keep this going, you know," Allenby said, more weary than angry. "This isn't natural. It's going to fall apart."

"Not while I live, I think," Aurens said, in his crisp, precise English.

"Well, when you die, then," Allenby retorted savagely. "And the moment you're dead, we'll be waiting—just like the vultures you called us in there."

If anything, the smile only grew a trifle. "Perhaps. Perhaps not. There is wealth here, and wealth can purchase educations. In a few years, there will be men of the tribes who can play the politicians' game with the best of them. Years more, and there will be men of the tribes who look farther than the next spring, into the next century. We need not change, you know—we need only adopt the tools and weapons, and turn them to our own use. I would not look to cut up the East too soon, if I were you." Now he chuckled, something that surprised Kirkbride so much that his jaw dropped. "And in any event," Aurens concluded carelessly, "I intend to live a very long time."

Allenby swore under his breath, and turned on his heel. The rest, all but Kirkbride, followed.

He could not, for Aurens had turned that luminous blue gaze upon him again.

"Oxford, I think," the rich voice said.

He nodded, unable to speak.

The gaze released him, and turned to look out one of the windows; after a moment, Kirkbride recognized the direction. East.

Baghdad.

"I shall have need of Oxford men, to train my people in the English way of deception," the voice said, carelessly. "And the French way of double-dealing, and the German way of ruthlessness. To train them so that they understand but do not become these things."

Kirkbride found his voice. "You aren't trying to claim that 'your people' aren't double-dealing, deceitful, and ruthless, I hope?" he said, letting sarcasm color his words. "I think that would be a little much, even from you."

The eyes turned back to recapture his, and somewhere, behind the blue fire, there was a hint of humor.

"Oh, no," Aurens said, with gentle warmth. "But those are *Arab* deceptions, double-dealings, and ruthlessness.

They have not yet learned the ways of men who call themselves civilized. I should like to see them well armored, before Allah calls me again."

Kirkbride raised an eyebrow at that. "You haven't done anything any clever man couldn't replicate," he replied, half in accusation. "Without the help of Allah."

"Have I ever said differently?" Aurens traded him look for ironic look.

"I heard what happened before the battle." Aurens, they said, had ridden his snow-white stallion before them all. "In whose name do you ride?" he had called. "Like a trumpet," Kirkbride's informant had told him, as awed as if he had spoken of the archangel Gabriel.

And the answer, every man joined in one roar of response. *"In the name of Allah, and of Aurens."*

Aurens only looked amused. "Ride with me to Baghdad." This had less the sound of a request than a command. "Ride with me to Yemen. Help me shape the world." Again, the touch of humor, softening it all. "Or at least, so much of it as we can. *Inshallah.* I have Stirling, I have some others, I should like you."

Kirkbride weighed the possibilities, the gains, the losses. Then weighed them against the intangible; the fire in the eyes, the look of eagles.

Then, once again, he looked Aurens full in the eyes; was caught in the blue fire of them, and felt that fire catch hold in his soul, outweighing any other thoughts or considerations.

Slowly, knowing that he wagered all on a single cast of the dice, he drew himself up to attention. Then he saluted; slowly, gravely, to the approval of every one of the robed men in that room.

"To Baghdad, and Yemen, Aurens," he said. *"Inshallah."*

Mel. White, a lovely Texan who is known to fans of both science fiction and comic art, has frequently wondered, like many Americans, what Samuel Clemens might have done had he found himself enmeshed in the Civil War. In the following story she uses some imagination, some history, and a lot of Mark Twain's flavor to answer the question.

Sam Clemens and the Notable Mare
by Mel. White

The Civil War was in its last stages when I became a millionaire for the first time. I was living in Nevada at the time, with my brother Orion, who had been appointed Secretary to the Territory. With the Union and the Confederacy determined to settle their differences in the most uncivil fashion possible, Nevada seemed like a nice quiet spot for a vacation. So I traveled West as my brother's secretary and left my betters to conduct the war in my absence.

Nevada proved to be a land of endless opportunity. I had the opportunity to be secretary to the Secretary, the opportunity to go broke prospecting for gold and silver, the opportunity to broaden my experiences with travel away from Nevada, and the opportunity to expire from Indians or heat or overwork. However, my budget soon felt the pinch of this riotous living. Desperate for income, I sent some articles of carefully edited truths about the locals to the eastern newspapers. The eastern newspapers printed these modest essays and sent money back, an arrangement that suited me very well. I continued in this amicable fashion until 1864 and the Great Clarendon Silver Mine Rush, when my mining partners and I had the opportunity to be millionaires.

Unlike many mines dug around Silver City, the Clarendon was a rich claim, yielding both gold and silver in good quantities. My partners and I had acquired a bundle of the stock in a swap a year before, when the Clarendon was a mere gopher hole, worth exactly nothing. But the first assay of the mine's ore showed that the Clarendon's owners had hit pay dirt and the value of the mine's stock certificates shot up to astronomical heights. Bill, Jack, and I counted our shares of Clarendon stock and realized that we had a profit of about four million dollars if we could get the stocks to New York, where there was a shortage of silver mine stock certificates and an abundance of cold hard cash. So we cut the cards and determined in the most democratic of ways that I should have the dubious honor of returning to the States to arrange an exchange of certificates for silver. Bill volunteered to arrange for my transportation while Jack and I assessed our financial situation.

To our dismay, we found that we were a hundred dollars shy of the price of a stagecoach ticket East. As we were moping over the possibility of having to send our stock to an eastern stockbroker to sell, Bill came bounding in, waving his hat and yelling.

"Hold on, fellas!" he howled. "I got a horse for Sam to ride! Only cost five dollars! That Injun over at the stables sold her to me an' threw in a saddle and bridle as well!!"

Now, Bill was one of the world's Original Innocents. He believed that Santa Claus came down the chimney, that stump water cured warts, and that a man could buy a good horse for five dollars. We harassed him for spending one twentieth of my traveling funds, but he insisted that it was a truly notable animal and led us off to see her.

We found the Notable Horse standing disconsolately in the corner of the stable yard, mumbling on a wheat straw, a skinny mare with a lanky neck and untrimmed hooves. It was plain even to a pack of non-horsemen such as ourselves that Bill had been had. We said as much to Bill and he protested strongly.

"Red Hawk says she's the fastest horse in the whole territory," he said, giving her a pat and slipping the bridle over her bony head. "He says he stole her from a tribe east of here and that she's one of their big medicine horses. He wants to get rid of her so she don't bring him bad luck."

We expressed our opinion that it was Bill who'd gotten the bad luck and demanded our five dollars back. Bill's response was to set up a loud roar for Red Hawk, who slowly emerged from the shade of the stable.

"Here now, Red Hawk," Bill yelled at him, "my partners are saying that this horse is no good."

"This notable horse. Plenty good," the Indian answered, and leaped lightly aboard her. The mare flicked one dusty ear back at her rider but took no other notice until he leaned forward and whacked her ribs soundly with his heels. Then that dust-colored mare stretched out her bony neck and took off like a prairie falcon, clearing fences, dogs, three wagons, and a stray church steeple on her way out of town. We stared after her, mouths agape, like men who had lost their senses.

After a few minutes, Red Hawk and his notable mare came ambling casually back up the street. He turned her into the stable yard and handed the reins to me. "Good horse. Get you there fast," he said.

"Goes like a reg'lar comet, don't she?" beamed Bill. Jack eyed the bony mare warily.

"Now, Bill, you know that Sam ain't the bestest rider

in the territory. Mebbe if we got Sam something a little more see-date . . ."

"Or if I got myself some sedation," I added.

"No problem," Red Hawk said as he took out his medicine bundle. "You no fall off. I fix this." And with that, he began to leap and howl around horse and saddle like he'd blundered into a beehive. When he felt that he'd satisfied his spirits and himself with the noise, he bounced to a halt, tossed a pinch of tobacco at the horse, and handed me the reins again.

"You ride now. No trouble," he said grandly, "but you remember one thing. This is medicine horse. You no speak of white man's gods near her."

I must have looked skeptical, for he repeated his instructions sternly. "This horse is Indian spirit. Powerful totem. White man's gods offend her. Do not speak of them near her."

"C'mon, Sam," Jack teased. "It's a five-dollar horse. We can't afford to be too particular at those prices."

In the end, there was nothing left to do but mount the beast, bid farewell to Nevada, and head eastward on the Notable Mare. Whether it was the Indian's intercession or my own practice since coming out West, the ride was not as rough as I expected. Notable covered the ground with an easy stride, making nearly as good time as a stagecoach. I did test the Indian's injunctions once by singing a song about the angel Gabriel, but at the first mention of angels she snorted like a volcano and humped her back. The coincidence made me uneasy so I began a song I learned from George Walsh: a cheerful little tune that you wouldn't repeat in front of children, women, preachers, or the faint of heart. Notable seemed to like it just fine.

The inns and stations along the way were full of gossip about the war. Two names were mentioned frequently—"Bloody Bill" Anderson and William Quantrill, leaders of a pack of men called Patriot Raiders. After the war we were to hear more of them and the others in their band—including Jesse and Frank James and the three Younger brothers. At the time they were lauded as true sons of the South who would save Kansas from the Abolitionists, but after hearing about their interest in bloody mayhem and rapine, I thought that "murderer" or "butcher" came closer to the truth. Though others praised their patriotism, I saw little to indicate that killing people ever convinced them of the error of their ways.

It was an interesting notion, and I thought I might be able to work it into one of my letters from Satan to the archangels about conditions here on earth. I ruminated over it as Notable wandered down the trail and soon a few useful phrases and sentences worked their way into my awareness and virtually shouted for recognition. Grabbing pencil and paper out of my saddlebags, I began scribbling feverishly.

I was in the midst of a particularly fine diatribe about the qualities of heavenly mercy versus those of earthly mercy when a thundering of hooves proclaimed that I wasn't alone. I looked up and was greeted by the business end of a navy revolver about the size of a field cannon, held by the leader of a scruffy flock of gray-clad men. My mouth went dry as the dust in the road.

"Howdy, stranger! You out here alone?" he asked with an affable grin. "It's not a good idea to be traveling by yourself hereabouts. You might be accosted by undesirables."

I could think of fewer companions less desirable than these felons, but had the deep sagacity to keep my opinion to myself. "Undesirables?" I quavered.

"Absolutely," he smiled. "And your presence disrupts several well-laid military plans. I'm afraid we're going to have to hold you under arrest for a while. But don't you worry." He smiled again. "You'll be fine. You have the word of Frank James on it."

As proof of this last, he cocked his revolver and leveled

it at my face. "You don't mind if Cole and Jesse check your things for contraband, now do you?"

I managed a very faint "Nope" around a smile as weak as dishwater.

The youngest hooligan waved me from Notable and began to go through my pockets while his companion examined my saddlebags. My weapons were judged inferior to their own considerable collection. They laughed a great deal at my pepperbox derringer, which was an excitable weapon with seven barrels and prone to firing off all its seven chambers at once. It generally missed what I was shooting at, but hit enough of the surrounding landscape to discourage the target. Indeed, one of the ruffians had the poor manners to suggest that the pepperbox was fit only to throw at the cats.

Though they were unimpressed with my choice of guns and horseflesh, they found the mining stock certificates intriguing and my traveling money downright fascinating. The one called Cole handed my saddlebags over to the leader of the troop, who eyed the contents with a grin.

"We do thankee kindly for your contributions to Quantrill's Raiders and the glorious cause of the Confederacy," he said with a smile and a tip of his hat. Then he slung my saddlebags and my fortune across his saddle and motioned down the road with his gun.

"Let's go."

We rode in silence for perhaps a quarter of an hour, through a stretch of summer prairie land as flat as a deaf tenor. As we topped a ridge that overlooked their camp, I was staggered to see how large an organization Quantrill had. I had expected an outlaw gang of perhaps fifty thugs and instead found in front of me an entire Confederate battalion, numbering perhaps five hundred men. Rows of orderly tents stood near the shade of the trees along the creek's edge, and there was an air of military professionalism about the camp.

The baby-faced cutthroat named Jesse led me to Quantrill's tent and presented me and my fortune to his commander. I noted that he forgot to present his commander with my sixty-three dollars that he took from the saddlebag, but decided against bringing the subject up. William Quantrill didn't appear to be the sort who'd let an honest citizen have a refund.

Quantrill squinted at me as he cleaned his gun with an oily rag. "What's your name?"

"Mark Twain, Gin'ril," I said, using the alias I'd recently concocted. It was useful to have my articles written under a pseudonym, in case my subjects felt themselves obliged to straighten out the true facts of events in question with a gun.

"Never heard of you," he said, loading his weapon.

I certainly hoped to high heaven that he hadn't heard of me. If he ever connected me with the Secretary of the Territory of Nevada, I would no doubt be used as a political pawn or held hostage for ransom. He and his cutthroats would be mortally annoyed when they found out just how little my brother and kinfolk were willing to part with to save my life. I twisted my hat brim in my sweaty hands and tried to look poor and harmless and desperate—which I was.

A sudden commotion outside drew his attention away from me. Throwing aside the tent flap, he roared a vow to the Almighty to bring domestic tranquility to the camp by ventilating the brawlers. Men scattered before his threat, and the camp calmed down except for the squalling of an angry horse in the picket line. Stalking back into the tent, he eyed me sourly.

"Put him with the rest of that lot, Jesse," Quantrill said sourly. "We'll deal with them after the raid tomorrow."

From the look in his eyes, I figured that young Jesse was all for shooting me then and there, but he sketched a rough salute and escorted me to a large tent in the middle of the camp. "Your quarters," he sneered, shoving me headlong into the interior.

Hands helped me up from my ungraceful sprawl. "I'm

afraid you've missed lunch," drawled a very aristocratic British voice, "and you're nearly late for tea. You should have wired ahead and let us know you were coming."

I dusted myself off and glowered at the tall Englishman. "If I'd have known I was coming, I'd have taken the other route," I grumbled.

"So would we all," he said brightly. "By the way, I'm Andrew Massey, corespondent for the London *Times.* Our companions in misfortune are Ted and George Ingram, Henry Anserine and his daughter, Miss Katherine."

"Twain. Mark Twain," I responded.

Massey stared at me thoughtfully. "That's an unusual name," he observed. "Are you the Mark Twain who wrote that piece about the stagecoach trip from Hannibal to Nevada?"

"Well, yes," I confessed warily, unsure if he meant to embrace me or fling a rock at me for sullying the journalistic field with my prose. But he grabbed my hand, pumped it enthusiastically, and burbled along about my article until I began to feel a warm rosy glow of embarrassment.

Miss Katherine stared at me, wide-eyed. "An *author*? How wonderful!" she gushed.

"I've had a few things printed in the eastern newspapers," I confessed, having no idea of just how much mischief a statement like that can create.

"Why, I just love books!" Miss Katherine caroled. "Papa can tell you that I read Goodey's *Ladies' Book* all the time. As I was telling dear Mr. Massey, a writer would find so many good stories in my life as it has been lived so far . . ." and with that she launched into one of the longest sentences since the beginning of history, innocent of punctuation and the listener's desperate hope that she would contract laryngitis. I tried nodding, but that only kept the verbal downpour running. Then I lapsed into inarticulate grunts, but this merely fueled her enthusiasm. Finally, I wandered over to one of the small camp beds to sit. She treated this as an invitation and began spicing her monumental sentence with girlish confidentialities. The Ingram brothers glowered jealously at me. Massey gave me a sympathetic glance as he made a hasty retreat for the other corner of the tent.

The long hot afternoon dragged into an equally long and hot evening, punctuated by the unending clatter of Miss Katherine's tongue. She did pause for breath once or twice, and Massey and I tried to divert the conversation elsewhere. I began the tale of my fortune and the Notable Mare, but this only served to inspire Miss Katherine into serving up another endless anecdote. Papa wiped the sweat from his forehead and beamed at his daughter. I wondered if he was deaf. It began to look as if death or sudden deafness were the only forms of release from the grip of Miss Katherine's nonstop conversation.

As I began studying how to slit my wrists with my pen, it occurred to me that I still had a small flat razor in the waistband of my pants. That piece of good fortune inspired me to concoct an impromptu escape plan. I leaped to my feet in great excitement and silenced Miss Katherine by producing both razor and plan with a flourish. The others stared at me as though I'd lost my wits.

"Cut a hole in the tent?" Papa spoke, giving lie to my speculation that he was deaf.

"Yes. And sneak out of camp while it's dark," I said as boldly as I could.

"Are you sure this'll work?" Ted Ingram queried.

"Like a charm."

"There's a full moon tonight," he observed. "You arrangin' for an eclipse?"

I was saved the embarrassment of swallowing my own words by the loquacious Miss Katherine. "Now, Ted, Mr. Twain's absolutely right," she cooed, giving me a doe-eyed look. "Authors have to be up on these things so they can get them right in their books."

"Why, moonlight escapes are all the fashion in Europe, boys," I said confidently. "When Wellington's men were captured by Napoleon they pulled a moonlight escape and made an express run back to their own camp to tell them where that Frenchman was hiding. That moon was so bright that the British were able to shoot holes in Napoleon's cook stove and spoil the disposition of his soup."

Massey cocked an eyebrow at my improvised history but to my vast relief said nothing. Then Miss Katherine turned the full charm of her smile on the farmers, and the poor love-struck things began smiling and nodding like a pair of mechanical puppets.

Thus reassured, the rest of the group turned their thoughts toward the escape plan. We were in the midst of discussing whether we wanted to sneak out quietly or ventilate Quantrill's tent as we made our exit when a young man in a Confederate uniform entered, carrying plates of stew. We looked up guiltily.

"You're lucky that I am the one who overheard your plans," he declaimed in accents that suggested he'd ruined his vocabulary by attending too many melodramas. "This gray cloth covers a true-blue Union heart.

"Colonel Pinkerton sent me to watch these ruffians and warn him of their plans. Quantrill intends to pillage Lawrence tomorrow, but I have sent Pinkerton news of this and he is riding here with his troops to turn the tables on this butcher. This will be a lively area in about two hours, so we must make hasty plans for your departure."

He talked with us for a while, drawing pictures in the dust to show us how the camp was laid out and where the sentries were posted. While he stood guard at the back of the tent, I quietly slit the back seam open. When the evening sentries showed up for duty, our friend groused at them about having to move the remuda to a pasturage further up the creek. Then, bold as brass, he paraded a group of horses past the rear of the tent. While he paused to pick a stone out of the hoof of the horse he was leading, we slipped out of the tent and darted into the midst of the horses. Then he hauled on the lead reins and, bold as brass, led us and the horses to the tree-sheltered creek, like Odysseus leading his men out of the

Cyclops' cave. We found our steeds still saddled and bridled among the remuda and led them quietly away. Miraculously, no alarm was sounded.

After perhaps eighty yards, the young sergeant drew his horse up alongside mine and pointed to a dark mass that crested a small hillock. "Lead your horses around that thicket of trees," he whispered. "There's a little road there, not much more than a path. You follow and it will lead you straight into Lawrence. You got about one hour, maybe less, before our attack begins."

"You can't come with us?" pouted Miss Katherine.

"No, dear lady. My comrades wait for me to lead the charge against these Raiders," he said, and touched his hat. Miss Katherine fluttered her eyelashes and sighed after him as he strode away into the dark.

Massey, who had been keeping watch in the rear of the group, suddenly hissed and pointed back to the camp. "By Jove!" he exclaimed. "They're going to hang one of those poor slaves that they caught!"

"Oh my God!" shrieked Miss Katherine, loud enough to wake the damned. I would have shrieked too, but I was having other problems. Massey's exclamation had started a very unwelcome transformation in Notable, and Miss Katherine's screech had made things considerably worse. The dusty little mare set her ears back, kicked her heels at the astonished stars, and suddenly tripled in size. The saddle girth creaked ominously but didn't break. I teetered, staring down at the ground that was suddenly fourteen feet below me.

"What the devil?" I said.

This was not the most intelligent choice of words I had ever made, for Notable snorted and turned a head the size of a roast pig toward me. Her eyes glowed like alabaster globes, alight with internal fires. She chuffed at me like a steam locomotive through nostrils the size of my hat. I frantically searched my mind for the names of any gods related to sudden deafness.

"Sweet *Jesus*!" I looked toward the sound, and saw a

soldier, Bible in his hand, staring dumbfounded at me and my steed. Notable turned her incandescent gaze from me to him and he blanched and backed up, holding his Bible in front of him. She took a long step forward into the edge of the firelight.

Behind me there came a sudden thundering of hooves. I twisted my head and saw the moonlit figures of our noble turncoat and a troop of perhaps forty Union soldiers cresting the hill. They paused in consternation at the size of the Confederate forces encamped in the little valley.

It was at this moment that Quantrill himself stepped out of his tent to see what all the noise was about. He took one look at Notable and me and gave forth a string of commentary and suggestions and supplications to the entire Christian heavenly hierarchy so creatively profane that I would have applauded the effort if I could have untangled my fear-frozen hands from the reins. Notable apparently found this last offense too much to bear, for she shrieked like a Commanche and charged him.

"By God, Mr. Twain has more nerve than any seventeen colonels!" I heard our Union spy shout. "Follow him, boys!!"

Whooping enthusiastically, the small band of Union soldiers followed in my wake.

Quantrill cut loose with a bullet and another string of profanity. Squalling like a warehouse full of cats, Notable tore toward him, jaws opened wide. He dodged behind a clump of trees and we lost sight of him for a few moments. Frustrated at missing her original target, Notable ploughed to a halt, glared about her, and then charged back through the camp again, scattering bedding and horses before her. I swayed and jolted from side to side, praying first that I wouldn't fall off. But when she took out a row of tents and headed straight for the ammunition stockpile, I began to pray that I *would* fall off. Alas, by this time the gods had finally approved my petitions for deafness, and turned a deaf ear to my latest request.

You never saw anything quite like that horse for clearing the territory of Confederate soldiers. She seemed to feel that everything in camp was responsible for the offense and showed her annoyance by hopping like an oversized bullfrog on top of a field cannon. Quantrill scrambled aboard a horse and Notable chased after him, dancing a fandango through two campfires and the cooking tent and starting a dozen small fires in her wake. I bounced around like a flea aboard a tornado as we pranced throughout the camp. Quantrill's men promptly decamped, searching for a safer war to join.

By the time Notable paused to see if the camp was flattened to her satisfaction, the Patriot Raiders were in considerable disarray. Hoofprints as big as hogshead barrels wandered all over the campsite, and the landscape looked as though a hurricane had come calling. Quantrill's tent was blazing merrily, sending burning scraps of my Clarendon stock certificates into the sky. As I sat watching my fortune go up in flames, Notable's saddle girth broke and I tumbled to the ground near Massey's feet. He gaped at the dusty brown mare, who towered some twenty feet over our heads.

"Ho-o-o-o-o-ly—" he began.

"Don't say it!" I screamed frantically. Notable gave me a last disdainful stare down the length of her bony nose and turned and began trotting west.

"That's the Indian medicine horse?" he wheezed. "The one you weren't supposed to talk about Christian religion in front of?"

"Pretty strong medicine, isn't she?" I replied.

"If you knew she would do something like this, why didn't you set her off when the Raiders first caught you?"

"I frankly never tested it," I explained. "I'm not a man given overmuch to sacrilege."

"I find that hard to believe," he grinned. "I heard your rather colorful commentary while that horse was leveling the camp. I can't believe you rode all the way from Nevada without practicing it in some small measure."

"After she humped herself so at the mention of angels, I decided to play it safe and stick to nonsacrilegious profanity. After that, we got along tolerably well," I replied as we watched Notable vanish over the horizon.

The Union spy came over to us, a lieutenant in tow. "Lieutenant Ford, this is Mr. Mark Twain. He's the brave man who led our charge," he explained.

The lieutenant grabbed my hand and pumped it vigorously. "By God, sir, you saved us all! We heard the cries in the camp below and thought the rest of our forces were already attacking. If it hadn't been for your brave routing of the enemy, they would have mowed us down like wheat."

Massey eyed me archly. "Care to explain this one, Mark?"

"Frankly, Horatio, there are things in this world better left *un*explained," I declaimed, waving my hands at the mangled landscape.

"Why, I have had *piles* of unexplained things in my life!" Miss Katherine began.

I looked at Massey, and he looked at me, and we decided that the bonds of sanity were stronger than the call of ethics. Appropriating Papa's horse, we left Miss Katherine to entertain the others' ears with stories of her not-too-distant childhood and rode like the wind for other parts.

Tony Lewis is never one to make things easy on himself. Instead of merely attending the 1971 World Science Fiction Convention, he was its chairman. Instead of merely enjoying recursive science fiction, he assembled a truly monumental bibliography of it. And in keeping with that attitude, when it came time for him to choose an alternate warrior, he chose one of the least likely in history: St. Francis of Assisi.

... But the Sword!
by Anthony R. Lewis

Francis Bernardone knelt in a pool of drying blood as he prayed forgiveness of Christ Jesu. It was the Monday after Palm Sunday, the twelfth day of April, in the year of our Lord 1204, and about him the city of Constantinople was burning. The great Crusade, the fourth of its kind, had changed its goal from the liberation of Jerusalem and the land oversea, to the purification of the degenerate heart of the remnants of the Roman Empire. Two years ago, when he first traveled to Venice from Umbria to join the Crusade, he would not have thought of fighting fellow Christians. Yet the Pope, Innocent III, had justified the battle. Were not those who had been accepted into Christian fellowship and then betrayed it more hateful in the eyes of the Lord than those who had never accepted Christ? Yet did not the Guelphs and Ghibellines still fight in fragmented Italy?

It was hard for a man to know what to do—except in battle. In battle, all was clear. The very act of fighting against the enemies of the True Faith was an act of worship. A truer act of worship than most celebrated in the churches—a complete trust in the Lord to keep on earth or take to heaven, even as He decided.

And how many of his twenty-three years had he done anything worthy of the name Christian? His father, Pietro, was a successful merchant in Umbria. His son had been well educated and was slated to follow his father's profession. But then Innocent III had succeeded Celestine III to the papacy in 1198 and wrested the Crusades from the secular control of the German emperors. This was a Pope that a spirited boy would follow.

Francis begged of his father training in the military arts and was delighted in 1202 when Innocent called for a Crusade to free the Holy Land. Francis had, with his father's blessing, hastened to Venice to join the great undertaking; he was twenty-one years of age. He had been disgusted by the mercenary attitude of the Venetians. At times he believed that the money changers that Christ had driven from the Temple had settled at the head of the Adriatic.

After they set sail in October, the Crusade became a nightmare for Francis—all but the battles themselves. They besieged and attacked a Christian town for no reason other than money—Zara in Slavonia. The fleet had divided, with some going directly to Syria, leaving the remainder to proceed to Constantinople. How could the land oversea be freed until Christians learned to work together obeying one military leader and one spiritual leader—the Pope in Rome.

For Francis, the Crusade ended with the fall of Constantinople. Let the Venetians and their Frankish allies divide the Empire or fight the Bulgarians. None of this would free the land oversea, nor hold it against the horde of unbelievers who pressed upon it from the East. More was needed. God had granted him a tantalizing glimpse and laid upon him the task of recovering Jerusalem. As yet, it was not time to reveal this. But it *was* time to go home.

"Must you leave, Francis, when glorious deeds may still be done? When this Greek Empire may still be brought back to its proper obedience to Rome?"

"It is not my will, my Lord Marshal, but rather God's that I must obey. I believe that He intends a different path for my life."

"Then go, Francis, with God's grace upon you. And let no man say that you leave for cowardice. For, on the day that any man says this, then that man must answer to me, and then to God. For I know you to be a brave knight. Do as the Lord bids you." Here Geoffroi de Villehardouin embraced Francis and the two parted with much sadness and tears such as are appropriate to warriors.

The only ships available were Venetian, and sailed to Venice. No remission of passage was granted to those that had taken the cross. The Marshal knew, as did many goodly knights and lords, of Francis' lack of worldly wealth, and it was he who arranged the details of the passage. The trip was uneventful, as was the journey overland south into Umbria.

During the next two years Francis threw himself into a frenzy of prayer and study. Lengthy vigils and fasts were interspersed with trips south to Salerno and north to Bologna and Modena. He traveled to Rome to study and had audience with the Holy Father himself.

At the end of his twenty-fifth year upon this earth, Francis left his father's house. He traveled the land of Italy, into the German states of the Empire, France, and Christian kingdoms of Spain. Always he spoke of the need for true soldiers, soldiers who fought only for Christ and the glory of battle, who cared nothing for wealth or pleasure. He did not garner many recruits. He had not expected many, nor had he wanted them. Had Francis permitted himself the analogy (which he would not), he might have thought of Christ, who chose twelve disciples only, though there were many good, though lesser men available.

There were many who opposed his mission, but the Pope, imbued with the spirit of Christ, supported him. In a bull in 1209, Innocent III sanctioned a new order—the Order of the Knights of the Church Militant, with Francis as its Commander-General. Francis at first refused the position, knowing he was unworthy. The Pope did not argue, but ordered him to accept—and Francis did as he was ordered.

The knights, upon joining the Order, gave up all possessions. Some refused upon learning that this included their swords. Francis argued that to trust one's life to a piece of metal was rank idolatry, and for idolaters there was no place in the Order. The first chapter house was established in Rome, but all looked forward to the day when it would move to Jerusalem.

In 1212, with the Order firmly established in Italy, Francis and some of his companions took ship from Ostia for the Holy Land. But God had not willed that Francis should be in the Holy Land yet. The ship was wrecked and they returned to Umbria.

The next year, the Pope sent Francis to Spain to the Kingdom of Navarre. While there, he traveled through the Moorish kingdoms and was appalled to see Christians living in peace with Moors and Jews, whom they should be making every effort to convert, expel, or destroy. He did not let this distaste prevent him from visiting the libraries at Zaragoza, Toledo, and Granada, where he read everything he could find dealing with military tactics and strategies.

At the great Fourth Lateran Council in 1215, Pope Innocent III once more called for a Crusade to free the Holy Land from Saracen dominion. The canons of the Third Lateran Council, forbidding trade in munitions with the Saracens, were invoked once again. The time had come. Then, in 1216, his mission accomplished, Innocent was called to Christ, and a new Pope, Honorius III, took up

the cross. The death of Innocent III had delayed the start
of the Fifth Crusade until 1218. Honorius followed Innocent's plan to begin the attack through Egypt, although
the Hungarians and Austrians sent troops into the north
at Acre.

Pope Honorius III called upon his Commander-General
of the Knights of the Church Militant. "Francis, take the
Brothers of your Order to Damietta. Take that city, and
may God be with you."

The Pope had not told Francis that crusaders from Germany and Italy would be in the attack. He recognized the
problem of divided leadership and prayed for guidance.
The Lord provided that there were no lords of note
amongst the crusaders. Armed with the Commandership
of the Order of the Knights of the Church Militant and
backed by the authority of the Pope—not to mention his
own charisma—Francis was able to alternately awe, bully,
and flatter those not under his command. By early winter
of 1219, he had moved his unwieldy host into position
around Damietta. The siege was thorough, but in the end
it was necessary to take the city by force. Many noble and
valiant feats of arms were performed as acts of selfless
worship to the Lord by young and old, noble and common alike. The defenders were brave, but the Lord was
not with them and they could not prevail.

Having taken Damietta with the aid of the Lord, Francis
asked of the priests of the Order that they should lead
the host in a mass of thanksgiving. And this being done,
the knights and soldiers entered into the city on the eastern delta of the great river Nile. But with the success came
division. Some wished to consolidate their position and
await the arrival of the Holy Roman Emperor Frederick II.
Others wished to march immediately upon Babylon (as
the Franks called Cairo) and smite the Soldan there. And
so matters stood early in the year of our Lord 1220.

A soldier entered the council room where Francis Bernardone, Commander-General of the Knights of the

Church Militant, studied a map. "My lord," he said, "a messenger comes to you from the Pope." The Cardinal Pelagius entered the room. Francis crossed to the legate, kneeled, and kissed his ring.

"Your Eminence, you are very welcome here. Please sit. Perhaps you would like some wine to wash the dust of travel?" Francis did not himself imbibe, but realized that the Lord had not made all men with the same strengths and weaknesses.

"Thank you." The Cardinal sat silently while a brother of the Order brought in his drink and then left. "Saracens do not know the pleasures of wine." He looked at Francis across the dark surface of the cup.

"But they may have many wives," the Commander replied gravely.

Was there a touch of humor there? thought the Cardinal. No, more's the pity. It is so hard to deal with living saints. The dead ones could be more carefully defined and circumscribed. "The more fools, they," he told Francis. "I know of no woman with the lingering appeal of a Rhenish white."

Francis smiled. "You are jesting. Our Lady was pleased with such. But you did not come here to pass the time in idle conversation."

"No." He put down his cup and took a scroll from his purse. "This letter from His Holiness places me in command of the Crusade." He extended it across the table.

Francis took the scroll, examined the seal, broke it, and opened the letter to read it. When he had finished, he rerolled it and put it down. "What are your orders, Your Eminence?"

"No arguments, no questions, Francis?"

"None. I am a sworn soldier of the Church and the Pope. Order me and I obey."

"The Pope is minded to wait until Frederick of Germany arrives before advancing."

"If those are the Pope's orders, then here we will stay until the Emperor arrives."

Pelagius raised his index finger, pointing it nowhere in particular. "Those are the Pope's thoughts, not his orders. His is unaware of the details of our situation. What would you do?"

"March immediately upon Babylon. Move before the knights and soldiers here are ruined by the soft corruptions of Egypt. The Order will hold together. We understand, as most do not, that the purpose of war is in the waging of it for God's glory. Any looting or rapine afterwards that is not part of the next campaign lessens us in the eyes of the Lord. The Soldan Malik al-Kamil is worried by the loss of this city."

"He has offered terms, Francis, including the return of the holy cross taken by Saladin in 1187."

"No!" He slammed his fist upon the table. "Your pardon, Eminence, but to haggle over holy relics like a Venetian—no! If he offers such terms now, how much better they will be when we are in Babylon as conquerors."

"Should we not wait for reinforcements from the Emperor?"

"With all respect, I do not believe the Emperor will come. He has his own problems in Sicily. And, what could be worse, the Venetians (who are called Christian only as a courtesy) could form a commercial alliance with the Soldan."

The Cardinal finished his wine. "Strange. The Saracens produce Saladins; the Venetians produce Doges. I will consider your council."

"I will speak to you again when you leave the chapel, Eminence."

"Oh?"

"Surely, you are going to pray for guidance."

"Of course, Francis, of course."

Two weeks later, the Frankish knights and soldiers, led by Cardinal Pelagius, and Commander-General Francis Bernardone and the brothers of the Order of the Church Militant, left Damietta and marched along the coast. They overwhelmed the unfinished fortress at Mansura. The Soldan sent messages, as Francis had predicted, offering better terms. But now the Cardinal had been convinced, and ordered a willing Francis to advance until they reached Babylon. As they reached the outskirts of that city, the Soldan was so affrighted by the glory of the Franks that he fled for Jerusalem in the land oversea. Easter was celebrated in Babylon.

As Francis had predicted, the German knights never came. However, the word of the great deeds in Egypt reached the heartland of European chivalry: France. There, led by the two noble sons of Geoffroi de Villehardouin, Marshal of Champagne, a large number of noble lords and knights and their attendants took the cross. Wishing to avoid the Venetians, they departed, by ship, from Marseilles, even the same port used by Richard Coeur de Lion of England thirty years before. This goodly body of men arrived in Egypt a few weeks before the Mass of Christ. Francis and Pelagius and all the leaders in Babylon greeted them warmly, for they were a welcome addition.

Now it was the common wisdom that the host should sail to Acre or Tyre and there join with the knights of Austria and Hungary who had reinforced the lords in Tripoli and Antioch some two years ago. So it was before Easter, early in the spring of 1221, when the host took to its ships and left the harbor at Babylon to sail east, then north along the coast. When all the ships were at sea, Cardinal Pelagius called Francis to his cabin aboard the flagship.

"Francis," he asked as the commander entered, "when do we reach Acre?"

"Never," came the short reply. "We land at Jaffa."

"But I thought we were going to Acre."

"Yes, so do they at Acre and Tyre, and so have the spies told Malik al-Kamil. Even now, I believe, God willing, he is marching his troops north to meet us. I will land at Jaffa and strike due east to Jerusalem. The march from Jaffa is how the First Crusade took Jerusalem from the

Saracens. This is how I intend to take it once again, and this time it will be forever Christian."

"And if I order you to go on to Acre, Francis?"

"I will, of course, order the captains to continue there. Is that your will?"

The Cardinal looked again into his wine, searching for the answer there. "No, keep to your plan. It cannot be worse than what has been done before, and at least we have the advantage of a single commander. That would not be the case at Acre. Continue. And may God be with you."

"May God be with us all."

The landing at Jaffa was chaos, for nothing had been prepared. It saddened Francis to see his men drown rather than die in battle. But he was sure that Christ would intercede for them at the Throne just as if they had been spitted by a Saracen. Cardinal Pelagius said mass and the army moved east.

Jerusalem is about thirty English miles east of Jaffa and there were few along that route to oppose Francis' troops. Jerusalem surrendered to yet another invader on April 15, 1221. Francis set about organizing the city. When Malik al-Kamil returned with his army, it was to a fortified city garrisoned with tried troops who were rested and well fed. His own were tired; they had marched north and done nothing. Now, upon returning home, they found that home barred to them. Malik al-Kamil launched three unsuccessful attacks, dying in the final futile assault. His captains sued for peace. Francis sent some into exile in Damascus, allowed some to stay in the Kingdom of Jerusalem, and disbanded Malik al-Kamil's army, setting many of the soldiers to farming or exile. Many were so awed by victories given by the Lord to the Commander of the Christians that they converted to the True Faith. Both Francis and the Cardinal sent messages to the Pope telling of Christ's triumph.

There was great happiness throughout Christendom

(save for the Venetians who dealt better with the Saracens than with their brother Christians). Many children were named Francis or Pelagius. John of Brienne, King of Jerusalem, heir to Amalric, entered the city on New Year's Day, 1223, and took command of his Kingdom. Francis was happy to turn the administration over to King John; it was not work for a warrior of the Lord. For the next year or so, he was in the field with the Order. They drove east from Jerusalem and extended the boundaries past Amman, then north to the Sea of Galilee, and they were on the march to Damascus when King John recalled them. He had signed a treaty of peace with the Emir of Damascus. The Order was to patrol the boundaries. Most could return to Jerusalem or Bethlehem or Jaffa or Ascalon. Francis went to Jerusalem, where the Order's headquarters had been established.

Although it was almost autumn in the Holy City, the day was still warm. The Commander-General traced his way along the Via Dolorosa, stopping at each station to thank the Lord and His Son for the liberation of Jerusalem from the rule of Malik al-Kamil. As he knelt at the site of the Crucifixion all became dark, and then a glory appeared, and a vision of seraphim. The hands and feet of these seraphim were shaped like those of men; but he could not look upon their faces for the beauty and light. And their voices, praising God, were wondrously beautiful to hear as they spoke to him. Then he knew no more. It was the fourteenth day of September 1224.

"Commander," a rough voice tried to speak softly, "would you have some wine?"

Francis tried to sit up, but he had not the strength. "What happened?" He reached for the wine and found his hand was bandaged—both hands were.

"We found you on the street in a swoon. The Order carried you back, although many in the city fought for the honor."

"How did I injure my hands?" He looked at them in the soft candlelight.

"A miracle," the rough voice quavered. "Your hands and feet began to bleed, even as did those of our Lord, who was crucified where you lay." The brother crossed himself and knelt by the bedside to pray.

Francis realized that his mission was at an end. He had accomplished the task that the Lord had set him to do. It was time to go home. He resigned his office of Commander-General to his second and retraced his steps back to Jaffa, where a ship of the Order took him swiftly to Rome. After a brief meeting with Pope Honorius III, Francis returned home to a hero's welcome. He was still a hale man, but retained the celibacy of his Order and refused to marry. He wrote ceaselessly, filling many pages. These, gathered into a Rule and Testament of military matters, approved by the Pope, form the foundation of the Order even unto this day.

After sending his manuscript to Rome, Francis had nothing remaining to do in this world. On October 3, 1226, aged forty-five, in his home in Umbria, he ascended to glory. Those who were present swore that they saw him taken up a shaft of light with an honor guard of angels bearing flaming swords.

In 1227, Pope Honorius III died in Rome. Cardinal Hugolino of Ostia, Protector of the Order of the Church Militant, became Pope as Gregory IX. The next year, having set his house in order, Gregory sailed for the land oversea upon a ship of the Knights of the Church Militant, coming at last to the coast of the Levant. From there he proceeded overland to the accompaniment of a joyous throng, both cleric and lay, both noble and common. Finally, the first pontiff in modern times to do so, he entered into the Holy City of Jerusalem and said mass there. At the end of the mass, he announced the canonization of Francis Bernardone, to be known as St. Francis of Assisi, patron saint of warriors, and further, that the Order of the Knights of the Church Militant would now be known as the Order of the Knights of St. Francis—the Franciscans. Great rejoicing met this proclamation among all true Christians who honored the saint for his chivalry and courage.

I BRING NOT PEACE BUT THE SWORD!

The author of such classics as *Galaxies, Beyond Apollo,* and *Herovit's World,* Hugo and Nebula nominee Barry Malzberg needs no introduction to a science fiction audience. And come to think of it, his alternate warrior, the late Leonard Bernstein, needs no introduction to *any* audience.

Fugato
by Barry N. Malzberg

Copland said that he could have gotten Leonard Bernstein out of it, that he could reach people on the draft board. Or, Copland said, failing that, Koussevitzky could pull some strings. No one messed with Koussevitzky in Massachusetts and Leonard was Sergei's boy that summer. But Leonard had said no, no, damned fool that he was, didn't want word getting around that he had dodged the draft or used influence to get out of any Jewish boy's obligation in these terrible times. Besides, Leonard had what he took to be secret knowledge, there was a punctured eardrum just like Sinatra, and if that didn't do the job there was a long history of back trouble. Oy, your lower back, Sam Bernstein used to say to him, you'll inherit your lower back from my lower back and that will be the end of this conducting for you. Better think of sitting in a nice chair in a stockbroker's office. Punctured eardrum. Lower back trouble. A sure ticket out and no scandal, that's what Leonard had thought, had told Aaron not to be so helpful, had told Jerry Robbins when he had

gone off to the draft physical that morning in 1942. And
now here he was. Here he was, all right. So much for
punctured eardrums and the lower back, so much for dis-
daining Sergei's close contacts with the gentry in Massachusetts, a long way from Tanglewood, Lenny, and no
way back that he knew.

In a farmhouse somewhere near the Ardennes forest,
pinned down with the remnants of his company by the
snipers' fire being laid down with terrible precision from
high ground, rolling somewhere in the mud of that forest
now become the floor of that farmhouse, Leonard had no
time to reflect upon his destiny or the look on his friends'
faces when he had come back from that physical and had
said, They found me 1-A. They didn't even want to look
at my eardrum, they asked me to jump up and down
three times, checked for a hernia, and that was it. Incre-
dulity had sprung from Adolph Green's face. Jerry Robbins had been speechless when Leonard had called him.
Seventeen months later now and he was a rifleman, a
private first class, part of the massive attempt to liberate
France, fighting for the spirit of liberty in the land of
Ravel, Charles Munch, Bizet, Hector Berlioz; the screams
of the riflemen around him, the terrified, choked cries of
men who had lost their way and stumbled into this gloating, final darkness in the farmhouse surrounded him with
noise and heat, odd flashes of light which Bernstein had
never seen before, a light which seemed to sever him not
only from any sense of his past but from the very conditions which he thought had organized his life.

Medic! someone screamed, *I'm hit, I'm hit,* and there
was the dull throbbing of the guns then, the sound of
demolition inside this wretched place, and it occurred to
Leonard as he hunched himself below the eaves, clinging
to the side of the fireplace, watching the odd and flickering cast of light through the windows, a light which
was neither dawn nor the darkness but composed of the
constituent parts of his own death, externalized, that he
was facing conditions which were utterly out of his con-

trol. He had pushed away that insight, that possibility for all of these months, told himself that it was impossible for Leonard Bernstein to lose that fine sense of propriety and balance which he had always equated with his destiny, but now it had gone from him; with a sudden and awful conviction Bernstein knew that he was going to die in this place, surrounded by sniper fire and the bellowings of animals, alert to the whimpers of men unmanned. *Te deum, laudamus. Dies Irae, dies illae.* The sound of all judgment. Berlioz and Mozart, *tuba mirium.*

In Tanglewood in the summer of 1941 Tallulah Bankhead had stolen him from a rehearsal and they had gone to a curtained bower where one by one she said she would reveal to him all of her great charms and secrets and in that great, damp clutch, her musk and necessity flooding around them, Leonard Bernstein had felt himself as with the deaf and dipsomaniacal Beethoven, hunched over the quartets, hunched over the actress, at some final certainty and apprehension of his life. Berlioz's drug-maddened poet dragged off to the gallows. How far from there to here he could not apprehend, but he could make a guess in the darkness. It was less, far less distance than he might have measured. All of his life this dark and terrible thunder, like Tallulah's gasps and secrets, had been waiting to envelop him. The stunned look on Adolph's face, all teeth and regret. Lenny, Lenny, what's going to happen to us? I don't know, Leonard Bernstein had said. What do you think, Adolph, that war is for the dopes, for the guys who can't hear things inside their heads? Because they die too, they die, you die, we all die, even Adolph Green and Jerry Robbins and Betty Comden and Berlioz, Beethoven and Nijinsky. The sound of clattering now and the sound of weapons recocked. The Hun was coming in.

At Tanglewood in that summer of 1941 he had met Britten for the first time. Britten, the British composer and his great friend Peter Pears, draft-dodging it in America and going the concert circuit while cursing Churchill and

Hitler and Tōjō and Roosevelt too, all of the war-lovers, Britten had said. I'm sitting out the war in Massachusetts and New York and points west, Britten had said. Peter and I aren't going to serve their purposes, give them fodder. It is an abomination, all of it. War is an abomination.

Well, of course it was, Leonard had thought, always was, always would be; World War I had knocked out a generation in Europe and now the same thing was happening again. It was the obligation of the artist to oppose war with all his being, to fight against the mania and the stupidity, there was no disagreement there. Don't go, Koussevitzky had said, Lenny, you do not have to go, something can be done. That had been in 1942, after the draft notice had come in, but back in 1941, Bernstein hadn't thought of anything like that at all, the war had still been at a distance and Britten's prediction that Roosevelt would keep the United States out of it until Germany and Japan had fallen into the pit of their exhaustion and corruption had seemed reasonable. Everything about Britten seemed reasonable even though Leonard could not get around the hard, derogatory feeling that the Brit and his lover were draft dodgers with no other name to put on it. They had had fun that summer though, all of them, they had taken over Tanglewood, he and Jerry Robbins and Copland, who had made Leonard his most honored, his favored pet. He conducted the student orchestra and once the Boston Symphony in the *Eroica* with Koussevitzky sitting out in the audience applauding, and it had all seemed very clear and open to him then; he was twenty-three years old and music was opening to him along with everything else and Sam Bernstein, his father, had been a fool. It *was* possible to make a career; Koussevitzky said that he had everything he needed and had arranged for him to go to New York, meet Rodzinski, apply for the assistant conductor position with the New York Philharmonic. How was he to know that it would lead to this? Schumann had heard that *A* within his head at the beginning of his final descent, the 440-cycle *A* sounding all day and night, cleaving his brain to shreds, warning him of the end of all possibility, but Leonard had had no warning at all. There was the chaos about which he read occasionally in the *Globe* and the *Times* and then there was the smooth and certain, sometimes convulsive tread of his own life as whispered by Koussevitzky, murmured by Copland, gasped by Bankhead. How was he to know? How were any of them to know? Europe fell on their heads, Britten had said, talking about Wilfred Owen and the poets of death, and now it has fallen on ours, but we must have the constancy to say no. To say no, to say no. Lying in this rotten shgingling, hearing the sure and certain sounds of those coming to end one's life, what was constancy? What was the nature of fortitude? It was one thing to talk about it in an undergraduate seminar or to discuss metaphysics with Britten in the empty tent pitched for the concerts but vacant after rehearsal with the sound of insects murmurous in the air but it was another, it was quite another, to face this disaster five thousand miles from Tanglewood or a century and a half from the spangled and heaving Europe which had made Beethoven a celebrity and had turned to Napoleon as liberator. I didn't want this, Leonard Bernstein said hopelessly, I never wanted to make these choices, never wanted to face any of this, but no one in the platoon was at that moment interested in discussing the issue or even debating with him, the pounding outside, the increasingly desperate and imperious shouts had shed notice now: the Hun was coming in.

You can't do this, Copland had said, you have some misguided air of patriotism, Leonard, but patriotism is not going to sustain you under rifle fire nor feed any of those ambitions and purposes of yours. Aaron of course had been in his early forties so it was easy for him to make abstracted debate, even though to his credit Copland had not—as Britten had—aspired to any moral plane or purpose. If Haydn had enlisted in the barricades in Paris in

1789, Copland had said, and had gotten himself killed for the cause of freedom, we would never had had the London symphonies; if Leopold Mozart had put little Johann Wolfgang into the king's service in 1775, what would have become of him when the tides of revolution came asunder? If you have any obligation, Leonard, Copland had said, it is to survive this war intact and serve your career; you can give something unique to the world like Haydn or Mozart, or you can lie somewhere overseas under a cross and to what benefit? To whose benefit? We know people, Leonard, Copland had said, there are things that can be done, and even if they cannot be done you can play the piano for the USO and direct shows, you don't have to take a rifle and start shooting at strangers, even if you're a good rifleman and I think you're a lousy one. Listen to me, Aaron had said, his face intent, as intense as Koussevitzky's when Sergei had said to him, Lenny, you must not put yourself beyond our reach, let me try to help you. It is not too late for this, not even now.

But it had been. It had already been too late, basic training completed, out on ten-day leave, waiting for the orders that would send him over. Bernstein knew that the infantry would be heading for France, every dogface knew that, there were no secrets. Home on leave with the orders cut and the maws of the ships waiting, he had flirted only briefly with the thought that Copland could save him from this, Sergei, even Sam the industrialist who had fought against his son becoming a musician but now wanted to save Leonard for the cause of music at all costs. But it wasn't possible, he had seen that sometime during the infantry training, staggering through the mud, hearing the curses around him and the screaming of the sergeants, the things that they had said about the Jews in the platoon when they thought that the Jews weren't listening. Or *knew* that they were listening but just didn't give a shit. Don't you understand, Aaron? Leonard had said. I can't dodge out. It's not my option. Maybe it's Ben

Britten's, he's got a long history of resistance behind him, and anyway everyone knows about him and Peter, and he could probably get out on that basis. But it's different here. It's different for Jews too, don't you see?

Aaron shook his head. Being Jewish has nothing to do with it, he said. It's irrelevant.

No, it's not irrelevant. I've been training with people who think, a lot of them, that the reason we got into this thing, the reason we're going to get killed is because of the Jews, to defend the Jews. So how would it look if this Jew tried to head out of it now? The only way I've shut them up is to say, well, then I'm going to be killed too. This is one Jew who is going to die because of the Jews. You think I want that?

You're being ridiculous, Copland said. You're making more of this than possibly exists. You're a musician, Leonard, you could be a great conductor, maybe even as good a composer. You think that these are outweighed by the necessity to look good for the Gentiles? The Gentiles are going to hate us whatever we do, getting killed for them will just make them hate more. There's nothing we ever could have done to have pleased them, don't you understand that? But Leonard hadn't understood that, he hadn't understood much of anything, he supposed. He had stopped understanding when the 1-A notice had come through and he had known with an utter sense of conviction and completion, maybe the same sense that had come over Britten's idol, Wilfred Owen, in the fox-hole, that he was going to die and that there was nothing personal about it, that his death was a large part of a great historical movement. *Te deum, laudamus.* The *kyrie* of the Mozart Requiem had moved hugely within him at that moment, peering at the glazed surfaces of the draft notice and after that it had been a straight plunge down the tube of circumstance to this moment. No, Aaron, he had said, it's too late. I am going to serve this out because it is beyond us. All of it is beyond me now. *There is no counterpoint, it is all monothematic.* Aaron had stared at him

beyond the thick glasses. If it is monothematic, he had
said, it is because you want to die. It is in your hands,
Leonard. You selected the infantry, you allowed this to
happen to you. Don't talk about historical inevitability.
They had not discussed it again. Aaron had gone back to
New York, talking about getting poor old, sick Charles
Ives to try to talk some sense into his head. But old, sick
Charlie Ives was too deaf and crazy by then to talk to
anyone. Leonard had served out the leave time and had
shown up at dockside in full field gear, waiting to ship
over. He knew that this had been a small surprise to some
in the company, they had expected the Jew to go AWOL
or to make some heavy arrangements during the leave.
But no, here he was. Not that this made any difference or
that any increased respect gave him even two inches more
space in the dead cubicle below deck where he sweltered
and vomited through the terrible weeks of the voyage.

The fantasy had been that he would get to Salzburg, to
Vienna, to the haunts and birthplaces of Beethoven and
Mozart, that he would somehow give testimony by his
presence to their own transcendent meaning in his life.
But that had not been in the plans, there were no com-
munions with dead composers on the slate, no commu-
nion with live ones either. Schoenberg and Bartók and
Rachmaninoff had had the sense to leave these places of
blood and dishonor already, but Bernstein had put a rifle
in his hand and had headed, not at all stately, the other
way. There was something of cosmic humor in this,
something as grotesquely and transcendently humorous
as the ghostly shrieks and spasms which Beethoven had
put into the Opus 135 quartet, sounds which no violins,
viola or cello had ever been meant to play, but he could
not see the humor. He could not see Tallulah, either, it
had been months since he had been able to summon her
image, or Koussevitzky's, or anyone from that vanished
part of his life; now it was only the close, dense, dank
pallor of the troops and the stink of the countryside and

now, coming slowly to a kind of frenzied attention, he could see the Germans pouring through the door, the Hun enormous in his uniform, consequential and brutal in his solidity, the sound and stink of the Hun grandiose as in multiple he poured through the door. They were coming to clean out the farmhouse, coming in fact to clean out the whole of Europe, and Bernstein had only the insufficiency of his corpus and a rifle he could barely fire to stand between them.

He came to firing position then, listening to the bellowing of the servants below or from the sides, the screaming and cursing of the men coming in all directions around him and then as the waves and grinding insistance of the attackers came over him, he felt himself sunk into a moment of fierce and total embrace, a sense of absolute collision with a destiny which always must have been there, waiting for him. Fired once. Fired twice. Shouted with the recoil and heard the bullet over his head, fired again and heard the return fire spaced around him, and then at last, the spasm as the bullet hit him cruelly and precisely in the targeted area. He shrunk over the bullet, scrambling against the wall, then felt himself beginning to fall. *Showed them,* Leonard Bernstein thought. *Showed them that a Jew could take the same shit as the Gentiles, showed them that even the Jewboy musician could take it from his gut.* Whether he survived or not seemed at this moment to be a very small thing, almost incidental, *completely* incidental to this moment of gigantic enclosure, his body a fist gripped around the bullet. Shouts for the medic. *Medic, medic! I'm dying!* Conduct the Philharmonic, Leonard Bernstein thought. Conduct the Philharmonic in Avery Fisher Hall in May 1962, the last concert of the first season at the new hall, the Berlioz *Symphonie Fantastique,* on a Sunday. March to the scaffold, the drug-wrecked poet dragged to his new destiny, spin and leap on the podium, leap as if all heaven was watching, the snarl and scream of the trombones and hang in the air, hang at the top of the leap, never falling, never falling: it is October 14, 1990, and high in that leap Leonard Bernstein waits with perfect resignation and acceptance to see, beyond the clutch of the respirator tubes running in and out of his shattered lungs, to see where or if he will land. *Te deum, laudamus.*

7 June 1992: New Jersey

in his sacred memory

David Gerrold, Hugo-nominated author of *When H.A.R.L.I.E. Was One* and *The Man Who Folded Himself*, is my secret Hollywood weapon. Along with his excellent science fiction output, David has been scripting movies and television shows for the better part of a quarter century, and whenever I edit an anthology, I always ask him to give me something with a uniquely Hollywood twist. With this book, for example, I suggested that he might take one of Hollywood's World War II heroes— John Wayne leading a charging squadron of marines, or Errol Flynn sneaking in under the cover of night—and see what he could do with the notion.

Well, as you're about to see, Hollywood has taught David to Think Big . . .

The Firebringers
by David Gerrold

The gunners, Taylor and Johnson, stood apart by themselves, whispering about something. I wondered if they were going to take their traditional good-luck piss under the tail of the plane before takeoff. Would they even dare with all the guards looking on and all the brass who were supposed to be here? The rest of us stood around under the plane like we always did, smoking, worrying, and pretending not to care.

There were twenty armed marines spaced in a circle

around the plane, so most of us in the crew stayed close to the boarding hatch and kept our eyes averted from their weapons. We weren't sure we appreciated the honor. Were the guards there to keep everyone else out—or us in?

We looked from one to the other and traded lights off each other's smokes. We talked about whiskey, poker, women we had known, chocolate, beer, cigarettes, everything but what really counted. Our terror.

Meanwhile, the fog kept rolling in. It was so thick that even the specially outfitted B-32 above us was only a darker shape in the gloom. The ground crew would be putting out flares all the length of the runway. If we went. I was beginning to wonder. The case under my arm, with all my weather charts and maps, was getting heavy. I didn't know if I wanted to go or not. I didn't want my work to be wasted. On the other hand . . .

The sound of an engine was followed by the ruddy glare of headlights, and then three trucks came rolling up to the belly of the ship. The middle one had a flat bed, with a tarp-covered shape clamped securely into place. The other two trucks were hooded and carried more armed marines. They spilled out of their vehicles in silence and quickly formed a secure circle around the loading operation.

Ollie, one of the two ordinance officers, climbed out of the shotgun side of the second truck and began gently cooing instructions to the bomb crew; he was so polite it was eerie. The scuttlebutt was that you could roll a Jeep over his foot and he wouldn't even say ouch. He was a corpulent man, but he moved like a dancer—and he was scrupulous about the loading, watching over every move like a mother hen with a single egg. He demanded precision and delicacy. Before the war, he and his partner, Stan, had been piano movers. Stanley was the quiet one. Once we were in the air, they'd actually arm the device.

Bogey, the bombardier, chewed an unlit stogie and looked skeptical. He'd had that stogie since the war started and he wasn't going to light it until he was sure he could get another one to replace it. He held a couple of steel ball-bearings in his right hand, which he rotated nervously while he waited. Despite our incessant drilling and practicing and studying, Bogey remained outspokenly skeptical. He was only going along for the ride, he said. After the war, he was going to reopen his gambling salon in Morocco. Uh-huh. Most of us didn't believe he'd ever been farther east than the Brooklyn Bridge. But it was his finger on the button. He'd look through the Norden bomb sight, he'd press the release when the moment came. Maybe his tough-guy attitude was his way of not letting himself think about it too much.

While we watched, the bomb crew lowered specially designed clamps from the plane and attached them to matching hooks on the bomb, then they locked each one carefully into place, with two men checking each clamp. The clamps wouldn't be unlocked until just before release. They handed one set of keys to Lieutenant Bogart. The other set of keys would be given to Colonel Peck.

As soon as the last clamp was secured, they began the arduous and delicate process of hoisting the bomb up into the belly of the ship. The chains began to clank. The slack was taken up, there was a hesitation, and then the vehicle eased itself and sighed as the weight was lifted away. Simultaneously, the plane groaned. We could hear its back straining. That baby was *heavy*.

Slowly, slowly the bomb rose up, hanging precariously in the space between us. We watched its studied ascent with a mixture of curiosity and fear. We had all seen the test in Nevada. We were still dazed by the memory of that white-flashing roar of heat and wind. We were terrified what it would do to a city. White-faced, Jaeckel had screamed to Bogey, "Holy smokes! What is that?" Bogey had answered grimly, "It's the stuff that screams are made of."

Even now, it was still difficult to believe that so much destructive power could be contained in this solid black cylinder. Someone had written in bold white chalk on the side, "Heil *this!*" But as it rose, I saw that someone else had carefully inscribed in bright yellow paint: *"Sh'ma Yisrael, Adonai Elohainu Adonai Ehod."* Beside it was a list of names—the men who had actually designed and built the bomb. I'd heard there had been quite a fight about the prayer and the names; but apparently Dr. Karloff and Dr. Lorre had told General Tracy, "No prayer, no names— no bomb." I couldn't imagine "Spence the Fence" saying no to either one of those two grand old gentlemen, and I was glad he hadn't.

But there were a lot of rumors floating around. We weren't supposed to repeat them, but we did anyway. We'd heard that Dr. Lugosi was already designing a more powerful bomb. We'd heard that Dr. Karloff was having second thoughts, that he'd written to the President and asked him to demonstrate the bomb on an uninhabited island so the Axis nations could see its power before we actually used it on a city. Rumor had it that Secretary of War Capra had advised against that as "too humanitar- ian." We needed to hurt the enemy *hard*—so hard that the war would come to a screeching halt.

President Cooper never said what he was thinking throughout the entire debate, but when the question was finally asked, he simply issued his characteristic "Yup" and that was the end of that. The prayer on the side of the bomb probably represented a compromise.

It bothered me. I understood—at least I thought I did— the urge behind it; but at the same time, I didn't think a bomb, and certainly not *this* bomb, was the right place to paint a prayer of any kind. But then again, I wasn't Jewish. I wondered how I'd feel about it if I were.

All of us were volunteers. At the beginning, we hadn't known what we were volunteering for, only that it was dangerous and important. Then they'd taken us out to Nevada and shown us. We were going to end the war. We were going to obliterate a city. We were going to kill a hundred thousand people in a brilliant bright flash of light.

We had dark goggles to protect our eyes. And radiation meters. Jaeckel, the new kid, would have the best view of all. He was the belly-gunner. He'd been issued a 16mm Bolex loaded with special Eastman-color film. He was supposed to photograph everything we saw. He was excited about the opportunity, even though it meant he had to wear lead-foil underwear.

And then the bomb was secured and the trucks were rolling away. We still hadn't seen Colonel Peck. Or Colonel Reagan, our copilot, either. And the fog wasn't clearing up. Worse, it was getting thicker. My shirt collar was sticking damply to my neck. I checked my watch. So far, we were still on schedule, but time was tight. If we were going to get in the air at all this morning, it would have to be soon.

I was pretty sure that Colonel Peck was uneasy about the mission. I knew him too well, all his mannerisms. He'd been brooding about this ever since Nevada. And the closer we got to takeoff, the more irritable he became. He kept ordering me to check the maps, over and over, plotting alternate courses, fuel consumption figures, alternate targets, everything. His tension was infectious. None of us were happy.

And now this. A morning so gloomy it felt like twilight. Could we even get off the ground?

We stood around underneath the plane, an uncomfortable clump of men in baggy flight suits, and listened to the awful stillness of the fog. Faraway sounds were simply swallowed up. Nearby sounds were amplified. Lieutenant Hope—I was suddenly struck by the irony of his name—wouldn't shut up. Even when I moved away to the other side of the bird, I could still hear his inane little jokes. "This is Bob 'Fogged-in' Hope calling anybody. Is anybody out there? Say, did you guys hear the one about the leprechaun and the penguin?" There were groans and a *thump* as somebody hit him with a parachute. "Don't

worry about me, fellas," he said, climbing back to his feet.
"I'm goin' home after this. I'm not spending *my* Christmas
with the army."

A chorus of hoots and catcalls greeted this response. I
turned away in annoyance and saw the headlights coming
out of the fog. I stubbed out my cigarette and called out,
"Ten-*hut*!" The crew snapped to attention where they
stood.

Generals Gable and Donleavy climbed out of the Jeep.
Colonel Peck and Colonel Reagan climbed out after them,
followed by the new sky pilot. "At ease," said General
Donleavy; he looked unhappy. General Gable stepped
forward and spoke gruffly. "I just wanted to come out
here myself and ... wish you godspeed. I know some of
you have been having second thoughts about this. I don't
blame you. I would too. I've been having second thoughts
about this since the day I was first briefed.

"But I want you to know that despite all my fears and
concerns, I fully support this operation. In fact, *I envy
you*. You men are going to save a lot of lives today. If this
device works as well as we hope, then millions of young
men—on both sides of this terrible war—will not have to
meet on the battlefield. You have it in your power today
to save millions of lives, both civilian and military, and
spare the world years of suffering and destruction. Just
keep that thought in mind and you'll do fine." He glanced
over at Captain Fonda. "If any of you want to see the
chaplain before you take off ..."

At first, most of us were too embarrassed, but then Stan
and Ollie stepped over to Captain Fonda and bowed their
heads. And then Bogey. And Colonel Peck. I followed.
And the others came behind me. All except Taylor and
Johnson, the skeptics. They strode down to the tail end
of the plane and ... upheld their military traditions. General Gable glanced over, decided not to say anything, and
deliberately turned his back.

Captain Fonda was slim and gentle, almost too gentle
for a war. He had a long, lanky way of speaking; the

words came softly out of him like honey poured from a jar. He was a different kind of sky pilot. He didn't talk about God so much as he talked about the spirit of God inside each and every one of us. "You know what's right in the world," he said. "Stand for it. And others will stand with you." It made me feel good to listen to him.

Afterward, I noticed, Jaeckel, the new kid, hung behind and knelt to confess. Captain Fonda made the sign of the cross over him, then helped him back to his feet with a friendly clap on the shoulder. That was what I liked about him; he knew how to be just an ordinary guy.

Colonel Peck collected his keys from Ollie, then the two of them, the pilot and the copilot, walked slowly around the plane, shining flashlights up into the wheel housings and looking for oil leaks under the engines. When they finished, they came back, saluted the generals and shook their hands; then they ordered the rest of us up into the bomber. From here on out, the responsibility for delivering the device was all ours, nobody else's.

The solemnity of the moment left us all subdued. That plus the unusual circumstances of two generals and a chaplain coming all the way out to the end of the field for our departure. There was none of the usual wiseass chatter as we climbed into our seats, hooked up our oxygen, and buckled our harnesses. We went through our checklists without the usual banter. Even Hope kept his mouth shut for a change. Finally, Colonel Peck started the engines and they clattered explosively to life. They sputtered and smoked and then abruptly caught with a bang. The bird began to vibrate like a 1932 Ford on a rutted road. Colonel Reagan fussed with the fuel mixture to compensate for all the water vapor in the air.

We rolled out onto the end of the runway and turned into the wind. Colonel Peck closed his eyes for a moment—a silent prayer?—then picked up his microphone and asked the tower for permission to take off. The tower's reply was crisp. "Go with God." It would be our last communication. From here on out, strict radio silence would be observed.

Colonel Peck ran the engines up, louder and louder until the plane was howling like a banshee. He turned in his seat to look at the left wing; Reagan turned to look at the right. Satisfied, they both turned back. Colonel Peck put his hands firmly on the wheel, bit his lip, and let the plane leap forward. I glanced out the front windshield, but all I saw was a gray wall of haze. He had to be steering by the line of flares along the sides of the runway. I glanced out the side window and tried to gauge our speed by the passing red pinpoints. Faster and faster—they leapt out of the gloom ahead of us and vanished into the gloom behind. Colonel Reagan began calling out airspeed numbers.

At first I didn't think we were going to make it into the air. The bird was heavy and the air was thick and wet. The engines weren't happy. The bird was bouncing and buffeting. Colonel Peck must have been having a hell of a time keeping us on the concrete. And the end of the runway had to be getting awfully close . . . but at the last moment, the Colonel gunned it, grabbed hold of the sky, and pulled us up over the trees—so close, I could feel the branches scraping our belly.

We bounced up through the damn fog, shaking and buffeting and cursing all the way. But the bird held together and at last we climbed up into the clear blue sky above the gray blanket. Suddenly, the warm June sun poured down on us like a welcome smile, filling the plane with lemon-yellow light. The air smoothed out and the bird stopped complaining. Colonel Peck glanced back to me with a smile. I gave him a big thumbs-up.

We were on our way to Germany. And Berlin. And history.

Crossing the Channel, we saw some fishing boats. Even in the midst of war, men still cast their nets into the sea to feed their families. I wondered if they looked up and wondered about us in turn. Did they ever think about the planes that crossed back and forth across the Channel, and if so, did they wish us well—or did they just resent the burden of the war.

I scribbled notes in the log. Time, position, heading. At the opposite end of the plane, Van Johnson was probably writing another love letter to his fiancée, June. He wrote one every mission and mailed it as soon as we landed. She wrote back every time she got a letter from him. We teased him about it, but we envied him the letters and the connection to someone back home.

"Okay, Jimmy," Colonel Peck turned around to me. "What's it going to be? Paris or Amsterdam?"

I pulled out my lucky silver dollar, flipped it, and caught it on the back of my wrist. I lifted my hand away to show him. "Uh—ah—it looks like Paris," I said. I glanced at the compass. "Uh, you wanna come right about—ah, forty degrees, skipper."

This was part of the security around this operation. Once we were in the air, not even the ground stations were supposed to know where we were. We had been instructed to plot three separate courses to the target; we were forbidden to choose our final heading until we were out over the Channel, away from all possible ground observers. Of course, all the flight crews knew that there were U-boats in the Channel, tracking the comings and goings of all flights, but we didn't worry about it. Much. Colonel Peck and I favored two different courses, Amsterdam and Paris, each named for the city we'd head toward before turning toward Berlin.

Our group had been sending single flights out over the Continent for months, spotting troop movements, checking weather conditions, dropping leaflets, taking photos, surveying bomb damage, all that stuff—a lot more flights than we needed to. They were decoys to get the Jerries used to the sight of a single Allied plane crossing their skies. Some of the fellows resented the duty. They'd rather have been dropping bombs, and nobody would tell them why their flights were so important, but they were.

We'd flown a lot of the flights too, mostly the missions over Berlin and our secondary targets. In the past week, we'd even made two leaflet drops, dropping the package and then pulling up and away sharply to the right exactly as we would do later today. The leaflets had warned the Berliners to leave the city, because we were going to destroy it. We implied that we'd be sending a thousand planes across the Channel, darkening their skies with the roar of engines and the thunder of bombs. We'd heard they were installing ack-ack guns from here to the Rhine and we wondered if they'd test them on us today.

Once, we'd also dropped an agent into Germany. A fellow named Flynn. His job was to contact members of the underground and warn them out of Berlin before the sixth. I wondered where he was now. I hoped he had gotten out. A nice fellow, I guess, but I wouldn't have his job. He'd seemed foolhardy to me.

Colonel Peck glanced at the altimeter, tapped it to make sure it wasn't stuck, and then spoke into his microphone. "All right, Stan, Ollie. We're at cruising altitude. You can start arming the device." He waited for their confirmations, then switched off again.

We'd heard that the Nazis had forbidden the civilian population to flee Berlin, but our intelligence sources were telling us that at least a third of the civilians had evacuated anyway and more were streaming out every day. Even if the bomb failed, we would still have seriously disrupted the economy of the Reich's capital. Most of the overlords of the Reich had already moved themselves away from the city—except for that pompous turnip Goering. He had publicly boasted that not a single Allied bomb would fall on Berlin. I wondered if he would be in Berlin today. I wondered about all the others too. Goebbels, Heydrich, Eichmann, Hess, Himmler, and the loudmouthed little paperhanger. Would they be close enough to see the blast? What would they think? What would they do?

Some of the psych boys believed that Corporal Schicklgruber would sooner die in the holy flames of martyrdom than ever let himself be captured and put on trial for war crimes. Worse, he would take the whole nation down with him.

If the bomb worked—

Of course it worked. We'd seen it work in Nevada. I couldn't get it out of my head—that terrible mushroom cloud climbing into the morning sky, churning and rising and burning inside. It was a preview of Hell. Afterward, we were given the chance to withdraw from the mission. None of us did. Perhaps, if we hadn't already been a crew, some of us would have, I'd have considered it, but I couldn't let the other fellows down. Later, we spent long hours talking among ourselves. If we ended the war, we'd be heroes. But ... just as likely, we might be war criminals. Nobody had ever used a bomb like this before.

But never mind that—if the bomb worked the way we wanted it to, we'd paralyze the Third Reich. The armies would stop fighting. The generals would surrender rather than let their troops be incinerated. Perhaps even, they'd overthrow the murderous bastards at the top and save the rest of the world the trouble of hanging them. Perhaps.

And perhaps they'd do something else. Perhaps they'd launch a ferocious counterattack beyond our abilities to comprehend. Perhaps they'd unleash all the poison gases and deadly germs they were rumored to have stockpiled. Who knew what they would do if they were scared enough?

But that wasn't our worry. All we had to do was deliver the device. Behind us, taking off at fifteen-minute intervals, thirty other planes would be following, each one equipped with cameras and radiation detectors. The visible aftermath of this weapon would be on movie screens all over the world within the week.

I tried to imagine what else might be happening today. Probably the French Resistance was being signaled to do whatever they could to scramble communications and transportation among the Nazis. Our ambassadors were probably preparing to deliver informative messages to other governments. Everybody expected us to invade Europe before the end of the summer. I wondered if our troops were massing even now to follow us into Germany.

Lieutenant Bogart came forward then with a thermos of coffee. It was his habit to come up to the cockpit for a while before we reached enemy territory. Today, he had more reason than ever. Despite his frequent protestations otherwise, the thought of the bomb in our belly clearly disturbed him as much as the rest of us. Perhaps him more than anybody. He looked burnt and bitter. "Which way're we headed, skipper? We going over Paris?"

Colonel Peck nodded. "It's the long way around, but I want to give Stan and Ollie plenty of time to arm the device."

I looked at Bogey suddenly. There was something odd in his eyes, but I couldn't identify the look. Anger perhaps? Some long-remembered hurt?

"Uh, ahh-h—you've been to Paris?" I asked.

He nodded. "I was there. For a while. Just before the Jerries moved in."

"I never made it myself. I always wanted to go, but something always came up. I had to stay home and help Pop with the business."

"After the war is over," Colonel Peck said, "we'll all meet for champagne on the Champs-Élysées." He got a wistful look on his face then. "It's one of the most beautiful streets in the world. Lined with cafés and shops and beautiful women. You could spend your days just sitting and sipping coffee. Or you could stuff yourself with mushrooms and fish poached in butter. You could follow it with little thin pancakes filled with thick rich cream. And the wine—we had champagne and caviar on toast so crisp it snapped. I never had a bad meal anywhere in France. Even a potato is a work of art."

He looked to Bogey for agreement, but the bombardier just shrugged. "I spent most of my time on the Left Bank, drinking cheap wine. I didn't get to the same joints you did, Colonel."

"You saw a lot of Europe before the war, skipper?" Reagan asked.

Peck shook his head. "Not as much as I wanted to. But I have good memories." He stared off into the distance as if he were seeing them all again. "I remember the tulip gardens in Copenhagen—so bright they dazzle the eyes. And the dark canals of Amsterdam, circling around the center of the city, all the buildings are so narrow that the staircases are almost ladders." He shook his head sadly. "I can still taste the thick layered pastries of Vienna. And I remember wandering through the sprawling parks of Rome—do you know there are wild cats living all over the ruins of the Colosseum? They've probably been there since Caesar's time. And the rumpled hills of Athens, the Parthenon looking down over the city, and ouzo in your belly like licorice fire. Berlin— the beer halls and the nightclubs. The screech of the trains. The smell of coal. The old opera house. On Sundays, you could go to the afternoon concerts; if you were a student, you paid half price. That's where I first heard Bach and Beethoven and Wagner. What a marvelous dichotomy the Germans represent, that they could produce such sublime music—and such incredible horrors too."

"Uh, ah—you've seen Berlin?" I asked. This was the first time he'd ever admitted it.

Colonel Peck nodded. "A long time ago." His eyes were shaded grimly. "It's a funny old town. When I was there it was full of students and workmen, shopkeepers and grandmothers in babushkas. No one was angry then. The streets were clean and the people were stolid and happy. It was spring and the world was green and fresh and full of butterflies and hope. It was a long time ago, and I was very . . . young."

Bogey and Reagan exchanged a look then. Worried. Was the colonel having second thoughts?

Almost as if in answer to their question, Colonel Peck added, "It was the music. I was sure that Berlin had to be the most marvelous city in the world that such incredible music lived there." And then, as if realizing again where he was and what he'd just said, he shook his head grimly. "I've never liked this idea. Bombing a city. Civilians. It's—" He didn't finish the sentence. Instead he reached over and flipped the fuel tank switches. It was time to lighten the left side of the plane for a while.

After a moment, he turned around again and looked at the three of us. First Reagan, then me, then finally Bogey. "All right," he said. "What is it?"

"Ah, uh—are you feeling all right, skipper?"

Colonel Peck nodded with his chin, in that grim way of his. "If you're worrying if I can do the job, stop worrying. This is what we've trained for."

"Right," said Bogey, clapping one hand on the colonel's shoulder. "We don't need Berlin. We'll always have Paris." I couldn't tell if he was joking or not.

Bogey was the weirdest one in the crew, always saying things that were either bitter jokes or just plain bitter. Colonel Peck wasn't sure what Bogey meant either. He just looked at him sideways for a long moment. The two of them studied each other the way two men do when they first meet, sizing each other up, getting a sense of whether they're going to be friends or enemies.

These two jokers had known each other for a long time, but right now, at this moment, it was as if they'd never really seen each other before. Bogey shifted the cigar from one side of his mouth to the other and grinned fiercely at Peck. Peck's expression relaxed, widened into a matching grin. And then suddenly, we were all grinning and laughing nervously.

"We're starting to take ourselves a little too seriously," said Peck. "Take over, Ronnie, I'm going back to check on the boys." He levered himself out of his seat and climbed past Bogey into the rear of the plane.

We waited until we were sure he was gone. None of us dared speak. Finally, I had to ask it. "Ah, ah—do you fellas think he's gonna be all right?"

Bogey shifted his cigar from one side of his mouth to

the other, then back again. "I dunno. I've seen a lot of men do a lot of strange things. When the crunch comes, that's when you find out what a man's made of." He added, "He's got a look in his eye, all right."

Reagan didn't say anything for a moment. He looked like he was rehearsing his next words. At last, he said, "I had a private briefing with General Donlevy last night." We waited for him to continue. "He said ... he said that if for any reason Colonel Peck was unable to carry out the mission ... I was to take over and make sure the device was delivered. I asked him if he thought that was likely. He said no, but ... well, the top brass just wanted to cover every possibility, that's all."

"Ah, uh, you can't be serious," I stammered.

"Well, General Donlevy suggested that if I thought I had to do such a thing, I should talk it over with the bombardier and the navigator and maybe the flight engineer. I wouldn't have said anything, but—" He glanced backward.

"Uh—you *can't* do it," I said. "You just can't. The colonel didn't mean anything by what he said. You saw him. He's just—I mean, anybody'd feel bad having to do this. *You* would, wouldn't you?" I looked to Bogey, alarmed at the way the conversation was going.

Bogey's expression was dark. "I'm not going to have any trouble dropping this bomb. I've seen the Nazis face-to-face." He looked to Reagan.

"Well," said Reagan. "I guess ... a man's gotta do what a man's gotta do."

"Ah, uh, you can't do this, Colonel. You gotta give him a chance. You do this, you'll wreck his career—"

Bogey poked me hard in the shoulder then and I shut up just as Colonel Peck climbed back into the cockpit. If he'd heard anything, he didn't show any sign. He glanced around at us with gentle eyes, and I *knew* he knew.

"All right, men," he said. "Let's talk about it."

"Eh?" said Bogey blandly. "We don't know what you're talking about."

Peck let out his breath in a sigh, glancing downward while he collected his thoughts. When he met our eyes again, his face was grim. "I wanted to have this talk with you before," he said. "But I realized that there was no safe way to have this talk until we were safely in the air. From here on in, this *thing* is our responsibility. It's up to us. We've been entrusted by our government with the single most important mission of the war. But I want you to think about something for a moment. There is a law that transcends the laws that mere men can make."

I glanced to Bogey, then to Reagan. Bogey's grim smile revealed nothing of what he was thinking. But everything Reagan was feeling was written on his face so clearly he could have been a neon sign.

Peck saw it. He put his hand across the intervening space and laid it on Reagan's shoulder. "Ronnie, I want you to think about the precedent we're about to set. We'll be validating that it's all right to bomb civilians, to wipe out whole cities. This is the first atomic war. If we do this, it won't be the last. Yes, I've been thinking; maybe the most courageous thing we can do today is *not* drop this bomb. Maybe we should jettison it into the ocean. It'll be three months before the next one is ready. But we could take a stand today, that soldiers of the United States will not kill innocent civilians. And if we did that, our government leaders would have three months to change their minds about using the next one. Perhaps they'd think differently if we gave them a reason to reconsider—"

"And perhaps they'll just put us in Leavenworth and throw away the key," said Bogey. "Count me out. I've seen enough prisons, thank you."

"You're talking treason, sir," said Reagan.

"Yes, in one sense, I guess I am. But is it treasonous to place one's loyalty to God and all humanity above everything else? If our government is about to do something terribly, terribly wrong, shouldn't we oppose it—just like all those brave men and women who have been trying to oppose the evils of the Third Reich for so many years? Do two wrongs make a right?"

"Ahh-h-h," I stammered. They all looked at me. "Ah, I hear the sense of your words, Colonel, but this is the wrong time to have second thoughts. The time to bail out of this mission was before we took off."

Peck looked to Bogey. He raised an eyebrow questioningly: what do you think?

Bogey chewed on the soggy end of his cigar for a moment before answering. "Colonel, you're one of the most decent men in the world. Perhaps too decent. You're certainly too decent for this job. And I wish I had your courage, because you're speaking what a lot of us have been thinking. But ... I'm also a realist. And there comes a time when even decent men have to do indecent things. That's the obscenity of war. Especially this one. Lives are cheap. We drop this thing, they're going to get cheaper still. But if we don't—well, I don't see there's much decency in the alternative."

Colonel Peck nodded thoughtfully while he considered Bogey's words. He nodded and kept nodding. I could see that he was thinking through the logic step by step. That was Colonel Peck. Careful.

But he never got the chance to finish his thinking. Colonel Reagan unbuttoned his jacket pocket and pulled out a set of orders. He unfolded them and handed them to Colonel Peck. "Colonel, you are hereby relieved of command of this mission. I'm sorry, Greg. I was given those orders last night by General Donlevy. If you showed any signs of not being able to carry out this mission, he told me to place you under arrest and take over." And then he added, "I hope you won't make this difficult. Sir."

Colonel Peck read the orders without comment. "These appear to be in order," he said. He passed them to Bogey, who glanced at them, and handed them to me. I pulled my logbook around and wrote in the change of command. My hand shook as I did so.

"Colonel Reagan, your orders appear to be valid. The

mission is yours." He folded his arms. "You've helped me make up my mind, and I thank you for that. The fact that General Donlevy felt that such an order might be necessary confirms the ugliness of this mission." He glanced at his watch. "We still have two hours before we're over Berlin. You might spend it thinking about what kind of a world we'll be living in after you drop that bomb. You too, Bogey, Jimmy." He looked to Reagan. "Do you want me to ride in the back?"

"If you promise not to interfere with the operation of this mission, I'd rather you stay up here, sir."

"Thank you. I'd like that."

Ronnie picked up his microphone then. "Attention, all hands. This is Colonel Reagan. Colonel Peck has been taken ill. I'm taking command. We will proceed with the mission as directed." He put the microphone down.

Colonel Peck nodded. "Thank you, Colonel Reagan."

"Thank you for your cooperation, Colonel Peck."

We flew in silence for a while. The plane droned across the bright green fields of France, heading toward the distant blue mountains and then the long run north toward Berlin.

"Colonel?" Lieutenant Laurel's softly accented tenor came through our headphones.

"Yes, Lieutenant?"

"Ollie and I would like to report that the device is armed."

"Thank you, Lieutenant." Reagan glanced at his watch. "You're ahead of schedule. Good job."

Reagan looked around at me, at Bogey. "Either of you fellows having second thoughts?"

I shook my head. "I'm fine." Bogey held up his thumb. *The* thumb. The one he'd use to press the button. I glanced at my watch, then wrote the time in the log. *Device armed.* The words looked strange on the page.

I wondered what the people of Berlin were doing now? Were they going about their daily lives without concern, or were they studying the skies and worrying? Did the husbands go to work this morning? Were they busy at their offices? Were the children reciting lessons in their classrooms? Were the wives and housekeepers out shopping for sausage and cheese? Were the students sitting in cafés, sipping coffee and arguing philosophy? Did the orchestras still rehearse their concerts of Bach and Beethoven and Wagner? Or was the music canceled for the duration?

We flew on in silence. The engines roared and vibrated. The big machine talked to itself in a thousand different noises. We had our own symphony, here in the sky.

Colonel Peck looked curiously relaxed, as if he were finally at peace with himself. The bomb might fall, but it would not be his doing. Reagan, on the other hand, could not have looked unhappier. He must have felt betrayed by the colonel. Worse, he must now be feeling the same burden that Colonel Peck had been carrying around for the last few months.

Reagan exhaled, loudly. I could tell he was trying to figure it out. "I don't get you, skipper. You're one of the smartest guys I know. How can you betray your country like this?" He had an angry edge to his voice.

"I'm not betraying my country. I'm holding her true to her principles. We're not killers."

"The Germans started this war," Reagan said. "The Nazis are an evil empire. This bomb will destroy them. We have to follow our orders."

Colonel Peck nodded. "Ron, it's an officer's duty to refuse to obey any order that he knows is wrong. We're about to drop the equivalent of fifteen kilotons of TNT on an unarmed civilian population. Do you think that's correct?"

Reagan didn't answer. Even from the back, I could see the expression on his face; he was so angry his hair was clenched.

"Maybe the whole idea of war has gone too far," Peck said. "Maybe it's time for someone to just say no."

"That's got to be the stupidest thing I've ever heard you say," Reagan replied, shaking his head. I could tell he wasn't thinking straight anymore. I'd seen him get like this before. He'd get so angry that he'd refuse to listen to anyone, even when he knew they were right.

"Maybe. Maybe it is—and maybe someday, someone else will have an atomic bomb—maybe the Russians or the Chinese or even some crazy little Arab hothead—and maybe they'll be thinking about dropping their bomb on an American city, maybe New York or Chicago or Los Angeles. I don't know. But whoever it is, they'll have the precedent of our actions today, Ron. They'll know *exactly* what the horror will look like. The whole world is watching. If we turn back today, we'll be saying that this bomb is too *terrible* for anyone to use.

"But—if we use it, then every nation will want to have one—will *need* to have one—if only to defend themselves against the United States, because we'll have demonstrated our willingness to inflict such horror on our enemies. Oh, if it were only the war, Ron, I'd drop the bomb. What's the difference between a bellyload of little blockbusters or one big city-killer? Only the size of the boom. But it's not just this war, Ron. It's everything. It's all the consequences. It's tomorrow and tomorrow and all the tomorrows that come after."

"We'll be over Germany soon," Reagan said to Bogey. He hadn't heard a thing that Colonel Peck had said.

Bogey grunted a noncommittal response.

Reagan looked to Peck. "It's time. Give him your keys."

Peck nodded. He unclipped the keys from his belt and handed them to Bogey. Bogey clapped the colonel on the shoulder, a gesture of respect and affection, then ducked out of the cockpit.

We flew on. The engines droned and roared. I bent back to my table, my charts, my numbers, my logbook, my frustration. They were both right, each in his own way.

"How long to Berlin, Jimmy?"

"Uh, ah—ah-h, twenty minutes."

"Thank you." Reagan spoke into his mike. "Bombardier?"

Bogey's voice came through the headphones. "I've got a problem—I'm coming back up."

Reagan and Peck looked at each other in puzzlement. Peck glanced back to me. I shrugged.

Bogey pulled himself back into the cockpit, scratching the stubble on his chin. "I dunno how to tell you this, Colonel," he said to Reagan, "but I dropped the keys. I can't unlock the bomb."

"Well, find 'em, dammit!" Reagan was getting red in the face.

"Uh, that'll be a little hard, Colonel. I dropped 'em out the window."

For a moment Reagan didn't get it. Peck realized it first, and a big grin started spreading across his face.

Reagan started to unfasten his seat harness. "All right, I'll cut the damn chains if I have to—"

"That won't work either, sir. Stan and Ollie are already disarming the bomb." Bogey looked to Peck. "We're going to have to turn back."

"You'll be court-martialed for this! Both of you!" Reagan snapped.

"Oh, hell," said Bogey. "Let 'em. If they want to put me in jail for standing for what's right, then our country's got a lot bigger problem than this little war. You and I, Colonel—our problems don't amount to a hill of beans in this crazy world. But if I let you take this plane to Berlin, I'll regret it for the rest of my life . . ."

Colonel Peck put his hands back on the controls of the aircraft. He looked over to Ron—

"Dammit! We have our orders—" Reagan protested.

"I know, Ron, I know," Colonel Peck said softly, regretfully. He picked up his microphone. "Lieutenant Hope. This is the captain speaking. Break radio silence. Send the mission-aborted signal. We're coming home." And then he began banking the plane around to the left.

The first atomic war had ended before it had begun. Not with a bang, but a whisper.

George Alec Effinger, Hugo- and Nebula-winning author of *When Gravity Fails* and *A Fire in the Sun*, does not see the world quite the way anyone else does. In fact, the creator of "Maureen Birnbaum, Barbarian Swordsperson" does not see the world even remotely the way anyone else does.

So I had a feeling when I suggested he write about Albert Schweitzer that I was not going to get your typical run-of-the-mill alternate warrior story (if such a thing can be said to exist)—but even I had no idea just how deeply George could warp history and how much fun he could have doing so . . .

Albert Schweitzer and the Treasures of Atlantis
by George Alec Effinger

The hot equatorial sun blazed down on the sleepy village of Lambaréné in French Gabon. The shrill screeches of jungle birds split the air, and from somewhere not far away came the roar of Simba the lion. Then, as if the challenge of the king of the jungle had frozen every other creature, silence fell once again. There was only the eternal buzzing of insects, and the complex rhythms of Johann Sebastian Bach played on a portable pump organ.

Ngele, the young man who pumped the organ for the world-famous scholar and doctor, Albert Schweitzer, paused in his labor. "What is it?" asked the kindly missionary in the dialect of the Wagomvi.

"Look, great Mganga, it is Adiri. She is hurt!"

Schweitzer turned around quickly, and indeed a young woman, dressed in a colorful cloth wraparound called a *pagne,* limped into he room that served as both church and clinic.

The famed theologian, musician, philosopher, and physician hurried to the young girl's side. "What happened?" he asked.

"The Europeans," she said, wincing with pain and holding a hand to her forehead. "The Europeans have returned."

Schweitzer felt his blood run cold. In the rest of the world, a great world war was raging, a war in which he had little interest. He desired only to be left alone to do God's work here in the great rain forest of French Equatorial Africa. The problem was that Albert Schweitzer had been born in Alsace, on the border between France and Germany. His official nationality was German, and when war broke out in Europe, the French officials in Gabon had interned both Schweitzer and his wife. After a time, bowing to world opinion, the French had released them, and the humanitarian had hoped that he could pursue in peace his errand of mercy. It was not to be.

"They did this to you?" he asked, gently touching the long gash above Adiri's temple.

She nodded. "I tried to run from them, from their trucks and guns. I caught my foot in a tangled root and fell. I almost tumbled into the Ogooué River, where Mamba the crocodile would have made short work of me, but I had to come here quickly. I had to bring you the news."

"You did well, Adiri," said Schweitzer, feeling an unaccustomed rage building in him. "My wife will tend to your wound." He stared after her as Adiri went in search of Helene Schweitzer.

"What will you do?" asked Ngele.

"I will need the help of the Wagomvi," said Schweitzer coldly. "I will not submit again."

"The Wagomvi will give you anything you need," said Ngele confidently. "You are as the brother of our chieftain. You are Mganga." Mganga simply meant "doctor," but when used in reference to Albert Schweitzer it conveyed so much more. It was a title of respect and reverence, a display of love that the Wagomvi offered to no other white man. Indeed, their own tribal name meant "quarrelsome people," and it had taken Schweitzer a long while to earn their trust and admiration. Now, though, they looked up to him as a leader who had but to voice a command and it would be done.

Before Schweitzer could begin forming a plan of action, he heard the racket of the French trucks breaking through the thick foliage that hemmed in the narrow road leading into the village. "And so it begins again," he murmured. He stood up slowly and gazed at Ngele. He knew that he had an urgent responsibility to the young man and the rest of the Wagomvi, who now looked to Schweitzer for both medical care and moral instruction.

"Monsieur Schweitzer!" called a loud voice from the clearing near the clinic. "Monsieur Schweitzer, we have urgent business to discuss."

Albert Schweitzer put a finger to his lips, and Ngele kept quiet. Then the tall Lutheran missionary went out into the bright sunlight to meet his enemies.

"*Bonjour*, Monsieur Schweitzer," said a French army officer. "My name is Captain Duplantier. It is an honor to meet you. Your fame is celebrated worldwide."

Schweitzer frowned. "I do not work here for fame, Captain. I have no desire to be celebrated."

Duplantier smiled, but it was not a friendly smile. "Nevertheless, your international celebrity has caused a certain amount of difficulty for my government. And for me, personally."

"I am greatly troubled to hear that, Captain," said

Schweitzer. There was more than a touch of irony in his words.

"Perhaps there is somewhere more comfortable where we may speak? In private? I am still not used to this damnable African climate."

Schweitzer shrugged and indicated that the French officer follow him into a small office at the back of the clinic. The two men seated themselves at a rough, unpainted table. "Would you care for some fruit juice, Captain? I'm afraid that's all I have to offer you. Ngele, fetch the captain something to drink." Schweitzer shook his head. "Captain Duplantier, I'm sorry that I have no ice to cool you. We have only the most primitive of comforts here on the edge of the jungle."

Duplantier waved a hand impatiently. "That is no matter. I would like to get down to the business at hand. My government has become concerned once again about your loyalties. Confidentially, the colonial government has never received the slightest bit of information that you, an Alsatian by birth, of German nationality, have any political motives in what you are accomplishing here. Speaking merely for myself, you have my complete admiration. However, the colonial minister in Paris is of another mind. He has suggested a second internment. Purely as a matter of security, you understand."

"Security," growled Schweitzer through clenched teeth. "How does your minister in Paris think I am a threat to his security?"

Duplantier shrugged. "That is not for me to answer, monsieur. I am only an army officer. I am given my orders, and I must carry them out. However, the colonial governor did amend the order slightly. It was pointed out that if you could provide an adequate bond, you might be permitted to remain here to do your work in Lambaréné. Otherwise, I'm afraid I'd be compelled to place you under arrest, and see that both you and your wife are transported to France for the duration of the war."

"France?" cried Schweitzer. "But we are the only source

of modern medical care for hundreds of miles around! Not only the Wagomvi but other tribes as well depend upon us! It would be criminally inhumane to close the hospital now!"

The French captain rubbed his brow with one hand. "I, for one, quite agree with you. Still, as I've explained—" He merely shrugged to complete the statement.

Schweitzer's entire philosophy was based on his concept of "reverence for life." This reverence for life sometimes extended even to the germs and bacteria he was forced to kill in order to protect the lives of his patients. Yet now, faced with this dilemma, he could begin to understand the need to take up arms and fight for liberty. However, there might still be another way open to him.

"You mentioned a bond," he said slowly. "What did you mean?"

"Oh," said Duplantier, "something of value. Something of great value to you, that you would give over to our safekeeping. A bond that would prevent you from acting against the French interests in this conflict. Naturally, at the conclusion of hostilities, this bond would be returned to you, provided the colonial minister is satisfied with your conduct."

Schweitzer made a fist and pounded on the table. "Look around you, Captain!" he cried. "Great value, you say! If we had anything of great value, do you think our hospital would be so poorly supplied? Do you think we would not build a more magnificent church to the greater glory of God? Value? We have nothing of value here, except knowledge and faith."

"And Bach," said Duplantier simply. "I share your love of Bach."

Schweitzer relaxed a little. "Ah," he said. He wondered if perhaps he could trust this man. A great deal would depend on it.

Just then, Schweitzer's wife, Helene, entered. She was a trained nurse who helped her husband administer the clinic at Lambaréné. "Albert, what is it?" she said anxiously, looking from him to the French army officer.

Schweitzer frowned. "This ... gentleman had just told me that we are to be interned again, unless we can provide the colonial government with some financial bond to guarantee our neutrality."

Helene looked stricken. "They want money from us?"

"Yes," said Schweitzer, coming to a decision, "and they shall have it."

"But what we've put away is dedicated to the continued operation of the hospital!"

Schweitzer went to his wife and put a comforting arm around her shoulders. "Yes, yes, *mein Liebchen*, I know. Without the bond, however, there will be no hospital. It must be done."

Duplantier let out a grunt. "I'm glad you're being reasonable about this, Monsieur Schweitzer."

"Just a moment then." The great white doctor left the small office and hurried into the main room of the combination clinic and chapel. Near the pump organ there was a small wooden door in the floor, hidden by a thick woolen rug. Making sure that no one was able to see him, Schweitzer moved aside the rug, threw open the wooden door, and descended into a secret vault beneath the hospital.

Here he kept the wealth he had carried away on his most recent adventure to a lost city deep in the jungle fastness. At the dawn of time, this city had been a colony of the now-forgotten continent of Atlantis, and even in the twentieth century it was still populated by the degenerate descendants of that ancient race. Stored in this lost city were fabulous treasures—even the rumors of their existence had been immortalized in oral and written mythologies throughout Africa and the Near East. Schweitzer had been given but a minute fraction of the gold, silver, and jewels stored up over the centuries by the Atlanteans. The riches had been a reward from the High Priestess of the cult of Atlantis, whose life Schweitzer had saved so dramatically—yet in this secret vault in Lambaréné he had enough to fund his missionary work for decades to come. Now he would have to part with some of it to prevent a second imprisonment by the French.

Quickly, Schweitzer filled a silver casket with gold coins, diamonds, emeralds, and great strands of pearls. He closed the casket, climbed back out of the vault and shut the secret door, and finally replaced the rug. Then, regretfully, he carried the ransom to Captain Duplantier. "Here," he said, placing the silver casket before the Frenchman. "This should be sufficient, I believe."

Duplantier's eyes grew large, and he raised half out of his chair. "*Mon Dieu,* what is this?" he cried.

"Money," said Schweitzer. "Money that should have paid for bandages, for medicines, for other necessary supplies. Instead it goes to satisfy the greed of your masters, to finance a war that is costing hundreds of thousands of young lives. Take it, and leave us to our important labor." The disgust in his voice was clearly evident.

Duplantier could barely speak as he opened the casket and examined the contents. "Why, there is enough wealth in here to . . . to—"

"Yes, yes," said Schweitzer angrily. "Now, be off with you, and don't interfere here again."

"But where did it come from?"

"Royalties from my husband's books on philosophy," said Helene Schweitzer simply. "His organ concerts. And donations from concerned and generous people around the world, of course. Although they're never enough. You have no idea what health care costs these days."

Duplantier stood. His brow was shiny with perspiration. He closed the silver casket and carried it securely beneath one arm. "Everything here seems satisfactory," he said. His voice sounded a trifle weak. "I will inform my superiors that you have cooperated in an admirable way, and that it is my opinion that you represent no threat to the security of the French government, the colonial administration of French Equatorial Africa, or the present war effort. I will say good day to you both, and please accept my sincere apologies for interrupting your good work here."

"Good day, Captain," said Schweitzer coldly. He watched as the Frenchman turned and left the shabby building. Schweitzer and his wife regarded each other for a moment. There was grave concern on her face, but only determination on his.

Later that night while his wife slept, Schweitzer lay awake and wondered why a war so many thousand of miles distant could cause so much disruption here in the heart of the African continent. He was not so naive as to believe that there was ever peace in the jungle—the constant struggle for survival continued every day beneath the equatorial sun—but there was a sort of tense equilibrium that nature maintained. Fisi the hyena had fierceness and cunning, but Swela the impala had speed to outrun her pursuer. Simba the lion was feared by all save such as Tembo the elephant, whose size and strength protected him against even the most ferocious of predators. Each animal had its own strategies to stay alive, to find its next meal, to breed and protect its young. No, there was never peace in the green world beneath the high, vaulting roof of the jungle, but there was stability. Life went on, day by day. Sometimes Simba made his kill and dragged the carcass of Pofu the antelope back to his pride; sometimes Simba failed and all went hungry. Only human beings upset this essential balance, and no one, man or beast, prospered because of it.

At last, Schweitzer tired of these fruitless speculations and fell into an uneasy sleep. His dreams were troubled, filled with images of marching men in French and German uniforms, marching into Lambaréné, forcing their way through the thorn *boma* that protected the village and Schweitzer's jungle clinic. When Ngele came to awaken the great humanitarian at dawn, Schweitzer felt as if he'd had no rest at all. Nevertheless, there were already patients to be seen.

The morning passed as they all did, with Schweitzer tending to the wounds and illnesses of his native charges as best he could, given the limited resources of his primitive hospital. At noon, when the missionary was accustomed to break for a modest meal, Ngele ran into the clinic's treatment room. The young man's expression was terrified. "O great Mganga," he cried in a pitiful voice, "she is gone!"

Schweitzer looked away from his noonday meal of bread and cheese. "What do you mean, Ngele?" he asked.

"He's taken her! The Frenchman! He left a note!"

Schweitzer took the sheet of paper from his assistant's hand and read it quickly. It told him that the French captain, Duplantier, had kidnapped Helene. "If you ever want to see her alive again, you will reveal to me the source of your treasure." Schweitzer crumpled the paper in one angry fist. In an instant, his benevolent philosophy vanished. No one—*no one*—would put his wife's life in danger!

Schweitzer's expression of resolve was so fierce that it frightened Ngele. The missionary doctor went quickly to his quarters. He searched in the chest of drawers that held his few personal belongings until he located the two items he thought he'd never have need of again: a leopardskin loincloth and a long, sheathed hunting knife Schweitzer had found in an abandoned cabin near the coast. Quickly he stripped out of his shirt, trousers, white lab coat, and shoes, and donned the loincloth. He wore the hunting knife low on his hip. Immediately he felt the thin veneer of civilization drop from him, and he stood before his mirror gazing at his reflection. He was now a cruel avenger, and the French captain would learn to beware his fury.

Hurrying from the village outbuilding, he leaped into a nearby tree and climbed quickly to the upper terrace. It had been years since he'd permitted himself the sheer exuberance of this atavistic life-style. He'd denied the ancient, even bloodthirsty side of himself for too long. Now,

however, the time of reason and peacemaking had come
to an end. Now was the time of violence—and vengeance.
He only hoped he wasn't too late to rescue his beloved
Helene.

Traveling more quickly through the leafy avenues than
the French invaders could on the ground, Schweitzer soon
caught up to the military caravan. It was now well past
noon, and Schweitzer knew the native bearers demanded
a rest period during the greatest heat of the afternoon. It
would give him time to plan his strategy.

It took him only a few minutes to traverse the distance
to the main village of the Wagomvi. He dropped lightly
to the ground near the hut of Mgobi, the chieftain. The
children of the tribe clustered around Schweitzer curiously, and their raised voices brought the headman from
his hut to see the cause of the disturbance.

"It is Mganga!" cried Mgobi. "Make him welcome! Prepare a feast! It has been too long since he visited us!"

"Mgobi, my friend," said the theologian, "I do not have
time for a feast. There is trouble around us, and I require
your help."

The old black man's expression became grave. "When
you call upon us, Mganga, we are ready. You have done
much to preserve our lives. We owe you more than we
can repay. Command me, and I will guarantee you the
utmost effort of each Wagomvi."

"I expected no less," said Schweitzer. He squatted in
the dust before Mgobi's hut, and they discussed what the
French captain had done, and how they together could
join in the effort to bring Helene to safety and punish the
European intruders.

In a short while, during which Mgobi organized the
superb warriors of the Wagomvi tribe, Schweitzer leaped
again into the arboreal highway. He still had to rally his
animal allies. Schweitzer's "reverence for life" did not permit him to take a life in anger, yet he felt at the same
time that anyone who offended the law of jungle should
receive the full penalty of the jungle. The execution of

that penalty could be more terrifying than any European was able to imagine.

An hour later, the Wagomvi had silently surrounded the French safari. The black Africans held silent, waiting for the signal to attack. All must be coordinated carefully to protect the safety of Schweitzer's wife, Helene. While the warrior tribe moved into position, Schweitzer communicated with Simba the lion, Tembo the elephant, Duma the cheetah, and others—even Chatu the python, and Faro the rhinoceros—to make certain that his human allies would be reinforced by the most dangerous creatures of the Dark Continent.

At Schweitzer's shrill whistle, the Wagomvi surged forward, screaming their ululating battle cry. Spears and arrows contended with the most modern weapons of 1917, yet the pistols and rifles of the French were soon overwhelmed by the sheer numbers and supreme courage of the Wagomvi. While the European soldiers were occupied by the Africans on one front, they were attacked on another by the savage creatures obeying the commands of the white man they knew as Mganga.

In the meantime, Schweitzer himself dropped from the limbs of a jungle tree into the midst of the battle. He took in the uproar and confusion quickly, and then spotted the single Frenchman who'd been left to guard Helene. The poor soldier's eyes were wide with terror as he watched his compatriots fall beneath the wrath of the Wagomvi on one hand and the bellowing beasts on the other.

Schweitzer rendered the man unconscious with one sure blow to the jaw. The missionary appreciated the irony that this single act of violence would likely save the soldier's life. "Helene, *mein Liebchen!*" he cried. "Have they harmed you?"

"No, Albert," she said. "They've treated me almost with deference."

"Then I shall take no retribution—this time." He picked her up easily and leaped into the nearest tree. He gave one shrill whistle and Simba, Tembo, and the other beasts ceased their murderous attack and melted silently back into the dense jungle that was their home. At another whistle, the Wagomvi stopped fighting and, saluting their honorary white chieftain, began jogging away from the battle scene. They returned to their village until Mganga should call upon them again.

Albert Schweitzer stood on the leafy bough and surveyed the scene below. Many of the French soldiers and their native bearers were dead or wounded. The captain, Duplantier, had perished with a Wagomvi spear in his chest. The silver casket full of Atlantean riches lay ignored upon the ground. "Helene," said Schweitzer, "I must leave you here. I will return to Lambaréné to fetch help and supplies. We must do what we can for the survivors."

"Of course, Albert," said his wife. "While you're gone, I'll try to make them as comfortable as possible."

"I thank God that you're safe. And I pray that nothing will ever interfere again with our simple, peaceful life." Schweitzer stared thoughtfully down at the scene of carnage below, shook his head at the folly of men, then swung easily away in the direction of the hospital.

One of Judith Tarr's passions is horses. Another seems to be turning out a steady stream of best-selling fantasy novels. Armed with a Ph.D. from Yale, she can find the most intriguing characters to write about, and supply enough details to make you think you're reading a true historical account.

As, for example, this tale of Sisygambis . . .

Queen of Asia
by Judith Tarr

I.

The tent was silk, heavy and rich, the pure deep-dyed purple of the Tyrian vats; its tassels were gold, and heavier yet, as heavy as the weight of the world on the Great King's shoulders.

The Great King was gone to battle on the field of Issus. Sounds of it reached even to the center of his camp, sounds remarkably like a slaughterhouse beside a smithy. Inelegant thoughts for the Lady of the Medes and the Persians, Queen Mother of Persia, but queenship gave a woman license to be practical.

Her eunuchs were calm because she was outwardly calm. Her women were less perfect in their obedience. Her daughters had had successive cases of the vapors; her daughters-in-law had indulged in proper hysterics. They were all banished to the back of this tent that housed the

Great King's harem. Only the child was with her here, the prince-heir sound asleep upon her knees, with his thumb in his mouth.

Confusion rang without. Voices raised. One was not the voice of woman or eunuch. It overrode the rest, advancing swiftly closer.

Sisygambis was prepared when he entered, prepared to forgive his lack of any but the most essential courtesies, his directness that was almost unthinkable in a noble Persian. She had been prepared all her life long, maybe, as a woman learned to be.

"Defeat," said the Lord Artabazos. His face was ashen pale. There was blood on his armor, and perhaps also on his sword that he had surrendered to the guards at the door. "The barbarian has conquered."

"And my son?" Sisygambis asked. Her voice was steady, a trained steadiness.

He paused. She watched the struggle, subtle as it was, a flicker of the eyes, a tightening of the lips in the iron-gray beard. At length he said, "The Great King, lady . . . the Great King . . ."

"He ran," she said. She had alarmed this good man, more direct even than he, and less delicate in his sensibilities. "He turned tail and fled."

His head bent, admitting it.

"And," she said, reading him as if he had been a scroll of the laws, "all was not yet lost, or even nearly. He lost his courage. He proved himself a coward."

"Lady," said Artabazos. "He might not have known—he might not have seen—"

"He was afraid," said Sisygambis. "He was always a bully, my great tall beautiful son. And bullies are cowards at heart. When they meet an enemy who is stronger than they—they run.

"And yet," she said, "this, to be his conqueror. A barbarian. A boy. A child."

"Not so much a child as that, this Alexander," Artabazos said. "And he has his father's army, which some reckon the best in the world."

He paused, perhaps to compose the rest of his speech. In the silence the prince woke, sat up in his grandmother's lap and frowned at the stranger. "You are not Papa," he said. "Only Papa can come here."

"This is Lord Artabazos," Sisygambis said, "and you will be polite. He is your kinsman and your friend."

The prince's frown did not lighten, but he forbore to offer further objection. Artabazos bowed to him in the proper degree before addressing Sisygambis once more. "Lady, the camp is chaos, and the Greeks are coming. If they take you, and worse, the prince . . ."

Sisygambis' eyes closed briefly. If, indeed. A defeated enemy's possessions belonged to his conqueror. Including his women. And his children. Menchildren, who could grow into avengers of their fathers . . . those were not permitted to live.

"Mind you," Artabazos said as if to himself, "he might be merciful. As I knew him, when he was a boy—he was odd, that way. He might not do you harm."

"And yet," said Sisygambis, "boys grow into men. And he is a barbarian." She rose, setting the prince on his feet but keeping hold of his hand. "We will stand bravely, at least, and die if need be."

"Lady, you need not," said Artabazos. "I have horses, a chariot. The enemy are confused, some galloping after the king, most running toward the prospect of booty. There may be hope; there may be a chance, if we run now."

Sisygambis' glance took in the tent, the eunuchs, the few women who remained in this outer chamber. "Can all this outrun the King of Macedon?"

"All this, lady," he said, "no. But a few of us, yes. The chariot will carry you, lady. The prince can ride before you."

"My place is here," said Sisygambis.

"To die? To become a barbarian's slave?"

She considered that. She was no longer young. She had

seen her son to the eminence of the throne; she had seen her granddaughters, and at last a grandson, a prince to be king when his father was dead. She had lived well. She could die in the knowledge of it.

But the child need not die; should not, and least of all for his father's cowardice. She laid his hand in Artabazos'. "Take him. Keep him safe."

Artabazos seemed ready to contest her, but a rise in the clamor without brought him to the alert. He swept the prince into his arms.

The prince was young, but his wits were quick. He apprehended much more than either of them would have wished. He lunged out of Artabazos' grasp, flung himself on his grandmother. "I won't go! I won't go unless you go, too!"

She struggled to pry him loose. He only clung the tighter, and began to howl.

Clash of metal outside the tent—deathly close. A woman's shriek, abruptly cut off. And the prince wailing like the baby he no longer was, as if he would summon his own death.

Sisygambis stuffed the corner of her veil into the child's mouth. No time to gather anything of use—time only to hope that Artabazos had provided for a woman and a child on the run, and to catch the eye of her chief eunuch, and to pray that he understood the command in her glance: to hold, to guard, to do what he must, when he must, once the enemy had come. The others were prostrate with terror. She strode over them, sweeping Artabazos in her wake. Out to the horses, the chariot, a road that might prove deadly; but better that than the death of a captive or a slave.

And suppose, she thought as the chariot rattled and lurched through blind night, running far from Issus. Suppose that Artabazos had never come, or that she had persisted in her refusal to escape while she could. She would be dead now, or worse. As her daughters and granddaughters must be; and her poor foolish waiting-women.

She took time for grief, there in her flight, as the dark deepened before the dawn. The prince was safe, his body warm against her, stiff with the jolting of the chariot. When it was lighter she would pass him to one of the soldiers who rode with them, let him ride for a while as a prince ought, on a horse rather than behind one.

His father had fled, her escort had told her, on the back of a new-foaled mare, so blind in his panic that he forgot honor, dignity, anything but saving his own skin. "We can excuse ourselves," she said softly to the drowsing child. "I am a woman; you are too young to bear weapon. But he . . ."

Bile drowned the rest. A mother raised her son to ride, to shoot, to abhor the Lie—that was simple, but sufficient. She also raised him to know the name of honor, and to be valiant. Not to run mewling from a field on which he held the advantage.

She wrapped the cloak tighter about herself and her grandson, and braced against a powerful lurch. Thanks to the Immortals, the chariot held together; the horses ran on, into the bleak morning.

II.

"He is the Great King," said Artabazos somewhat wearily after so many repetitions. "When he commands, we must obey."

"And when he commands nothing?" That was Prince Oxathres, with rare heat. He was a quiet one, was Oxathres, but he was losing patience. "He does nothing but sit and wait, and let the Macedonian run rampant down the coast of Phoenicia."

"He sends messengers to ask for his harem back," observed the Greek, Patron, whom Artabazos had brought to this meeting with brief introduction and no explanation. The nobles endured the mercenary general's presence in silence. Sisygambis, behind her screen, studied him when she might, and drew conclusions of her own.

"Ah, the harem!" cried Oxathres, whose sisters were part of it; for he was the Great King's brother by another mother than Sisygambis. "Can you believe what they say, that he never touched it or went into it, or let any of his men near it?"

"I can believe it," said Artabazos. "That would be very like Alexander. He has a noble heart, for all his outland breeding."

"Oh, he's a proper Homeric hero," said Patron with what Sisygambis had learned to perceive as dry wit. "Thinks he's Achilles and his lover's Patroklos. I'll wager he's planning a grand gesture, give all the women back like a noble king from the old days, and get himself written in an epic. But he'll keep the loot and the tents, don't any of you doubt that. He's practical under the poetry."

"And our Great King is reduced to begging favors from him." Oxathres began to spit, caught the Queen Mother's eye through the translucent screen, raked fingers through his beard instead. "He shames us, my lords. He shames us all."

"And what would you wish to do about it?" Sisygambis asked him.

He was fair as Persians went, and his color was high; it went higher, even to scarlet. But he spoke boldly. "I would see him punished as he deserves."

"With shame? Reprobation? The need to beg alms from a barbarian?"

"With death," said Prince Oxathres.

The silence was abrupt, and enormous. Sisygambis sat back in her chair, which for all its cushions seemed suddenly as hard as a rack. None of them could deny that they had come here to this secret meeting in the women's quarters of Persepolis, to talk of anything but disposing of a king who had proved himself a coward, and nigh lost Persia for it. But the blunt expression of their purpose was more than they were ready to confront.

Except for the Greek, whose nation knew nothing of subtlety. "That's logical enough, taking all in all. And it won't be the first time. I suppose you'll poison him discreetly, in the Persian way? Then what? Who gets the throne? Oxathres?"

"The prince's look of horror was quite unfeigned. "Ahuramazda, no! I'm no Great King."

"Who, then? Bessos? Nabarzanes? You, Artabazos?"

Artabazos raised a hand. "No, none of those. Bessos might be a logical choice, but I don't trust his judgment. No; I had another thought. Our prince is too young to rule, to be sure, but with a regency. . . ?"

They all turned to stare at Sisygambis behind her screen. She gazed levelly back. After some consideration, she signaled the eunuch who attended her. His glance disapproved, but he moved to obey, folding and removing the screen, leaving her with nothing between herself and these men but her thin veil. None of them was a stranger to her face, save the Greek; and he had manners enough not to stare.

"We speak of bitter things," she said, "but things that are necessary. Fate and the Immortals granted me escape from the debacle of Issus, and brought me here in safety, with the prince in my care. And as we rode, running like felons, ever wary for pursuit, I had time to think.

"Call it logic if you will, as a Greek might; or call it foreseeing. But I dreamed, my lords, as we rode through the dark. I saw us returned to the idleness of cowardice, the barbarian running like fire down to Egypt, and then when that half of our empire was cut off from us, roaring up out of the Black Land to overwhelm us all. And our Great King saw him, and feared him, and ran. Do you wish to endure that shame again, my lords? Can you?"

"He might be persuaded," said Artabazos. "He was brave once; he fought a champion and won. He might remember his courage again."

"My dreams deny it," said Sisygambis, and her voice was iron. "I saw this place in which we sit, this palace of

the thousand years, go up in flames, and Alexander dancing in the midst of it like a spirit of fire."

They shivered, even hardheaded Patron, who made a
sign against evil. It was he who said, "It never did anyone
any good to sit and wait for King Philip to come calling;
and Alexander's his get. Somebody could try to beat that
into the Great King's head."

"We have tried," said Oxathres. "Endlessly. He refuses
to hear us. He shuts himself in his chambers with his
women and his pleasure-boys, and drowns his sorrows
in wine."

"He will drown us all," said Sisygambis, who also had
spoken to the king, and not softly, either. The memory
of his face was bitter, and his voice crying against her,
calling her old woman, doomsayer, witch and unnatural
mother.

"If I am unnatural," she had said to him, "then so be
it. But I am the Queen Mother, and you are the Great
King. If you will not look to the safety of your empire,
then another must do it for you." And then she had left
him, mildly astonished that he had permitted it, or left
her living thereafter. She had increased her guard since,
and added a second taster, but nothing had happened. He
had put it out of his mind, perhaps, as he forgot anything
that discomfited him.

She looked into Artabazos' eyes. He was the best of the
men here, the wisest and the one most to be trusted. "I
see no other choice," she said.

For a long while he said nothing. His face was stony,
his eyes flat. What passed in the mind behind them, she
could not know, but it was simple enough to guess. She
had suffered the same, night after night, since she fled
from Issus. Honor was sacred, and truth divine. She asked
him to defy both. To acquiesce in a Great King's death—
a Great King who had been his friend.

Oxathres made as if to speak. Patron stopped him before Sisygambis could move. "He has to make up his own

mind," the Greek said in a rasping whisper. "Don't get in his way."

At last Artabazos stirred. His face sagged, seemed suddenly gray and old. "Yes," he said, almost too low to be heard. "Yes. It is necessary."

Sisygambis kept her own face still, but she knew the stab of pain, the voice of her heart that cried *No!* even as she said aloud, "It shall be done. Let none of you have a part in it; but be ready, when the moment comes, to move."

They bowed, all of them, except the Greek. He favored her with a sardonic glance and a soldier's salute. "I don't envy you at all, Mother. Luck to you; and buck up. It will work for the best in the end."

III.

Words were spoken. Commands were given. Matters were seen to. And Darius the king fell ill, and by the third day he was dead.

This was not unheard of in Persia. There were procedures for it, and proprieties. Certain slaves were interrogated; some were put to death, or died of the questioning. A lordling or two was disposed of, who had been heard to speak ill of the king. There might have been contention over the succession, and that too would have been in order, but Sisygambis saw it cut short. Prince Oxathres and Lord Artabazos were regents for the young prince; and Sisygambis, in the absence of the prince's mother—taken, alas, by Alexander—held the place of queen and regent.

Alexander, ignorant of affairs in Persia, had marched from Issus to take Sidon without a battle, but Tyre had given him greater resistance. It had, in fact, given the boy-king offense, and being still as much boy as king, Alexander had turned stubborn. He had sworn to take the city, the messengers said, if it took him a year. And since Tyre was an island, and impregnable, and Alexander had no sea-power, it might well take him the rest of his life.

"Which he would likely do," said Artabazos, "bone-stubborn as he always was." He knew whereof he spoke: he had been an exile in Macedon when Alexander was a child. "He'll mount the greatest siege the world has ever seen, and he'll do his utmost to take the untakable city. Alexander never does anything by halves."

"One thing about sieges," said Patron, who was never far from Artabazos these days, or for that matter from Sisygambis and the prince. He was paid to be loyal, he had told her once; and he had a feud against the Macedonians. "Sieges necessarily have just one direction, and that's facing whatever they're besieging. That, with Tyre, is the shore and the island. Take them from behind and they're all turned around wrong; they have to scramble to fight back."

"And we have sea-power," Artabazos said, "and Alexander does not."

"Yet," said Sisygambis. "That is an alarming young man. If he sees that he needs the sea, he will have it."

"But we had it before him, lady," said Patron. "He'll be at Tyre for a while, and it will keep him busy. That's time we can use—to get the army back together, muster the fleets, get ready to move."

"And then we take him," said Prince Oxathres. "At Tyre, still, if we can. The Tyrians will help us. They love us little, but they love him less."

"At Tyre," Artabazos agreed. "And if he moves from there, we follow."

The men immersed themselves in matters military, forgetful of the Queen Mother's presence. Sisygambis listened with absent attention, as she might to the babbling of children. War was a great matter, but she knew better than to expect to be listened to; time later to work on them as a woman could, softly, with the proper deferential words. Now it was enough that they went where she thought they should go.

Her soul would burn long in the fires of ordeal for the murder of her son. But necessity commanded, and the empire's preservation. She had never thought as others did that her son would be a strong ruler, but she had hoped that he would hold well enough in war, at least, to use his mighty advantage of numbers against the Greek invasion.

For that had been coming for a long while. The Greeks never forgave the Persians their taking of the Peloponnese, years ago, and in Philip of Macedon they had a man to lead them and an army to fight for them. When Philip died, murdered it was said by a disgruntled boy-lover—so untidy, these barbarians were, and so reckless with their loves and hates—Persia had hoped for a respite. But Philip's son proved as warlike as his father, with the wildness of youth added to it, and a dangerous edge.

All men had their weaknesses. Alexander's, she reckoned, was his youth, and the pride that went with it. That held him at Tyre, besieging it, when he might have gone round, or ventured something subtle.

The men were speaking of that. "He's stubborn," Patron was saying, "but he's not stupid. He knows he can't have a viper's nest of enemies at his back if he moves inland, or if he goes south to Egypt—and that's what Tyre would be."

"Still," said Artabazos, "he could be less . . . thorough. Joining the sea to the land, Immortals help us, and building a causeway from the shore to the island. That smacks of obsession."

"And he thinks we're hiding deep in Persis, coddling the baby king and squabbling over spoils," Patron said. "Let's make sure he keeps on thinking that. We want him cocky; we want him letting his guard down and giving us a way in."

"He can hardly ignore the advance of the Royal Army," said Artabazos.

"What if it wasn't?" Patron said at once. "Look here. No disrespect, lords and lady, but you people go to war

like ladies to a festival. You take your women, you take
your pretty boys, you take all the loot you own. It takes
you hours to march a furlong. While the Macedonians,
they just take what they can carry, and they march fast."

"Not any longer," said Sisygambis. She had startled
them somewhat with her woman's voice in this council
of war; they stared. "He has the baggage that was ours,
now, and the women and the eunuchs and the treasure.
All untouched, we are assured. All unharmed."

"Then the tables are turned," Artabazos mused. "His
siege and his newfound wealth would bind him. And if
we were to turn barbarian in our ways of war, march as
an army without women or servants . . ."

They said it could not be done. The army of Persia
would never submit to such discipline. Its princes knew
their prerogatives; its foot soldiers fought with little training and much use of the lash.

But Kyros the Great had set precedents, and precedent
in Persia was sacred. Kyros had had a mob of hill-warriors
and no conception of luxury. Sisygambis had a palaceful
of silk-clad princes and a horde of ragged countrymen.
But they came round swiftly, because she invoked the
throne and its power, through the men who spoke for
her.

She was not undertaking to be loved. She would end
this threat to the empire, and end it quickly. Then let
lordlings mutter against her, even send poison in the cup
and knives in the dark. They were nothing that she had
not faced before.

Now the winter was past, the spring begun, the season
of war. The army was on the march, and she was riding
with it. Strictest sense would have left her in Persepolis
with the prince, safe, protected, trebly and quadruply
guarded. Half a dozen of Artabazos' sons spoke for him,
and Sisygambis' chief eunuch told them what to say. They
were good young men, and obedient, and loyal to a fault.
They would do well enough.

And Sisygambis would go to the war. Dreadfully ill-attended for a woman of her rank, riding in a cart little better than a farmer's, sleeping in a tent barely sufficient for her handful of eunuchs, she was as happy as she had been since she was a girl. She even contemplated calling for a soft-gaited horse and riding like a man; but dignity forbade. Some things the Queen Mother must sacrifice to the necessities of rank.

They marched with speed that would have astonished her late and unlamented son. Patron the Greek led them. He knew how Greeks fought, and what Macedonians did that was different. Morning and evening and even on the march, he put the Persian levies through exercises that seemed preposterous, bullied their loose and shifting masses into ordered ranks, challenged the haughty lordlings of the cavalry to prove that they could charge together and on command.

He drove them without mercy. There was a matter of blood between Patron and Alexander, a city sacked that had been Greek, kinsmen dead by Alexander's command. But Patron, being Greek, had a talent for dividing his mind. The half that hated was servant to the half that calculated. She wondered if he ever forgot himself and uttered an unplanned word.

The Persians would not have suffered him without Artabazos and Oxathres. Or, she admitted, without her. They seemed to have decided that the Great King's shame was Alexander's fault. For them as for Patron, this had become a grudge-fight. When they spoke of what they fought for, they spoke of stolen treasure, captured women, defending the honor of Persis against a rabble of garlic-gnawing Greeks. That a Greek led and trained them they bore because they must, and because their princes and their queen commanded it.

Patron called that native servility. Sisygambis reckoned it the wisdom of civilized men. It would serve her well, she hoped, when at last they came to the battle.

Alexander was still at Tyre, still besieging it. He was

still building a causeway from land to island, not much
hindered by Tyrian resistance; and spies brought word
that he had been trying to win the Persian sea-forces to
his cause. Since those fleets were Persian only in name,
consisting chiefly of Phoenician ships under Sidonian and
Tyrian captains, and Sidon was already his at least in
name, that was less unlikely than it might have seemed.
If he took it into his head to build his own fleet in the
shipyards of Sidon, he might gain the sea-power that
hitherto he had lacked, and broaden the scope of the war.

Sisygambis could do little to help that, except to send
envoys to the fleets with gifts, bribes, and a reserve of
threats. Meanwhile she marched as swiftly as might be.
She could not hope for surprise, but Alexander might not
expect a Persian army with discipline. With luck he would
think it a gesture merely, a token of resistance from weakened Persepolis. It was a bare tithe of the host that Darius
had mustered, hardly enough to serve a satrap's pride, let
alone a queen's. Alexander need not know that this was
a trained army under a Greek commander, and not the
undisciplined rabble that he had met before.

She made sure that she was known to lead it, she and
a mercenary who might turn against her: a woman and a
hired soldier against a king by right and blood, suckled
on war. Let him feed his arrogance on that, and let him
grow swollen with it. Then when the battle came, let him
see what Persia had made of itself.

IV.

They came up over the mountains of the Lebanon, and
down through the great forests of cedar, to the narrow
plain and the long reaches of the sea. There had been
skirmishes, small bands of outriders and occasional bandits, but nothing of moment. Alexander they had not seen,
though he was known to ride in small companies against
reivers in the hills.

Sisygambis paused on the steep hillside. Her wagon went on without her, with much rattling and jolting. She fond an outcropping to stand on, well wrapped in veils, and looked out across the plain of Tyre. The siege was a sprawl of tents along the plain, a cluster of men like ants upon the shore, a causeway reaching well out toward the black rock of the island. Sisygambis wondered how Alexander meant to breach those massive walls when he came there. Siege towers alone would not do it, for the walls rose fifty yards out of the sea; and Tyre could burn or topple any that came within reach.

He had no ships, at least. Her coming had distracted him; and she had sent a lesser army to surround Sidon, where he must go if he would muster a fleet. Whatever he did, he must do from the land.

Sisygambis returned to the column winding down off the mountain. Alexander could not but have seen it. He had done nothing yet. Maybe he was too busy with the diversion from Tyre: the ships that came out of the two harbors, north and south, and descended on the causeway. Some were fireships. Some had rams, and all were full of armed and yelling men.

Sisygambis' own men picked up their pace. They were ordered to husband their strength, but there was battle ahead of them at too long last, and they were eager to fight.

The actual order of battle was the men's concern. Sisygambis had to trust to them, now that the time was come, and hang back with the servants and the noncombatants. They had plenty to do: making and securing a camp, fighting off stragglers from Alexander's forces, serving as runners and horseholders and physicians. If all went as they had planned it, the Persian army would close in on Alexander from the land and the fleet from the sea—not only the Tyrian ships but a great billow of sail out of Cyprus and Arados and even Sidon, with a good west wind. He, caught between, must fight for his life.

But there was no telling what Alexander would do once

he was trapped. He held hostages: the Persian women and
the treasure of empire. A Persian would have raped and
mutilated the women, destroyed the treasure or cast it
into the sea, anything to keep it from the hands of the
enemy. Alexander was less predictable.

Sisygambis should have sat with queenly patience in
her tent in the camp's center, and waited as queens did,
for the men to fight their battle. So she had done at Issus,
and at the Granicus before that. She was weary of waiting
in tents, with only eunuchs to bring her word of what passed
on the field. She wrapped her veils against the brisk breeze,
called for a chariot, and commanded the charioteer to place
her where she could see the battle.

It was confusion as battle always was. Ships on the
sea—sails, masts, smoke and flame from the fireships
grounded on the causeway, men in boats and men leap-
ing over the sides of ships to swarm onto the land. Chaos
on land—flash and glitter of armor and weapons, spears
upright or thrusting level, horses rearing and wheeling,
some mounted, some yoked to chariots. Men shouting.
Horses screaming. Banners lurching and swaying. Persians were easy to distinguish: they were wrapped from
head to foot, with scarves drawn about their faces. Phoenicians looked much like them, but smaller, more sinewy,
and half-naked if they had come from the ships. The rest
must be Greeks of her side or theirs, armor of leather or
bronze or, rarely, gold, ranks that held more often than
not, great spears that were the Macedonian sarissai, three
manlengths long.

Her eyes were not what they had been, not for close
work, but she still had the long sight of a bird of prey.
She saw Oxathres towering above a knot of bronze-
helmeted Greeks, Artabazos in his chariot with its
matched grays. And she saw the man in golden armor on
the black horse, seeming to be everywhere at once, now
spurring among the cavalry, now leaving his horse to fight
among the footsoldiers. He moved like a cat, with a restless energy that caught the eye even in the midst of the

press. Others paused to rest when they found a lull. He never did.

Oxathres saw him, too: she watched the tall prince close in on the smaller Macedonian, hacking his way through the men between. When they met, she had forgotten to breathe. Oxathres was mounted in a chariot. Alexander was still afoot, with his horse a furlong away.

Prince Oxathres, noble always, got down from his chariot and spoke to the king his enemy. Sisygambis felt her body go taut. It was no part of Oxathres' mandate to call for a battle of champions, as all too clearly he was doing. Yet it might resolve the matter. With their king dead and their army surrounded, the Greeks would surely yield— or fight at least with heavier hearts.

Oh, to be a man, to be out on the field with sword in hand, in the clean simplicity of battle—to live or to die, to slay or to be slain. A woman could only stand and watch, and pray the Good God that her people gained the victory.

It was swift, and yet unbearably slow. They drew back in a circle that seemed to have cleared for them, they stalked one another round it, at last they closed. It was as vicious as dogs fighting in the bazaar, and yet there was something like goodwill in it, even laughter as they leaped apart. It was not over then, not nearly; they only rested. In a moment they were at it again.

The battle went on around them, undiminished even close to them. But no one ventured their circle.

Sisygambis' awareness narrowed as theirs must have, focused upon them. If one of them fell, the rest would follow. Yet she knew distantly that a part of the Persian cavalry had broken through to the sea, and joined the mariners there in surrounding and battering a part of the Macedonian army. But elsewhere the Persians were falling back, the seamen driven to their boats, and some of those were burning.

The single, vital combat went on. It was slower now. Scarlet stained Alexander's bright corselet; he moved stiffly, but he was still cat-quick. Oxathres had lost his helmet and his scarf; his hair was on his shoulders, his beard a tangle on his breast, curled ringlets hanging limp with sweat. Beardless Alexander was crimson-faced in his helmet; then he tossed it away, shaking out his lion-colored mane, and called out something that might have had to do with fighting fair.

The end had come before Sisygambis knew it. Oxathres went down with dreadful suddenness. Alexander stood over him. Sisygambis swayed against the chariot's rim. The charioteer, daring greatly, braced her with his shoulder.

She straightened with an effort. The battle was still going on. Artabazos fought side by side with a man in Tyrian armor. Patron led his Greeks in a charge against a huddle of men in armor very like their own.

In the circle of combat, Alexander stepped back, sword still in hand. A Persian leaped on him, maddened perhaps by the prince's fall. Others followed. Alexander vanished in a knot of struggling men.

That was justice, Sisygambis reflected. Grief was remote, and very cold. The battle had not even paused, nor would it, it seemed, until the last man was dead.

They fought until the sun was low. The Macedonians had broken into scattered bands, fighting with their backs to whatever might protect them. The outliers of Persians and Phoenicians were already at work separating the wounded from the dead.

"Victory," said Artabazos, as if he had hoarded the word for all these bitter months since Issus, to bring forth now like a jewel set in gold. He was weary, wounded, staggering where he stood; but he was grinning like a boy.

Sisygambis did not make a habit of smiling; her teeth were not her best feature. But in the face of such joy she forgot vanity—and all the more for what he brought with him. Men of the army, battered but proud, bearing a litter, and Oxathres on it, expounding volubly on idiots who strapped a man down when he was perfectly able to walk.

"Certainly you are," Artabazos said. "With a knock on the head that would have felled an ox, and one leg all but hamstrung, you can walk to the surgeon's tents and not a step farther."

Sisygambis' presence silenced Oxathres if not Artabazos. She bent over the litter. "What is this I hear of your refusing to be sensible?"

Tall prince though Oxathres was, he was no match for her. He said not a word more as he was borne off to the surgeons.

Artabazos watched him go. "He'll be well, lady. There's nothing wrong with him that time and good feeding won't mend."

"I thought him dead," said Sisygambis.

"He was convincing, wasn't he? That last stroke of Alexander's sword should have cloven his skull. But he has a hard head."

"As hard as diamond," said Sisygambis. Then at last, slowly, wonderfully, she let it swell in her. "Victory," she said. "We have the victory."

V.

Sisygambis surveyed the tent that had been the Great King's, and then was Alexander's, and was now in Persian hands again. It was little the worse for wear. Some of the vessels had been put to uses other than they were intended for, and men in armor had been sitting on the couches, making rents in the silk, but there was nothing much missing, and nothing destroyed.

The women were tearfully glad to see her again. They swore that they had not been molested, or even visited, by the man who had captured them. "He doesn't like women," said Stateira, the mother of the heir, once she had been reassured that her son was safe, guarded, and

properly cared for—insofar as he could be without his
mother to look after him. "He has a lover who goes with
him everywhere, and no wife at home, nor any children.
He is very Greek."

Sisygambis had her own opinion of that, but she let it
pass. "And none of his men ventured any liberties?"

"Not a one," Stateira said. Her daughters, great-eyed
solemn creatures as lovely as does and as tall as young
trees, murmured assent. "He was always perfectly cour-
teous. He sent us presents through the eunuchs, little
things that he thought we might like. Tidbits—he sent us
apples once. He loves apples."

The eldest daughter giggled. "He sent us spindles, too.
He thought that we would want to spin and weave. We
were terribly insulted."

"And he was mortally embarrassed," her mother said,
"when he found out what he had done. In his country all
the women spin, even queens."

"How barbarous," said Sisygambis.

"Oh, he is very pleasant," Stateira said. "The eunuchs
like him. They dismay him a little, because there are no
eunuchs in Macedon, but he treats them like people. Our
own men seldom do as much."

"Interesting," said Sisygambis, and sent them away so
that she could think.

When the Queen Mother of Persia received the King of
Macedon, she did so in state, but not from behind the
screen that should have been proper. She stood regent to
the Great King in Persis; that set her outside of the common lot of women, and granted her liberty in the greeting
of captive kings.

He came in under guard but not in chains, walking as
easily as if the guards were his own. There was another
with him, a tall young man with a somber face, who even
in Persia would have been reckoned beautiful. That one
looked like a king, and moved softly and with grace,

walking somewhat ahead of the other as if to prepare his way.

The one who truly was king looked like a boy. He stood hardly taller than one, with his unruly bright hair and his high-colored face; he looked about with bright curiosity, smiling at any who met his glance.

And yet, Sisygambis thought, he was feigning at least a part of it. When his eyes turned to her, they were disturbing, one as pale almost as silver, the other almost black. They caught and fixed on her.

She allowed the liberty. For all his ease of manner, he was angry, and as wary as a lion in a trap. He had never lost a battle until now. He had never faced a victor.

Here was one with whom she must take great care. She did not smile or otherwise show him softness, but searched his face as he searched hers, seeking to know the man who wore this mask of boy and king. Restless, brilliant, ruinously spoiled—he was all of that. Full of prickles and crotchets: she knew the tales of his mother the witch of Epirus, his father the ram with a hundred ewes.

Still, she thought, there was something about him that fascinated her. It was not his beauty, certainly. He was too red for that, too broad of face, too nobly endowed with nose.

A strategy took shape in her as she considered him, a great strategy, as daring as anything that Alexander himself would try. It was young yet, half-formed. It was outrageous—preposterous. And yet it tempted her. It was like her dream of Persepolis burning: it had that force. She could not dismiss it out of hand.

He bowed before her, not mockingly, but not with any great awe, either. This might be how he bowed to a queen at home. He elected wisely to be silent until she should choose to speak.

When she did, it was not to him. She dismissed her attendants, all but a pair of trusted eunuchs and the Greek interpreter. The tall young Macedonian remained as well—his friend certainly. His lover? She rather thought so.

Once the room was cleared, Sisygambis said to Alexander through the interpreter, "Sit."

He looked as if he would ask where, until one of the eunuchs set a stool for him. He sat on it with no appearance of nervousness, although he must have been shaking within. The other Macedonian was not usually so pale, Sisygambis suspected, or so stiffly correct in his posture, with his hands fisted at his belt where a weapon should have hung.

She studied both of them until Alexander began to fidget, lacing his fingers together and clamping them between his knees. Abruptly he said, "Well? What are you going to do with us?"

The interpreter rendered that in Persian. She understood Greek tolerably well but did not speak it; she inquired in her own language, "What should I do?"

Alexander, when that had been presented to him in Greek, shrugged and said, "It would be simpler if you were my prisoner. I'd keep you as I kept the other women, and return you intact to your lord when the war was over."

"We can hardly do that with you," said Sisygambis, "since you are the instigator of the war. We could send you home, I suppose, in return for a sizable ransom; but I know well that that would only set you free to vex us again."

"I could swear oath never again to make war on Persia," he said.

"Oaths are easy, King of Macedon, and cheap at the price. How long would you keep yours? A year? Three years? Five? While defeat rankles deeper, and revenge grows sweeter. No; I think you would not keep such an oath."

Swift anger crimsoned his face, but laughter came as swift, and swept anger away. "You see me clearly, Mother." *Lady,* the interpreter rendered that, but that was not precisely its nuance. "If I were you, I'd get rid of me now. I'm a dangerous prisoner, as stubborn as I am, and as quick to find ways to escape."

"We could," she said, "render you harmless." Her eye slid toward the younger of the eunuchs. He was as fair as Alexander, if not as ruddy—his skin was like milk. He had been beautiful in his youth.

The color drained from Alexander's face, leaving him as pale as the eunuch. He showed no fear, for all of that. "I'd make a terrible slave. Stubborn. Thickheaded. Rebellious. No habit of obedience at all."

"So I have reflected," said Sisygambis. "What then shall we do with you?"

"Kill me," he said.

He thought he wanted that. In light of the alternatives, very likely he did.

"That would be a pity," Sisygambis said, "as young as you are, and as gifted a general. Patron says that you may be nearly as good as your father."

"I am better!" he snapped.

She suppressed a smile. "Patron also said that you would say just that. And maybe you are better, or you will be, with time."

He knew himself baited: he relaxed with an effort that she could see, and showed her his teeth in what might have been taken for a smile. "Well, then. I lost this battle, I grant you. Maybe he would have won it." He did not sound as if he believed it.

"You should have let Tyre be, and taken all else about it, and let it fall to you by default. Or if you had to take it, secured the sea from Sidon before we could close it to you, and marched against us while we were still disordered with Darius' death."

"Maybe," said Alexander. The interpreter's voice had become a part of this colloquy of theirs, the pauses imperceptible, but now there was a silence. Alexander had gained back a little of his ruddiness, but not all. His hands were still clamped between his knees.

"I could take the city yet," he said. "I saw how to do it, if I'd had the means. Rams, you see, mounted on ships anchored fore and aft. I'd have needed a fleet to start with, to keep the enemy's ships away, and to provide bases for the rams. Then when I'd broken the walls I'd march my men in along the causeway, and reign as king in Tyre."

"You are a dreamer," said Sisygambis. "I would call you mad if I did not see you clear. Are you such a hater of women as they believe you to be?"

He did not exchange glances with his friend, she noticed, nor did his friend change expression. "Who says that?" he demanded.

"You never touched the ladies of Persia," she pointed out.

"They were honorable captives," he said with no little indignation. "It would have been a disgrace to rape them."

"One would think you could not," she said. "That you have no ability to perform with a woman."

He was angry, that was obvious, but keeping it in check. "Are you insulting me?"

"I am inquiring," she said, "as to whether you can or will beget an heir for your kingdom."

"You sound exactly like my regent in Macedon." That was not a commendation: he snarled it. "My father tupped anything he could get his hands on, female, male, both or neither. I like to fancy that I have some small degree of restraint."

"From extreme to extreme," said Sisygambis, nodding slowly. "I understand."

Perhaps he did not think that she did, but he held his tongue.

"My lord king," she said, "it is clear that you cannot be set free, for you would only return, and renew the war. It is equally clear that you would make a wretched slave, eunuch or otherwise."

"Then I'll die," he said. He sounded almost resigned to it.

She fixed him with a stern eye. "I was not finished, sir."

He flushed, which charmed her more than she liked to admit, and muttered an apology. Of sorts. It said nothing of remorse.

"However," she went on, "there is another expedient. You would be a prisoner, after a fashion, but only if you chose to perceive it as such."

His brows went up. She had him at a loss, she was pleased to see. Yet surely his mind would leap in the proper direction soon enough. He was remarkably quick.

"You would not return to Macedon," said Sisygambis, "but you would remain king of it, if that suited your fancy. You would linger here in Persia. My son is dead, you see; his heir is a child."

"You want me to be his *paidagogos*?" Greek word; the Persian was difficult, somewhere between body-slave and trainer of children. Alexander sounded astonished and no little insulted. Perhaps in Macedon kings did not train children, as in Persia ladies did not spin wool.

"No," Sisygambis answered him, "you would not be a child's tutor. What is the word for a man who takes a king's heir for his own, and weds the child's mother, and takes oath to serve them both as he best may?"

He was slow to piece that together. Surprisingly so, if he had not had his wits scattered by everything that had come before. "I'd . . . marry . . . the Queen of Persia?"

"Could you bear the thought of it?"

He shook his head slowly, not in refusal but in disbelief. "That's preposterous. I'm a barbarian, I rode to war against you, I don't know a word of Persian or a bit of Persian custom. Persia would never accept it."

"Persia would learn to accept it," said Sisygambis. "The logic is simple enough. You won the harem by right of conquest. The harem included the mother of the heir. Her husband is dead. You inherit the wife, and therefore the child. And since I have conquered you in turn, I decree that you will marry the woman whom you won, and be father to the child, and rule as king on the child's behalf.

You will name him your heir, and let no other heir of your body supersede him."

She did not know if he understood. She thought that he might have begun to. But he was wary, and wisely so. "Do you always marry off your widowed queens to your defeated enemies?"

"It can happen," said Sisygambis. "Our king is dead. We need a man strong enough to hold this empire together, and wise enough to judge the limits of his power."

"I may be strong," Alexander said, "but I never pretended to be wise."

"Nor is any lord in Persia. We suffer a sad dearth of wisdom in these days."

"So," he said. "Why?"

She shrugged slightly. "Call it expedience. Alive and in Macedon, you threaten Persia. Dead at our hands, you threaten us—your countrymen would make you a martyr, and advance yet again to war. Alive, granted wife, son, titles, bound to us with oaths and courtesies, you would serve us well. And," she said after a moment in which he said nothing, perhaps could not, "I abhor waste; and waste it would be, to cut you down so young. You are intelligent, which is rare in royalty. And you are interesting, which is rare in any man."

He was beautifully taken aback, but as quick, at last, as she had hoped. "I came to conquer Persia, and you would make me king of it. Is this a story that I'm in, or the gods' jest?"

"Our gods seldom indulge in levity," said Sisygambis.

"Well then," said Alexander. "We'll have to teach them how."

He was laughing; he was elated. He had not forgiven the defeat, she thought, nor ever would. But he was safest here under her hand, and in the end, maybe, he would learn to be king in Persia.

It was a little like flying a new-trained hawk, and a little like laying one's head in the lion's jaws. She did not laugh, it was not proper, but she allowed herself to smile. The first king that she gave to Persia had proved to be no king at all. This one, the Good God willing, would be what Darius had failed to be.

Or—and she went grim again at that—she would dispose of him as she had disposed of Darius, with equal remorse but no more hesitation.

She rose. He rose a moment after, with an instinct of courtesy that would serve him well when he came to the courts of Persepolis. He stood barely higher than her shoulder; but size mattered little when a man was truly a man.

"Come, my lord," she said, "and meet your bride."

She spoke so to test him. He seemed no more dismayed than any man brought without warning to his wedding. He even smiled, although his laughter had died. It was coming to him, maybe, what he had won for himself, and what he must do to hold it.

He took her hand in his, a great liberty, but perhaps he did not know it. Nor did she mind it. It was he who led her to the harem and the younger queen, eager as he was when he went to battle.

He would do, thought Sisygambis. Yes, the Good God willing, he would do.

Bill Fawcett is best-known as the editor of a number of excellent anthologies, many of them having to do with the future aspects of the military—so I thought I'd pose him a problem by suggesting he write about a warrior not from the far future but the distant past. One who, instead of fleeing from the Pharaoh, decided to make a stand. One Moses, by name . . .

Zealot
by Bill Fawcett

Aaron tried not to shift as he watched the chariot and retainers move slowly beneath him. It was long after full sun on a cloudless spring day and any time the zealot moved the sunbaked surface of the rock shelf on which he was hiding burnt his hands. The Hebrew felt a stab of concern. They were barely over a dozen and they had expected fewer retainers to be guarding the Egyptian merchant who approached. Instead there were eight armed men, more than they liked, but not more than they could handle with the element of surprise. Experienced as a war leader, Aaron took careful note of the opposition. Each retainer carried a bronze-tipped spear, but wore little armor; that followed, as this was only a social call and the day was hotter than normal. Aaron would have thought they had learned better by now.

Completing this survey of their victims, the zealot scanned the horizon for any sign the merchant was simply bait in a trap. After two years of escalating battles between the escaped slaves and Pharaoh's guards, he had to be ready for any subterfuge. Nothing was visible. Aaron mouthed a prayer of thanks.

As the chariot clattered below, Aaron pressed himself against the burning rock and looked at his brother for the signal. Crouched a few steps away, Moses, as usual, hardly seemed to be paying any attention to the impending ambush. Still, Aaron knew to wait. Since they had both been thrown out of Pharaoh's court for demanding their people be allowed to return to the Old Lands, Moses had led the zealots on dozens of similar attacks. He knew that each strike was carefully planned to cause maximum discomfort for the noble families and god-king that controlled Egypt. And to exact maximum revenge on those who had cast them out of their court as unclean and inferior.

Since every household had a number of Hebrew servants, learning the movements of their overlords was easy. It had been one of these spies that had told them that an important representative of the rich merchant he worked for would be traveling alone this day and what route he would follow. Then Aaron's brother had sent the children to call the men away from their brickmaking. They had run for hours across the dry lands beyond the valley to get into position in time. They had needed to sneak into the rocks and crevasses before sunrise, or risk discovery by the many patrols of mercenaries and Nubians. It had already been a hard night and Aaron had twice dozed off as he lay well hidden beneath a gray cloth. The cloth rendered him unseen to the approaching party, but gave no real protection from being baked by the unrelenting desert sun. All the zealots had suffered and many must be near exhaustion, yet, as always, not a man had complained. Each time Moses had sent the children every man called had answered. They were the zealots, soldiers of their people and sworn to punish their oppressors until every tribe was set free, and lived for nothing else. Recently too many had died for their cause as well.

Aaron watched as his brother's eyes came into focus and then narrowed. His prayer had ended just as the merchant's party was in the center of their trap. Moses raised his hand a few inches above the boulder he was sheltered behind. Almost without thinking the zealot tightened his grip on the javelin he carried. Like all weapons they carried, it had been taken from the body of a dead Egyptian and paid for with the blood of other zealots. As always when combat was near, Aaron had to fight away nausea and his heart throbbed so rapidly that it hurt to breathe. This would pass, he knew, as it had on countless ambushes. The young, anxious war leader of the tribe of Judah forced himself to take a long, painful breath.

The chariot was almost at the center of the ten-pace-wide canyon. Aaron took a final look at the shimmering horizon, searching for unseen enemies. This way was little traveled and no other party of Egyptians was in sight. It would begin in only seconds. There would be a flurry of fighting and he would either live, or if the Lord so willed, die. They had lost two men only the week before while setting fire to a straw house that had been occupied by soldiers. Those had been good zealots, devoted but unable to outrun the lead bullets cast by the slingers of the town's garrison.

Moses signaled.

Suddenly Aaron found himself screaming and rising to fling his javelin at the nearest retainer. The other zealots were also attacking. Even before the javelin struck, Aaron was drawing a bronze sword and scrambling down the three man heights of the canyon wall to slay the survivors. To his frustration, Aaron saw his javelin fall wide of the mark, missing the startled retainer by less the width of a hand. He couldn't stop his scrambling descent and if the retainer had stood up, Aaron would be skewered on the man's short spear. Screaming what might have been his final appeal to the God of his people, the zealot tried to look as threatening as possible. To Aaron's relief the man turned and ran.

The Egyptian retainers were good. Half had survived. All were dressed like members of the regular army. The zealot guessed they were veterans of Pharaoh's recent Canaanite Campaign. By the time Aaron had reached the canyon floor and stopped to assess the situation the soldiers had formed themselves into a half circle protecting the chariot. One javelin had pierced the throat of the chariot's lone horse and the lightly built chariot had been flung on its side by the horse's death struggles. The young merchant who had been thrown from it seemed to have been stunned and was still trying to gain his feet. Outnumbering their remaining prey by almost three to one, the zealots slowly approached the leveled spears of the guards. A trickle of sweat teased down Aaron's face and stung one eye, but he was afraid to wipe it clean. A hardness set in on the faces of the soldiers. The Egyptians must have recognized whom they fought. In over three years Moses had never allowed a single prisoner to live.

With a bellow to their only God, the zealots charged at that circle of spears. Aaron hung back. His sword was useless until their own spearmen had broken apart the Egyptian's defense. He saw Samuel stumble backwards and hurried to help Deborah's son, but the bloody bubbles pumping from the deep wound on the young warrior's chest spoke of his close and inevitable death. All Aaron could do was to ease the man down and prop him in the shade at the edge of the canyon.

Two more retainers were down. The last two were trying to edge backwards protecting their still-dazed charge until they had the canyon's stone walls at their backs. The other zealots had seen Samuel fall and were shrieking threats of revenge, but keeping their shields ready. Cries of "Death to idolators" and for revenge on all slave masters echoed along the dry, stone canyon. Aaron found the threats redundant as both sides knew this was a battle to the death. As if to emphasize this, one of the men of Gad broke away and began slitting the throats of the Egyptian wounded.

A lull in the screaming and clash of spears on their shields allowed Aaron to hear Moses' whistle. His brother used whistles to give orders in combat since his speech was slurred from when he had burnt his mouth on a hot coal as a child when directed to do so by one of his divine visions. Moses was still standing on the ravine's wall. He rarely engaged in the actual fighting anymore, preferring to wait where he could see everything and give orders. When necessary, though, the older man had shown no reluctance to fight, often viciously. Aaron knew that the liberation of his people was a personal cause to his brother. He spoke of it as being the Lord's will, but Aaron knew there was another reason for his brother's zeal. It was a way for him to rejoin the people they had lost contact with while favorites in Pharaoh's court.

Moses was holding a javelin and making throwing gestures at the Egyptians. It took Aaron and the rest of the zealots a moment to understand what he was ordering. Then several began to smile and a few men left their ranks to retrieve the javelins they had thrown at the start of the battle.

The merchant was up and had drawn an ornately decorated sword, but Aaron knew that no longer mattered. The bronze weapon with lapis embedded on its handle would do him little good. The Egyptians had not only trapped themselves against a steep wall, but were all shieldless. Their only distance weapon was a bow that was still in the wreckage of the chariot. They would have no protection from the zealots' sharp, bronze-tipped throwing spears.

Those zealots who had left the arc surrounding their prey returned to where the rest still trapped th Egyptians against the stone wall. The spears were passed around as they withdrew a few paces further. There was a strange, painful silence as the Egyptians watched their deaths being prepared. One began a chant to their animal-faced god of the dead. The gesture was a bit premature, but not by much.

The men cast together on Moses' whistled signal. Every Egyptian was hit. Most were pierced by more than one of the newly sharpened spears. Only the young merchant still stood. He had been partially protected by his retainers. A javelin struck in his sword arm made that limb useless. Gamely, the well-dressed Egyptian drew a dagger with his other hand and continued to threaten the zealots as they closed in around him.

When they were a few steps from the hapless youth all the men stopped. Most could not later say why, but their steps slowed. Panic was clear in the eyes of the young merchant and he was now beginning to quiver and whimper as he faced death. For dozens of heartbeats no one moved to end the massacre. Aaron could smell an unmistakable, acrid odor and knew the rich Egyptian had fouled himself. Finally the young man simply folded up and lay curled, whimpering in the dust.

Aaron stood, unable to bring himself to strike. It was hard to accept that the death of this weakling would help free his people. He was startled when a strong hand gripped his shoulder and pulled him roughly aside. Moses growled a slurred curse as he pushed past his brother and with a quick lunge, drove his sword completely through the sobbing Egyptian.

The zealots' prophet and leader pulled a heavy purse from beneath the boy's body even as the Egyptian died. His hand and the leather purse were both covered in blood. With a look of disgust Moses wiped them both clean on his victim's white robe. Then, as always, he led the men in a prayer of thanksgiving for their victory.

Samuel's life had bubbled away while they had fought. With practiced speed the zealots gathered up the fallen Egyptians' weapons. These would join hundreds of others hidden under the floors of Hebrew homes or buried in the sands that lined the length of the Nile Valley. Aaron was pleased to see that the bow had survived the chariot's crash. They would need such weapons for further ambushes and wood was hard to find in the wastelands where the two brothers were forced to live. He offered the noble's inlaid sword to Moses, who rejected it with a fierce scowl.

In an act calculated to further outrage the Egyptians, they cut off the heads of their victims and buried them far from the canyon. They knew that the Egyptians felt that this robbed the dead of any hope of rebirth. That was how all the zealots preferred their oppressors, dead ... permanently.

The all-night, retaliatory search had ended and they were safe, but Aaron was troubled. He and Moses were hidden in a tiny, unwindowed room of Judith's house. Judith herself was a fierce zealot. This woman of their tribe was small, with long black hair that extended below her waist and an air of determination that made even Aaron hesitate to argue. She wore a sharp blade under her robes and swore she would use it on any Egyptian she found herself alone with. Her husband had been a zealot, captured and tortured a year before. He had died without even giving his captors his name.

The boy they had killed in the desert was the oldest son of the Keeper of the Grain, a very important noble here in Giza. Huge amounts of stored gain were needed to feed the thousands of slaves and poor farmers that struggled to build magnificent graves for the Egyptians' sacrilegious living god. Its Keeper had Pharaoh's ear, and the People of the True God had paid a high price for his death in the ambush. Small groups of soldiers had rushed through the crude huts of the slave quarters, setting fire to many and slaying anyone who resisted. Songs of lamentation could be heard even inside the dark, small room in which they crouched. Aaron feared the rising anger would be vented upon himself and Moses should they be seen. So he waited and tried to rest in the stifling heat that had crept through the mud walls and built up in their hiding place.

The only light the two brothers had were spots of lessening grey where the evening light came through small holes in the hut's thin roof. They sat with their shoulders touching, cramped and barely able to straighten their legs. Both were dressed as brickmakers and had taken care to stain their hands yellow. Now Aaron's back itched where the sweat ran down his spine and he found it nearly impossible to twist around and reach the spot. He settled for rubbing his whole back against the wall he was pressed against. As always, his brother seemed unaware of the discomfort. Sometimes, quite often lately, Moses made Aaron very nervous. Three years ago, playing in the palace garden in Memphis, Moses had dragged Aaron to their rooms. For a long time before this Moses had begun in secret studying the faith of his own people, something which had seemed to be of little concern while growing up as Pharaoh's playmates. There he had confided to Aaron that he had been spoken to by the one God and was to lead their people to freedom. At first Aaron had thought Moses meant Amon-Ra, the sun-god, but he had meant the God of Judea. The next day they had left the court and never returned. After a month in the desert, Moses had begun preaching in the slave quarters and raising his band of zealots, warriors of the people who were inspired with the zeal of knowing they were specially blessed, holy warriors.

Staring at the dirt floor, Moses had said nothing since they had sneaked into the slave quarters hours before. Finally Moses shifted, began to say something Aaron didn't catch in the slurred speech his abused mouth allowed, and then lapsed again into silence. He was clearly upset, and unsure as to how to proceed.

They had come to recruit new zealots after their victory. But there was no chance of that now. Aaron was more afraid that his own people would turn on them. Certainly many would blame them for the Egyptians' reaction. Most of the people were already unsure if the zealots were heroes or simply bandits. They could easily form a mob that quickly succeeded where Pharaoh's army had so often failed.

"We must flee or attack," the leader of the zealots finally announced to his waiting brother.

"Attack?" Aaron asked.

"We are fighting not only Pharaoh and his army, but also for the faith of our people. We must act with faith in the one God and us as His sword," Moses answered, then continued. "Ours is a jealous god, a warrior king that allows no other before Him. He is not the god of slaves and it is not right that His people be held in bondage."

Aaron noticed that, as often happened when Moses was filled with a vision, his speech cleared. He nodded in agreement. They had said this many times before. Somehow now it seemed more threatening.

"I must speak to the people," Moses continued. "It is time to arouse them to act. I was told that I was the instrument that would free our people. It is time to do as I was bade so long ago. There is no more the few of us can do against the Two Kingdoms. It is time for all the people to act."

"I'm not sure they will follow you," Aaron cautioned.

"I am the sword of the Lord. His people will follow me." There was an edge to the older brother's voice that allowed for no contradiction. "We must go now and lead our people to freedom."

Aaron sat astounded. He had thought they would flee back to their desert caves. Moses' eyes glowed with vision, and his brother and war leader knew there was no use arguing.

"Now," Moses announced, rising, "I will speak to my people."

The crowd filled the center of the slave quarters where hours before the merchants had sold overpriced wares to Giza's poorest dwellers. Moses had been speaking for several minutes. His words flowed unimpeded and his arms flailed as he spoke. Those who had gathered were in a restive mood. Standing next to Moses on an oxcart, Aaron was still worried they might turn on the two of them. For a while there had been mumbled threats and even calls for someone to summon Pharaoh's soldiers. But Moses had refused to leave and stood haranguing the growing crowd with the evening breeze snapping the ends of his brown robe.

"They have cast down your Lord," Moses shamed the crowd with a listing of Egyptian wrongs. "They imprison your sons and take your daughters, later to cast them aside like chaff. You build temples for their idols and so insult the name of our one God."

The crowd began to rumble. Moses' list of wrongs touched on each of them. Even after generations of slavery they had retained faith in their God of Gods. All realized that they served those who worshipped other gods, but their had been little they could do about it. Aaron could see Moses sensed this appeal to their ancient faith was succeeding where his promise of freedom had failed. His voice rose as he played to the crowd.

"Last night I was on a mountain."

Aaron nodded. They had spent the night eluding patrols in the hills. They had arrived in the city just before dawn. It had been an exhausting ordeal.

"A burning bush spoke to me!" Moses announced with an upwards gesture. The crowd gasped. All were familiar with the visitation to the prophets of old. Aaron tried not to look startled. They had set a bush on fire to distract some guards while they sneaked onto a ship. Aaron hadn't heard it speaking, but he had been preparing the boat. Moses had seemed a little upset as they crept on board and tacked up the Nile.

"It told me that we are the chosen people. We walk with the sword of the Lord over our heads, ready to smite our enemies." The zealot leader's voice softened. "But I was afraid and buried my face in the sand. Then our one, our true God, He spoke to me and said I was to be His voice, to lead my people to freedom, just as He had done years ago. Then I was afraid. I feared we were too weak and did not trust in His power to shield us." Moses screamed his final plea and pointed at the high walls of the Royal Palace. "The Lord of our fathers has spoken. Believe in Him. Follow me to the unclean palace of the idolators! We shall make it a temple!"

The mob screamed. Most had been slaves all of their lives. Even the oldest had been oppressed by the Egyptians for decades and all were anxious for revenge. Even the zealot leader found himself cheering along with the others. The last years had been hard and now they would gain the reward for all of his and the other zealots' sacrifices. Aaron had hurriedly sent for the other zealots when he realized Moses was determined to speak. They had been waiting in the streets at the edge of the crowd, ready to spirit their leaders away or provide leadership for their people. It was a moment all of the zealots had dreamed of, the day when the people rose and threw off the Egyptian yoke. Most had also been told to bring bags full of the cached weapons. Bellowing madly, they began to pass these out, generating an even greater roar of approval. Soon the mob streamed behind Moses and Aaron and toward the Royal Palace. Aaron grabbed a pole and placed on it a sheepskin, the old banner of their tribe. Aaron was exalted and enthused. He was filled with purpose. For the first time in two generations their war leader was leading an army of all his people into battle.

The few soldiers they encountered ran or were easily slaughtered. Thousands of men, women, and even children swarmed behind the two leaders. As they entered the wider avenues of the temple district, Aaron was amazed at the size of the mob that followed. It filled the hundred-paces-wide avenue and extended as far back as he could see. The sound of the crowd was like that of an oncoming storm.

The Royal Palace was rarely used, since most Pharaohs preferred to remain in Memphis. The wide entrance was almost always open. A thick, wooden door hung from one

side. This was just swinging closed when Moses and
Aaron rounded the corner of the paved way leading to it.
Moses gestured and the foremost men began to run. The
door had almost closed when the first reached it. They
pushed, but the heavy wooden door was still closing,
likely driven by dozens of frightened guards. It looked as
if the zealots would be trapped outside the palace's ten-
man-high walls. They would be slaughtered here. Aaron
looked around for the safest way to escape. With a feeling
of loss he almost tried to turn them back. Some of the
mob would be slain, but most would escape to their
homes.

One of the men pushing on the door bellowed the
Lord's true name and threw himself forward at the nar-
rowing space between the door and the wall. His scream
turned to one of agony as the heavy door ground him
against the unyielding stone, but the sacrifice prevented
the door from closing.

Aaron ran for the door, calling for everyone to follow
him. As hundreds of new hands pushed back, the twenty-
man-wide door began to open. When the door gave with
a start, the zealot guessed the guards had realized they
couldn't hold and would be slaughtered if they remained.

The sound of the mob as they swarmed through the
gate behind him frightened Aaron. There was a vicious
edge to it. Pushing past his brother, Moses seemed to
glory in the whole chaotic scene. He virtually glowed,
gesturing his approval as he passed knots of men and
women kicking or stabbing at fallen royal guards.

From the palace wall Aaron could see smoke rising
from many parts of the city. No one moved in the distance. The last of those who had joined the zealots were
entering the palace below. All others had fled the city,
hoping to be spared Pharaoh's wrath. Aaron was grateful
now that they had not destroyed the heavy door. Down
the wide streets he could see the first chariots of the Royal
Escorts deploying jut beyond bow range. They were easily

recognizable by the decorative gilt and silver inlaid harnesses. This meant that Pharaoh himself had finally arrived. Moses would be pleased. Aaron was less sure. He felt a minor stab of guilt. This man and his brother had been friends once, children playing together and tormenting the guards assigned to watch them. But, the war leader rationalized, even before they had left they had grown apart, Pharaoh realizing that he was to become a living god and the two finally understanding their station as mere servants.

On a practical level the presence of the Pharaoh meant that he had likely brought with him most of the army. Aaron understood. If the rebellion in Giza survived, then the greater number of slaves in Memphis and the lesser cities would follow suit. They had to be crushed, mercilessly. No one would leave the palace alive. Those who survived the siege would become public sacrifices to Pharaoh's need to maintain unquestioned control of all Egyptian life. The army's presence here also meant that there was little to stop slave explosions in other cities. Hopefully Aaron studied the distant horizon, hoping to see the masses Moses had promised would rally to them.

Using a forked pole, Aaron pushed yet another ladder from the wall. He had long since lost any sense of satisfaction at the screams of the soldiers that plunged to their deaths at the foot of the wall. Beside the war leader a Hebrew warrior fell, an Egyptian spear through his throat. Before anyone could react, two Egyptian soldiers were standing where he had fallen. Another was climbing over the edge of the wall even as Aaron turned. Bellowing for those who were less pressed to assist him, Aaron used the pole to push one of the soldiers off and into the courtyard below. The fall might not have killed the man, but he was sure the women gathered there would. He was barely grazed by the spear of the other soldier before he could recover his balance. Dropping the pole, which was useless now that they stood only a few paces apart, Aaron drew his sword and hurried toward the spearman. Already the third soldier was over the wall and fighting with his back to the man the war leader faced. A fourth and fifth were struggling to join them and enlarge the foothold.

If they succeeded, the few hundred remaining defenders would be overwhelmed by the thousands Pharaoh had gathered to destroy them. Recklessly Aaron dived beneath a spear thrust and drove his sword into the belly of the spearman. The Egyptian let out a wavering shriek as he clutched his middle and toppled into the palace courtyard.

A glancing blow from the sword of an officer who was still only partially over the wall almost sent Aaron after his hapless victim. But a hand steadied him and from behind a long spear reached out and smashed into the officer's chest. The man's armor stopped the soft bronze, but the force of the zealot's thrust pushed the officer off balance and he disappeared from site. Then the last of the Egyptians were down and their ladder joined the others in a broken jumble at the foot of the palace's granite wall. Two horns sounded and the assault was over.

Knowing what would come next, every defender crouched close to the wall. With a sound like the roaring of a storm wind through a temple a shower of arrows soon filled the air above them. Aaron hoped the women and children in the courtyard had found safety before the deluge. The hail of arrows lasted only a few volleys, then Aaron was free to supervise the carrying of the wounded to the comparative safety of the palace itself. While he did this each of his lieutenants, all former zealots from their years in the desert, found him and told him how many had died and how many remained in their band.

Beating back this assault had been especially costly: nearly thirty men were dead and that number again hurt too badly to fight. After two weeks they had lost over half their strength. Still no one suggested they surrender. After it became apparent that no further attack was planned for that day, Moses began moving among the small knots of defenders that Aaron knew were now spread too thinly along the wall. He spoke of having yet another vision even as the battle was being fought. In his vision he had seen a holy army, led by a legion of the Lord's messengers armed with fiery swords, approaching from Memphis. They would be saved, but they had to hold out until it arrived. The men nodded somberly. Some may not have believed, but no one argued. It was the only hope that remained.

When he had finished speaking, Moses approached Aaron. To the war leader's surprise, his brother gestured for them to step away from the others. Eventually he led them into a small room that had once been used by the wardrobe servants.

"How long can we hold out?" Moses asked. Aaron noticed then how weary the prophet looked. His eyes were sunken and his shoulders sagged.

"Perhaps one more such assault, no more. We have too few men left to hold the length of wall we are forced to defend." Aaron wondered if he looked as tired as his brother. Self-consciously he wiped a spot of Egyptian blood off the back of his hand.

"And the food is nearly gone. We have no hope," Moses said in a flat, almost emotionless voice.

"But your vision?" Aaron sputtered.

Moses shrugged. "Once I believed in these things. But I must have failed, misunderstood what our Lord required of me. He promised me the death of their firstborn, but no matter how many we slew it made no difference."

Aaron stared at his brother. On one level he had never quite understood or accepted what Moses had claimed to see. But on another he had accepted it without question. Now his world seemed to shake. He had wondered at the visions and believed in his brother's leadership. Toward the eventual success of their cause. Now it appeared he had believed in the wrong things.

"If we are taken," Moses continued, now visibly close

to collapse, "we will be tortured and made lessons of. If this happens our people will fear to set themselves free for so long that none will remember we are a people."

Aaron reached out to support his brother. He realized how rarely he had touched the man since they had seized the palace. Moses had stood alone, somehow a prophet and no longer his brother. Now they were brothers again.

"I have asked the women to prepare a poison from the herbs kept here to treat the dead," Moses continued. "None of us must be taken alive." His voice was flat, but despair edged every sound. "I have failed our God and our people."

Aaron could say nothing. He knew Moses was correct. They could be used to cow the people into submission. Better to be martyrs than prisoners. The people would remember martyrs, but disdain fools who had died.

"I really was given a final vision," Moses commented after Aaron nodded his agreement. His voice was slurred again, the first time since they had occupied the palace nearly a full change of the moon earlier. "But the fiery angels came not to save us, but to take us to the presence of the Lord."

Aaron began to say something to console his brother, but Moses pulled back. Again his eyes glowed with the vision of prophets.

"You and the others will be welcomed," he assured the zealot. Then he slumped onto a nearby bench. "I am called to explain my failure."

Aaron tried to protest again, but Moses would not hear. The war leader knew that if their final sacrifice was to be successful, they had to begin before the next assault. He called for all the survivors to join him in the open area in front of the palace. For a change Moses stood and Aaron spoke. When the zealot had finished, many women began to cry, but all accepted the judgment.

The commander of the next assault was astounded when his forces met no resistance. His amazement turned to horror as he walked through the palace and found only the dead. Even the wounded and children had been killed. A thorough search found one young girl alive. She had been hidden by her mother who was unable to bring herself to share the poison. The girl was barely able to walk and was too young to serve as the example that Pharaoh desired.

The ministers of the court tried to spread the tale that the God-on-earth had called down his magic to slay those who had revolted. But those who lived in the slave camps understood. Even as the army that had been gathered to retake the palace dispersed to its camps, a small boy herding sheep on the sparse, dry grass of the lower Nile had a vision: in which his people were free.

Marilyn Monroe is one of the less likely alternate warriors in this volume—and yet, consider these facts: she was on intimate terms with the political movers and shakers of the world, she may well have had access to certain secret information, and in the end, she might have been willing to fight and die for her beliefs much as any other man or woman of honor.

Jack Haldeman, author or coauthor of well over a dozen well-received novels of science fiction, here gives us the mid-twentieth century's favorite blonde bombshell in a totally different role . . .

The Cold Warrior
by Jack C. Haldeman II

The secure phone rang.

"Hello," she whispered into the mouthpiece. "Marilyn speaking."

"This is Sam. Can you talk?"

Sam Giancana. Mobster. Sometimes lover. Another someone to be used. She flipped open her phone ledger and wrote his code name down, along with the time.

"Sure, Sam," she said. "What's up?"

"I'm still worried about Saturday," he said. "This is a big one, and it's got to come down clean. You know how much we've got on the line here. I don't want anyone at Justice catching wind of this."

"Bobby doesn't have a clue," Marilyn said. "I talked to

him the other day. He knows something's about to happen, but he's looking at Hoffa, not you. I didn't have to do anything but agree with him. He's going to come out of this with egg all over his face, and it'll serve him right."

"But I thought you and him was—"

"You think too much, Sam," she snapped. "You can't believe everything you read or hear on the grapevine. My personal life isn't that simple."

"Look, this is important to me. I got to be sure. I can't have no cops or FBI guys wandering into this by accident."

"Local cops are your business. I've got the FBI covered. Richard is throwing a smoke screen in Newark on Saturday that will keep them real busy."

"Richard? Do I know this Richard guy?"

"I doubt it. He's Hoover's plant on the waterfront. He and I have, well, an arrangement."

"I don't like the sound of that."

"You don't have to like it, Sam. All you need to know is that Richard does what I tell him. It's the results that count."

"You may be right," he said.

"I know I'm right," Marilyn said, jotting notes in the ledger. "So don't worry. And give my love to Judith."

There was a pause on the other end.

"You can be one cold-hearted bitch," Sam said.

"I know. It's one of my more endearing qualities," she said, setting the phone down, and cutting the connection. She got up off the bed and walked to the window, pulling the curtains aside to look out at the California night. Things were happening very quickly.

Damn Mexico, anyway. Damn it all to hell.

She turned away from the window angrily, filled with bitterness, and upset with herself for even thinking of that time. It was history. And the payback time was getting very, very close.

She walked to her dresser and mixed a weak drink, lots of ice and soda, with only a hint of bourbon for the taste.

As the time approached and all the pieces started sliding into place, she had cut way back on her drinking. The pills were gone forever, thank God. Revenge was a much better drug.

The other phone rang. She didn't pick it up. That one was wired twelve ways to Sunday by the FBI, the CIA, the Justice Department, the White House, the Mafia, the Teamsters, three local detective agencies, and God knew who else. They all thought they were the only ones who had the tap. Talking on that line was often useful, to spread confusion or misinformation. But right now she had to be very, very careful as to who knew what.

"Are you going to answer that, Miss Monroe?" called her housekeeper from the other room.

"No," she said. "I'm not up to it tonight."

"Will there be anything else?"

"No, but thanks anyway. You might as well go to bed. I'll see you at breakfast."

"Very well. Good night."

"Sleep well."

Yes, sleep well. Good advice. It had taken her a long time to learn that lesson herself. There had been too many years of hiding from her devils, trying to chase them away with the booze and the pills and the random sex. Those days were gone. Now when she felt the pain in her chest, she turned it into action.

She tried to remember why in the world she had ever gone to Mexico in 1955. It was all a fuzzy alcoholic memory, like it belonged to someone else and she was trying to read a blurred carbon-paper copy of that two-week period. Something to do with a film, she was pretty sure, or a director, or maybe an actor. It went that way sometimes, back in the days she was struggling. Her mama had always told her to use what she had, and that was about the only thing she was good for back then. That was the sad truth.

Only those days in the mountains were clear. And that

was what hurt so much. If she could change anything in her life, or blot them out, those were the days.

It seemed so good at the time, sitting around the campfire with Fidel and Che Guevara and the rest of their crew, talking about the injustices in the world and how one could take the "rightness" from one's heart and turn it into a fire that would change everything. Batista had to go. Cuba belonged to the children of the land, not to the rich landowners. It was all so clear then. To die young for a cause that was right was far better than to live forever in dark shadows.

And the nights in Che's tent were the most painful memories of all.

He could be a brutal lover, taking his anger out in their savage embraces with his lean, hard body. She loved it all: the loss of control, the willing submission of an Anglo legend to a violent man of the soil, a man who carried death and hope in his heart. A rebel.

And then she would change the script and become the gentle and quiet lover, covering his body with soft kisses and caresses. Che was unprepared for that.

Both scenarios worked only too well. She fell in love. That was the fatal mistake.

She left Mexico. Che and Castro returned to Cuba and from the Sierra Maestra they waged a successful guerrilla war using a ragtag army that fought more with desire than anything else. When Batista fled on New Year's Day in 1959, Marilyn popped a bottle of champagne.

Then everything went sour. The threads unraveled quickly. Che quit sending messages. Castro embraced, of all things, Communism, and not the idealistic people's republic they had discussed in Mexico, but the sick and rotten brand of Russian Communism. A short time later the telegram from Che arrived.

It was over. He called her a bourgeois bitch, not fit to sleep in the dirt with pigs. The vile things he wished upon her ripped her heart from her body. She remembered the soft way he moaned in his sleep, the way he held her, his musty smell. She could not reconcile these things with the words on the telegram.

The bottle. The pills. Oblivion seemed far better than living with that. She willingly rode that chemical elevator down from the penthouse towards the basement. Just before she hit bottom she realized what had happened.

Castro. Fidel Castro had turned Che's heart to stone. The bastard would pay for that. And, remembering her mama, she knew how to get even.

It wasn't all that hard.

She had all the physical equipment, and it was prime material. She knew how to use what she had if she could get over the deep-rooted insecurity. She had done it before, for lesser goals. Now she had a mission. Fidel Castro would burn in hell.

The secure phone rang. She picked it up.

"Marilyn, this is Peter."

"Yes?"

"I'm having, uh, a visitor tonight. Perhaps you might like to drive over."

"Cut the crap, Peter. Who's coming, and what do you want?"

"Our mutual friend just came in by helicopter. He wants to see you."

Marilyn made a note in her phone log.

"So what makes you think I want to come? And why didn't he call instead of you? I'm not about to drive all the way over there and flop on my back just because some washed-out actor wants me to come see the Attorney General."

"Come on, Mare. This phone—"

"No. You come on. What's the scoop?"

"Those nukes in Cuba. He told me to say that if you asked. Please don't put me on the spot."

"I'll put you on any spot I want, Peter. I assume you and Mr. High and Mighty are talking the black wig and dark glasses."

"If you don't mind. And bring the Ford with the fake tags."

"How about I have a breast reduction before I come? You don't want much, do you?"

"Marilyn, I don't want anything. Bobby said—"

"Shut the hell up, you spineless bastard. I'll be there in an hour." She slammed the phone down, walked to the bathroom and tossed her unfinished drink into the toilet. A clear head was what she needed. And that she had.

Before she left, she called Ricardo in Key West. He had just returned from a speedboat run to Cuba and back. Mostly he confirmed what she already knew. Then she called Carlos in Miami to transfer two thousand dollars to Ricardo's bank from the blind account she kept there. It was all proceeding as planned. The only thing left was to put the screws to Jack, and she had a way to do that.

Marilyn put on the dumb wig, wrapped a scarf around her head and grabbed the dark glasses, as if it would fool anyone, especially in the middle of the night. But she needed Bobby in her pocket, and there wasn't much time. The Ford started with the first turn of the key.

The gates to Peter's oceanfront estate swung open as she approached and then closed quickly behind the Ford with a loud clank. Robert Kennedy was standing alone in the shadows by the front door. As he walked to her, her heart gave a little jump as she remembered how it had been. But this was business, she reminded herself, serious business. They embraced, and she held him a little longer than she should have. On the other hand, he did not resist.

They walked around the house and stood at the chain-link fence behind the pool, looking at the ocean without speaking for a few minutes. They were standing inches apart, and the old feelings were still there.

"I'm sorry, Marilyn," he said at last. "It was all getting too complicated. Jack said we needed to distance ourselves from you. And when Giancana—"

"Shut up," she snapped. "You didn't fly down here to

discuss damage control for the political ramifications of our sexual relationship."

He hesitated, and stepped back a little.

"The telegram," he said. "The one you sent under your Secret Service code name."

She looked at him and didn't reply.

"Nukes in Cuba," he said. "How much do you know?"

"I know the Russians are starting to move missiles into Cuba. I also know that you are trying to decide how to deal with this."

"How did you find all this out?" he asked.

"I have lots of friends," she said. "They tell me things. Some of them owe me favors, big favors."

"You're a strange woman, Marilyn."

"You don't know the half of it," she said. "The word I have is that you're about to blow it again, big-time."

"Again?"

"Have you already forgotten the Bay of Pigs?"

Kennedy winced. "That one wasn't ours. It was a deal that Eisenhower and the CIA had cooked up. By the time we came in, it was already in place."

"It was a mistake. You should have followed through. Now it's too late for an invasion. The beaches are fortified. You won't stand a chance."

"Hindsight is wonderful. At the time—"

"Hindsight has nothing to do with it, Bobby. You plain and simple blew it. Just like you blew those three attempts to poison Castro."

"How in the hell—"

"Bobby! Listen to me. You want Castro's head. I want Castro's balls. Let's work together."

"You're going too fast for me, Marilyn."

"And I'm going to move faster. Listen up. I know that Jack has already rejected the frontal-attack scenario. The most likely game plan is some sort of a blockade. And this is where you come in. I want you to nuke the bastard."

"You've got to be kidding, Marilyn."

"I'm dead serious. Look, there has to be a showdown. Russian ships are going to be stopped. Something will happen and you will have to respond."

"That could blow the world apart, and you know it."

"Wrong, Bobby. You and I both know that the CIA has predicted with near certainty that Khrushchev will back down, even if the island is leveled."

"God, Marilyn."

"I'll sweeten the pot. You want Sam Giancana?"

"Are you kidding? That would break the Mafia's back."

"I'll give him to you on Saturday."

"You can do that?"

"With one phone call. And how about Hoffa?"

Kennedy stared at Marilyn, stunned.

"I've got the hard numbers on Hoffa and the rest of those boys. Wiretaps, film, and a paper trail you would not believe. I've been a busy girl."

"This is too much."

"I'll throw in Hoover for free. I've seen his private file on us, and the one on Jack, too. He's dead meat. And I'll give you two Supreme Court justices. All you have to do is toss one bomb you're probably going to toss anyway."

"You must really hate Castro."

"More than you can imagine, Bobby. And there's one more thing."

"Yes?"

"You won't have a choice. If the Russians don't trigger this, I will."

"You?"

"My anti-Castro friends will blow a couple of your ships out of the water the minute I send the word. It's set up to look like the Russians did it, and there you are, backed into a corner. Just don't miss and hit Panama by mistake."

Kennedy looked defeated, deflated; he stood with his shoulders slumped and his hands in his pockets. Marilyn reached up and kissed him on the cheek.

"Have a nice evening, honey," she whispered to him. "I'll call you tomorrow after I've set up the trap for Sam

Giancana. I figure we've got a few weeks before we move on Castro. Oh, and give my love to Jack."

On her way out, Marilyn saw Peter looking out a bedroom window at her. She flipped him the bird.

Marilyn felt great. All the pieces had clicked into place. Castro would roast.

As soon as she drove up to her house in Brentwood, she knew something was wrong. Her housekeeper's car was gone. All the lights were off. The front door was open. She flipped open the glove compartment and took out the gun she kept there.

Going inside, she hit the living room light with a slap of her hand. The sofa was overturned and the wall safe behind it where she kept her files was open and empty. There were no sounds at all in the house. She walked carefully to her bedroom and stood at the door, listening. Total silence. She kicked her door in, paused, and hearing nothing, she reached around the door, turned on the light and stepped inside. Her phone log was gone.

Her back was turned when the man leapt from the bathroom and covered her nose and mouth with an ether-soaked rag. She felt the sharp sting of a needle and tried to struggle away. Her gun fell to the floor.

Everything seemed blurry and very far away. The man let go of her and she collapsed onto the bed.

"You," she whispered. "Of all people. Why you?"

On August 5, 1962, Marilyn Monroe was found dead in the bedroom of her home in California. In spite of some unusual circumstances, her death was ruled a suicide.

On October 22, 1962, President John F. Kennedy announced a naval blockade of Cuba. After two weeks of tension, no missiles were fired by either side. Nikita Khrushchev withdrew his men and equipment. Fidel Castro remained.

Michelle Sagara is the author of a quartet of excellent fantasy novels and a handful of short stories, all of which helped to make her a Campbell nominee for the best new science fiction writer of the year. Here she takes Thomas Beckett, who died for his beliefs, and examines what might have happened had he fought for them instead.

For Love of God
by Michelle Sagara

When they came to the place of which God had told him, Abraham built an altar there, and laid the wood in order, and bound Isaac his son, and laid him on the altar, upon the wood. Then Abraham put forth his hand, and took the knife to slay his son.

—Genesis 22:9–10

He has always loved Henry.

Not a moment passes when he is free from that knowledge, and even the solace of prayer is a double-edged blade, for Henry and God are ever intertwined.

The sun is high, and the sky so perfectly clear and beautiful, it might be the eye of God, all-seeing, ever beneficent. Herbert mumbles something; the wind catches and twists his words. For a moment, no more, Thomas,

Archbishop of Canterbury, Holy Legate of the Apostolic See, is caught in time and memory.

But a moment is enough.

The King's court is in London at this turning of the season, and Thomas, son of Gilbert Beket, a man he hardly knows and never claims as kin, has been sent forth from the house of Theobald, Archbishop of Canterbury, into the wider nets of the world. Theobald is old and canny; a monk by training and learning, a man to whom Latin comes almost as a mother tongue. He has instructed Thomas in the ways of the Church, has elevated him to a clerk of his household, has done what he can to hone and sharpen Thomas's able wit.

This is all he can offer Thomas; for reasons that were never made clear to Theobald, Thomas demurred when offered a place in the order and robes of the priesthood.

"Let me instead serve you in the manner of worldly law," Thomas had said, and to this, Theobald had grudgingly agreed. Thomas, styled Thomas of London, never gave the Archbishop any cause to regret his service—and in turn, when young Henry, Count of Anjou, had taken his place upon the high seat of England, Theobald had made haste to suggest his favoured archdeacon, Thomas, as likely Chancellor.

Thomas arrives, a single man upon a single horse, at the palace gates. In full sight of the guards of the King, he gets down from his horse, and kneeling in the cobbled streets, makes obeisance to the skies.

He is alone once again, but free from the duties that the Archbishop's house imposed upon him. He feels as if he has discovered freedom for the first time. These courts, this world—perhaps, perhaps they might be his.

He enters into His Majesty's court. Nothing will ever be the same.

He had not thought to like this Henry, this new, hungry King. They are worlds apart in almost all things. Henry is twenty-two, and Thomas thirty-five; Henry is worldly, the flower of English perfection; Thomas is an echo of that greater glory. He is nervous with the court routines; nervous with its many ladies and lords. Henry is at home among the wolves.

So he is surprised the first time that Henry requests a private audience with his new Chancellor. Worried, even. He has heard, for months now, the word "commoner," whispered at his back when people are sober, and more openly when they are not. He is not at home in the courts, any more than he was at home in the politics of the Church.

It is with misgivings that he makes haste to respond to the summons of the King. He wonders who will laugh at him in the audience chamber, as he tries to measure and calm his step. Who will be promoted to his office in his place?

But when he arrives at the audience chamber, it is empty. A page waits to announce his entrance to the King before disappearing into the wide, cold halls. Henry stands by the fireplace that takes up the entirety of a wall. He holds a goblet in his hand; he wears no crown. He does not look up as Thomas enters.

Quietly, Thomas walks over to Henry. He begins to kneel at his feet, and Henry sets the goblet down upon the mantel.

"Don't."

Half-crouched, Thomas freezes. "Your Majesty?"

"I did not call you here to have you scrape and bow," the King replies. "Stand up, Thomas. Look at me." Thomas obeys so quickly that Henry's lips quirk up in a smile; it is an odd one.

"Thomas Beket."

Thomas of London feels his knees weaken, but he nods.

"A hungry commoner. My royal Chancellor."

He nods again; his cheeks are reddening.

But then the jest stops, the King's face changes. "I know what it's like to be on the outside; to be hungry. There is

not another noble at this court that understands that so
well as you or I. I am not hungry any longer, but I am
not secure. I need one man, at least one man, that I can
trust. Will you be that man?" Before Thomas can reply,
Henry continues, his young voice deep and measured.
"Everything I have, you will have in my name. Everything
I know, you will know. Your enemies will be my enemies—and my enemies will be yours—if you assent." His
eyes are wide and unblinking as he meets Thomas's.

This time, when Thomas kneels, Henry does not demur. "Yes, Your Majesty. Yes, Henry."

Henry's laugh fills the hall with joy.

And no one, from that day on, calls Thomas a commoner where any ears friendly to the King can hear it.

Herbert settles one knee against the grass, and Thomas
forgets about the gates of Henry's grand estate. He shakes
himself, bitterly, against the chill in the air, and draws
his robes of office tight.

"It is almost time," Herbert says softly.

"Yes." Thomas does not look at his aide; he does not
need to. During the long years of exile, Herbert has been
one of the few constant and loyal voices. And at this
moment, God forgive him, Thomas hates that voice.

"Holiness," another voice says; John of Salisbury kneels
directly before him, coming like a sudden cloud before
Thomas can avert his eyes. "The book."

With shaking hands, Thomas takes the well-worn,
much-honoured Bible from the hands of his follower.
"That will be all, John."

John clears his throat and looks nervously at the grass
blades his knees are crushing. "The Queen is on the field,"
he whispers.

"Do you believe in God?" Henry, well satisfied after the
morning's hunt, leans back against the cushions that are
scattered before the burning fire. He is unattended, save
for Thomas, and that is agreeable to both of them. Before

Thomas can answer, Henry's loud and booming laughter
echoes against the heavy stone walls of his chateau.
"Thomas, you are still too easily scandalized! You are the
talk of the court." His laughter dies into the crackle of
broken wood. "But do you believe in God?"

Henry is never easily put off; Thomas, Chancellor and
royal favourite, knows this well. "Yes," he says, because
only truth will serve. "I do. But more, I believe in, and
serve, my King—the King of all England."

"Flattery?" Henry laughs again; wine trickles down the
corners of his lips as he drains his goblet and sets it
rolling across the floor. "Then let me tell you, Thomas,
I've a woman in my sights that only Divinity could explain."

Thomas smiles; this is the Henry the whole court
knows, and loves half in spite of itself. "Queen Eleanor
has barely forgiven the last."

"What is one more mistress? She'll accept it; what
choice has she?"

Thomas sees the standard of the Aquitaine. The
standard-bearer is a proud young boy, surrounded as he
is by pavilions and the ladies of the Queen's court. Even
at this distance, Eleanor is unmistakable; her deep, bur-
gundy gown trails artfully down her legs and across the
dais she occupies; her hair, swept up in jewelled combs,
catches sunlight, adorning the harsh, proud profile of her
face. He hears, or thinks he hears, her open laughter as
the strains of a lute take wing. At her right hand sits her
son and heir to the Aquitaine.

*Was it worth it, Henry? Was Rosamund worth Eleanor's
anger?* He has no way of asking the King of England, but
he wonders it nonetheless.

"Holiness?"

"Not now, John. Give me a moment's repose." There;
his voice is edged and temperamental. John, recognizing
this, retreats anxiously. But not before quietly pointing
out the standard of the King of France. Louis, Capetian

monarch, crosses the green, preceded by his most trusted advisors, and the bearer of his standard. He bows to Eleanor, and Eleanor, with great and elaborate grace, makes haste to curtsey. The King holds out his hands, and she places hers within them; words are exchanged, old allegiances reaffirmed.

Thomas knows that Eleanor intends her favourite son, Richard, to rule England at the end of this day. And Richard, youthful and brash, is very much his father's son; it is ironic that he, so like to the Angevin dynasty and not the Poitou, should be the one to find Eleanor's favour.

Richard has his father's skill at arms.

He has always loved Henry—but never so much as now: in the battle for Toulouse. Henry's wild, reckless grace, Henry's skill at arms, Henry's ability as a tactician—they fly in the face of sanity and order. On horseback, or on the field, unhorsed, Henry is a man to be reckoned with; a leader to follow.

And Thomas is his most trusted servant.

"What are you thinking, Thomas?"

Pensive, Thomas says nothing. Henry asks again, and Thomas shakes his head, gesturing with a ring-heavy hand.

"Come, tell me. I command it."

It is a jest between them, this lowering of the voice, this severity of chosen word. Thomas sighs. "I learned the use of the sword once. When I was young."

Henry raises a brow. "You've never mentioned it."

"There was hardly any cause. I never thought I would be on the fields of battle."

"Were you any good?"

Thomas shrugs, surprised at how the memories hurt him. "I was, once."

"Why did you stop?"

He does not know how to answer. Henry, however, will have an answer, and at length. Thomas says only this: "My father could not afford the lessons." It is a lie.

In response, Henry spits to the side. Then he smiles his dangerous smile, and his eyes narrow into blades. "You've a penchant for war, then? Make war for me."

"W-war?"

"Yes, w-war." Henry laughs. Thomas loves that laugh; it defies the very heavens with its depth and its savagery. "I have duties of import to attend to—and I would trust no other but you with this task. Take this province. In my name."

Thomas is silent.

"I know you've watched me; God knows you've advised me well in my course of war, though you claim to know nothing. Lead my men, Thomas, I trust you. You will not fail me."

Thomas the Chancellor bows low, and grasping Henry's hand tightly, kisses him. "No, lord. I will not fail."

Nor did he. But he never explained all of the truth to the Angevin monarch. He is weary; his hands shake; the Bible is suddenly too heavy, too weighty for him. He sets it down gently on the grass, and bows his head over clasped hands.

Earthly glory is not for you, Thomas. Shun it.

He had not listened.

He listens now.

He has always feared God.

As a child, even the angels were a terror; a dream of gilded death, a threat that only day absolved him from. But like each man in the night he would turn to sleep, and from sleep to the dreams of the will of God. Thomas Beket—for that is who he was as a youth, even if that child is long dead—met with angels in the shadows of sleep.

The angels were not kind. Cold and severe, like his father, they came with their golden keys, their painful words.

These we offer you, Thomas Beket. Only take them, and you will serve God, and by God be called to the Heavens.

He mouths the words of his refusal, silent now, where once he might have shouted them aloud. Although, in this memory, he is only a child, he knows the shape and feel of sin: It is the width and breadth of the world that he longs for. The angels are not happy, but they nod.

You will be God's warrior; you cannot turn from it. We will wait until you see the truth of this.

But he yearned for a life of adventure—every child's dream. He took his lessons with the sword far better than those with the book; his Latin, poor, was poorly loved. Only when Gilbert Beket sought the Church for his son did Thomas relent.

"A man of the cloth," his father had explained in cold and measured tones, "does not wield a weapon of the world."

By God's will, he set aside the sword, but by Henry's he had lifted it again. The sword is fasted to his hand; his hands are red, although only he can see it; he will never again be able to lay the weapon to rest.

"Henry," the King says to his oldest, and his dearest, son. "Tend to the ladies; Thomas and I must speak."

Henry the Prince nods to Henry the King, and smiles shyly at Thomas the Chancellor—at the man who has become almost a father.

Thomas bows to his liege-lord, but only his body rises from the posture when the time for its end has come. His eyes seek the grooved, dark wood of the floor at Henry's feet.

"Theobald is dead," Henry says, coming, as always, to the point.

Thomas feels his throat tighten; he has no heart for Henry's news. But he knows what it will be. To stave it off for a few minutes longer, he offers his monarch some wine. They are alone in the room; not even a servant remains to pour it.

Henry takes the cup firmly in hand, and smiles at his nervous chancellor.

"Henry," Thomas says, still looking away, this time at the inlaid surface of his fine study table, "I know what you come for. Do not ask this of me."

Henry shifts position, and after a moment takes one of the large empty chairs that grace Thomas's library. "I've no choice. The Church, as you know, has troubled us much; Stephen was too weak to handle it properly. You have served me well, Thomas; continue to serve me. I have already nominated you to the Archbishopric of Canterbury; the royal letters have been sent, summoning the bishops." He sets the drink aside, as he does when he speaks in earnest. "Thomas, I command you. Look at me."

Thomas does.

Henry starts in his chair. "In the name of God, Thomas." His voice is a whisper; he stares at his Chancellor as if he has never seen his face before. They study each other, the monarch and his servant, as if already sundered. Then Henry's lips lift in a self-deprecating smile; the moment is lost. "Thomas, you will be Archbishop. I need you."

"Do not ask this of me, my lord. I will serve you faithfully, loyally, as Chancellor. But this other office—it is not for me. Please."

"Nonsense."

Thomas has never been able to say no to Henry; not even in this. But they argue for another two hours before he at last acquiesces. And when Henry finally leaves, Thomas prays to a God that he knows will not listen.

Only upon June the 3rd, in the year of 1162, do the prayers die.

Thomas has been consecrated to God; the keys of the heavenly kingdom are in his hand. He takes his vows at an altar he can barely see through his tears; he hears the strain of the choir at his back; sees the proud face of the man who will never again be his master.

You shall not bow down to them or serve them; for I the Lord your God am a jealous God.

"Come, Thomas; the orders of battle will be given within the hour."

There is no way to escape those words; only God Himself has a greater power or a greater authority. Thomas, retrieving the Bible, takes to his feet. Waiting, with attendant cardinals and priests, stands Alexander, the Pope—the very voice of God. Alexander was, in youth, a handsome man; he has lost that bloom, but he has gained a measure of power that only experience grants. This he wields with great cunning; it has served him well in the past, and serves him well now, although the antipope, and the schismatics of the German Empire, have been laid to rest for almost a decade.

Thomas bows low before Alexander, taking and kissing the signatory ring upon his finger. Alexander gives him the words of blessing and bids him rise.

"You proved true to the honour of God," Alexander says. "And on this day, the fruit of that struggle will be made known. Come; the blessing of the battle is yours to give, as my legate."

"The honour," Thomas says, in a perfectly composed voice, "is yours, Holiness. When I escaped England, you granted me sanctuary in my exile, and upheld my case against the English bishops."

"Yet the perfidity of this King would never have been so clear without your grace. Come, Thomas. I insist."

John of Salisbury and Herbert of Bosham come to take their place at Thomas's right and left hand, urging him onward in genuine pride. Thomas cannot argue with the Pope. Very quietly, he makes his way down the slope of the grassy knoll, towards the pavilions meant for royalty.

But there is only one monarch for Thomas. Why is the sun so bright?

* * *

He does not want to remember when it first started to go wrong; but although surrounded, Thomas is always alone, and memories plague him.

He goes to Henry; it is dark, he is alone.

"Thomas?"

Thomas longs to laugh or smile, to join his former King at the tables. He does neither. "Your Majesty." Stiffly said.

"Have you come about the coronation of Prince Henry?"

"No." Thomas takes a step into the small room. "I have come to resign my position as Royal Chancellor." Each word is hard and cold; Thomas can barely speak at all.

"*What?*"

It is the only time, in their long years of friendship, that Thomas has ever managed to surprise his friend. "I can no longer continue in that post, Your Majesty." He kneels; his voice drops. "No man can serve two masters."

Does Henry hear the break in the words? Does he realize what it costs to say them? Thomas looks up, and sees in Henry's face a sudden, bleak loneliness. Bitterly, the King of all England says, "You've forgotten what it's like to be hungry."

"No," Thomas whispers softly, meeting his lord's eyes fully for perhaps the last time. "And I will never be free of hunger again." He loves this man, and he cannot love him. The price would be too high. "I will retire all offices and lands that were granted to me during my tenure as Chancellor, Majesty."

Henry's face stiffens; they speak business, like any two men who are powerful and solitary.

He knows Henry's pride and Henry's temper. He knows Henry's passions and pleasures, and knows his dealings with traitors. He has been hurt, and even angered, by the Angevin monarch. He has been humiliated, as Henry has sought to force what can no longer be offered: obedience to the King of England at the expense of the Church. But that part of him that knows this pain belongs more properly to another life.

He has never been able to escape its web.

It was hardest to make that first break; he hoped it would end with that. It did not. Henry in anger was his finest enemy and God's worthiest foe. Ashamed at even the thought, Thomas bows his head and silently pleads for forgiveness. Divine Grace.

Ah, there. Eleanor has risen to greet him. He is hardly aware of the ground that has passed beneath his feet.

"Thomas," the Queen of England says. "You look well."

"And you, most gracious Majesty." He bows in response to her curtsey, feeling her eyes upon him.

"Will God smile upon our undertakings this day?"

"If that is His will." He has never liked Eleanor, and in her icy eyes he sees the predator and the mother combined. She has never loved Henry, he thinks. Or perhaps, just as he, she did not love him wisely. He shakes his head.

Louis, the King of all France, comes forward then. "Will you inspect our troops?"

The Pope nods, and after a moment, Thomas also gives his assent.

"Holiness," the King of France says, and suddenly kneels in the sight of noble witnesses, "after this day, your exile is ended; you will return to your see with the blessings of God. The Archbishop," he cries, raising his voice as he stands, "will return to Canterbury!"

There is cheering.

Thomas has no stomach for battle anymore. Only in the shadow of Henry's glory did battle have any romance, any meaning.

He has spent these six years and more attempting to avoid this war, this place. He has written to Henry, as Archbishop, as Papal Legate, and as former friend. He has pleaded, cajoled, even threatened. Henry will not be moved. He must see the Church in its proper place— subordinate to the King of England.

And Thomas must see the Church beholden to none. He knows that Louis will gain all of the territories of

France and Normandy that Henry holds now. Knows that
Eleanor will keep for herself the Aquitaine, and for her
son, England. He knows that the Pope will declare this
an act of the glory of God, and take from this battle an
example and a heightening of prestige.

Men stand, in row upon shining row. Archers wait behind, and to the side, the nobility of France is mounted.
Their huge horses are restive; they snap and bridle at
each other as the cavalry officers play their games for the
best position.

The army bears the standard of France and the standard of the Holy Roman Empire. They bear the cross as
well. Solemn, almost infectious in their eagerness, they
await their final orders.

Thomas nods as he walks past them; they are already
forgotten. There, ten feet ahead, the ground tilts upward
just a little. He cannot help it; before he knows it, he
stands upon the gentle slope, looking down the valley.
Flying in the wind, and in the face of the Pope and the
King of France to whom he owes a nominal allegiance,
the Angevin standard can barely be seen. Thomas searches
for a glimpse of Henry.

Then, unrewarded, he turns away. The business of God
is at hand.

He has always feared God, but he has served what he
has feared for so long now, he does not imagine he could
live without that fear. Everything that he gave to Henry,
he gives to God. Even this gathering of the united duchies
and baronies of France, alongside the papal delegation, is
his work. It was Thomas who knew how best to approach
Eleanor; Thomas who knew when the timing was right
to seek the aid of the King of France. And it was Thomas
who knew best the mind of Henry, and knew how to take
advantage of the weaknesses in his strategies.

All of this, he has done for God. The sun is upon the
tufts of the eastern trees; the time has come. Thomas
opens his holy book and begins to read in the presence

of his allies. Then he stops as he sees the passage the book has opened to. It was not the one he selected.

It is Genesis.

His eyes cloud; it must be age. He looks up, and curses the sun quietly. There should be storms, he thinks; gouts of fire, earthquakes—some natural sign to bear God's witness to the bitter events of the day. Clear and cold, the sky gazes down upon him, an unlidded, inescapable eye.

Thomas struggles with the Bible, and in the end it is John of Salisbury who opens it to its marked place, and holds it aloft so that Thomas might read it without shaking the holy words.

God, Thomas whispers, as his eyes blur, *do You not yet know that I fear You? I have withheld nothing. Have I not yet passed Your testing? Give me a sign, Lord. Give me Your blessing.*

But although he listens, heart and breath suspended, God speaks no words to him; God does not grant him Abraham's peace.

He has always loved Henry.

Crying now, his voice so weak it is barely audible, Thomas, Archbishop of Canterbury and Holy Legate of the Apostolic See, gives his blessing to the battle.

Ever long for the day of the old pulp magazines? You know the ones—where Operator Five or Secret Agent X was always matching brawn and wits against the Nazis, where Eva Braun was Hitler's answer to Mata Hari, where the settings moved from palaces to trains to abandoned warehouses, and where the Good Guys somehow managed to win in the end?

Well, Lea Hernandez, well-known graphic novel scriptor and artist, remembers those days well, and comes up with the perfect tough-guy spy: Al Einstein—Nazi Smasher.

Al Einstein—Nazi Smasher!
by Lea Hernandez

(*From the pages of the December 1947 issue of* Spicy Jewish Secret Agent Stories)

The name's Einstein. Al Einstein.

My evening began as most of my evenings did during that blood-soaked time when Schicklgruber and his Nazi minions still held my beloved Europe captive: playing quartets with Queen Elizabeth and two of her ladies-in-waiting. I wasn't merely playing music, but also playing *at* being a glamorous dilettante who, finding his venues limited by the advance of Nazis over Europe, chose the social orbit of the crowned heads and dignitaries of the Allies.

Though I loved to tinker with mathematics, I had been a successful and popular violinist and pianist before the war. I played all over Europe, entertaining not only royalty but the common folk as well. I delighted in the thrill of the music, and I can't say that I minded the adulation of my audiences—especially the ladies. Hardly a performance would pass without a hotel key, calling card, or scrap of paper marked with a hastily scribbled address being pressed into my hand or delivered backstage.

But now I had a far different role: I was an agent for the underground. The reason for my close company with royalty was not social climbing, but, rather, to act as a liaison between the underground and the countries united against the Axis. This very night I would be undertaking what could possibly be, I knew, my last mission—even if I was successful. Our agents, at the expense of the lives of many good people, had finally discovered the location of Schiklgruber's V-2 launch site. In a short while, I would be meeting another agent, and together we would be traveling by train and motorcar to Dresden, Germany, there to destroy Schicklgruber's awful V-2 rockets and release Europe from his fiendish clutches!

One of the ladies-in-waiting caught my eye as she looked up from the piano. We were nearing the end of Mozart's Quartet in B-flat Minor, as well as the end of the evening. Our eyes remained locked as we led each other through the gentle climax of the piece. I sighed inwardly. She was a knockout, but tonight I was in the service of the Allies; we would both have to settle for mere musical partnering until I returned from Germany. I smiled and shook my head ever so slightly, and she looked away, obviously disappointed.

As the last notes wafted away, the Queen stood and her ladies obediently followed suit. She motioned them out of the chamber, and turned to me as the doors closed.

"Dearest Albert," she said as she gathered my hands into her own, "His Highness and I wish you the best of luck." She paused. When she could speak again, her voice was choked with barely checked emotion. "Oh, do be careful!" she whispered. "May God will that you return to us!" She turned away quickly and left the room with as much speed as her royal dignity would allow.

It was raining by the time I reached the club where I was to meet the agent who would lead me to Dresden. Our rendezvous point was unmarked, nondescript, a place where, before the war, the wealthy and famous met to share each other's company without the inconvenience of rubbing elbows with people they considered their inferiors. It served the same purpose now, but without the grandeur of those prewar years. The moneyed and the celebrities still came, to remind themselves of better days. I stepped into the foyer. At one time, I would have been greeted with a lovely woman to whisk away my coat, and a waiter with a tray of drinks. Tonight, I checked my coat myself and found my own seat in a darker corner of the club.

A waiter appeared promptly to take my drink order (service was abbreviated, but still excellent). After my drink arrived, I sipped it slowly, meditating on the task ahead.

"Mr. Einstein?" a woman's voice said.

"Nothing else, thank you," I replied without looking up. Then I recalled that the club had not had waitresses for several years. "Excuse me. I'm expecting some—"

"You are expecting *me*," she said softly.

I looked at the owner of the voice for the first time. She was wearing a dress both black and simple, and yet she looked like an American movie star. She gazed at me through the mist of the black veil that covered her face and clouded her eyes.

"I am Eva Braun," she said, extending a black-gloved hand. I stood hastily to receive her, and I have to admit I couldn't take my eyes off her. Her wrap was just slipping off of one white shoulder, a shoulder I suddenly wanted to kiss.

"Call me Al," I said.

She smiled ever so slightly as she slipped into the chair opposite my own. I followed her lead. As I sat, she opened her purse and pulled out an envelope, which she pushed across the table to me.

"This is your train ticket. I will contact you again when we are under way to Dresden. There will be a motorcar waiting for us at the train station. Do you have any questions?"

"I wasn't expecting a woman," I said. "Especially one like . . ."

"Now is not the time, Al." I could see a smile tugging at the corner of her mouth, but the tone of her voice was low and serious. "We will go over our plans when I meet you on the train. Farewell." She swept out of the club, never once looking back. I finished my drink, collected my coat, and stepped out into the rain, towards what promised to be one of the most dangerous nights of my life.

As it turns out, the ticket Eva had given me was for a rather comfortable berth on the train. I had the curtains open, watching treetops race with the half-moon. I allowed myself some time to think of what I might do if I survived the night. When I was on missions for the underground that I knew were particularly dangerous, I would find myself missing my touring days rather keenly. But, I would always remind myself sternly, I was in the service of a greater cause.

The train rattled on to Dresden. I took my violin (I always brought it with me) from its case and began playing it softly, so as not to disturb the other passengers.

I had been playing for only a short time when I heard a knock at the door. I went to the door, violin in hand, ready to apologize to the porter if there had been any complaints.

It wasn't the porter. It was Eva. She was attired in a cream-colored dressing gown that was not exactly a mod-

est cut; hell, it was almost too low to be *immodest.* I tore
my eyes away from her bosom and stepped back to allow
her to enter the room.

"Ah. You brought your violin."

"I find that playing calms my mind when I have difficult work ahead of me."

"Playing at what?" She smiled. Not the predatory smile
of a vamp, but the teasing smile of an old friend.

I decided to ignore her remark for the time being. "We
are supposed to go over our plans for disarming or redi-
recting the V-2 rockets, aren't we?"

"We have time. Would you play for me?"

I struck a romantic pose, designed to make her laugh,
which it did, and began to play, softly, my favorite Mozart.

The notes hovered about the room like fireflies, soared
like swallows. I lost myself in the playing, and Eva had
to repeat herself several times before I heard her.

"Al!"

"Yes?" I looked at her.

"I'm frightened, Al!" She stood and pressed herself to
me, her hands twisting in the cloth of my shirtfront. "We
may die tonight . . ." she breathed. "I do not want—"

She was trembling. I laid the violin down, to put my
arms around her. I realized as I touched it that her dressing gown was silk. I had no time to question how Eva
had come by a silk garment during a time when others
were giving up the precious stuff for parachutes. She
pulled my face to hers, and all questions disappeared.

When I woke up, Eva was gone. According to my watch,
only a short time had passed since our lovemaking, and—
blast it! We had yet to review our plans for eliminating
the V-2 rockets. I cursed my carelessness as I dressed.
The train wasn't a large one, so I knew I'd soon find her.
I attributed my uneasiness to my anger at faltering.

But the sense that something was very wrong increased
as I entered the last passenger car, and there was no Eva.

Near the end of the car, however, a door opened, and she stepped out, fully dressed. She was more surprised to see me than I liked.

I grabbed her arm. "What the hell is going on here?" I snarled.

"I don't know what you're talking about! You're hurting me!" She tried to twist away, but I held fast.

"I want to know what—" I saw Eva look over my shoulder, and I tried to turn, but it was too late. I heard the distant crack of my own head as someone behind me hit me with a sap. Stars exploded, black and painful, and I sank to the floor of the train, senseless.

I awoke in darkness, with cloth pressed against my ears, and a terrible ache in my arms and wrists. I felt as if my arms were being wrenched from their very sockets. To relieve the agony, I tried to move them and found out that I couldn't. I realized that the cloth pressed against my ears was my shirt sleeves, and that my wrists ached because I was tied up and dangling by my hands! My head throbbed where the sap had landed, and my back was pressed against something cold, smooth and unyielding.

Suddenly lights blazed. I squinted against the glare, trying to make out my surroundings. The first thing I could tell, from turning my head to the left and the right, was that I was on a launching pad, and that on either side of me were two V-2 rockets. The second thing was that I was hanging about five feet from the ground from a fifth V-2. Looking forward, I was able to make out six figures, standing in front of the bunker from which the V-2 rockets were controlled. The shock of the light subsided, and I could make out a person in a coat, head down, and four tall men in the uniforms bearing the twisted cross. The Nazis had holstered Lugers, and were carrying machine guns. The last was a man, impressive in neither stature nor carriage, but one I knew well.

Adolf Schicklgruber.

"So you are awake, Einstein," he called cheerfully. "I am flattered that someone of your prestige and notoriety would choose to visit me." He had the joviality of a person in a decidedly superior position.

"What is this, Schicklgruber?" I demanded. "Aren't you brave enough to shoot me? Give the cheap theatrics a rest."

Schicklgruber's smile faltered, as he tried to control his famously short temper. "My dear Albert! I merely wish to return you to England. My lovely V-2 will reduce England to rubble—and you," he feigned sadness, "I do not think you will survive the trip. Ah, well."

"Launch all your rockets, you foul fiend! Try to grind Europe beneath your heel! Europe will prevail, even if I perish!"

"Ha ha ha! I win tonight, Ein*schwein*!"

"A petty taunt from a *minuscule* man!"

Schicklgruber turned beet-red. So, I had drawn blood! I had heard rumors of his stunted manhood, and his reaction proved me correct. Through my pain, I laughed.

"You will not be laughing when you see who is with me!" he raged. He turned to the person whose face I could not see, and led him forward.

Suddenly the person lifted *her* head, and I could see it was Eva Braun.

"I am to marry Eva tomorrow. If you were to live, perhaps Eva could compare us. She would then be able to tell you that I am not so small. Eh, Eva?"

"Of course, Adolf," she purred, leaning her head into his shoulder.

"My Eva led you straight to us, Einstein," crowed Schicklgruber, his ego bolstered by Eva's obvious affection. "And now I will finally wipe England from the map and eliminate the underground's greatest agent in one fell swoop!" He paused, his eyes glowing like hot coals. "And after England, the countries that do not bend their knee to me will also feel the fire of my rockets!" He continued to spout his nonsense, gleefully naming off locations of other V-2 sites and their targets.

This careless discourse of facts so valuable to the underground should have interested me, but I was focused, instead, on Eva's betrayal. Her alliance with Schicklgruber explained her silk gown, for example, but it did not explain her fear, or her passion—both of which had seemed very real.

I could think no more. The pain in my head and arms had become dizzying. There didn't seem to be any way out of the trap I had so foolishly allowed myself to be led into.

Then, suddenly, the most amazing thing happened. Eva moved away from Schicklgruber, and two of the Nazis stepped back quickly. Eva reached into her coat pocket and whipped out a Luger, which she leveled at Schicklgruber. The two Nazis that had separated themselves from the group raised their machine guns. Schicklgruber sputtered, staring in disbelief.

"Thank you, Adolf," Eva said sweetly, then shot him through the heart. Before his body hit the ground, the first two Nazis had machine-gunned the second two.

"Good girl, Eva!" I grated. "Now cut me down!"

But it wasn't to be that easy. More Nazis, attracted by the sound of gunfire, came boiling out of the bunker. Eva picked up a machine gun from one of the fallen guards and mowed them down as they came out.

"Hans!" she commanded. "Inside to see if there are any more! Fritz, help me free Al!"

The two of them ran across the pad to the rocket. Once there, Eva tossed away her coat and nimbly climbed the gantry, while Fritz waited below. When she was near my hands, she pulled a knife from a sheath tucked into her garter. I couldn't think of a place I'd rather be if I was a knife.

"Fritz, get ready to catch him!"

She sawed away at the rope that held my hands. The strands parted quickly, and I fell into Fritz's arms.

"Can you walk?" he asked me.

"Yeah, I think so," I said, and he set me on my feet.

Eva had climbed down, and began cutting away the rope on my wrists. "Will you be able to disarm the rockets, Al?"

My hands were numb, and my wrists raw, but as the rope was removed I began working the fingers and wrists, and finally feeling returned to them.

"Let me give it a try," I said grimly.

"Good," she said. "Fritz and Hans are my brothers. We have been working in the underground, just like you. They joined Schicklgruber's army, and when the underground discovered he was looking for a wife, I made a play for him, hoping he would take me into his confidence, and reveal the sites of the V-2." She paused. "When Schicklgruber found out that the underground was sending you to disarm the V-2 rockets, he had me 'infiltrate'"—here she laughed—"the underground. I was to seduce you and lead you to him—which was precisely my intention all along." Suddenly she blushed. "The part about leading you to him, that is."

"I like the other part better," I said.

She ignored my remark. "I was playing out Schicklgruber's script in the club and on the train. I had no idea you would be the one to goad Schicklgruber into revealing his V-2 plans!"

I stopped, and turned to her. I could feel Fritz lurking behind me. Eva waved him away.

"Was it all pretend, all play?" I asked, searching her eyes.

She had been looking directly at me, now she lowered her lashes. "No," she replied, a now-familiar smile crossing her lips. "It was not."

Fritz coughed and discreetly turned his back. The sun was just beginning to touch the horizon as I gathered Eva into my arms and covered her lips with a passionate kiss.

"Now, my dear," I said as I led her to the bunker, "I shall disarm Schicklgruber's rockets, and then I think I owe myself a little vacation." I looked at her. "Perhaps you'd like to join me on it?"

"I'd like that very much, Albert," she said.

"Call me Al."

A few weeks after Jack Nimersheim had handed in his Mother Teresa story, he called me on the phone and told me he had another idea for the anthology, and if I liked it better I could substitute it.

If you can come up with a more unlikely warrior than Mother Teresa, I'll buy both stories, I told him.

He did.

And so here is the story of Stephen Hawking, Warrior . . .

Mind Over Matter
by Jack Nimersheim

A stranger might pity him. He certainly cut a poignant figure, his all but useless body folded unnaturally into a high-tech wheelchair. The best of the brightest humanity had to offer, held hostage in a rolling prison.

I first met Stephen Hawking in 1989. We were an odd pairing, indeed.

I owned nothing but an old, portable typewriter and the clothes on my back. He had everything a brilliant physicist could ask for. I was a struggling writer trying to complete the first free-lance assignment I'd landed in over six months. His landmark book, *A Brief History of Time: From the Big Bang to Black Holes*, had already spent a year on the *New York Times* best-seller list. I never knew where my next paycheck was coming from. He held Sir Isaac

Newton's chair as Lucasian Professor of Mathematics at Cambridge University.

But professional accomplishments, or a lack thereof, only told half the tale. Contradictions also marked our personal lives. I ran eight miles each morning, rain or shine. Over the years, I'd cut the time required for this daily regimen to slightly under an hour. It took Stephen almost as long just to get out of bed and dress for the day. Like most serious writers, I enjoyed my solitude. He was rarely alone. Not by choice, but by circumstance. Someone—a nurse or associate, sometimes both—attended him constantly. Stephen accepted their supervision with characteristic wit and warmth. It demanded no great genius, however, to recognize that he did not relish his dependence upon others. Who would?

Despite these differences, Stephen and I became fast friends. We filled several evenings following our initial meeting with quiet conversations and cordial debates. Our discussions embraced topics far beyond the scope of the short celebrity profile a well-known New York magazine had assigned me to write about him. I soaked up each idea and opinion he offered. I treasured every word translated into emotionless, electronic speech by the portable computer and voice synthesizer mounted inconspicuously beneath his wheelchair.

For more than a week I drank from this fount of knowledge and wisdom, savoring every drop. And then I departed. As did most people who met Stephen Hawking, however, I carried away a small part of this extraordinary man with me.

That should have been the end of my story. No doubt, it would have been, had an event that occurred almost a decade later not written a tragic epilogue to this brief moment in time.

Stephen and I kept in touch with one another, off and on, throughout the intervening years. Occasionally, our paths would cross at some scientific conference I'd been

assigned to cover. But this happened only infrequently.
To my surprise, however, Stephen tracked the forward
momentum of my career. Intermittently, he would tender
on-line congratulations for some accomplishment or another of mine. I never knew quite how to respond. I'd
sold a few articles and books; he had uncovered previously hidden secrets of the universe. Where was the par-
ity in that? And yet, Stephen always made me feel his
equal, as he did everyone.

Stephen's last note was waiting for me on the network
one evening when I signed on for the regular, Thursday
night writer's conference. The header revealed it to be a
broadcast message—that is, a single communiqué transmitted concurrently to multiple destinations. My copy had
been routed through an Internet gateway only moments
earlier.

I did not know who else he chose to share his final
thoughts with. In truth, I had no clear idea at the time
what Stephen was thinking about, as he composed the
message that scrolled across my display that fateful night:

> They're going to do it. The bastards are really go-
> ing to do it. Now I know how Einstein must have
> felt. Or Oppenheimer. Or Pauling. Or every scientist
> who's ever watched his theories transformed into a
> loathsome reality—every one except maybe Teller,
> that is.
>
> They took my ideas and twisted them. I should
> have realized they would. Albert. Robert. Linus. It
> happened to each of these, all better men than I.
> The eagle and the crown have banded together to
> destroy me. I offered them order. They wanted ord-
> nance. Using my own theories as ammunition, they
> have accomplished what ALS could not, these past
> thirty years.
>
> I know that few of you comprehend what I'm say-
> ing. Soon, however, you'll realize the gravity of the
> situation. (The gravity of the situation . . . any irony

contained in this statement was unintentional, I assure you.) I can offer no excuses, no apologies. It's far too late for that. There may have been a time when I could have stopped it somehow. Although I doubt it.

These things take on a life of their own, you know. Just like children do. They're conceived as theories, the ideas as zygote. They're nurtured within the sterile womb of incomprehensible equations scribbled on a blackboard or tapped into a computer keyboard. And when the theory is tested and proved, when the equations are solved, the results are born into the world. Once there, they become our mental progeny, but not our property. The intellectual child is father to the corporeal man.

Our children. What's to become of them? Where are you, Robert, Lucy, Timothy? Someplace safe, I pray.

And yet, even this solace is denied me. I once stated that religion is based on revelation, while science relies on observation. I went on to claim that, since I've never experienced the revelations that lie at the heart of the former, I had to rely on the latter. You can't pray to science. For sadly, the ends to which men use it all too often are obscene.

And so, I go gently and quietly into the night. My future resembles the crowning glory of my past, as I descend into the deep, black hole of death.

Stephen

I didn't sleep at all that night. Stephen's cryptic note unnerved me and, try as I might, I could not contact him to ask what was going on. It wasn't until early the next morning that I fully grasped the meaning of his missive. That's when Tripoli imploded. A half hour later, Baghdad blinked out of existence—followed in short order by Tehran and Beijing.

The President and Prime Minister held a joint press

conference at noon. Together, they announced the successful deployment of the Hawking Device, named in honor of the man whose revolutionary theories on singularities paved the way for the secret development of this equally revolutionary weapon. No, not a weapon, the President corrected himself, almost as an afterthought, but the ultimate instrument of global security and world peace.

Beth Meacham is arguably the most influential science fiction book editor of the past decade—which simply means that the field lost an excellent writer when she opted for the other side of the transom. In this story, we have a true alternate history, with a true alternate warrior: the mighty Tecumseh.

One by One
by Beth Meacham

Walks Softly slipped between the great, shaggy boles of two beech trees. The bright morning sun of a spring day shone slantwise through the forest, lighting the lower trunks of the ancient trees, and the faint, narrow path she followed. This woodland was part of the People's land, primeval forest tangled below with fruit-bearing brambles and spring-flowering herbs, sheltered under the great trees—oak and beech and elm towering up, with their great, strong arms making a canopy of leaves that, at noon, would cast the forest floor into the dusty gloom of a forbidden attic. But not now, not this morning. Now the sun's rays slid along the forest floor, and the wind made the pale green new leaves above sing a gentle song, and Walks Softly's Reeboks made hardly a sound on the cushion of last year's leaves.

The forest, and the People's lands, curled around the lands they had lost to the whites like a hand with a thousand fingers, stretching hundreds of miles; the lost lands were held within its compass, but were forever separated from it, and the People. She could smell the taint from the factory just over the rise behind her. The plant was on reservation land, forced on the People by the white government of the state, who wanted the factory, but didn't want to smell it. It was almost time for the morning shift, and the Rockwell factory was coming on-line. She glanced at her watch, a little worried. Soon. Soon. She was flung suddenly to the ground by the force of the explosion behind her. The great trees swayed and bent, and one white oak cracked and fell. A cloud of smoke and fire rose up over the ridge, and though she knew that the noise was loud, she could hear nothing at all. Walks Softly leaped back to her feet, and shouted her joy and triumph. She had struck a blow in the Two Hundred Years War between the Shawnee Alliance and the European invaders. She had set those bombs in the crucial points of the factory during the last hours of the night. Now the murderers knew that they would not be safe behind their fences and their hateful laws. Now they paid for the death of her little brother, mowed down by the ACT. Walks Softly was fifteen years old today, and the outlawed Alliance Warriors Society had a new member.

She shook her head to try to restore her hearing. It would come back soon. Then she looked again at her watch. Seven o'clock, and she had five miles to cover to get to school before eight. She was in the tenth grade in the county high school, and she didn't want to attract any unusual attention today. She smoothed her dark brown braids, picked up her day pack, and set off at a run.

Walks Softly's grandfather, John Walker, lived with his granddaughter in a tiny little house on the outskirts of Chillicothe. The old Shawnee village had grown over the centuries into a thriving town, with shops and markets, a glass and pottery factory, mills and a big new power plant. Chillicothe was still the center of the Shawnee Alliance, but a stranger would never have realized that this was red territory. All across the state, the People farmed and traded as they always had, lived in their towns and villages, and mostly kept the peace with their white neighbors. Mostly. John Walker was one who made the sign against evil when he had to go down the Scioto to the white towns along the Ohio. The bustling little city of Cincinnati wasn't a place to make one of the People feel at home.

But Walker stayed on the Reservation these days. His son had died three years before, lost to an Army Counter-Terrorist raid. The ACT claimed that Russell had set the bombs that blew up the bridge at Zanesville and killed a dozen whites. Walker hadn't been terribly surprised— Russell had been a strong warrior for the Alliance. But Russell had left two children behind. The boy, only twelve years old, had been killed two months ago, mowed down in an ACT raid. The young men had been in winter camp, preparing for manhood in the traditional way, fasting and praying, and learning the histories of the People, just as they had done for two hundred years, ever since the Prophet revealed the rites to unite all the warring tribes into one, against the invaders. And the ACT came in with their poison gas and automatic rifles to mow down two hundred unarmed twelve-year-olds. Thirty of the boys had died. ACT claimed it was a training camp for terrorists run by the Alliance Warriors Society. Now John Walker watched carefully over Russell's daughter, helping her to grow strong and brave, and never forget her father and brother, or the cause of freedom they had died for.

He turned on his TV set. It was about time for that Johnny Carson show. He had to admit Carson was a pretty funny guy for a white man. Ed Ames was a guest on the show tonight, doing his phony Indian shtick. Walker almost turned it off. He had no patience with reds who played the white man's game of patronization and stereotype. But on the other hand, Ames was rich and successful, and had financed a good school up by Sandusky, along the lake. His own nephew had been killed in the same ACT raid on the boy's society camp that had taken

Walker's grandson. Carson was introducing Ed now.
Walker sat straight up in his easy chair when he saw
Ames walk out onstage. The tall, hatchet-faced man was
dressed in genuinely traditional clothing, and his face was
painted with the lines of mourning and vengeance. He
stood and smiled genially when Carson quipped that he
looked like he'd been mugged by an abstract expression-
ist on the way to the studio.

The stage hands hauled out the traditional target. They
were going to do the tomahawk-throw routine again. John
Walker thought that he sure wouldn't let a man painted
that way throw hatchets at him. But Carson didn't know
any better. They went through the routine—Carson standing against the target, Ames throwing little razor-sharp
tomahawks at him, striking close but not too close. Just
like always. But then Johnny just had to make a joke.
"Now we know why you people lost the war," he said
with that little dry laugh. "It's because you never could
hit what you were aiming at." The audience cracked up.
Ed stood real still. Then he turned to the camera with his
eyes lit up like fire, staring right into the heart of white
America.

"The People are still fighting the war." His voice was
strong. "It has never ended for two hundred years, and it
will go on for another thousand years until the last invader is driven from our sacred land. The Prophet and
the Alliance he made are still alive, and we will never
forget what has been stolen from us."

Then he pulled the big hatchet out of his belt, whirled
and threw it at Johnny Carson. The blade went right through
Carson's skull, it was that sharp and heavy, and lodged in
the target. It happened so fast, and the director was so
shocked, that the image stayed on the air long enough to
burn into John Walker's memory: the talk show host hanging there twitching, blood pouring down his body.

The Shawnee town of Pataskala had been uneasy for
months. It was getting harder and harder to keep the peace

between red and white, even for those whose families had been living side by side for generations. The enormous state of Indiana, from the Ohio to the Mississippi to the Great Lakes, was carved up like a piece of lace; the treaty that the U.S. had finally signed with Tecumseh's grandson, just as the Civil War broke out, had guaranteed that the members of the Shawnee Alliance kept their traditional village sites and traditional farmlands. It also gave them "corridors of passage" between villages for communication and trade. Somehow, Molly Evans thought, she just knew that the men in Washington who had made that treaty hadn't been looking at the maps. There must have been hundreds of villages for the Reservation to be as big as it was, boxing the white settlers into only half the land in the state. You couldn't go from one white town to the next without crossing the Reservation. Her father said that the savages had taken advantage of the North's weakness during the Civil War to grab far more land than they had ever occupied before America was discovered. And when the ten-year-long war had finally ended, the exhausted victorious North had been in no shape to try to take back any of the land, especially with the Canadians funneling British money to the Alliance, and the Cherokee coming in from the devastated South to reinforce them.

Molly's family had been in the state for a long time—some of her ancestors had been killed in the Columbus massacre of 1798 along the Scioto River. She had been taken to the graveyard that was all that was left of that village, and shown the tombstones. She wondered, sometimes, why they kept living in a red town if her dad hated it so much, but when she asked him he laughed and said he didn't hate the reds; hadn't he married a girl who was part red? He just tried to be realistic about them, he said. He had no patience with people who romanticized the Alliance. Her mother pointed out that she was different—her red ancestors hadn't set themselves apart from the

white immigrants, but had taken them in and married
them. "Half the people in this state are related by blood
or marriage to the other half, Molly," she'd say. "I suppose
that's what makes things so tense. There's nothing worse
than a family fight."

But now even Mom was getting nervous. That factory
bombing near Chillicothe two days ago had been bad.
Usually the outlawed Alliance Warriors Society phoned
in a warning, making sure that people got out. This time
the whole start-up shift had died. And the Carson Atroc-
ity last night made it worse. If even a successful red like
Ames could turn into a crazy savage like that, for no
reason at all, no one was safe, anywhere. Molly's parents
were talking earnestly about selling the farm and moving
away from Indiana, or at least off the Reservation and into
the big white town of Newark.

"It's happened before, you know," Molly's best friend,
Jennifer Marlin, whispered. The girls were up in the hay-
loft above the cattle barn, just talking, and there was no
one else to hear. Molly bent close. If it was that secret, it
was worth listening to.

"What? What's happened before?"

"Reds going crazy on TV. There was a show once, called
The Lone Ranger. My cousin Steve, the one that's in the
army? Over in Newark? He showed me videos of it last
year."

"It was about reds?"

"Nah. It was about a guy in Texas who was kind of like
Batman. He wore a mask, and went around fighting crime.
He rode a beautiful white horse called Silver. This horse
must have been seventeen hands, and could do some
amazing stunts." Jennifer loved horses more than boys.
Molly could see the story slipping away.

"Jen! What's that got to do with it?"

"Oh, nothing. But see, the Ranger went around with a
red, called him a 'faithful Indian companion'—I remember
that 'cause Steve played the line over and over, play, reverse, play, reverse, play . . . made me nuts. Anyway, the

guy they had playing the red really was red, and one day he just went berserk on the set and started shooting people. He killed all the actors and the cameramen, and then he shot himself."

"Wow."

"Yeah. Nobody knows why. He just went crazy, I guess."

"Did he kill the horse?"

"Grandfather." Walks Softly had come in quietly and stood in front of the old man.

John Walker looked up at her and smiled a little. "Granddaughter."

She sighed, and sat on the floor in front of him. This wasn't going to be easy.

"Grandfather, school will be over for the year in less than a month."

He didn't say anything, just looked at her the way he did when he knew she wanted something and wasn't going to make it easy.

"I would like to take a vacation, just a few weeks, before I look for a job this summer."

"Vacations are for rich people," he said. We can't afford such a thing, he meant.

"I don't mean a trip like white people take. It's more like a . . . a retreat." This wasn't coming out right. She sounded defensive.

John Walker leveled a fierce eye on her. "Where do you want to go, and who do you want to go with?"

She'd blown it. She'd have to think fast now.

"Some of the kids in school—"

"Red kids or white kids?" her grandfather asked.

"People, Grampa. You think I'd want to go away with white kids?" She was scandalized.

"Your best friend in grade school was that white girl who moved to Pataskala. You two got along real well." Walks Softly was silent. She hadn't thought of Jenny for years. They'd been like sisters till just before Jenny moved away. But it all ended the day that Jenny's mother phoned,

the day before Jenny's ninth birthday party, to tell Walks
Softly that she was sorry, but she just couldn't come to
the party. Jenny's grandparents would be there, and some
of Jenny's friends from church, and she was sure that
Walks Softly wouldn't want to embarrass Jenny by being
there. She hadn't told her father about the call. She had
been afraid that he'd go there and make a big scene and
make it even worse. It occurred to her that if she had told
her father, something real unpleasant might have happened at that party, but back then she hadn't known he
was an Alliance Warrior. "Granddaughter?" The old man
had leaned forward. She must have been thinking too
long.

"Sorry. I haven't thought of Jenny for years." She flashed
a smile up at him, false as the masks that hung from the
rafters in the Medicine Society lodge. Her grandfather
made a funny noise.

"No, a bunch of us want to go upriver, and over toward
Newark for a summer camp. We want to look at the
Mounds." He should like that, she thought. John Walker
was big on ancient history—he'd made her learn all the
names of all the tribes that made up the Shawnee Alliance, their leaders and their territories. She could still
chant them all, if asked.

"The People who built these mounds are a long time
gone." His voice sounded far away. She smiled a genuine
smile, which faded as he continued, "Granddaughter, I
think there's more to this than a history trip."

"Oh, Grampa! We just want to get away into the woods
for a little while. It's summer," she said, "and Sam Miller
is going too." Hoping he'd take that for an explanation.

"Be careful, child," was all he answered, finally, but she
knew she had permission.

Walker stared at his granddaughter. He was proud of
her. She was doing well in school, she didn't run around
with boys like half her friends did, she didn't drink or
take drugs. His friends told him that there was a good

chance she'd get a scholarship to Indiana University in Chicago, the state capital. That would be something, to have his granddaughter go to school in a big white city with half a million other people in it. But she was still grieving for her brother, and she was up to something with this summer camp stuff. She was fifteen now, a young woman, and maybe she did just want to go off with a boy. But on the other hand, Sam Miller's uncle was sachem of the Warriors Society this year. And they'd lost a lot of young men to ACT's guns.

"Be careful, child," was all he could bring himself to say. He would discover the truth in time, and meanwhile the Alliance Warriors Society valued discretion.

Across the Canadian border, near the city of Detroit, Ontario, there was a monument to Tecumseh, Hero of the Thames. It had been erected, the plaque said, in 1850, by a Grateful Population. The great bronze statue of the General stood larger than life on a base of native stone. His feet were planted squarely, in their high boots. His uniform buttons were polished to a higher sheen than the rest of the statue. He held his plumed hat cradled in one arm, revealing the distinctive haircut of the Shawnee warrior—a high, stiff roach and braid down the back. The hat would never have fit over it. His eagle's beak of a nose and his high cheekbones made his eyes seem deeper, darker, more penetrating as he stared off to the east, across Lake St. Clair, toward the battleground along the Thames. He and his warriors had come just in time to rally the British army, near retreat, and spur them to victory. It was a turning point of the War of 1812, and some people said that if the British had lost that day, Detroit would be an American city.

At the base of the statue were a dozen little leather pouches full of cornmeal, decorated with feathers. Jack Lind kicked one as if it were a tiny soccer ball, and watched it soar and then impact against the General's shoulder in a puff of the fine-ground meal.

"Now, if that had been red paint—or better yet, blood—you'd have made a point," one of his companions said. "Why do they want to have a statue like this to a red, anyway? Do they want to encourage the Alliance?"

"Shut up," Jack said. "We're supposed to be quiet, wait to see who shows up." He patted his rifle. The three men were dressed in ACT's dark military fatigues, with black berets. They each carried a small pack, and their belts were hung with knives, binoculars, night scopes and other small electronic equipment. Jack had a transmitter. They'd been sent across the border after one of the leaders of the outlawed Alliance Warriors. Rumor had it that the man, who was responsible for dozens of deaths in the Chicago area, was going to make some kind of ceremonial visit to the statue.

They faded back toward the bushes; in the daylight they wouldn't have been able to hide anywhere nearby, but night deepened the shadows of the hedges.

Half an hour later, a faint noise brought the three Americans to attention. Jack could just make out two figures until he pulled his night scopes on. He leveled his rifle at them as they approached the statue.

There were two reds, a man and a woman. The woman was carrying a basket in both arms. The man seemed to be unarmed, though he was wearing a nylon windbreaker and could hide anything under one of those. Jack looked from side to side at his two men. They nodded, ready.

Jack took a breath, coiled, then sprang up with a shout. In two steps he stood in front of the two reds, rifle poised against the man's throat. His men shifted around to the side, grabbed the startled reds and slapped restraints on them. It took ten seconds. The basket the woman had been carrying was on the ground, the contents spilled out toward Jack: more bags of cornmeal, little locks of hair, some wooden carvings. He kicked them aside. "Surprise," he said softly. The woman made a noise, something between a gasp and a moan. The man holding her slapped his hand across her mouth, none too gently. "What do you want?" the red man asked, stiff in his captor's grip. Jack shifted his rifle barrel a little bit away from the red man's throat and up, pushing the man's head up and back. The man shivered but said nothing more. This was going well.

"Is your name Logan Bates?" Jack waited for the red's response. When the man said nothing he moved the rifle barrel away to the left, and then swung it back against the man's jaw, hard. There was a satisfying little crunch, and a trickle of blood started out of the corner of the red's mouth. The red closed his eyes for a long moment, but did not cry out. Then he opened them and stared at Jack.

"Yes," he said, his speech a bit slurred. "I am Logan Bates. What do you want?"

"You are charged with acts of murder and terrorism, and with making war against the United States of America. You have been identified to the Army Counter-Terrorism department by reliable witnesses, and have been found to be guilty." This was the first time Jack had been in charge of a grab like this; he found that he enjoyed reading off the charges. There was a brief flurry as the woman struggled to get away. It ended with the soldier's hand down her shirt. Jack gave it a minute before he said, "Cut it out, Bob."

"Aww, come on, Lieutenant. Who's gonna know?"

"We will. So will the people who find her. And then the captain will know, and you know how he feels about people who play around on duty. Come on—we don't have a lot of time here."

Bob pulled his hand out of her shirt.

The two reds were forced to their knees in front of Tecumseh, and shackled hand to foot. Then Jack moved around behind them, and fired one bullet through the back of each head. As they crumpled, he thought of his cousin, Sarah, who had died in an Alliance Warriors bombing in Zanesville, three years ago. This was for her, and for all the innocents that the savages had murdered.

Then the three American soldiers made sure they had left no evidence behind, returned to their jeep and headed back across the border.

It occurred to Jack Lind as they left that he hadn't asked what the woman's name was. He shrugged. She was associating with a known terrorist, and that was enough.

Army Counter-Terrorism's Eastern Indiana headquarters was located in the white town of Newark, in the old county courthouse. The ACT offices were on the ground floor, and their arsenal was stored in the basement. The upper stories were empty—rotting wood and old fire damage made the floors and stairs too dangerous. The old courthouse was a baroque extravaganza of carved stone and spires, built in the heyday of the railroads in the center of the small city, set in the middle of a small square lined with stores and offices and churches. Though the city fathers had tried to turn Newark into a manufacturing town in the early part of the century, the town's economy was still based mostly on the surrounding farms, and on the air force base just outside of town. The government had had to take some Reservation land to build that base; the surge of violence that had followed was what prompted ACT to set up their headquarters here. That was thirty years ago.

Steve Marlin lounged on the east steps of the courthouse, off duty for an hour and enjoying the early summer sun. It was quiet at headquarters today, with the Commander away and most of the units out looking for trouble. His rifle was propped up to one side, with his beret hanging on the barrel. Steve was twenty-two, six feet tall, blond and handsome in his black fatigues. There was a group of teenage girls, shopping, who had walked past him three times, giggling and giving him sidelong glances as they passed. The scenery had improved, Steve thought, since school let out for the summer.

"Hey, Marlin!" He turned toward Jack Lind, calling him from the doorway. Jack had transferred in from the Western Indiana division just last week. "Someone here to see you."

"Who is it?" Steve wasn't expecting visitors.

"Looks like family to me, buddy. You got a cute little sister?"

"No. Wait. Maybe it's my aunt and uncle." Steve swung to his feet, grabbed his rifle and headed inside. He didn't see the two vans that pulled up to the curb behind him, nor the dozen red teenagers who piled out.

Steve made his way through the ground floor, past quiet offices and the ready room where Jack rejoined the on-call soldiers who were reading and playing cards, to the west entrance and the official reception area. The old wooden floors were scarred and worn, and the GI green paint was flaking off the woodwork and window frames. There were his aunt and uncle, all right, and his cousin Jennifer.

"Hey! Uncle James, Aunt Dot. What brings you here?" he asked. James Marlin worked for the BIA, in the office over in Pataskala. He'd never seemed very happy with his job.

"Steve, good to see you again." James smiled and punched at Steve's arm in a good-natured avuncular way.

"Just thought we'd stop by and leave a note for you— we didn't expect to find you here." Aunt Dot was smiling like she didn't mean it.

"Leave a note? Why?"

"Dot and Jennifer are moving into town. We've rented a house a ways out on Church Street." Uncle James seemed disturbed.

"Steve," Aunt Dot interrupted, "it just isn't safe for Jennifer anymore on the Reservation." She shuddered, delicately. "I never liked living there, but Jim's career, you know . . ." She trailed off meaningfully.

His uncle picked it up. "I was wondering, Steve, if you could give us a hand getting the girls settled in. This won't be permanent, just till things settle down again."

"Huh," Steve said. "I would've thought the Reservation

would be the safest place for you. They never bomb the
red towns." He stopped as he noticed his uncle's gestures
to keep quiet. Aunt Dot had made up her mind, that was
clear, and she was a powerhouse of conviction. Jennifer
had wandered away and was looking at the posters on
the walls, identifying known terrorists. The sergeant on
the desk made a meaningful gesture toward his watch.

"My break's about over," Steve said. "Why don't you
give me the address and I'll come by when I'm off duty
and help you unpack."

"Thanks, son. Jenny! Time to go!" James Marlin's voice
rose to call his daughter.

A sudden crash like thunder shook the floor, Steve's
knees began to collapse under him and a window exploded into shrapnel. There was a cloud of smoke billow-
ing up through a floor vent, followed by one bright lick
of flame. He dropped and rolled, keeping hold of his rifle.
As he came up again, he saw his aunt and uncle on the
floor, and beyond them, in the front door, three young
reds aiming rifles at him. He couldn't see the sergeant. A
sudden rapid burst of automatic fire from somewhere behind him in the building was followed by an ominous
silence.

Jennifer started to turn away from the photograph of
the terrorist that she'd been looking at when her father
called her name. Then something slammed against her
feet and there was a loud noise and suddenly she was on
her ass on the floor, leaning back against the wall. Her
head hurt. As her eyes came into focus she saw a red man
with a gun standing in the doorway that led back into
the building. He looked like the man on the poster. Then
there were other reds with guns crowding behind him,
laughing and elbowing each other. Steve had been standing with his back to them, his rifle pointed past her at
someone in the front door. Now he lowered his weapon
and looked around, startled. Jennifer suddenly couldn't

breathe, and she felt like she had a stone in her stomach. This was it.

"Okay, all of you up and over there," the man shouted while the younger reds jostled around him into the room. They fanned out and linked up with the other groups of reds who had come in the other doors. Her mom and dad were hauled to their feet, but she couldn't move.

Walks Softly stood near the floor vent, where smoke was coming up from the basement. She'd been part of the group that snuck in and set the incendiaries in the basement, well away from the munitions storage areas. The whole thing would blow eventually, but they had time to make sure that the ACT goons didn't get away. The blond soldier hadn't fired; this was going to be easy. The scent of smoke in the air grew stronger as the old dry timbers of the basement caught below them. The sachem had better hurry—they hadn't counted on the floor collapsing from fire before the munitions went up.

Then she got a good look at the civilians being herded across the room toward the front door. She moved to where the girl was still huddled against the wall.

"Jenny?"

The white girl looked up, her brown eyes dilated with fear.

"Soft?" Jenny's voice cracked, and she swallowed convulsively. "Soft?"

Nobody but Jenny and her brother had ever called her that.

"What are you doing here, Jen?" Walks Softly couldn't believe that of all the times and places in the world, she'd find her old friend again here and now. And her mother, the bitch. It would be so easy just to pull the trigger, wipe out the years of bitterness in one burst of automatic fire.

"Soft, please don't kill us."

Jenny's voice was cracking again. The smoke was getting thicker, Walks Softly's eyes were watering. She couldn't do it. She turned away quickly.

This was suddenly a lot harder than she had thought
it was going to be. Setting the bombs was a puzzle, an
adventure, and the resulting explosions were better than
fireworks. She hadn't had to shoot the soldiers, or even
see it, though she knew her friends had killed them all.
All but the sergeant and the blond soldier here in the
front room.

She held out her hand to the girl on the floor, and
pulled her to her feet. As Jenny came up, her mother
screamed, "Oh my God, leave my daughter alone!"

Walks Softly turned toward the woman. Dot Marlin was
struggling in Sam Miller's grip, while another red girl tried
to get hold of her arms. Dot broke free and launched
herself at Walks Softly, screeching, "I know you, you filthy
little savage!" Sam lunged after the woman. Walks Softly
raised her rifle and fired one burst, right into Dot Marlin's
face.

The dead woman collapsed, taking her screaming
daughter to the floor under her.

Steve Marlin saw his aunt's head explode in a spray of
blood. He shouted "No!" and pulled free of the red teen-
ager who was leading him toward the door. Grabbing up
the red's rifle, he crouched and fired a burst at the boy
who had jumped after Dot. The red fell, his back spat-
tered with black holes.

Jennifer struggled to get free of her mother's body and
away from the shooting. She couldn't think; someone was
screaming. She saw her cousin fall, the front of his black
uniform suddenly all wet.

Then the red leader shouted something, she couldn't
hear what. A rifle swung toward her.

"Shoot them all," the sachem shouted. "We don't have
time for anything else, and they know some of us."

Walks Softly closed her eyes when he shot Jenny, one
bullet to the head. Then a gout of flame burst through

the floor near one wall. That was enough. The sachem raised his rifle and everyone who could ran for the door to the hallway that would take them back through the building. Sam Miller and two others they left behind.

They made it out of the courthouse, into the vans and out of the square before they heard the sirens going off. They were close to the city limits when they heard the explosions start as the arsenal caught fire. Twisting around in her seat, Walks Softly could see the great cloud of black smoke rising from where the courthouse had been.

"For my brother," she thought. "For my father."

Pope John XXIII was one of the most cheerful and best-loved figures of this century, easily the most popular Pope with both Catholics and non-Catholics alike.

But he wasn't always John XXIII. Once he was just an Italian priest named Angelo—and, as Tappan King, editor and novelist suggests, he might have had another name as well.

A code name.

The Mark of the Angel
by Tappan King

1961

His Holiness Pope John XXIII, Vicar of Christ, Bishop of Rome, Successor of St. Peter, Patriarch of the West, Supreme Pontiff of the Most Holy and Apostolic Catholic Church, was feeling a bit dyspeptic.

"Almighty and most merciful Father," he gasped, suppressing an afflatus that was less than divine, "though I am weak and frail and unworthy of Thy trust, lend me just a bit of strength to do Thy work this day, eh?"

He had succumbed to temptation again that morning, a half dozen of Father Vincente's notorious pistachio cannoli, in direct defiance of his physician's orders—and his conscience. He would have penance to do when this long day was done—though surely the indigestion itself was penance enough?

He might have avoided this harsh temporal judgment

if he'd been able to spend the day in fasting and prayer, but he had foolishly agreed to a breakfast meeting with some of the more conservative Cardinals, who were urging him to issue an encyclical forbidding the faithful to vote for Communist candidates. That intense young fellow from Krakow—Wojtyla, was it?—half seriously advocated excommunication. To fortify himself, he'd consumed too much black coffee beforehand, and far too much pastry during the meeting.

Though a few of the hard-liners were raving *fascisti*, he certainly understood their concerns. In every corner of the globe, socialist and Communist movements were gaining popularity—many of them defiantly atheistic. Algeria had elected a Communist government after the abortive right-wing coup by the OAS. In Cuba, Ernesto Guevara's National Liberation Party stood a real chance of defeating the Batista regime in the fall. Here in Italy, Aldo Moro was making overtures to the Communists to form a new coalition government. Worst of all, it now seemed possible that Jean-Paul Sartre, the Communist mayor of Paris, might actually win the election next month against General de Gaulle and become President of the Fourth Republic. Sartre was the worst sort of intellectual, a man who had used the talents given him by his Creator to deny His very existence. The conservatives insisted that only a papal decree would ensure Sartre's defeat.

Yet there were arguments for tolerance. In Latin America, *Liberación*, the local arm of the Catholic Workers' Movement, was the only force strong enough to oppose the ruthless exploitation of the poor practiced by the military dictatorships. And in Southern Africa, so his delegates told him, Communists—some of them priests!—dominated the leadership of the African Christian Socialist Party, which had done so much to end colonial rule on the continent. One thing was certain: Whatever decision he made would be unpopular.

His guts roiled, and he rested his head in his hands, massaging his throbbing temples, his fingers finding the old scar that still twinged in times of great stress. Lately he'd begun to wonder if he might be entitled to a bit of rest after eight decades of devotion. But clearly the Lord was not finished with him quite yet.

"Father, help me," he prayed. "Give me some sign that I might understand Thy will in this matter . . ."

There was a knock at the door.

He raised his head, folded his hands over his agitated stomach. "Enter!" he called out.

His secretary, Father Domenico, entered and deposited a diplomatic pouch on his desk without speaking, and quietly exited. Inside the pouch was a single sealed envelope, containing an urgent request from the Archbishop of Paris, on behalf of one Brother Jacques Michel, S.J., for a private audience "on a matter of grave moment." The name was familiar, but he could not quite place it.

He was about to set it aside with a dozen other such requests when a small piece of paper fluttered out from among the folds of the letter. It was weathered and creased and lined with age, blank save for a primitive drawing scratched in black ink upon it—a stick figure with a halo and a "V" suggesting a pair of wings . . .

1943

A mortar shell crashed in front of the lorry, opening a crater in the already-pockmarked road leading from Dijon to Paris. Archbishop Angelo Giuseppe Roncalli cringed as shrapnel rained down on them, clutching the rosary about his neck. The young Italian soldier who drove the vehicle was unperturbed, steering quickly around the hole, mindful of the valuable cargo he carried. In the leather satchel beside Archbishop Roncalli was a secret communiqué from Pope Pius XII to Marshal Pétain, the French Premier. And, in the pocket of his robe, papers identifying him as Brother Angelo Apollinaire, a Dominican friar being transferred from St. Peter's to Notre-Dame de Paris.

Diplomatic missions were nothing new to Archbishop Roncalli. Nor was war. He'd seen the worst of it in the

Great War as an ambulance driver at Vittorio Veneto. He'd had his life threatened by Macedonian terrorists in Bulgaria and freedom fighters in Greece, been held hostage by Atatürk's men in Turkey, during his years of service as legate to Pius XI. But at fifty-two he was surely getting too old for this sort of cloak-and-dagger business. It was absurd—as if he'd awakened in a chapter of the suspense novel he'd been reading last night before bedtime.

The Pontiff hadn't chosen to share the contents of the message with him, but Roncalli had enough friends in the Curia to deduce what it contained. His Holiness was hedging his bets, suggesting that Pétain might wish to sue for a separate peace with the Allies, as he'd counseled the Italian King, Victor Emmanuel, to do. *Il Duce*'s campaigns in Greece and North Africa had been disastrous, and there were rumors that Allies would soon make a beachhead somewhere in the Mediterranean—Corsica, perhaps, or Sicily. The Germans had fared no better in Stalingrad, and every day the Resistance was gaining strength in France. The winds of war were shifting, and prudent men knew when to trim their sails.

Prudent men, indeed. Cowards was closer to the mark! Archbishop Roncalli knew the Church was supposed to be neutral in the affairs of nations, but Fascism was a new thing, something more than mere nationalism. In its ruthless arrogation of power, its venomous doctrine of racial purity, he could see the hand of the Adversary clearly at work. When Hitler invaded Poland, Roncalli had urged Pius XII to read the denunciation of totalitarianism his predecessor, Pius XI, had been laboring on at the time of his death. But the Pontiff had demurred, maintaining that the Church wielded more power in this conflict as a neutral party. Though Roncalli was bound by his vow of obedience, a part of him rebelled, feeling that silence at a time like this bordered on collaboration. As the conflict had progressed, he had grown more vehe-

ment in his opposition to the Church's policy of nonin-
volvement. Perhaps this assignment was his reward.

The day had grown damp and raw as the sun disappeared behind the hills of Champagne. His white robes
did little to cut the chill. Now night had fallen, and the
sound of shelling had begun again. He was hungry and
tired and more than a little afraid, and Paris was many
miles away. Archbishop Roncalli bowed his head and
prayed: "Watch over me, O Lord, and—"

But the prayer was never finished. As the vehicle
rounded a bend in the tree-lined road, a mine exploded
under its wheels, hurtling the truck down the bank into
the ditch below.

It was night. At first he thought he'd been blinded, but
as consciousness returned, he could see a few stars in the
cloud-strewn sky above out of his left eye. His right eye
would not open, and there was a stab of fire at the side
of his head. He tried to sit up, but he could not move.
His arms and legs felt as if they were swathed in lead.
Lifting his head, he saw that his body was trapped under
a vehicle of some sort, which had turned over on its side.
Still, at least he was alive.

Slowly, he dragged his right arm up, clawing through
the damp soil. After long, agonizing minutes, both arms
were free. He fell back, feeling dizzy and faint with hunger. The thought of a good, hot meal brought tears to his
eyes. It was always his stomach that betrayed him. But if
God had given him a great appetite, He had also given
him great strength. That strength would have to save him
now.

Murmuring an Ave Maria under his breath, he placed
his hands on the edge of the truck body and pushed.
There was a creaking sound, and the massive weight began to tip to the right. When he let go, it rocked back,
knocking the wind out of him. Not good. He might have
the strength to push the vehicle off of him for a moment,
but he would have to use that moment to slide out from

under it, or risk being crushed when it settled back down again. Well, so be it.

He closed his eyes, resting. A light rain began to fall. It would make the soil softer, but it would make it harder to grip the metal. There was no time to waste. He inhaled again, braced his broad hands on the chassis, and shoved hard, crying out to his God with a great outrush of breath. The truck lurched, and he pushed down, dragging his body upward. Then his arms shuddered, and he let go, curling into a tight ball as the great mass of metal came hammering down again.

It was near dawn. The clouds overhead were ruddy with the first hints of sunrise. It must have rained most of the night, for the ground was sodden and muddy.

But he was free, somehow. The truck lay on its side a short distance away. He could see a soldier's arm dangling from the window, pale in the first light, and whispered a prayer for the poor man's soul. He gingerly touched the side of his head, wincing with pain as his hand came away sticky with blood. He lifted himself up on his arms, dragged himself to his knees, then fell forward, kissing the sweet earth in gratitude for his deliverance.

A moment later he heard a low droning sound from the road above. A vehicle was approaching slowly, its headlamps dark. He was too weak from blood loss and hunger to cry out. If it was God's will that they see him, they would.

It was an old truck filled with hay. It slowed as it passed him, picking its way carefully around the pit in the road. He thought he could make out a white-haired figure seated behind the wheel, and managed to lift one arm in a feeble wave. But it was a young boy's voice he heard instead, speaking in French.

"Grandfather, stop! There's a man down there to the left. No, really! He's alive!"

The man's reply was lost to him, but the truck stopped. Two figures climbed down, a wiry old man with an unruly shock of snow-white hair, and a boy of about ten or eleven years. They stood by the bank for a moment, just staring at him. Then the old man looked about him, almost furtively, pulled a pistol from his belt, and began to make his way slowly down the steep slope.

He went first to the young soldier's lifeless form, searching it for valuables. He stripped off the soldier's wristwatch, stuffed his pistol into the pocket of his coat. Then the old man was bending over him.

"Shit!" he spat in thickly accented French. "A damned priest."

"A priest?" The boy laughed. "With that great nose, he looks like a Jew!"

The old man spun, slapped the boy fiercely. "You shut your mouth! Where did you learn that shit, eh? From the damned Nazis?"

The boy sniffed, but did not cry. "I'm sorry, Grandfather."

The old man dug deep into his pocket, pulled out a tobacco pouch, rolled himself a cigarette, lit it, and inhaled deeply. "Who are you?" he demanded. "What is your name?"

"I—my name is—?" What was his name? He couldn't remember. "Angelo," he said at last. That was right. But the other names wouldn't come.

"Can you walk?"

"I—I think so." He rose to his feet, dropped to his knees again with dizziness. The old man swore. "Jacques!" He gestured to the boy, pointed up the steep slope with his pistol.

"Go! Quickly now!"

Leaning heavily on the boy, Angelo made his way slowly up the steep earth to the truck. Halfway up he paused to rest, and looked back. The old man had ripped a sleeve off the driver's shirt, stuffed it into the fuel can on the back of the lorry.

"No! Wait!" he cried.

"What is it?" the old man demanded. But Angelo could find no answer.

Striking a match on the sole of his shoe, the old man set the cloth afire, then made his way swiftly up the slope, shoving the priest before him. A moment later, the lorry exploded in flame.

It was full day by the time they arrived at their destination. He'd drifted off among the bales of hay, and now was wakened by a rude shake. The truck was stopped in front of an old farmhouse. A young woman in her late twenties had come running out as they pulled up. She was a pretty girl, with black hair bound up in a blue kerchief, and fierce dark eyes.

"Thank God you're safe!" she scolded. "I should never have let you take Jacques with you! What have you found, Papa?"

"I've brought you a surprise, Marie," the old man called back. "A guest. I found him wounded by the road."

"You're mad! Why did you bring him here? Henri will be back at any moment!"

"He's a priest. You want me to shoot a damned priest? Or leave him there to die?"

The young woman had come around the back of the truck, and was glaring at him. "Shit!" she said. "He is a damned priest! What are we going to do with him?"

"Didn't I tell you? He's hurt. Get him cleaned up. And make us some breakfast. We're hungry."

With a scowl at the old man's back, Marie led Angelo into the house. He was relieved to discover he still had the sight of his right eye. It was just swollen shut and covered in blood. She was none too gentle in cleaning up his head wound, scouring out the cut with a soapy rag, stitching it up with a needle singed over the flame of an oil lamp, bandaging it with a pad of soft linen soaked in brandy.

"Thank you very much, mademoiselle," he said, when

she was done. "I owe you—I owe all of you my life. May God bless you."

"He speaks very pretty French, Papa," she said. "How do you know he's not a Vichy spy masquerading as a priest?"

"Are you a spy?" asked Jacques, his eyes alight.

"Jacques! Be still!" the old man shouted, lifting a hand to strike him.

"Don't you touch my son!" Marie shouted back.

"Aah! You coddle the child. He'll be a man soon enough in this world. He'll have to learn to take it!"

"How old are you, Jacques?" Angelo interjected, acutely uncomfortable with the dispute.

"I will be twelve in August! You know what I'm going to be when I grow up?"

"No," Angelo answered.

"A saboteur, like my papa!" he answered, face flushed with pride.

"Jacques, hush!" Marie snapped, her face stricken. "He was making a joke, Father," she added hastily. "It's a crazy world, no?"

"It's all right," said Angelo. "I understand."

The woman searched his face with her gaze, then shrugged.

"Come. You must be hungry. Can you eat?"

Angelo burst out laughing. "I think so," he said. "It's been more than a day since my last meal."

He'd just sat down to a plate of fried bread and honey when he heard the sound of a motor in the distance.

"It's Henri!" cried Marie, running toward the door. But the old man shoved her aside, peering warily out the window.

"Shit," he said. "It's a damned Kraut. Jacques! Go back to your room and don't come out until I tell you! Marie! Put away the guns, and get those bloody rags out of sight! You!" He was holding his pistol close to Angelo's face. "Not one word or I kill you, you understand?"

There was a knock. Marie busied herself at the stove.

The old man tucked the pistol behind his back under his jacket. The knocking grew louder.

"Open the door!" a voice shouted in German. *"Schnell!"*

The old man slumped his shoulders, seeming to gain a decade of age in an instant, then slowly opened the door.

A dapper young man in the garb of an SS officer stood outside. A motorcycle emblazoned with a crimson swastika gleamed behind him in the morning sun. He was slim and blond, with a neat mustache and sleek hair. He raised his hand in salute.

"What do you want?" the old man answered in a feeble, cracked voice.

"I am looking for Henri Michel," the officer answered in crisp, clipped French. A black Luger was just visible at his hip under his leather trench coat.

"I am Henri Michel," said the old man. The officer laughed.

"You? The Henri Michel I seek is half your age."

The old man coughed and spat, barely missing the officer's glossy black boot.

"I don't know where my damned son is," the old man answered. "I haven't seen him for more than a week. And I hope I never do again."

"Why not?"

"He's no good. He—"

But the SS officer did not wait for his answer. He turned in Angelo's direction, taking in his mud-stained priest's robes, his bare feet, the bandage on the side of his head.

"Papers, please!" he said, gloved hand outstretched. For a moment Angelo was uncertain of his meaning.

"Papers, please!" he repeated in German, growing more impatient.

Angelo fumbled in the pocket of his robe, found a small leather wallet. The officer snatched it out of his hand, unfolded the paper it contained. He looked back and forth from the paper to Angelo.

"So, Brother Angelo, you go to Paris? To Notre-Dame?" The officer's manner was suddenly light, cordial.

"I—yes, I think so . . ."

"You *think* so?" He grabbed Angelo's broad jaw in his gloved hand, wrenched his head to the left. "What are you doing here? How did you get hurt?"

"Stop!" cried Marie. "He is my cousin!"

The officer turned. A smile spread slowly across his lips. "Well! What have we here?" He walked quickly across the kitchen. "Your cousin, eh? An Italian?"

"He is Swiss," she lied smoothly, eyes demurely downcast. "My great-aunt's son, from Geneva. His vehicle struck a mine. These roads are so terrible these days, you know. Those dreadful Partisans—"

The officer had insinuated himself close to her, trapping her against the stove. "So, your husband has left you all alone, with no protection save a priest and an old man, eh? Doesn't he know that the countryside is a dangerous place for a young girl?" He lifted her chin. "Some young man might come along and steal a kiss, no?"

She twisted out of his grasp. "Please, sir. The food is burning!"

"Damn the food!" the officer answered. His face was tight with anger at her rejection. As he bent over her, she groped blindly behind her, smashing the hot cast-iron skillet in his face. He howled, and slapped her backhanded, knocking her to the floor, falling upon her, and pressing his seared and bloody cheek against her face.

The old man dove toward him with a cry of rage, but his shoulder exploded in a spray of blood as the officer turned and fired. Without thinking, Angelo was on his feet, lifting the young officer bodily, turning him about, and striking him hard with a clenched fist, knocking him against the edge of the table. The German lay dazed for a moment, then sprang to his feet, the Luger cocked, and aimed between Angelo's eyes.

Without thinking, Angelo grabbed the officer's wrist, bending the gun back. They struggled for a moment, then there was a sharp report, and the SS officer slumped to the floor, a bloody hole in the side of his head.

"My God!" cried Marie. "You've killed him!"

Stunned, Angelo dropped to his knees beside the German, probing for any hint of life. But the soldier was dead. He bowed his head and began to pray.

"What are you doing?" said Marie.

"Praying for his soul," said Angelo. "I—I've never killed a man before."

"That pig never had a soul! Help me here! Are you all right, Papa?"

The old man lay on the floor, blood welling from his ruined shoulder. "This damned arm!" he said. "Quick, woman! Help me before I bleed to death!"

Leaving the dead soldier, Angelo bent over the old man, probing the wound with his fingers. A moment later, he lifted his head. "It's pretty bad," he said. "We'll have to get him to a doctor."

"A doctor!" Marie answered. "And tell him what? My father was shot while trying to kill a German soldier?"

Angelo looked up again. "You don't understand. He's got to have help. He won't—"

The door flew open. A young man in black was crouched against the door frame, a gun leveled across his arm. "You!" he shouted. "Get back or I blow off your damned head!"

"Henri, no!" said Marie. "This man—he saved our lives!"

The young man froze, his gaze raking across the kitchen to rest on the lifeless form of the German officer.

"What happened here?" he demanded. "Where's Jacques?"

"He's safe, Henri. We're all safe, though your papa has gotten himself hurt."

"Jacques! Come here!"

"Papa!" The boy came running out. "You missed everything! There was a Nazi with a big gun who tried to kiss Mama—" His words faltered when he saw the dead soldier, his grandfather's ruined arm. He wedged himself between his mother and father, clutching them tight.

"Who is this?" Henri asked, pointing to Angelo. "What are you doing here?"

"I—I don't know," he answered. "I think I was on my way to Paris, but I can't remember . . ."

"Well, none of us can stay here," said Henri. "The Germans will be here soon. They found us after we blew up the bridge. I was the only one who got away." His face darkened. "Anton and Louis were killed, but they captured Pierre. They'll make him talk. We've got to get out of here fast. Get to Paris. They've probably blocked the roads already—and they have my description. I don't know how we'll get through."

"Let me drive!" whispered Henri's father. "You can hide in the hay."

"Don't be a fool, old man!" said Marie. "You're half-dead! You'd only kill us all—"

"Wait!" said Angelo. "I have an idea—"

"Talk quick, priest," said Henri. "We don't have much time."

"The German soldier," said Angelo. "You are about his size. His uniform should fit you—"

"Go on," said Henri with a slight smile, understanding dawning in his eyes.

"I'll drive the truck," said Angelo. "You take the motorcycle. You can tell the Germans we're your prisoners—"

"Pah! It's madness!" said the old man. "You don't know this man! He might betray us to save his own skin!"

"Shut up for once in your life, Papa!" said Marie. "This man has already risked his life for us!"

"Quiet, both of you," said Henri. "I like your idea, priest. And we don't have time to think of a better one. Get your things, everyone, and let's get out of here!"

By some miracle, the deception worked. Henri set fire to the farmhouse, hoping their pursuers would accept the charred body of the German soldier as the remains of the notorious Partisan, Henri Michel. There was a tense moment at one of the roadblocks, but Henri managed to conceal his limited knowledge of German with a stiff and officious manner. No one seemed suspicious of Angelo.

By nightfall, they'd found the Partisan hideout in an abandoned factory on the outskirts of Paris. Angelo volunteered to help out in the makeshift infirmary there. He was shocked at the carnage—boys barely older than Jacques blinded, maimed, and crippled in their secret war of liberation. And he was deeply angered at the stories he heard of atrocities committed at the hands of the Germans. Refugees slaughtered and buried in mass graves. Food stolen from the mouths of the hungry. Children conscripted as slave labor. Whole villages exterminated simply because they were Jews, or Gypsies, or Poles. The images troubled Angelo's sleep that night. But so did the face of the young German soldier.

"We can't stay here," Henri told Angelo the next morning. "This place is no longer safe. What will you do now, Angelo? I am sending my family to stay with relatives north of the city. You are welcome to go with them. Or will you go on to Notre-Dame de Paris? Abandon this troubled world for the tranquility of the cloister?"

Angelo was silent for a while, then finally spoke.

"I'd like to come with you, Henri, if you'll have me."

"We can use every man we can get—even a priest!"

"I must warn you," Angelo continued. "I—am a man of peace, not a man of war. I won't willingly take a life. But I'll help in any other way I can. I can drive, and tend to the wounded . . ."

Henri extended his hand. "I owe you more than I can ever repay. I'd be proud to have you beside me. You're twice as strong and ten times as brave as many who carry a gun. And you drive like an angel—ah! That's it! That's what we'll call you!"

"I—I don't understand."

"Your code name. Your *nom de guerre*. Me, they call *le Spectre*—the Ghost. You, we'll call *l'Ange*. The Angel."

* * *

And so he became the Angel. Once the name got about, it stuck, first as a joking reference to his pacific ways, but later as a term of respect. Henri's little band was a chaotic alliance—Communists from the French Section of the Workers' International, Socialists from the Popular Front, members of the criminal underworld of Paris, followers of de Gaulle who hoped to be bosses when Paris was liberated. But they all listened to the Angel, because he was the least interested in reckless heroics, the most concerned about saving human lives.

In the months that followed, Angelo became one of Henri's closest confidants. Henri would talk out his plans for a mission, and Angelo would listen carefully, pointing out the weaknesses in the plans, always arguing for solutions that did not require killing. And though he sometimes came along on missions, as a driver and medic, he always kept to his vow never again to take another human life.

But one night he had to break that vow.

Henri's little band had grown larger. Fortified with donations and supplies smuggled to them from the Free French in London, they had become a well-trained group of commandos, fighting a relentless shadow war against the Nazis. Outraged by the constant sabotage, the Germans had grown more determined to stop them. There were rumors of spies and traitors in their midst, of a reward of a million francs in gold for the man who killed *le Spectre*. But Henri scoffed at the rumors. He'd laugh and say: "Who can kill a ghost?"

This night they were to stop a train. Though the Germans had done their best to conceal its departure, word had leaked out that a train would be leaving Paris sometime after three A.M., carrying thousands of conscripts to the front to be used as slave labor.

Angelo had come up with an ingenious plan to stop them. A small group would attack the train at the station as a diversion, to throw them off guard. The larger group would blow up a section of track near Gagny, and liberate the prisoners as the crew attempted to repair the rails. Henri was surprised when Angelo volunteered for the mission.

"There will be shooting tonight, Angel. Are you sure you want to come along?"

"I want to go," he said. To his relief, Henri did not probe further. He could not have explained his reasons if he had.

The ambush was to take place in a sheltered valley a half mile or so from the river. One group was to take out a small trestle bridge with explosives about an hour beforehand. Another group was to arrive about a half hour before the train and build a bonfire across the track so that the engineer would be sure to stop in time. Henri's men would attack the train crew, while Angelo's group led the captives to safety.

So far, everything had gone according to plan. They'd taken up their positions at the top of a rise, where they would have the first view of the train when it appeared. It was a clear night, pleasantly warm. His partner, a young Communist code-named Scaramouche, a French Canadian, had thoughtfully brought along some bread and cheese, which they ate as they lay in the long grass beside the track, waiting for the train to come.

"Tell me, Angel," he said. "You ever think what you'll do when the war is over? Me, I think I'll go to Russia, see if it's as good as they say over there. What about you?"

"I don't know," he answered at last. "I suppose I'll be a priest, just like I am now."

"Don't you have any ambition? Don't you want to be a Bishop or something? Hell! Why not Pope?"

But Angelo wasn't listening. Far up the track, he saw a glimmer of light. He raised his field glasses. The train was racing toward them. He waved to Scaramouche, who whistled the signal: three short high notes, one long low note. The opening notes of Beethoven's Fifth Symphony. Morse code for the letter "V"—for victory. In the still, clear air, Angelo could hear the signal passing along the track, the faint rustling as the Partisans took up their positions.

Then the train was roaring past them, its engine loud as thunder, screaming to a stop just short of the blaze in a shower of sparks and a cloud of steam.

Silence. Then curses from the engine. Then lanterns swinging as the engineer and tender climbed down and walked slowly along the rails, surveying the damage to the track. From his high vantage point, Angelo could just make out the dark forms of Henri's commandos making their way across the wet grass toward the front of the train.

Wait. There was a flash of metal in the engine cabin. All along the train, the doors were opening, and dozens of German soldiers were pouring out.

"Get down!" Angelo shouted, his voice booming out across the valley. "It's a trap!"

Alerted by the Angel's cry, the Partisans scattered into the shadows. But Henri's men were surrounded. Angelo started running, his lungs heaving as his stocky legs propelled him down the hill. A half dozen soldiers swarmed down from the engine, lighting the night with their machine-gun fire. As Angelo drew near, one of Henri's men spun in agony, and crumpled at his feet. Angelo threw himself at the nearest soldier, knocking his head against a steel rail, ripping the machine gun from his hands, and turning it on the rest of them, watching in horror and exultation as they fell like reaped wheat before him.

There was a sharp cry behind him. Angelo spun to see Henri fall forward, his body ripped by a hail of bullets. With a quick burst, Angelo felled Henri's attacker, then dropped down beside him.

"Are you all right?" he asked, clasping Henri's hand.

Henri shook his head, coughed blood. "I'm gone," he said. "It's up to you now, my friend."

"Me?" said Angelo. "But I can't. I—"

"You must!" he said, his face tight with pain. "Be an

avenging angel for us tonight, eh?" he whispered. Then his limp hand fell from Angelo's grasp.

Angelo sat motionless for a moment, staring at his friend's blank gaze. Off in the distance he heard cries of pain and the sound of gunfire. Then, with a whispered prayer heard only by his God, he gathered up the fallen weapons of the German soldiers and started off down the track.

It was all over by dawn. With the Angel leading them, and Henri's name on their lips, the Partisans fought with passion and ferocity. More than a hundred of the German's best soldiers were slaughtered. The Resistance fighters lost only a half dozen. As they walked through the mists along the track, stripping the soldiers of their weapons and ammunition, a few of the younger Partisans scrawled slogans on the side of the stilled train. Angelo watched as Scaramouche chalked a hammer and sickle on one of the cars.

"Hey! Angel! Ain't you going to make your mark?"

"My mark?"

"You know. Like Kilroy. Let 'em know you was here!" He held out the chalk, a broad grin on his face. Angelo stared at it for a moment, nodded, and took the chalk out of his hand. With broad strokes, he chalked a stick figure wearing a halo. Then he crossed it with a broad "V" to make a pair of wings, and wrote the word "angel" beneath it.

"Come on," he said. "Let's get out of here."

The mark of the Angel appeared all over Paris in the months that followed. No one contested Angelo's leadership of Henri's band, though some of them chafed under his exacting rules. No unnecessary killing. No indignities against civilians. Warnings to bystanders. Sharing everything they gained with the people.

By winter, they'd gained widespread support among the citizens of Paris and the surrounding countryside. As the long months passed, the mark of the Angel began to appear all over France, as Partisans acted in his name, adding to his growing legend. By spring the Vichy government was under a state of siege, and the Germans were wary about venturing into the streets of Paris after nightfall.

In June the Allies landed at Normandy. Throughout the summer rumors circulated that Paris would be free in a matter of weeks. The Germans redoubled their efforts to track the Angel down, but without avail. Angelo moved constantly, never allowing the Nazis to find him, frequently receiving sanctuary in the city's churches and synagogues.

But the long months of struggle had taken their toll on the man they called the Angel. One sleepless night, curled up in a borrowed blanket in the choir loft of an old Left Bank church, Angelo looked up at the figure of the Savior above him on the altar, and cried out:

"Lord, on the mountain You blessed the peacemakers, granting them the Kingdom of Heaven. Forgive this, Your servant who has taken up the sword in Your name, but I grow weary and long for rest. If it is Thy will, take this cup from me now. Let this struggle be ended soon, and peace prevail again."

The following morning, he was waked suddenly by a young priest.

"Monsieur! Get up!" he cried. "The Germans are on their way here! You must go!"

He could hardly move. He was groggy from lack of sleep, and his back was stiff from the hard wood bench. With a great effort, he lifted himself up.

"What's going on?"

"The world has gone crazy! The Allies are advancing on Paris!" he answered. "The whole city is in revolt! Hitler has ordered his generals fight to the last man, to burn the city down rather than surrender!" Wild hope stirred in Angelo's breast, but he'd heard such rumors before.

"You said the Germans are coming here?"

"Yes! Yes! Some traitor has told them that the one called

the Angel is to be found here, in this church! Whoever you are, you must go now!"

Angelo stood up, grimacing at the pain in his aching limbs. There was shouting in the street outside, followed by the sound of gunfire.

"Is there a back way out?"

"No! Yes—maybe! Through the vestry! Go!"

Two dark figures had appeared in the door of the chapel. Angelo turned and ran through the great oak door to the small room beyond. There was no exit. The only way out was a narrow stained-glass window overlooking an alleyway far below. He smashed the glass with his elbow and forced his body through. The sharp glass caught on his clothing and bit into his soft flesh. It was always his stomach that betrayed him.

For a moment he was stuck fast, then the frame gave way, and he was falling, striking his head against a pillar of stone. The world went red, then black.

A woman's face was leaning over him. A face framed in black.

"Good morning, Your Excellency," she said. "Are you feeling better?" She was a nun, and her words were Italian. Somehow he'd expected they would be in French.

"Where am I?" he said suddenly, sitting up. She pressed gently on his chest, and he fell backward.

"In the hospital. You've been very ill, and you need to rest."

"How long have I been here, Sister?"

"Here? About two weeks. But you've been ill longer than that. It wasn't until three weeks ago that the doctors felt it was safe for you to return here to Rome."

"I'm in Rome?"

"In the Vatican, yes," the nun answered. "His Holiness has been so worried about you! Do you know that he actually came to visit you while you were ill, and prayed over your bed? Perhaps I shouldn't mention this, but I think he holds himself responsible for what happened to you. When you didn't appear in Paris last year, we all feared you were dead. If the Archbishop had not recognized you in that field hospital, we might have lost you for good! Our dear Lord must certainly have been watching over you to have brought you home safely to us again."

"Yes," said Archbishop Roncalli, "I suppose He must have been."

1961

"A Brother Jacques Michel to see you, Your Holiness," said Father Domenico. "Would you like me to stay and record?"

"That won't be necessary, Father," Pope John XXIII replied. "This is just an informal meeting with an old friend. Please send him in."

A few minutes later a young bearded priest in his early thirties entered, and stood hesitantly at the door.

"Come in! Come in! Please sit down—Jacques?"

The priest looked about awkwardly, then sat in the chair on the other side of the great desk.

"Tell me, how is your mother?" asked the Pontiff, his mind drifting back over those long-ago years.

"Very well, Holy Father," the priest answered. "She—she asked me to convey her warmest regards, and her thanks for all of the help you've given us." His voice was full and strong, and his Italian was very polished. The boy had done well, thank God.

"Let us come to the point, Brother Jacques. What is this 'grave matter' you wish to discuss with me? A matter so grave, you felt compelled to send me—this?" He lifted a letter from a tray on his desk, unfolding it slowly and laying it on the edge of the desk where the young man could see it. The drawing of the angel rested in the middle, fluttering in the faint breeze. The young priest grinned with embarrassment and lowered his gaze for a moment, then looked up intently to meet the Pontiff's gaze.

"Very well, then, Your Holiness, I'll be frank," said the young priest gravely. "We've heard that certain members of the College of Cardinals are pressuring you to denounce certain—progressive elements—"

"Communists," said the Pope. "They want me to issue an encyclical forbidding members of the Church to vote for Communists. Tell me, Brother Jacques, do you feel that a vote for a Communist should be grounds for—excommunication?"

"Of course not!" the young priest protested. He looked genuinely frightened.

"You wouldn't happen to be one of these—how did you put it?—'progressive elements' yourself, would you, Jacques?"

"No, Your Holiness—though several of my friends are."

"I see," said the Pontiff. "You know that the Communists say God does not exist?"

"Only some of them," the young man answered. "Others feel they are following Christ's commandments to share what we have with the poor."

"And you?"

"A number of us—including my mother—feel that there is a great danger in this world of ruthless materialism and greed. In my own country, the generals plot to restore Fascism using de Gaulle as their puppet."

"You would rather by ruled by that cynical atheist Sartre?" cried the Pope.

"At least he cares about the people—as I thought you did also," said Brother Jacques, rising to his feet. "Perhaps I was wrong."

The Pontiff spread his hands. "What do you want me to do? I am not a master here, but a servant of the Church. I must do what is best for all members of the Church, not just a few vocal upstarts. You don't think you can blackmail me with a bit of paper, do you? It is God's will that rules here, not mine."

"I want you to remember, that's all," said the young man, his eyes alight with fire. "I want you to remember my father, and my grandfather, and all of the brave men and women who followed a man they called the Angel. I want you to remember what they were fighting for, and how fragile a thing freedom is. I want you to remember who you once were, and what mattered to you then—and then do what your conscience—and your God—tell you is right."

He stood for a moment looking deep into the Pontiff's eyes, and then his gaze fell.

"Your Holiness, I humbly ask your forgiveness," he said at last. "I have been guilty of the sin of pride. I had no business speaking to you as I did. I've disgraced myself, and my cause, and I ask your permission to leave—"

"Not yet," said the Pope firmly. "What you said may have been tinged with pride, but it was also spoken out of love for your fellowman. If one in a hundred of my Cardinals had such passion, we could convert the whole world in a week. Sit down, son."

Brother Michel sat heavily, his face flush with shame.

"Tell your friends—and your mother—that I will consider your request seriously, and ask them to pray for the Lord's guidance in this matter. And tell them—tell them I remember."

"I will, Holy Father."

"Good. Now go with God's blessing. Find some more dragons to slay. The world needs people like you, Jacques."

"Yes, sir," he said, rising. "Thank you—Your Holiness."

A moment later, Pope John XXIII was alone with his God.

He looked down at the crude drawing on his desk, a flood of memories washed over him. He closed his eyes for a moment and then opened them again.

"So. This is how You answer me, eh?" he said softly. "Well, You never promised me it would be easy . . ." He reached for the bell on the corner of the desk and rang it. A moment later Father Domenico entered.

"Yes, Your Holiness?"

"Get me Cardinal Montini. Tell him I have some bad news for him . . ."

Barbara Delaplace has been writing science fiction for less than two years, and has managed to sell almost a story per month. You don't do that if you're not a talented writer, and she was recently nominated for the Campbell Award, given to the best newcomer in the field.

In a field known for huge themes and vast canvases, Barbara has specialized in small, human stories of hearts and minds in conflict. Which made Neville Chamberlain, the great appeaser of the twentieth century, right up her alley . . .

Standing Firm
by Barbara Delaplace

Neville Chamberlain sits in his office, brooding as he has brooded for the past three weeks. The press wants an answer. The King wants an answer. Parliament wants an answer. More to the point, the Austrian Corporal demands an answer. And he hasn't any. His last hope is Churchill. Churchill, who loves the spotlight as much as Chamberlain hates it, is coming to advise him.

Churchill, the man who became an overnight celebrity at twenty-five, thanks to a daring escape from his Boer captors while covering the South African War as a correspondent. Who began his political career as a Conservative, then "crossed the floor" to become a Liberal, then crossed the floor again to rejoin the Conservatives. (It takes a remarkable man, Chamberlain reflects, to face your political opponents and make them willing to accept you as an ally not once, but twice.) Churchill, who has served his country in war and peace, in the military and in political office, through prosperous times and lean ones.

Surely, Chamberlain hopes, such a man will be able to suggest a way out of this dreadful situation.

Chamberlain stands up and paces about the office, furious at his own indecision. *Leaders are supposed to make choices. It comes with the territory. I've made difficult decisions before. Why is this one so much harder?* He smiles grimly to himself—he knows the answer to *that* question, at least. It's harder because this decision will affect more than just Britain, it will affect millions of citizens of a country not his own. And though he's never even seen them, he can feel the weight of all the fears and hopes of the people who live in that country pressing down on him, heavier than any burden Atlas ever bore.

At least, for Chamberlain it's a dreadful burden. "The public," that fine collective noun, has never been a mere abstract entity to him. Always he's been blessed—or cursed, depending on the point of view—with remembering that any group is made of individual human beings, each one entitled to consideration. More than once he's been told by those more realistic, or perhaps just more cynical, that this is a disadvantage for a politician. At this moment he agrees with them. In fact, right now he considers it a curse.

I went into politics to help people, not to get them killed, he thinks for the hundredth time. But this time, he can't see any alternative. For no matter which decision he makes, people will die. Because of the provocative demands of one man in Berlin, a sovereign and democratic nation will be ripped apart. And that, appalling as it is to consider, is the *less* dreadful of the two paths. If the other is taken, all of Europe could be plunged into war.

I've never been a soldier, he thinks. *I've never served under fire or seen men die. Perhaps that makes a difference.* Perhaps when confronted personally and immediately with death, one becomes more resolute, decisions become easier.

It's possible—but somehow he doubts it.

His secretary taps on the door. Churchill has arrived. "Show him in, please," says Chamberlain.

"Good to see you, Prime Minister," Churchill says as he strides into the room, radiating self-assurance.

Chamberlain wishes he felt as confident as Churchill always seems to be as he crosses to shake his guest's hand. *He looks the part of the British bulldog,* he reflects. *More than I do, certainly.* "It was good of you to come on such short notice, Winston. Please be seated." He returns to his desk and sits down himself.

"Thank you, Prime Minister." Churchill lowers his bulky form into the offered chair. "I'm always happy to offer advice, even when I'm not holding office."

"Well, Winston, this situation with Czechoslovakia is a terrible business, and I wish to hear your thoughts on the subject. Oh yes, smoke if you like."

"Thank you, sir."

Chamberlain clasps his hands upon the desk. "Now, I want you to understand I haven't fully made up my mind yet"—an untruth, but one any politician would use—"so please speak frankly. You're aware, of course, of Chancellor Hitler's latest position regarding the Germans living in Czechoslovakia—the so-called reunification with the 'Fatherland.'"

Churchill shrugs. "I read the newspapers, and listen to what my fellow members of Parliament have to say." He smiles. "Sometimes they say quite a lot."

"I have no doubt they do," says Chamberlain dryly. He pauses briefly. "Well, now. It seems to me no matter what we do, the situation is fraught with disaster. If we go along with the Chancellor's demand to let German forces occupy the Sudetenland, we're consenting to what amounts to an invasion of Czechoslovakia, a peaceful country with a legally elected government. If we refuse to accede to his demands, there's no question in my mind that Germany will invade Czechoslovakia anyhow, under the pretext of 'protecting' the ethnic Germans living there."

"Which of course the Czechoslovakian government would resist, leading to civil war."

"Exactly—and which I fear could easily spread and involve much of Europe." Chamberlain pauses again and studies his hands for a moment. Then he raises his head and looks at Churchill squarely. "What is your advice, Winston? If you were sitting in my place, what would you do?"

The stern-faced man sitting opposite him returns his gaze. "Prime Minister, I would accede to Hitler's demand."

Chamberlain finds he is shocked. *Was this the advice I was hoping to hear?* he asks himself. But he keeps his voice calm. "And why would you do that, Winston? The occupation of a sovereign nation is not something I want to be party to without an excellent reason. And the Czechs are prepared and willing to resist—President Beneš has made that clear to me. The reason would have to a very good one indeed to pay so high a cost."

"Sir, I agree. The cost is a horrifying one. But to defy Germany would exact an even higher price, one paid in more valuable coin—the lives of Europeans of many nations, rather than a comparatively few lives of a single nation. As you said a moment ago, refusing German's demands would lead us into another Great War."

"The Second Great War," Chamberlain agrees somberly. "I never imagined we'd have to begin numbering them."

"We won't have to begin numbering them at all, Prime Minister. Give Germany what it wants, and there will be peace," says Churchill.

"You sound very certain of that."

"I *am* certain of the vital need for peace, sir. War brings its combatants down to a common, hideous level. When I served, I saw the bodies of both my comrades and my enemies bloated and stinking in the sun. They looked no different. They smelled no different. I heard men scream-

ing in agony. I couldn't tell which side they were on by
the sound—their suffering was the same. And it's not only
the soldiers who suffer in common, either. The weeping
of those left behind for their lost sons and husbands and
fathers—that sounded identical too. War extracts too high
a price, Prime Minister."

"Come now, Winston, I didn't ask for a speech." *You
can take the politician out of office, but you can't stop him
from* being *a politician,* he observes wryly to himself.

"Forgive me, Prime Minister. But if you'd seen what I
saw in Africa and Egypt, and in the trenches, you'd understand my feelings. I'll do everything in my power to
prevent Britain from going through anything like that ever
again."

"I'd hardly argue with you regarding the importance of
peace," replies Chamberlain. "But I'm not sure giving in
to Hitler's demands will secure it. Have you read *Mein
Kampf*?"

Churchill dismisses this with a wave of his hand. "Many
politicians write books. I have myself. It's a way to keep
one's name in front of the public."

"It can be a useful tool," Chamberlain agrees. "But the
man has outlined his foreign policy goals in that book,
and they call for conquest and genocide."

"Nonsense. It's a book written by a man before he came
to power. Once in office, one's perspectives change. It's
very different when you're actually *in* command—as we
both know, sir."

"Indeed we do. Still, I'm not as sure as you are that
Hitler's priorities have changed since he took office. Germany invaded Austria only a few months ago. Another
'reunification'—exactly as he said he would do in *Mein
Kampf: 'Anschluss,'* he called it."

"But what possible grounds can he have for demanding
further concessions once he gets his way regarding the
Sudeten Germans?" asks Churchill. "He'll have none. And
he's promised to hold plebiscites and follow the will of
the ethnic Germans."

Chamberlain frowns. "We don't know that he'll do as he says."

Churchill replies, "We cannot *know* anything for certain in this world, Prime Minister. But let me ask you again: what possible justification can he have for further expansionism? It would only lead to war—and only madmen go to war. Certainly no madman could rise to be the head of the German Republic. Hitler may be a boor, but he's ultimately a rational man. No, this will be his last demand, you may rely on that," he concludes confidently. "Give Germany what she wants and there will be peace in our time."

There is a moment's silence, and in the distance a clock can be heard tolling. Chamberlain rises. "Thank you, Winston. I'll consider what you've said carefully."

Churchill stands up. "You're welcome, sir. I'll send you an *aide-mémoire* of our conversation today," he says as Chamberlain escorts him to the door.

"I would appreciate that. Thank you again."

"Good day, Prime Minister."

And the door closes, leaving Chamberlain alone again with the decision no one else can make.

I wish I were as sure as he is. He knows what he would do—but I feel caught between Scylla and Charybdis, the rock and the whirlpool. Which is the lesser of the two evils?

He returns to his desk and sits down.

Of course Churchill is right: only a madman would seek war. Two reasonable men should be able to sit down together, discuss things in a straightforward manner, and come to some mutually agreeable solution.

But then Chamberlain remembers *Mein Kampf*, and how closely Hitler seems to be following his own blueprint, laid down years ago. *He broke the Versailles agreement, just as he said he would. He's reuniting all Germans into that "Greater Germany" of his, just as he said he would. And we've done nothing but stand by while he's done it. Indeed, we've given in to his every demand. Why on earth should he stop making them?* In fact—the thought chills

Chamberlain—why should he even bother to make demands at all? When a bully isn't faced down, he keeps on bullying. Why shouldn't Hitler simply start *taking* what he wants by force?

But that would lead to war, and only an insane man would want that.

Chamberlain stands up and begins pacing the length of the office as he considers reports he's received from the Foreign Office. Reports of concentration camps where hundreds, perhaps thousands of people are dying. Much as he loathes the very idea of such a barbaric concept, he has to admit that Germany is far from the first country to use such camps to detain those considered undesirable by the state.

But most of those imprisoned are there solely because they are Jewish. There are whispers that Hitler wants to wipe out *all* Jews. Why would any sane man be obsessed with destroying an entire people?

And he remembers the most important thing of all: his face-to-face meetings with Hitler, meetings which Churchill has never had. There were those mood swings, the screaming rages, the sullen silences. Is it possible that Hitler *isn't* sane?

No. Germany is a civilized country—it would never elect any but a reasonable, rational man to office.

But civilized or not, sane or not, Chamberlain's mind keeps going back to *Mein Kampf.*

And the lights in the Prime Minister's office stay lit far into the night.

The hubbub in Parliament dies down and the Speaker of the House recognizes the Prime Minister. Chamberlain stands up to speak.

"Mr. Speaker, my family motto is 'Standing Firm.' And I believe with utter conviction that this is what our nation must do. We must stand firm against Adolf Hitler, or any other leader with grandiose dreams of empire, and show them they dream in vain. That they cannot be permitted to encroach upon free peoples who have freely chosen their own governments. Czechoslovakia is such a people: they have a democratically elected government. A government that is now being besieged by Hitler's claims of abuses against ethnic Germans in that country.

"Mr. Speaker, can we doubt that these claims are merely an excuse for Hitler to press for the so-called reunification of the territory occupied by these Sudeten Germans with Germany itself? A reunification spelled out in his terrible manifesto, *Mein Kampf*? Austria was not enough for him. Czechoslovakia will not be enough for him. If any of the honorable members here have read that book, they have seen into the mind of Hitler, the modern Genghis Khan. A Khan who will stop at nothing to achieve his ends.

"Mr. Speaker, it is imperative that we stand firm against Hitler and his Nazi Germany. When I go to Munich in a few days, it will be to inform him that we will not permit German forces to occupy Czechoslovakia."

Amid rumbles of approval and cries of "Hear, hear!" he sits down again. Chamberlain, who all his life has believed in the goodness of man and the triumph of reason, smiles grimly inside. For sometime in that long night when the lights burned late, he lost his belief.

Neville Chamberlain, who has never been a soldier, knows he has just led his country into war.

Brian Thomsen, the editor/creator of Questar Books, and now the editor of TSR Books, chose Sidney Reilly, the famed World War I spy, for his alternate warrior—and then gave him an alternate, and perhaps more important, cause to fight for.

A Sense of Loyalty, a Sense of Betrayal
by Brian M. Thomsen

London, 1918

To: Captain Mansfield Cumming, CB, RN
     Chief of British Secret Service
From: Prime Minister David Lloyd George

I am becoming increasingly concerned about the current situation in Russia. It is imperative that this situation stabilizes. We must be able to count on them as our Far East ally, and the doctrine being preached by these so-called Bolsheviks casts some doubt on their reliability.

The special envoy, Robert Bruce Lockhart, that I assigned to negotiate with the Bolshevik Party has fallen out of contact with the Foreign Office after having acknowledged the receipt of several hundred thousand pounds for negotiating purposes, and quite frankly I am quite worried.

* * *

To: Prime Minister David Lloyd George
From: Captain Mansfield Cumming, CB, RN

Let me set your mind at ease, Prime Minister. Lockhart is in the hands of one of my most capable men,
Sidney Reilly, whose competence I am sure Winston Churchill has already relayed to you. He and
Lockhart have something in the making which
Reilly assures me will stabilize the Russian situation
and guarantee their future cooperation in diplomatic matters for many years to come.

Moscow, August 30, 1918

Sidney Reilly was as at home in anarchy-torn Moscow
as he was in the boudoir of any of his married para-
mours. After years of living by his wits, gathering intelligence, and mastering deceit in the name of the British crown,
Reilly was pleased to return to the land of his birth. Born
Sigmund Rosenblum near Odessa in 1874, the son of a Tsarist
colonel's wife and her illicit lover, a Jewish doctor named
Rosenblum, Reilly relished the idea of finally assisting the
land of his birth in the overthrow of the anarchistic tyranny
that had come to pass after the deposing of the Tsar Nicholas.

The so-called Lockhart Plot had really been Reilly's plan
all along. With the exception of having put him in contact with the forces that would act as the catalyst for his
plan, Lockhart had been of relatively little help, with constant reservations about the plan's success and whether
they should really be acting without further consultation
with the PM, proving the old adage that envoys and diplomats are best suited for kissing and making up, once
the real men of action have already changed history.
Lockhart had, in fact, ceased coming to the meeting of
their cell, preferring to coordinate things from his em-
bassy office. As Reilly saw it, he was a cowardly bureau-
crat, and prayed that he would just stay out of their way
until the approaching zero hour was over.

The Lockhart Plot was relatively simple. Several weeks

ago, Lockhart had sent to Reilly two Latvian officers named Berzin and Shmidkhen, who wanted to surrender their troops to the British consulate and thus withdraw themselves from the so-called revolution. Instantly the plot had begun to form in Reilly's mind.

The Latvian forces had been permanently assigned as the bodyguards for the ranking Bolshevik leaders, and with their cooperation Reilly knew he would be able to kidnap both Lenin and Trotsky, and engineer a British-controlled and financed coup of the Russian government by the close to sixty thousand Latvian officers under General Judenitch, who could restore to power the White Russian faction currently in exile in England. With the help of Berzin and Shmidkhen, and several hundred thousand rubles in bribes, he had managed to bring the close of the revolution to what he saw as a few days off at best.

The kidnap and coup were set for September 2, and Reilly was having the final meeting of the team that would succeed in overthrowing the government. The meeting was pro forma. Everybody knew what their jobs were, and Reilly fully expected it to be over in a few minutes. As a result, he decided that a public meeting would provide a minimum risk at best, and therefore the concerned parties had chosen the back table in an old wineshop in one of the poorer sections of Moscow as their meeting place.

As always, Reilly had shown up first and taken the chair against the back wall to provide unlimited observation of both the front door and any parties seated at the bar. Second to arrive was his lieutenant, George Hill, who had managed to insinuate himself into Trotsky's immediate circle as an advisor on the creation of a new Soviet air force. They were soon joined by Dmitrievich Kalamatiana, an American of Greco-Russian origins, who was the head of U.S. Secret Intelligence in Russia; Colonel Henri de Vertement, the head of the French Secret Service; and another Frenchman whose identity Reilly planned to learn fast, or he would immediately call the meeting off.

"Henri," said Reilly sternly. "What's the meaning of this? Who is your companion, and why have you brought him here? New faces are not appropriate at this late stage in the game."

"Don't worry, Sidney," explained Henri. "He is only a correspondent for *Figaro*, back in France. I have known him for years. We learned Russian together. Besides, you yourself said that it would be important that we have the rest of Europe's public support once the trap has been sprung, and what better way than having a correspondent in place to release the good news as soon as it happens?"

"I don't like it," Reilly replied.

George Hill intervened. "Sidney, don't worry. Our meeting is supposed to be short anyway. There is no reason to go over the particulars at this point. Therefore, unless our French friends have already conversed on the subject, all should still be intact."

"George," Henri responded, "you do me a great disservice. Réné here knows nothing of the particulars of the plan. Once the trap has been sprung, I will fill him in, and the rest will be the subject for history books."

Reilly brought the banter to a quick end, trying to ignore the presence of the man named Réné. "Enough," he said. "Is all in readiness?" His coconspirators nodded. "Good. Any questions?"

Dmitri, who had been acting as an unofficial liaison with General Judenitch, spoke up. "Our Lettist friends are a bit nervous, and asked that I reconfirm the financial matters once again, as the funds will be needed immediately upon the execution of the plan."

Reilly quickly held up his hand for silence. "Say no more," he ordered. "All is in readiness. Only George and myself know where the cash is. When the time is right we will repay our Lettist friends, in cash and in full. If there are no more questions, let us go. The next time we shall meet, we'll be running the place."

His compatriots laughed, and one by one made their way to the street, where they quickly went off in different directions to avoid being noticed . . . that is, all except for Reilly and Hill, who lingered at a street corner bonfire to assess the events of the last few minutes.

"Do you think we're compromised?" asked Hill.

"I don't know," replied Sidney. "Everything is in place. Barring some act of God, nothing should stand in our way. I do wish that Henri had been a little more discreet with his friend Réné."

"Henri only knows about the post-plot matters. You had assigned him that, specifically knowing that no Frenchman was ever reliable when it came to showing up on time. If the operation is breached by him, all we have to do is use a different safe house until the new order is in place."

"I know," said Reilly, "but I can't help feeling uneasy. Three days from now the men entrusted to guard Lenin and Trotsky with their lives will hand them over to us, and General Judenitch will seize control of the government. Nothing must happen to disrupt the normal course of events until that time. Only then will Russia be ours."

"You mean England's," corrected Hill.

"Of course," said Reilly.

The two brothers-in-conspiracy went back towards Lockhart's flat, where they had, unbeknownst to the envoy, successfully hidden the half million pounds that they had requisitioned in the name to finance the coup. A bread riot had resulted in the closing of the most direct route from the wineshop to the consulate, and they decided to stop by a café until the area had been cleared. Once inside, Reilly quickly recognized a comrade from one of the social revolutionist cells that he had used to disrupt the Bolsheviks' efforts and keep him informed of other underground activities. Reilly and Hill joined the man, whose name was Pietor, and ordered glasses of tea laced with spice.

"Comrade Relinsky"—the alias by which Pietor knew Reilly—"have you heard the latest?"

"What, comrade?" Reilly replied.

"Uritzsky, that Cheka bastard, was killed in his office today. It would appear that the day of the rope has finally arrived, and he will not be the last Bolshevik fiend brought to justice, I assure you."

Reilly tensed. "Go on, comrade."

"That is all I know ... but the revolution is at hand. At last the voices of the masses will be heard without these Bolshevik bastards interpreting everything to fit their own agendas."

The fanatical Pietor downed his drink, and with a quick *"Comrades!"* exited the café.

Hill sipped from his glass and whispered to Reilly, "What do you make of that?"

Reilly replied in an equally cautious tone, "He'll probably be in the Cheka's custody before he's gone three blocks from here. We should leave quickly."

Hill went to drain his remaining tea when Reilly leaned as close to him as the small tea table would allow.

"Uritzsky is an obvious target for any enemy of the state," Reilly whispered. "Still, we can't be too careful. Nothing must jeopardize our plan, not even the day of the rope. You trail Trotsky and I'll trail Lenin. Nothing must happen until zero hour. Once they are in the custody of our Lettist friends, we'll rendezvous at Lockhart's, where we'll disperse the payments. No one else's plans must come between us and victory."

"Should we warn the others?" asked Hill.

"Tell no one. Just be prepared to intercede if anything unusual should happen," ordered Reilly. "Status quo must be maintained until we are ready."

Dora Kaplan had been a student when the Tsar had closed the universities due to the increasing unrest brought to the streets by the student uprisings. Her lover/mentor/philosophy teacher had been arrested by the

Tsar's secret police not two weeks before the storming of the Winter Palace, and since then she had drifted from radical cell to radical cell, each time moving farther and farther to the left. Not surprisingly, she had also drifted from lover to lover, devoting both her zeal and her body to the cause. She knew Reilly as Metternick, a student leader in the radical socialist cause from Odessa, and though they had never slept together, it was not due to any lack of desire on her part.

She saw Reilly waiting outside the Moscow factory where Lenin was speaking at a meeting. She longed to approach him, to share the zeal of her plans with him, but decided against it.

First things first ... then, if she survived, there would be plenty of time to share comfort in another comrade's arms.

Reilly had been up all night and had reconciled himself to not sleeping for the next two days. He had done this before during a mission, and though he realized that it slowed him down a bit, it seemed to be the only workable solution. Before the meeting with Berzin and Shmidkhen, assassination would have furthered his cause. Now, with control of all Russia in sight, he had to make sure that nothing happened to Lenin until zero hour. He only hoped that Pietor was wrong, and if not, he hoped that he'd be able to recognize the assassins before they succeeded.

All was quiet save for the usual huddled masses waiting for a glimpse of their savior/dictator. A hush came over the crowd as the sound of a bolt being thrown signaled the opening of the factory doors. The meeting was over, and soon Lenin would be coming through the doors, the Latvian Guard trying to maintain a wedge between him and the crowd, as he hurried to the waiting coach that would take him back to his office.

Reilly pushed through the crowd, parallel to the intended target. All seemed routine until he spotted a vaguely familiar face out of the corner of his eye.

Dora knew that Lenin would be passing within a few feet of her in the next few seconds. Her hand gripped the pistol that she had hidden under her shawl. As she slowly withdrew the weapon, her eyes unexpectedly met those of Reilly. She smiled quickly and returned her attention to her target.

Her weapon was now drawn, and Lenin had moved into position to provide her with a perfect point-blank target.

Dora Kaplan, from the student's group, Reilly remembered, turning his attention to her in just enough time to see her withdraw a pistol from beneath her shawl.

Reilly leaped forward with a scream, hoping to throw off Dora's aim. Two shots went off as Reilly continued to push forward, knocking guards to the ground, until he himself was pinned down.

His body racked with pain from kicks and blows, the last thing he remembered was seeing Lenin being helped to his feet, where he brushed off his coat and looked down at his assailant.

Lenin's and Reilly's eyes met just before the pain of the beating became unendurable.

Reilly closed his eyes and thought of England. Then he passed out.

Helsinki, September 1918
   To: Captain Mansfield Cumming, CB, RN
   From: George Hill

   The plot has been blown. Lockhart has been arrested, and Reilly is missing and also believed to be in custody. The attempt on Lenin's life has thrown the city into an unproar, and all foreign nationals are being rounded up.
   Am en route to London with the suitcase.

London

To: Prime Minister David Lloyd George
From: Captain Mansfield Cumming, CB, RN

Hill is on his way back from Moscow.
Lockhart and Reilly are believed to be taken into custody by the Cheka.
The plot has been blown, but the money has been secured.
Moscow is in an uproar.
How do you wish us to proceed?

To: Captain Mansfield Cumming, CB, RN
From: Prime Minister David Lloyd George

Our official position is that we have never been involved with any plots or conspiracies in Russia, nor will we take sides with any of the parties involved in the revolution.
Lockhart has obviously been the victim of some misunderstanding or conspiracy to discredit or jeopardize British-Russian relations. We will offer to trade their envoy Litvinov for Lockhart in the spirit of diplomacy between the empire and an emerging government.
To our knowledge, Sidney Reilly left the employ of the British Secret Service in 1914.
Send our condolences to Mrs. Reilly. His work while in our employ was exemplary and we owe her at least that much.
Please brief Mr. Hill on this as soon as he arrives in London.
I trust you will perform the necessary editing on all pertinent files.

To: Prime Minister David Lloyd George
from: Captain Mansfield Cumming, CB, RN

Orders received.
Will comply under protest.

Moscow

I came within an ace of being master of Russia, thought Reilly.

He'd had plenty of time to think over the past few weeks. After the initial interrogation-beating, he'd been pretty much left alone in the solitary cell far beneath Cheka headquarters. Last week, one of the guards had informed him that Dora Kaplan had been executed. He remembered that this had been an old trick of the old Tsar's secret police, letting a prisoner know of the fates of others in order to increase the dread and uncertainty concerning one's own future.

Reilly had to believe that they had only linked him to the students' group, and that Hill and the others were still safe. The plot must have either failed or been aborted. Forty-eight more hours and the coup would have been in place, and he would have been pulling the strings. Now the only string that awaited him was a rope . . . only this time the Cheka would be the ones tightening the knot.

It had not been a bad life, he thought. He had always anticipated that his luck would eventually run out. He just wished things would move along. Hill, Cumming, and the others were safe, and he had no intention of betraying them. Even a spy owed his employers some loyalty.

Reilly heard bootsteps coming down the hall. Four, no five, pairs, echoing down the narrow corridor. *Well, I guess this is it,* he thought. Normally the guards only came in pairs. The party of five must be his firing squad. At least the waiting was over.

Reilly remained seated on the floor, his back to the wall, facing the door. The lock's wall-bound mechanism was turned, the bolt thrown, and the door pulled open. Instead of rousting him to his feet and dragging him into the corridor to meet his fate in the courtyard that was two hallways and a staircase away, the two Cheka guards set two chairs facing each other on the cell's bare floor. They then dragged him to his feet and placed him on one of the chairs, taking stations on each side of him. When all was in readiness the other three members of the hall party entered the cell. Due to the dim light from the hallway which provided the small chamber with its only illumination, only when one of the three took the seat directly opposite him, did Reilly realize that this was not a Cheka guard, but Bolshevik Party leader Lenin himself.

"Leave us," he commanded the guards. "We must talk in private."

The four guards left the cell, though the hallway's echo revealed that they had only retreated a few paces from the door. The corridor was the only way out, the prisoner was unarmed, and they could safely assume that he wouldn't be going anywhere without permission.

"It appears that I owe you my life, Comrade Relinsky," said Lenin, then adding, ". . . or should I say Reilly, or perhaps Rosenblum?"

Reilly remained stone-faced, though he was intrigued. It was quite unexpected that he would be interrogated by the party leader himself, let alone that they would have already correctly established his identity.

"Of course, I didn't expect you to react," the inquisitor continued. "I have much too much respect for you, comrade. Nor do I expect you to, as the Americans say, 'spill the beans.' Instead of my asking you questions, why don't I provide you with some answers? I know that your name is not Relinsky, it is Reilly, and that you are in the employ of the British Secret Service. Your name was originally Sigmund Rosenblum and you were born in Odessa. Though you no doubt had a passing acquaintance with the recently deceased Miss Kaplan, you were not involved in the assassination attempt on my life. No, you had much bigger fish to cast your net for in the following two days."

He knew about the plot.

Lenin continued, "A good friend of the party, Réné Marchand, who you may remember as a friend of your comrade de Vertement, let us know that your time was soon at hand, your zero hour, as I believe you refered to it. You should also know that Comrade Berzin was also loyal to the party, and had supplied us with the names of all of the Latvian traitors who were rounded up the next day. We also took into custody your Mr. Lockhart, a terribly weak man who quickly told us all we needed to know with just the most gentle of prodding."

Envoys and diplomats are best suited for kissing and making up, once the real men of action have already changed the course of history.

"You see, Mr. Reilly, loyalty cannot always be bought, no matter how extravagant the bribes. By the way, we assume that you must have had a tremendous cash reserve. It was never recovered."

At least George got away.

"Which brings me to you, Mr. Reilly. Normally we would have had you shot as a spy ... but you did save my life, and I am sure that that counts for something in the greater scheme of things, no matter what your motivations were."

Lenin rose from his chair and started to pace, circling the two chairs.

Reilly kept his eyes forward. He was sure that Lenin had not finished saying his piece.

"You may be surprised at this, Mr. Reilly, but I have grown to be quite a fan of yours. I particularly appreciate all of the work that you have done over the past few years providing the government with arms for the war in the west. No doubt the Tsar was also appreciative, but when it comes to war, it is the Russian people who suffer, and I am sure it was they who you were trying to help."

Lenin resumed his seat, saying, "Face it, Mr. Reilly—when all else is stripped away, you are still a Russian."

Lenin had hit a raw nerve with Reilly. The truth was unexpected, and never before had an adversary been so insightful. Reilly couldn't wait to see where this was going.

"Yesterday, Comrade Litvinov, one of our intelligence men stationed in London, who had been exposed by your

BSS, was returned to Moscow in exchange for Robert Bruce Lockhart. Your Prime Minister seemed to be in a great deal of hurry to retrieve him. You, on the other hand, are another story. According to a memorandum we intercepted from 10 Downing Street, you have not been in the employ of the BSS for at least four years. No trades are to be made to guarantee your safety, nor will your— how shall I say?—loyalty be rewarded. In the eyes of your superiors, Mr. Reilly, you no longer exist."

Lenin offered him a cigarette, which he accepted.

"Is this to be my last cigarette before I am executed as just another non-person in the eyes of the crown and the state?" he asked, some of his bravado returning.

"No, Mr. Reilly," Lenin assured him. "It is only to your superiors that you are a non-person. To me you are another son of Russia, a comrade who has finally returned to the fold. You and I both have a lot in common. Our Jewish blood, our time in exile, the new identities and aliases that situations have forced us to adopt. By the way, why did you ever change your name to Reilly, of all things?"

Reilly chuckled at the memory. "The BSS requested that I change my name to something less Jewish for diplomatic reasons. I chose the name Reilly. Cumming, the Service head, asked why I chose it, and replied that it was only fitting, since after the Jews, the Irish were the most oppressed people in the Western world. I am sure he never reported my reasoning to his superiors."

"I think not," Lenin agreed. "Well, enough of our bourgeois chitchat. I am here to make you an offer."

"In lieu of my execution as a spy?" Reilly asked wryly.

"Sidney Reilly was a spy, and the British government disavows his existence. My offer is for Sigmund Rosenblum. You are a very smart man, and Russia needs such men."

"I will not betray England," Reilly answered.

"They have already betrayed you," Lenin countered, "but there is no need for you to do the same. As you well

know, there are a great many who wish to see me dead.
Not just the enemies of the state, but factions within my
own party as well. I could not help but notice the disappointed look on Stalin's face when I emerged un-
scathed from Miss Kaplan's attack. He already fancies
himself as my successor, and I shudder to think what
would become of the revolution under him."

"You want me as your bodyguard, then?" Reilly asked.

"Nothing that simple. I want you to be the bodyguard
for the Russian people. Help me to keep the revolution
on track. Dzerzhinsky and the Cheka will keep the party
secure from sabotage. I want you to keep us free from
infiltration and corruption from abroad, and from within.
I want you to be my watchdog."

Reilly thought for a moment. It was true that he had
never expected loyalty from his employer. Cumming had
more or less told him that from the beginning. It was not
as if he was a British subject. Russia had always been his
first love. Instead of a death sentence, Lenin had offered
him a cause.

A life for a life.

Sigmund Rosenblum offered party leader Lenin his
hand.

"I accept, comrade," he said.

London, 1943

*An excerpt from the private journal of Kim Philby, MI5
(unpublished):*

While sorting through documents that had been
stored without proper indexing due to the exigen-
cies of the Blitz, I came across a startling memorandum linking Sigmund Rosenblum to a certain
Sidney Reilly who had once worked for the British
Secret Service. Imagine that! A former British agent
is now the ruler of all Russia, Lenin's successor, and
leader of the Bolshevik Party.

Any doubts I had previously about my destiny or

allegiance to the cause have been completely dispelled. I will bide my time as the party wishes. Who knows—some think I have quite a promising future working for British intelligence.

Brad Linaweaver has been toiling in the vineyards of science fiction with considerable success for a number of years—so when it came time to assign him an alternate warrior, I decided not to make his life too easy.

We now present the story of a warrior who finally decided not to turn the other cheek: Jesus of Nazareth.

Unmerited Favor
by Brad Linaweaver

And there are also many other things which Jesus did, the which, if they should be written every one, I suppose that even the world itself could not contain the books that should be written.

—*The Gospel According to St. John*

As long as anyone could remember, the Holy Land had been hot. That's why it was good to live in Jerusalem. The old city had a lot of water—so much of it that the occupying Romans could have their fill (and Pontius Pilate, the procurator, could grow all the roses he wanted); and there was still plenty left for the Arabs, Syrians, Egyptians, Greeks and, of course, the people whose land this was.

Thomas wasn't thinking about any of that right now, although he was as patriotic as his comrades. Like them, he dreamed of the glory that had been the birthright of the ancient Hebrews. But right now he was only thirsty, wishing that he wasn't in such a rush to get to the secret meeting.

He had been to a lot of secret meetings. None of them had changed anything about these depressing modern times in which he and his friends found themselves. But he was in the habit of lending support to any organization that would make a show of resistance against the order of things. Not too long ago, he'd been content to be a fisherman, and not think about politics except to grumble at tax time. Then he'd rediscovered deep wells of religious faith in himself, and had drunk deep; and he knew the one absolute fact of human life was the unity of politics and religion.

The rekindled passions coursing through Thomas could be blamed on the man from Galilee. Some perfectly sensible people were starting to believe that this strange rabbi was the Messiah. There was nothing unusual about the rabble pinning their hopes on the next charismatic man in line. But this new one, this Jesus, was achieving a level of credibility that Thomas found hard to believe. It's not that the man offered a specific plan. He could deflect any talk of revolution into a soliloquy on redemption. He could answer any concrete question with a mysterious parable that left everyone scratching their heads. And yet there was always something subversive in these parables. Primarily, Jesus had the enviable knack of being different things to different people, at a level of sophistication worthy of the most wily emperor. Maybe Jesus *was* the One!

Thomas didn't want to miss a word the Nazarene might speak. Heretofore, the speeches had been scheduled in easily accessible places. Or they had happened spontaneously—if one didn't believe the cynics—as a natural response to the love, and hunger, of the crowd. This time there was secrecy. Thomas counted himself fortunate to have been told at all! The place was a secluded garden on the outskirts of the city that had been allowed to go to ruin. It was the perfect location at which to harvest a crop of Roman spies.

Despite his haste, Thomas was late. A Zealot was already addressing the crowd that filled the tattered spaces of the unkempt garden. Thomas felt his dry tongue against his drier lips, and suddenly, as if a miracle, a cup of water was pressed to his mouth by a young lad who was working the crowd, jug in hand. They also serve those who stand and wait.

Refreshed, it was easier for Thomas to pay attention to the Zealot's speech, who even now was saying, "The emperor will hang on to this area if we put up five times, *ten times*, the resistance. Our sacred land of Judea is central to his trade routes. We all know it! Worst of all, our aristocratic Sadducees know the economic realities too well. And the Pharisees know it . . ."

There was some muttering at the last comment. The speaker quickly demonstrated his political sense. "Yes, I know it never pays to be overly specific when one is being critical. I am of the Essenes. The children of Israel have our little differences . . . and we Essenes are often criticized for our ideas on purity. But you've never seen a squabble until you've got Sadducees and Pharisees debating the afterlife!" A few chuckles near Thomas helped defuse the tension.

Then they were treated to Zealot humor, an oxymoron if there ever was one: "The Roman Empire first became involved in this part of the world when she tried to solve the conflict between Mesopotamia and Egypt. Well, she's had nothing but trouble since. You think she would have learned." He wasn't a bad-looking man, this Zealot, and as he laughed at his own remark, Thomas was tempted to join in, if only out of politeness. It was just that no one saw anything funny about a perfectly accurate historical remark.

The Zealot was quick to recover. Nostrils quivering at a breeze that brought with it a whiff of distant salt and sea, he felt like a fisher of men. This was the moment to cast his net: "You know what binds us together," he said with passion. "Our national pride will never be crushed!" Thomas could feel the shift in the crowd, as a tidal pull has you before you even notice. A murmuring of agreement rose up, sighed against swaying palm leaves as if they were so many knives. The voice grew louder, more reckless of being overheard. "Our willingness to stand together is our power; and we will resist a hundredfold, even beyond counting, until there is no military occupation of Palestine!" Now there were cheers, as predictable as the marching of Caesar's legions.

Thomas found himself wondering why they hadn't sent out special invitations for the enemy to join them, considering the noise. Then he reproached himself for his lack of patriotism. Surely every precaution had been taken. The Zealots had posted their own guards. Now if Thomas could only make himself stop doubting the likelihood of spies in their midst.

The Zealot was sufficiently carried away that he probably thought he could convert any renegade among them who would sell their future for damned Roman coin. Perhaps he was capitalizing on the work Jesus had done, when the Master told His followers that they didn't have to deal in Roman money at all; and if they didn't like the coins with Caesar's graven image, they could always render them back to the Roman state. More people were trying to live by barter than ever before.

And yet it couldn't be said that Jesus preached against money *per se*. He didn't. Someone had observed that He spent more time talking about money than about Heaven. Thomas found Jesus the best possible guide for legal advice, when He had said that it was better to give the shirt off your back than allow another to take you to court, where you ran the risk of imprisonment and endless fines. No one gave more practical advice.

"All that is wanting is a leader," cried the Zealot. "We have waited long for a warrior, the greatest warrior, to lead us against the Roman evil. Have our prayers been answered? Has the true leader come among us?"

With a buildup like this, Thomas expected the appearance of Jesus very soon. Yet how would the man handle the spot he was being put in by the speaker? Up until now, Jesus had avoided direct confrontation with those expecting a martial solution to their problems. Thomas felt uncomfortable.

Thomas was also uncomfortable over the many stories circulating about Jesus's propensity for working wonders. Thomas hadn't seen any miracles. Too much emphasis on this sort of thing seemed like playing to the lowest common denominator of the mob. And yet, could all this be part of a clever strategy? After all, the military prospects were bleak. The only reasonable plan was to combine a military strike with a political solution at the same time; so that the costs of putting down the rebellion would be greater than Rome was willing to pay.

Out of two discomforts Thomas found a new sense of security. He was too pragmatic to really expect any sort of unqualified success. Despite these reservations, he believed that a devious leader could improve the situation. Better someone reputed to work miracles like Jesus should take charge, than this Zealot whose hotheaded approach would guarantee disaster. A failed rebellion could make things worse. After all, Jerusalem enjoyed an almost anarchic freedom compared to any city in Egypt. The latter was a senatorial province with practically no freedom for anyone. Here, at least, they had the legal protections of a client state with some small degree of autonomy. It was easy for Jewish officialdom to keep the peace on purely practical grounds. Only a man skilled at fooling a lot of the people a lot of the time could shake the establishment out of its lethargy.

Thomas had stopped following the Zealot's words. Hear one of these tirades, and you've heard them all—the call for violence against a superior foe when it was not at all clear that the man crying for sacrifice would be spilling his own blood into the contested earth! Then there was a moment of blessed silence as the Zealot fumbled to find a new cliché, and was spared any further thought. A new voice spoke, the voice that Thomas had come to hear.

The crowd's attention was seized by Jesus of Nazareth as a child's fancy might turn to a delightful new color, and even finer sounds. No one had a voice like Jesus. Thomas felt himself smiling just because he was hearing the voice. And then he gazed again upon the only face that captured in its every line a perfect serenity and confidence.

Jesus said: "If you bring forth what is written within you, what you bring forth will save you. If you do not bring forth what is within you, what you do not bring forth will destroy you."

That was certainly a conversation-stopper. Not only did the crowd maintain a studious silence, but the Zealot moved his lips and no words came forth. Another miracle! The first time Thomas had heard Jesus speak, he had thought the man was merely skilled at stating *non sequiturs*. But anyone who could make a person think, the way Jesus did, was not merely spinning meaningless tapestries of words. It was Jesus who had made Thomas recognize the full humanity of women; who had made him feel a degree of sympathy for the poor and the ill that he would have condemned as weakness in himself until the strange rabbi made him accept his own emotions as strength!

Jesus had not come alone. Simon Peter was with him, and also Judas Iscariot. Thomas had once overheard Peter in an unguarded moment tell a friend that the Master often spoke in parables because the people weren't ready to understand the mysteries which must be kept secret. His friend had replied that Peter had a better understanding regarding the people's limitations than anyone else, including the Messiah! The conversation had then wandered into areas touching on Peter's organizational skills; and Thomas had wandered off in search of wine.

There seemed nothing secretive about what Jesus did next. Sometimes he could be so direct that his followers could scarce credit what they heard. He asked who among the gathering they trusted. Naturally, there were cries of His name. He seemed not to hear. Again, as if speaking to unruly children, he asked them to look at one another, and look into their hearts, and say, truly, if they trusted one another.

Thomas noticed a grim expression on the face of Judas Iscariot. Clearly this was a man of principle who was prepared to judge his neighbors. And yet hadn't Jesus admonished everyone to avoid judging anything but their own hearts? The more Thomas tried to understand Jesus, the more mystery he found.

Holding up his pale, white hands—hands that had an almost feminine quality about them—Jesus gestured for everyone to come closer. Above the hands smiled His face, a face that encompassed every imaginable quality of the masculine. No one hesitated to move forward.

He did not speak to them for very long; but every word seemed a revelation, burned into their minds. He told them that the time had come to take up arms against their true enemies. The crowd sighed as if releasing their collective soul for Him to fondle. Then He let silence reign, and it, too, became a palpable presence.

The Zealot was the first to find his voice. He asked: "Are you the new Moses?" Another asked: "How shall you lead us?"

Thomas was surprised to hear his own voice asking: "What of the law?" There were times when Jesus seemed to challenge the traditions of His own people as thoroughly as He brought subtle criticism against Rome.

Jesus answered them all with: "I am not come to destroy, but to fulfill." Thomas seemed to recall that He had said that before. It probably wouldn't be the last time. Then He spoke of bringing a sword in his hand and the Zealots cheered. Their fear that He would lead His followers in the path of peace seemed an empty worry this day.

The voice of Jesus changed then. The lofty quality was replaced by something more worldly—as if insinuating things, hinting things ... making plans in nasal tones, plotting faction against faction and anticipating the worst. He said that any who wished to take up arms should meet back at this place tonight and they would be well satisfied.

Standing at the edge of the crowd was a sinister-looking merchant who grinned through broken teeth. Thomas had heard that this unsavory fellow was gifted at providing weapons for the right price. As to how the transaction might be arranged, Thomas had sufficient wisdom not to question a worker of miracles.

Jesus finished with a reminder that He demanded Faith from those who would follow Him. Faith was not about the fog of half-formed aspirations and dreams floating in a young fool's head. Faith was about confidence translated into action. Tonight would be an important test for everyone.

As the sun hung over the smooth, round hills of the Holy Land, it looked like a golden Roman coin placed against a woman's body. Thomas would not have as far to travel to reach the meeting place this time. He had simply remained behind. Although the heat of the day still clung about his sandaled feet, he wished that he'd brought extra clothing because the nights could be cold. Although born and bred in desert lands, Thomas often felt that he had too narrow a range for comfort where temperature was concerned. He envied his friends their toughness; and he also felt intimidated by the adaptability of the cursed Romans. They seemed suited to any climate, with their long, hard faces and souls of marble.

The merchant returned with a minimum of fuss and a heavily laden cart. When one wheel bumped over a broken piece of statuary, there was a sound of metal on metal from under the cloth that covered the contents. It seemed incredible that Jesus was really going through with it. All this talk of Faith would be put to the test tonight. Thomas prayed that his last doubts would be as a dried husk, falling away to dust.

Two of the Zealots, left to guard the meeting place, had no compunction about arguing the usual: Was this man really the Messiah? If so, why did He waste time criticizing the natural order of things? Whence came this bizarre predilection for worrying over prostitutes, children and other no-accounts? From the point of view of these two pragmatic gentlemen, it was just about time for a leader to either put on the armor of a warrior or just shut up about odd hobbies and obsessions. Thomas rubbed the stubble on his round chin and smiled over the subject the Zealots were avoiding: the most disturbing behavior of Jesus was the man's willingness to talk to Gentiles as if they were human in God's eyes.

Here were dangerous waters to navigate; and more than one person had wondered out loud about the Nazarene's parentage. There was no doubt about the mother. His mother was not the source of controversy. At first Thomas had thought an Egyptian father might explain some of the Master's more exotic features. More recently, he had inclined to the dreadfully heretical view that there might be a Roman father skulking around the silver fountains. Perhaps this would explain the tolerance of the imperial authorities for some of the more provocative preachments of this latest man of destiny.

Hatred of the Romans was such that one didn't openly talk of such matters. Besides, the growing cult was putting out the idea of a supernatural origin for Jesus—one that didn't preclude a human mother but insisted on something far more transcendental for the father. This sort of notion played better with the Romans, actually, than with those who owed their allegiance to King Herod. The Romans believed that Zeus sent more of Himself earthward than just lightning bolts. Who ever dreamed a rabbi could be spoken of in a manner reserved for mythical figures, such as Heracles?

The heretical implications of the Jesus movement could undermine any political advantages if everyone wasn't very, very careful. There were plenty of mystery cults sniffing around. No one took them seriously. You had the followers of Mithra. You had the followers of Zoroaster. You had all sorts of followers . . . but not all of them wielded swords, like so many flashing scythes, to mow down the greatest army in the world.

We'll probably all be crucified, thought Thomas, but there comes a time when a man must choose to spend his life, if not wisely, then with a full measure of devotion. That was the kind of commitment Thomas noted on the faces of the men who were gathering in the garden. As night drew its shadows close around them it was harder to make out details. There was no moon yet. A few, lone stars winked overhead. And while visions of spies and solemn treachery made a chaos of Thomas's mind, Jesus walked among them.

It was that crucial moment in any military campaign when the commanding officer must inspire confidence. This would have been an auspicious moment for the leader to appear, surrounded by his entourage. But He had come without Matthew, without Luke, without Mark, without John, without Peter or Judas, who had been with him only a few hours earlier; but it was worse than that. The leader might be expected to make a surprise inspection of the troops. That wasn't so bad for morale. But Jesus had a woman with Him.

Thomas had met Mary Magdalene once before when she would occasionally join the small group that followed Jesus around Palestine. By that time, she was no longer plying the trade that had caused so much controversy. Respectability held no charms for these disciples of the new. Thomas regretted that Mary was no longer available to a hardworking man with coin to spend.

In the fading light, he could make out her long, delicate fingers. He wanted to touch them. Her raven-dark hair hung loose about her face instead of being tied up and properly out of view. A torch was lit near her face and in the dancing light he saw the hint of a smile as she noticed the discontent she inspired among the men. She glanced at Jesus but He seemed not to notice.

Thomas couldn't understand why the Master would make an error regarding something as important as the men's morale. Jesus had a worldly side, as he'd demonstrated when he put a stop to James and John angling for greater authority of their own. Bringing a woman along seemed not the wisest move at such a time but Thomas reminded himself that it was not his place to pass judgment.

Without saying a word, Jesus walked over to the cart and uncovered swords and spears and shields. Silently, he gestured to the warriors. They came forward, one at a time, to receive the offering. Jesus passed out the weapons with the greatest solemnity. When it was Thomas's turn, he hesitated. They had been told nothing of what to expect. This small group could be part of some large, coordinated plan—a rebellion that might stretch from Jerusalem to Jericho. Or it could be one more pointless act of terrorism to be followed by the usual reprisals.

With a sensation of tingling in his fingertips, Thomas reached for a sword and prayed that no one would notice his hand tremble. Jesus's face was blank and unreadable. Thomas felt Mary's eyes on him, and his cheeks burned under her sight. The call to Faith was never easy.

When everyone was armed, Jesus, still unspeaking, walked out of the garden. They followed Him. Thomas waited until last. He couldn't take his eyes off Mary, who showed no inclination of joining the procession. To his surprise, she approached him right before he left and whispered in his ear: "You will be protected by His grace." Then she retired behind a sorry-looking specimen of an olive tree.

Thomas was still trying to figure out what she had meant as he trudged along the ancient hills, a would-be liberator with the rest. The sky had turned from gray to black and more stars were visible. For purposes of surprise, it would be best to have a cloudy night or, failing that, at least a moonless one. The credibility of the mission was not further enhanced when the round orb of the moon did rise like a sleepless eye to watch their progress. The moonlight cast their shadows before them like streaks of oil. Thomas felt like a ghost.

Jesus was leading them God-knows-where. At first it seemed that the objective might be a garrison, but as they marched out into the desert sands, in a direction that even Thomas knew promised nothing but more desert, the worst kind of grumbling began—patriotic grumbling.

Thomas was about ready to rethink his position on Faith when the ragged line stopped dead in its tracks. So there they were, remote from the cares of the city, all alone in the still, windless, desert night. The grumbling of the men subsided as easily as it had begun. They waited. The moon washed them a pale white as if they were statues from antiquity.

Jesus said: "You see but do not perceive." His tall figure seemed almost to hang over the desert, like a mirage, while Thomas was bogged down, uncomfortable with the sand filling his sandals and getting between his toes. Thomas waited stupidly. They all did; the way many of them had reacted the first time they saw the Master lower Himself to wash the feet of mere followers. *Now what?* screamed a thought in Thomas's mind.

Jesus sat down in the sand. Some joined Him there. Some stood uncertainly, shifting from foot to foot. Thomas was one of these. The Zealot who had made the speech that got everyone's blood boiling stared with undisguised anger at the latest turn of events.

"The enemy will be coming through here?" he asked through clenched teeth, not bothering to disguise the sharpness of tone. Jesus said nothing, which only served to feed the other's anger, who grew more shrill with: "You're not going to tell us there is no enemy, are you?"

Another man asked, just as testily: "You're not going to ask us to turn the other cheek?" Jesus did not respond.

So they waited. All that could be heard was the rasping sound of heavy breathing, the breath of anger. Still Jesus did not respond. He let the quiet settle about their heads, and sink into their bodies, and slow the breathing, before he spoke to them. Then He told them about the enemy.

He promised they would face the enemy, here, tonight, as He had faced the ultimate enemy in this place. Then He pronounced forbidden names of the most loathsome Demons. He said the Demons would soon come among them and they must gird their loins to do battle with the foe. He closed His eyes and bade them pray.

"I knew it!" screamed the Zealot demagogue as if recovering the tongue stolen from him in the garden. "We cannot put our Faith in this man. We should have known better. Here is a prince of fools who wastes time warning those without power about the pitfalls of power! He's a madman who says prostitutes have a better chance at entering Heaven than those who administer our sacred moral law! Now we see what sort of warrior 'He' is. We are to make war against demonic possession rather than Roman oppression!"

Suddenly Thomas had every reason to believe that there would be bloodshed this night. For every man who seemed deranged in anger, another was either confused or willing to defend the rabbi, come what may. "He has no use for these weapons," the Zealot continued, "but we do!" He waved his sword so that it gleamed in the moonlight. "We'll leave 'Him' here with any other madmen who care to face invisible hordes."

Not a few men cast nervous glances over their shoulders as if expecting monsters to rise up from the ancient sands or descend from the even more ancient stars. The first to look up mistook the large cloud that had drifted into the otherwise perfectly clear night sky for a supernatural manifestation. He screamed.

The cloud covered the moon, and the confusion down below was almost perfect. At the same moment, a cold wind slashed at their faces. There was shouting, another scream and the clash of steel. Thomas panicked at the thought they might be fighting each other. He tried to run and collided with a massive chest. A pair of hands shoved him from the side and he fell to the ground, tasting sand and getting grit into his eyes. Listening to the melée, he wasn't at all sure he wanted to stand up again.

The Zealot was evidently disappointed by the absence of *esprit de corps* in the face of bad weather. He screamed above the wind: "You stupid children! You'll never stand up to the Romans. You'll . . ." He coughed. Then he made a gurgling sound and fell near Thomas, who reached out and felt the other man's inert body.

"Demons!" shrieked another. "Demons took him!"

"Death to the evil one," said a voice much quieter than the rest. "There will be no more sorcery."

There were men for whom the life of Jesus was a poem, and His words echoed in them as His actions guided them. For others, He was a danger not to be borne. When the cloud passed on into the night, and the moon shone down again upon the disorganized company, two bodies lay in the sand. The first was the Zealot, eyes staring in horror at what no one could guess. The other was Jesus, prone upon the ground with a spear piercing his side.

No one had kept track of who was armed with what weapon. No one admitted to the crime. Thomas stumbled forward, as in a dream, and reached out to pull the lance from the side of the only man in all the world in whom he had placed his Faith. Then Thomas reached down and touched the red, gushing wound and he cried at the sight.

Many threw down their weapons and ran off in all directions. They were a mob now. Thomas knelt beside the body. A few others joined him there. They sat that way for at least an hour until a hand touched Thomas on the shoulder and he turned to see that, somehow, Mary Magdalene had joined them. Her hand was firm, and without thinking about it he pressed his face upon her arm.

"What will we do?" he asked her. "It's all over."

"No," she said, "it is not over." She sat down beside him and joined the long vigil. "It is only beginning," she whispered. Thomas thought she was speaking to him but she wasn't.

Jack Haldeman is back, and so is Martin Luther King. Very few men of peace have had such an impact on the American people, and very few writers have been able to avoid wondering what might have happened had Dr. King's life taken a somewhat different direction.

Death of a Dream
by Jack C. Haldeman II

St. Patrick's Day. Chicago, 1975.

Twenty minutes past midnight.

Martin Luther King, Jr., broke down the rifle like an expert. He oiled it and rubbed it with a soft rag, even though it didn't need it. It had only had a single box of ammunition run through it to check the sights and the scope. He was amazed at how easy and natural it all seemed.

The bare light in the cheap hotel room cast sharp shadows against the fading and peeling wallpaper. It was a dump. He'd hoped to find something better, but this was the only colored hotel on the motorcade route.

It didn't matter. By noon, nothing would matter. It would all be over.

He was hungry. He set the rifle down and opened a diet soda, pulling a cold hamburger from a carry-out bag. He would have liked to have his last meal sitting in a fancy restaurant, but this was the wrong neighborhood for a black man to eat. He could have gone to the ghetto in the South Side, but that wouldn't have been the same.

Last meal, he thought as he chewed the hamburger. Some last meal.

He had no illusions. In the morning he would die. But he would take the President of the United States with him.

He finished the hamburger and walked to the window, pulling the tattered curtain aside to look out into the Chicago night. It was cool, the air was clear. There was a pleasant breeze off the lake. The traffic was light on the street below, and most of it consisted of black and white police cars.

Chicago was a law-and-order city. Which was just another way of saying they were very good at keeping the niggers down.

He washed, and stretched out on the bed, removing his shoes, but remaining dressed. He left the bedside lamp on, having turned out the overhead. He imagined he could feel the cancer chewing his gut.

Things could have been so different. Way back then, he still had a dream. Now all he had was a nightmare.

Hoover had done it. Not the FBI, not the bureaucracy, but J. Edgar Hoover himself. It all blew up in Washington, He had already written his "I have a dream" speech. He never got to give it.

As a Baptist preacher he could cry for equality from the pulpit, and as long as he was addressing only poor black people, he attracted little attention. But he'd had a golden voice back then, and the vitality and the passion. People listened. People believed.

And other people started paying attention.

The crowds had grown, and were no longer all black. People all across the nation were joining hands and walking together. Freedom rides. The Montgomery bus boycott. It was all so close.

Then Hoover, who had also been paying attention, held

that press conference in Washington the day before the march. The dream shattered like broken glass.

Monstrous lies were built from half-truths. They painted King as a sleazy manipulator, a man without principles or morals, a calculating coldhearted bastard.

In the uproar, the truth got buried. If it had been anyone other than Hoover, perhaps he would have had a chance. As it was, King was broken, crushed. Even his most trusted friends backed away from him, apologizing as they went, but going anyway. Rap Brown. Stokely Carmichael. The Civil Rights Bill died with Kennedy. Everything flew away like dust in the wind. His heart turned bitter.

Washington never happened. The crowd that would have filled the Mall went home. There was no joining in spirit. There was no speech. There was no dream.

Then Malcolm X stepped in and the backlash from his assassination of George Wallace killed any hopes the civil rights movement had. Those were days of riots, arson, murder, lynching. Harlem was surrounded and burned to the ground, as were parts of Baltimore and Los Angeles. The resistance from the black community was feeble, and with a few exceptions, unorganized.

A surprising number of politicians showed their true colors and rode the crest of public hatred and fear. They rode it into the White House. The Senate. The House of Representatives. Only they didn't call it bigotry, they called it law and order.

I still can't drink from water fountains with the white folk, King thought bitterly. The police have a mandate from the people to keep us in our place. The Senate is seriously considering a "back to Africa" bill. The world has gone crazy.

And I'm dying of cancer.

Then Martin Luther King, Jr., fell asleep for the last time in his life.

He woke with a start and looked at his watch. He had overslept. There was not much time. He went to the bathroom and washed up. Then he went to the chair by the window and pushed the curtain aside.

One half hour to go. Green bunting and shamrocks were everywhere. People were gathering on the sidewalks below, white faces waiting for the President, anticipating his annual "Drive the snakes out of Ireland" speech. King was doing much the same. Waiting. He loaded the rifle and set the extra shells on the table beside him. Not that he'd have a chance to use them, nor a reason. It would only take one shot.

His stomach burned as the cancer gnawed his life away. In better times, a poor black man could have had medical treatment. But complicated and expensive medical care was for white folks. Let the blacks take care of their own. Never mind that no black person had graduated from—or even been accepted to—medical school in five years. It was the American way. Let the blacks get treated with voodoo magic or herbs and berries.

And for God's sake, don't give them the vote back.

King popped the top of another warm diet soda and grinned a little as he sipped it. He should have bought a regular soda. What difference could a few calories make now?

It bothered King how comfortable the rifle felt. All his life he had been nonviolent. But the fallout from Washington had crushed him. The loss of human dignity and respect had embittered him to where he could see no other option. It had brought him to this place, sitting in a cheap hotel and waiting to kill the man who had let his blind search for power divide a wounded country.

President Richard J. Daley was sitting pretty. Not only had the all-white electorate given him a sweeping mandate for a third term, but a convenient airplane crash had left four empty seats on the Supreme Court. He would start to fill them next week—if he lived—if he lived to cut another deal, lived to sell more souls for his rotten political empire.

His Vice President was a former Georgia governor who

had been added to the ticket at the last minute as a compromise to those who didn't share Daley's extreme viewpoint. So far in this term he had been kept in the closet, being dragged out only when some bleeding-heart liberals needed a bone tossed their way.

But King knew the man, knew him from years back. He was a decent man, once you got past the political crapola. He played the party game only to get to a place where he could do some good. As a Vice President, he was in a blind alley.

As President he might be able to change the country. Change the world.

King winced as his stomach took another bad turn. The crowd started yelling. It was time.

First the motorcycles came by, sirens wailing and flags flying. Then two cars filled with men from the Secret Service cruised past, scanning the crowd. Next was the open car with the President and his stooge, the mayor of Chicago. King braced the rifle against the window ledge.

It would be an easy shot. He lined the cross hairs on the back of the President's head.

"Smite thy enemy," he said softly as he pulled the trigger. As the President's head erupted in a red spray, Martin Luther King, Jr., threw the rifle out the window, closed his eyes, and cried while he waited to die.

Josepha Sherman, author of science fiction, fantasy, young adult, and nonfiction books—and also a full-time editor in the science fiction field—has chosen for her alternate warrior no other than Jules Verne, who may never have faced a Martian invasion but was probably better prepared to than any other man of his era.

Monsieur Verne and the Martian Invasion
by Josepha Sherman

It was a bright, virtually windless morning in the year 1887, and Monsieur Jules Verne, inventor *par excellence*, thought with great satisfaction that surely life could not be finer. France was at peace again after what had seemed like an infinity of wars without and within, aeroships, their upright, multiple rotors slicing smoothly through the air, once again plied the skies, en route to all of Europe and the Americas, and three brave aeronauts were even now on their way to the Moon.

Yes, and today, Verne added to himself with an inner smile, he and these chosen few political and military men had come to this isolated field for the testing flight of yet another Jules Verne invention.

"What a pity this must be done in secret," said a voice.

Verne glanced at the speaker, his fellow inventor, the

artist-turned-balloonist who called himself simply Nadar. "What's this? Jealous, my friend?"

"No, no, of course not!" Nadar hastened to reply. "I know as well as you that ... certain powers must not know of your warrior aeroplane till it has been perfected."

"Exactly. And—"

Verne broke off in midsentence at the approaching sound of powerful rotors. "Ah, here comes Bertrand now."

Bertrand Dufy was, the inventor thought dourly, probably the finest aeronaut in all of France. He was also tall, golden, elegant of dress and style—and brainless as a bird.

If he dares foul things up now ...

No time to worry about that now. All about him, Verne could hear the startled gasps as his aeroplane, his *Terror*, roared across the sky. Commercial aeroships were just that: stately, thirty-masted ships of the air, differing only from their sisters of the sea in that those masts bore rotors, not sails. But the *Terror* was more bird than ship, more predatory bird, its wings swept back like those of a diving eagle. Its dark metal hull gleamed dully in the sunlight as its rotors sped it, beautiful and deadly, over the viewer's heads.

Now Bertrand banked sharply to the right, bringing the *Terror* back in a second pass, and the audience gasped anew. Never had an aeroship shown such fantastic maneuverability! Bertrand banked again, flying the *Terror* in a tight figure eight.

"Flying her yourself?" Nadar teased his friend in an undertone. Verne glanced down at his hands and reddened, realizing for the first time how he had been moving them as though holding a pilot's wheel.

Yes, he admitted ruefully to himself, *I wish it were I flying the* Terror, *or even her younger sister, my new, untested* Eagle.

Surely it wasn't vanity to know one was more than a competent pilot? That one was the only other soul yet capable of handling his warrior aeroplane?

But I am hardly in Bertrand's caliber. Besides, he is young

*and dashing and the darling of reporters. While I, alas, am
not.*

Still, Verne reminded himself, it would be *his* warrior
aeroplanes that would, in time, defend France and perhaps all the free world. What more could any man possibly want? But just then Bertrand brought the *Terror* back
in yet another pass, this time throwing in a quite unau-
thorized up, over, and down again loop. As the audience
burst into spontaneous cheers, Verne felt himself grinning like a boy. Yes, that young idiot had no business
risking his invention like that—but ah, how such stunts
proved the *Terror* all that more versatile!

Ah yes, surely life could not be finer!

*This was not going well. This was not going well at all.
The star charts It had managed to stow aboard the ship had
turned out to be all but useless, and the vessel itself—oh, if
this wasn't a clear case of sabotage, It was a flesh-slave!
They had known It would try to escape, they, the so-moral
ones who thought to free all the slaves and live in peaceful
coexistence with the solid creatures—bah, the idiots!*

*Not such idiots. When the revolt had torn It from power,
It had had no intention of suffering the tearing-from-any-
flesh-host execution due traitors. But they, the cursed victors,
must have known the only vehicle It could reach was this
one. It had done the best It could to repair the ship, but It
was a warrior, a ruler, not a worker! The power drive sputtered and staggered like a dying flesh-slave. The ship had
already lost its ability to soar through hyperspace, and now
It wondered if the feeble thing would be able to reach the
only planetary system It had been able to find. And Its own
flesh-slave was beginning to suffer from radiation leakage. If
the creature died, with no other host within reach ...*

*It refused to consider that, forcing the flesh-slave to study
the flickering vision-screen. Ha, look, look! The third planet
bore signs of life, reasonably intelligent life—yes, oh yes! Now,
if only this faltering wreck of a ship would hold together long
enough ...*

But now the power drive was failing altogether. Despairing, It realized there was just enough energy left for an emergency landing on the natural satellite circling the planet.

So be it. If the creatures on that world were civilized enough for space travel, It would live. If not . . .

Fear was for the weak. Whatever came to pass, at least It would not die at the wills of Its foes!

"Good God." Robert Duval, the oldest of the three aeronauts en route to the moon for humanity's third lunar landing, nearly banged his nose against the thick, spaceworthy glass of the *Lucille's* view screen. "Did you see that?"

His two comrades crowded against him, staring out. The vast, pitted gray surface of the Moon filled the entire view screen, so close that for the last day they'd had to keep forcing themselves to accept it wasn't about to fall on them. But what had been that sudden flash of light, there on the edge of the sunlit side?

"A meteorite strike," thoughtful Georges Nantes decided.

"That didn't look like a meteorite strike! I could have sworn I saw a rocket flare!"

"Impossible. We are the only ones out here."

Duval shot a disapproving glare at the man who'd just spoken. Albert Legrand was the youngest aeronaut—and as far as Duval was concerned, he was also the shallowest, most disgustingly egotistical know-it-all of the lot. It had *not* been exactly a peaceful voyage so far. "And you think we of Earth might be the only explorers of space?"

"Oh come now, Duval! You're not going to say we just saw some of Monsieur Wells' space fantasies come to life, are you?"

"I am saying," Duval said, biting off each word, "that whatever caused the flare, it is something worth our investigation."

A pity their radio communications could not reach as far as Earth. But since there was no way for them to consult with scientists back there ... "Georges," Duval commanded, "alter our course, if you would. We shall see just what is down there."

It lay trapped within the heavy, motionless body of the flesh-slave. At the last few moments, the power had failed completely, and only this satellite's lesser gravity had kept It from total disaster. As things were, the flesh-slave was clearly too badly injured to survive, and the ship itself was—bah, the ship had always been wreckage. But now it was ruined beyond all hope of repair.

But that didn't matter. For now the strange, teardrop-shaped capsule It had sighted during those last frantic moments before the crash had landed, not too far away. And two flesh-creatures wrapped within cocoons of protective garments were making their bounding way forward.

Soon, It promised Itself, ahh, soon ...

"Well? What is it, Duval? What's out there?" Nantes' voice, transmitted by the *Lucille*'s radio, sounded reedy and thin in the earphones of Duval's helmet, but the man's impatience came through clearly enough; someone had had to stay on board the *Lucille*, and Nantes had lost the toss.

"A ship, by God!" Legrand cut in before Duval could answer. "It must have hit pretty hard, but—"

"Legrand, come back here!"

Too late. The younger man was already crawling into the wreckage. "There's someone in here!" His voice shook with excitement. "Or ... something. But he—she—it—whatever it was, it's dead, and—damn!"

"Legrand! What is it?"

For an agonizingly long time, there wasn't an answer. Duval was just about to dig into the wreckage himself to pull the younger man out when Legrand said weakly:

"A headache. Damned powerful one, too. Came on just like that. Something must be going wrong with the air in my suit ..."

"Get out of there, man, now!"

As Legrand staggered free of the wreckage, Duval caught him and practically carried him back to the *Lucille*. As he worked on getting Legrand out of his suit, Nantes set about firing up the *Lucille*'s engines. Enough for a first visit, Duval thought. Enough to keep the scientists on their toes for days!

"There, now. How do you feel, Albert?"

"Better." The younger man rubbed a hand feebly over his eyes. "But I still feel groggy."

"I . . . uh . . . smuggled this on board," Nantes said, almost shyly.

"Wine!" Duval exclaimed. "Just the thing! Albert, this will—"

"No! No. I—I don't drink."

"Since when—"

"My head hurts. I . . . think I need to take a nap."

Duval and Nantes exchanged worried glances. "Of course," Duval said soothingly. "Just take it easy. We'll be back on Earth soon enough."

"Since when does Legrand not drink?" Nantes whispered. "Remember that night back when the three of us were in training and—"

Duval waved him to silence. "You saw the pain in his eyes. If his headache is that bad the best thing for him is sleep. He'll be fine when he wakes." *Please God.*

But if anything, Legrand seemed worse the next "morning," lying strapped to his bunk in weightlessness, staring blankly at nothing. *Almost,* Duval thought uneasily, *as though he's forgotten who and where he is.*

"Nantes," Duval said slowly, "we can't tell anyone back on Earth about finding that . . . vehicle."

"We can't just pretend it never happened!"

"Oh yes, we can. A sick aeronaut, a wild story about otherworldly visitors—my God, man, think about it! We have no concrete proof of what we saw. Either everyone *doesn't* believe us, and we're locked up as madmen, or they *do* believe us and we start a panic! No, what happened here is that we merely went for a walk on the lunar surface. Legrand became ill. And that," Duval said fiercely, "is all!"

After a moment, Nantes bowed his head in reluctant agreement. Now all they could do was pray for a swift, safe return to Earth. Yes, and pray that the doctors would know exactly what had gone wrong with Legrand—and that whatever he might have contacted wasn't contagious!

Who would have expected the flesh-slave, the human, as it called itself, to have such a strong sense of identity? The initial casting-of-self-into-slave had gone well enough; just as with the flesh-slaves of Its own world, there had been a weakness that allowed It entry, in this case a bizarre dream of self as hero, seeing all the rest of humankind adoring it. The creature had known so little of what was happening to it that it had put up only a token resistance. But now the slave had begun fighting back against domination so constantly It had to clamp down on everything but those actions that kept the host body alive. Worse, the others of the humankind were self-aware as well, and aware that something was not right with this one. Best to stay as quiet and still as possible till the creature's home world was regained. These beings might be self-aware, but of course they could never reach the level of true sentience. No, no, It would stay quiet for now, and bide Its time . . .

For once Verne was very glad that the science of communication had not advanced as quickly as that of aeronautics. When he first saw the *Lucille* splash safely down in the Pacific, to be neatly retrieved and returned to France by aeroship, he'd been full of pride. After all, the Moon missions had been his concept, the small yet efficient space capsules mostly his design. The first two missions had gone so spectacularly well, and now, it would seem, so had the third!

But then the aeronauts had been smuggled away without being allowed to speak to anyone. Something was wrong, Verne knew, something was very wrong ... He made inquiries, spoke to the right people, and was reassured:

"Oh, it is nothing, Monsieur Verne. You know that some men readjust to Earth's pull more easily than others. Albert Legrand is under observation for a few days, that is all."

"Observation? Observation where?"

"Why, l'Hôpital de St.-Denis."

"The hospital near Millais?" Verne asked incredulously. "But that's in the middle of nowhere!" It was also near the empty fields where his *Terror* and *Eagle* were stored. "Why on Earth wasn't he taken to Paris?"

And what, I wonder, is everyone trying to hide? I think, Verne told himself, *I shall pay a small visit to l'Hôpital de St.-Denis and find out for myself.*

It fought down surges of wild impatience. Yes, It was here, on this living world just full of potential hosts—but which one should It pick? Which would be the most useful? Yes, and what plans should It make? The flesh-slave—the human in which It was encased—was fairly young as its kind measured time, that much It had learned, and seemed to have a reasonably healthy body. But the creature was so—so stupid, full of pride yet nearly empty of intellect, and so maddeningly limited in its worldview! If It could have sighed in frustration, It would have done so. The flesh-slave knew it belonged to a country called France, which was one of many others in something known as Europe, which in turn was part of Earth. Barbaric! All these countries, each with its own government! Where was unification? Did no one being rule the world?

No one ... yet.

Of course, of course! It would make Itself ruler here as It had been on the Home World. But here there would be none of them! Here there would be no one to stop It!

Easy thought. But how to accomplish such goals. . . ? It was rapidly learning how to tap into the memory and speech functions of Its host. Of course, such usage meant that once

It *left, the host* would no longer be able to function. But that was usually the fate of flesh-slaves. More important was the fact that while this human *creature* was useful for its youth and strength, it had no real power among its kind. And because its fellows thought it had fallen ill, it was being kept in seclusion. Yet there must be some visitor, someone as weak of will as this host had proved, but with greater intellect. Someone to carry It out into the world. But who? And when?

It settled restlessly down to wait.

"Ah, Dr. Mireau, thank God you're here!" The harried head of St. Denis' Hospital shook his hand so fervently Mireau though the man surely meant to remove it.

"What is all this hysteria? I receive a mysterious message that you urgently need a specialist in matters of the brain—and that message comes from the National Aeronautic Department. But no one will tell me anything! Now I learn you have a sick aeronaut hidden away in this provincial little hospital!"

"True, true. But as far as any of us can tell, his sickness is of the mind." The man paused, eyeing Mireau like a nervous little bird. "You understand why the need for secrecy?"

"Bah, of course. You fear that if word of this sickness reaches the public, there will be a panic. And that would put an end to any future lunar missions."

"Exactly." The worried little man shook his head. "I tell you, *monsieur le docteur*, this is the most baffling case I've seen. The young man has no sign of fever or any other physical ill. He eats and exercises, does everything he's told. But all the while it's as though . . . as though there's no one at home in there." The man tapped his head. "Or rather, it is as though someone *else* were trying to make himself at home."

"What on Earth are you saying?"

"What *can* I say? If this were a different age, I would swear that poor young man was possessed!"

"Oh, what nonsense," Mireau said sternly, looking

down his nose at the man. Ridiculous, dragged from his comfortable home, his lucrative practice, to listen to some superstitious little provincial fool ... "There are no such things as devils. Come, let me see this 'possessed' young man."

"In here." It was said in a whisper.

Mireau impatiently pushed his way past the man. The aeronaut was sitting quietly in a corner, staring at nothing. He barely moved as Dr. Mireau bent over him, the blank stare never wavering.

"Well, young man," Mireau began heartily. "How are you today?"

No response.

"I am Dr. Henri Mireau, come all the way from Paris to help you. But I can do nothing unless you tell me what troubles you."

Still no response.

Odd, odd. According to the records, there had been no injury to the head, no physical trauma at all, no sign of illness. Madness? Or could this all be part of some manner of perverse game? Impatiently Mireau took the young man's head in his hands, forced the blank gaze to meet his own ...

Verne stared at the hospital director in disbelief. "He's *dead*? Legrand? But—but he was so young!" *Stupid what does mere youth have to do with anything?* "What was the cause of death?"

"I wish I could tell you, Monsieur Verne. But ..." The man gave a weary little shrug. "Who can say? At least there was no sign of plague."

"There would hardly be," Verne said drily. "Unless Legrand decided to suddenly remove his suit in the airlessness of the moon—in which case he would hardly be alive—the only germs to which he could have been exposed were those the aeronauts carried with them from Earth. And neither Duval nor Nantes show any sign of ill-health, do they?"

"Uh ... no."

"Well? Go on. I assume an autopsy was performed?"

"Of course. It revealed no signs of physical harm. But then, we already knew as much."

"Who was the doctor in attendance?"

"Besides myself, Dr. Henri Mireau of Paris."

"Ah." *Mireau, you idiot! I remember you from Paris: so sure you know everything there is to know about the brain and all its functions.* "Let us go see good Dr. Mireau."

"I ... don't think we should just yet, Monsieur Verne. Dr. Mireau was apparently hit quite hard by poor Legrand's death.'

Verne stared. *The man I met was hardly the sort to let a patient's death affect him.* "So be it. Let me speak with Duval and Nantes instead."

"I don't know if—"

"I am not some fool of a reporter looking for some scandal! I am Jules Verne!"

"Well, yes, of course, but—"

"But nothing! I *invented* the space capsule and planned its missions! Now, let me see those aeronauts!"

The two men were hiding something. They were definitely hiding something. Verne forced back his impatience and said with great restraint:

"Once again, gentlemen. Did either of you see or hear anything peculiar while you, Duval, and the late Legrand were out on the surface of the Moon?"

The aeronauts exchanged nervous glances. "I was in the capsule all the while," Nantes said softly. "I saw nothing."

Verne sighed. "And you, Duval, what did you see? No, wait. I think it only fair to warn you that should it become necessary I mean to call in the services of a trained mesmerist to bring forth hidden memories. But that will *not* become necessary, will it?"

The aeronauts exchanged a second glance. Duval's shoulders sagged. "No. It will not. Monsieur Verne, we decided back on the *Lucille* to say nothing for fear of causing a panic. But . . . what we found on the Moon was the wreckage of an alien space vehicle . . ."

This was a far more intelligent host than the first, and far more stubborn. Oh yes, it had been relatively easy for It to spring from one slave to another, since this one, too, had a blatant weakness: it was a scientist of sorts, a doctor (what foolishness, to waste time healing the feeble!), and saw itself as far superior to its fellows. It had gladly accepted an image of itself accepting honors for some great discovery of the brain it had made.

Of the brain, indeed, It thought drily, and continued the struggle to bend the stubborn will to Its own. Information flooded It: the country was, indeed, a separate entity, the government was based in Paris. The leader, It thought hungrily, what of the leader? Was this some mighty warlord who—

Elected? Their leader had been elected? Was such—such weakness possible? Surely there was some concept of war in this world, some fierceness on which It could seize and build. . . ?

Yes. There was a military cast among the humankind, some representatives of which were here, at this very structure-for-the-sickly. Quickly, It abandoned the idea of maneuvering this flesh-slave back to its home in Paris. No, no, why risk Itself trying to take over a mere weak elected leader? It would find a good, strong, military host, one who knew something of the war weapons of this world.

Its struggle with this slave, though, had done irreparable damage to the creature's mind. Already sections of it were beginning to fail. It dared wait no longer. As soon as It could get the recalcitrant creature under total control, It must begin the search for a new and better host.

"And that, Monsieur Verne," Duval finished wearily, "is the whole story. The true story, I swear it."

"And I," Nantes seconded.

Verne looked from one to the other, seeing the sincerity in their eyes, and shook his head in wonder. "Fascinating ... You say Legrand was in the wreckage for ... what, five minutes?"

"At the most, yes."

"And of course at no time could he have had his suit open, which, as I told the head of the hospital, rules out some space-borne disease ... Doctors screen all aeronauts carefully before a mission, which rules out Earthly disease as well. From what you've told me, Legrand was hardly the sort to be harboring the seeds of any mental disorder."

"Hardly," Duval echoed, with the faintest touch of what might have been sarcasm. "Whatever else Legrand might have been, God rest him, he was most assuredly sane."

"So. That does leave only one possible solution, fantastic though it sounds."

The aeronauts stared at Verne like two small, frightened boys. "You ... don't think it could be an invasion from Mars...?"

"Bah, no! Leave such nonsense to Monsieur Wells and his fantasies. We know far too much about Mars these days for that! No ..." Verne added thoughtfully, "whatever occupied that ship, whatever attacked poor Legrand, was surely from much further away than Mars."

Yes! Now It had the knack of controlling a human flesh-slave! Why, it was almost simple, once one realized the creatures were endowed with a fair amount of cunning. Now, secure in Its new abilities, It forced this new flesh-slave up and out of the structure-for-the-sickly, fending off the comments or inquiries of the other humans with monosyllabic mutters that seemed to satisfy them; apparently this creature hadn't been known for friendliness with its own kind.

Ahh, but the sense of military was nearby, drawing It on and on.

* * *

"What do you mean, Dr. Mireau is gone?" Verne roared. "Gone *where*?"

The orderly cringed back from his fury. "I—I don't know, *monsieur*, truly I don't. The last I saw of him, he had left poor Monsieur Legrand and had retreated into a private room with the door closed."

"The door that is now open and the room that is empty." Verne let out a great, angry sigh, struggling to regain his patience. "So. You were in the room when Mireau spoke with Legrand, weren't you? Exactly what happened?"

The orderly hesitated, plainly wondering if Verne was going to attack him if he said anything wrong, then began warily, "Dr. Mireau said something, but I wasn't close enough to hear what it was."

"And then. . . ?" Verne prodded impatiently. "*Something* odd must have happened."

The orderly hesitated again. "Not really. Except that all at once Dr. Mireau straightened, his hands going to his head as though it pained him—"

"*What!*"

"Yes, but then we all realized Monsieur Legrand had fainted—so we thought, only fainted, we didn't know he was dead yet and—Monsieur Verne! Where are you going?"

"Thank you, my friend! You've been very helpful!"

The sudden headache, just as Duval had described, the just as sudden death—as though something or some*one* had transferred neatly from one mind to the other. Dear God, this meant they were faced with an invasion, indeed! How did one fight an unseen, hostile alien being, presumably one made of energy, not matter, one to whom other lives obviously meant little? It plainly had a plan, using Legrand to get it from its wrecked ship (that dead body within: the being's "host?") to Earth, and Mireau to get it out into the world. But what would such a hostile being want? Where would it be heading?

"Dear God," Verne repeated aloud. "The *Terror*."

And it had been armed for one last test ...

Verne looked frantically about for a vehicle, any vehicle. Nothing, of course. With a groan, he broke into a run.

Bertrand Dufy frowned. This middle-aged, grim-faced fellow in the white coat was clearly someone from l'Hôpital de St.-Denis. But he had no business being *here*!

"Excuse me, *monsieur le docteur*," Dufy said politely. "I'm afraid this territory is off limits to hospital personnel."

The doctor muttered something. Dufy blinked. "I'm sorry, *monsieur*, I didn't hear that. Would you mind—hey now, what are you doing?"

The man had suddenly caught him by the arm, pulling him forward. Corpse-cold hands closed on his head ...

God, his heart was going to burst, or his lungs fail ... he was not meant to be a runner, not with his solid middle-aged physique ...

"Verne! What's the rush, man?"

"Can't—can't talk now, Nadar. Have to—have to get to the *Terror* before—"

The roar of powerful rotors cut into his words. Helpless with horror, Verne watched the warrior aeroplane storm up into the sky.

"What in *hell*?" Nadar gasped. "I didn't know you had any testing planned for today!"

"I don't!"

"Then what does Dufy think he's doing? Has he gone mad?"

"Not mad, my friend. Something much, much worse." Quickly, never taking his attention from the *Terror*, Verne sketched in the tale the aeronauts had told him, the tale he had confirmed with his own eyes by almost literally stumbling over the crumpled body of Dr. Mireau. "Dufy must have met him, or rather met the thing possessing him—and been in turn possessed."

"My God, man, it sounds like something out of Monsieur Wells' stories!"

"It's real. Too real."

"But—but then this *thing*, this alien intelligence, has just taken command of the most terrible war machine yet built!"

Verne groaned. "Exactly. It hasn't quite gotten Dufy under perfect control, you can see that in the way he—it's flying. But once the thing figures out the aeroplane is armed . . . God! It probably already knows all about the government, and where the President is staying—I have to stop it!"

"But—wait—where are you going?"

"There's only one other aeroplane as mighty as the *Terror*."

"The *Eagle*? Jules, you can't! That plane has never been fully tested!"

"I designed the damn thing! Who better to test it now?"

Almost no wind . . . cloud cover building to the west . . . never realized this cursed seat was so small . . . the whole thing seems so fragile . . . glass windscreen, composite material fuselage, not much good, solid metal . . . ah well, no time to worry about it now. Here we go . . . gently now . . . gaining speed, more speed . . . Now!

Verne pulled back gently on the pilot's wheel. The *Eagle* seemed to leap into the air with its namesake's delight, roaring up, pushing him back into the uncomfortable seat. All around him, the machine was creaking, complaining, but it was flying, by God it was flying!

Now was the most dangerous time, though, when he hadn't yet gained enough height. If the alien controlling the *Terror* realized what he was doing and figured out just how to fire the on-board rockets, Verne knew he was dead. But either the creature didn't know about rocketry, or Dufy was giving it a good fight, for the *Terror* kicked and bucked its way across the sky, threatening at every moment to stall.

But so was the *Eagle*. He was forcing it to climb at too steep an angle. Level out, now . . . gently . . . yes. A little more power . . . a little steeper climb . . .

Lightning seemed to explode to his right.

Damn! The thing's won control!

Quick bank to the left, sliding through the air, level out, quick bank to the right: yes! The *Terror* was before him and if he fired his own rockets now—

I can't! Dufy . . .

Dufy was already as good as dead. The alien killed whomever it possessed, Legrand, Mireau. He must fire before—

Too late! A second blast from the *Terror* struck home, sending the *Eagle* tumbling end over end. Feeling the ever-increasing pull of gravity trying to tear his hands from the controls, Verne fought the plane, bit by bit turning the mad tumbling to a smooth dive, then leveled out, checking dials and switches frantically. Minor damage, some scorching of the fuselage—*damned strong composite after all*—

But the *Terror* was diving after him, and if he didn't do something, he was doomed.

All right, my winged child, you were designed for speed. Let us see what you can do.

The *Eagle* sped across the sky, almost, Verne thought with a flash of fancy, as though enjoying the race. Far behind, the *Terror* followed, but Verne, judging distance with what he hoped was an accurate eye, was almost sure he was out of range—ha, yes! That last blast had missed by a good quarter-league. Both aeroplanes were fully fueled; theoretically they could travel nearly to America without trouble.

Travel over the ocean, the empty Atlantic . . . What if . . . Yes, yes, yes! The alien needed a human host, that much was clear. If Verne led it out over the ocean, far from any other possible fleshy home, then destroyed it (and Dufy; no, he wouldn't think of that), the creature would be left without any host.

Save me. And I, if need be I will dive into the ocean and die before it can gain control.

(God, I don't want to die, I don't want it to come to that . . .)

Water glinted far below them. The Bay of Biscay . . . not far enough . . . needed open ocean . . . yes, yes, here we were . . . But the air was becoming rough, buffeting the *Eagle*, making Verne very glad of a steady stomach. The cloud cover overhead was growing ever thicker.

Ha, just what I wanted!

He had enough of a lead over the pursuing *Terror* to start climbing, climbing, feeling the wind shaking the *Eagle*, wrenching at its rotors, straining its wings, trying to break it and toss it from the sky.

A little more, my child, a little higher . . .

He was in the clouds now, surrounded on all sides by heavy gray. Cold up here, the chill stealing into the cramped pilot's cabin . . . the air thinner than he would have liked, but still breathable. Not a thing else to be seen but that damp cold grayness, not a clue of *east* or *west*, only the instruments on the panel before him telling him which was *up* or *down*. Somewhere below him was the *Terror*, and if he strained to hear over the roar of the *Eagle*'s own rotors, Verne thought he could hear that second roaring.

Now, now, before the creature follows me!

Decrease forward motion . . . stall. Wheel forward, nose down. Dive, yes, dive down and down, faster, faster, one hand on the firing switch of the rockets . . .

The *Eagle* broke out of the clouds so suddenly Verne nearly gasped. And, dear God, thank you, there was the *Terror*, some half-league below and to the right.

"Forgive me, Dufy. If this doesn't work, I'll see you before God in just a few moments . . ."

Gritting his teeth, Verne fired one, then the other rocket, waiting, waiting, sure he had missed, sure he was going to die.

With a roar of thunder and a flash that tore the sky

apart, the *Terror* erupted into a ball of flame. Dazzled, Verne turned away to save his eyes . . .

"But what happened then?" Nadar insisted.

Verne took a luxurious sip of his Bordeaux. "The alien attacked. Oh, that was a desperate struggle, I don't have to tell you. We both nearly died in the waves by the time I regained control of the *Eagle*."

"But *what happened*?"

Verne shrugged. "My will was stronger. I don't mean to belittle poor Legrand or Mireau, but they were single-minded men, easy to understand. An inventor, as my wife Hortense teases me, is half-mad to begin with. The alien couldn't figure me out! I felt the thing lose its grip on my mind again and again, as much as screaming to me that if it didn't find a sentient host quickly, it was lost. The thing was so terrified by this point I could almost have pitied it—if I hadn't known it was a merciless killer.

"And then the creature made a fatal error. It tried to make me think reality had changed."

"What do you mean?"

Verne smiled. "Why, the poor, bewildered thing tried to make me think all this wasn't true, that there weren't any such things as aeroships or warrior aeroplanes. It tried to make me believe this was all part of my imagination."

"How foolish."

"Wait, there's more. With its last effort, the alien tried to get me to believe I was nothing but a—a writer! A writer of scientifiction!"

"What!" Nadar let out a roar of a laugh. "Not really!"

"Oh yes." Verne settled more comfortably into his arm-chair, smiling into his wineglass. "Can you picture me as a writer of fiction? Me, Jules Verne? Can you think of anything more ridiculous?"

Kristine Kathryn Rusch probably expends enough energy in the course of a week to power an entire city. She is the editor of *The Magazine of Fantasy and Science Fiction*, she has written and sold at least seven novels in the past two years, she is a Hugo and Nebula-nominated short fiction writer, and she teaches a writers' workshop in her spare time. (Spare time???)

It's difficult to say which of these many things she does best, but after you read her memorable history of Sojourner Truth, the freed slave who campaigned for abolition and women's rights, I have a feeling you'll be hard-pressed to vote against her short fiction.

The Arrival of Truth
by Kristine Kathryn Rusch

I first heard the story the morning they took my third child. My body, half-hidden in the feather bed, ached from the effort of birthing a baby I would never raise. My breasts dribbled milk that would soon feed a white child. The Missus and Old Sal, the midwife, took my new baby out of the room so I couldn't hear it cry. I reached for it—all small, bloody, and wrinkled—but wasn't strong enough to get out of bed. As the door closed, I turned my face against the Missus' feather pillow and wished I had died.

A breeze rustled the gingham curtains on the open

window. Voices echoed in the yard, and from Big Jim's yelp, I knew I had had a son. The voices hushed for a moment, then Big Jim cried, "No! No! That's my boy! You can't take him away! That's my boy!" and I tried to sink deeper in the soft bed, softer than I was used to, the bed the Missus used when a girl gave birth to a baby she could sell and make more money for the House. Big Jim's shout got cut off mid-word as a whip snapped and cracked through the air. Big Jim would get another scar because of my baby, and the child wasn't even his.

The door creaked open, and Nesta stood there, eyes sad as eyes could be. She snuck inside and let the door close quietly. She was big and soft, and I wanted to bury my face against her chest and cry until no more tears would come, but when her hand caressed my forehead, I couldn't look at her.

"Oh, baby," she said. "All that learning didn't save you. It don't save none of us, long as we look different from them."

She took a cornhusk doll, painted black, with frizzed yarn hair and a sackcloth dress, and tucked it in my arms. "Sojourner's coming," Netta said. "And when she gets here, all them white folks are going to learn the Truth."

Then she slipped out the door, quietly as she came. I buried my face in the doll's rough skin and I wish, Lord how I wished, it could move and cry and pat its little fist against my cheek.

Some days I can still remember the feeling of being a child, the closest to white I'll ever get.

The old Missus, she had Ideas that her son, Master Tom, said was dangerous and harmful to his way of life. But when he was a boy and had no say in the house, the old Missus would teach some of us. She taught us how to read and spell and how to talk proper. She read to us from the Bible and said we needed to know God's Word so we could get into heaven. She made us promise we would never tell nobody what she done because she would have to stop, and some of us could get killed because of her mistakes. So we practiced reading in private, hiding the books when the old Master or Jake the overseer or any guests came to the House. The old Missus talked to us like we were the same as the white folks she spent the rest of her time with. And she loved us, each and every one. No babies got sold when she ran the House, and she promised that when she died, we would all go free.

But she died one sunny afternoon when her horse stumbled and threw her. The old Master said her will was written by a crazy woman who didn't understand money, and he wouldn't abide by her wishes. So none of us got our papers, and none of us were set free. The old Master brought us—the ones she educated—into the House and made us "the best House niggers" in the state of Carolina. We were never allowed to leave, never able to talk with the field hands or any of the others, as if he was afraid our knowledge would spread like pox through a room full of children.

Three days later, when I could stand alone, the Missus let me return to my cabin behind the House. I took the doll with me, clutching it like the child it had replaced. The Missus had promised me to the Wildersons down the road, and I was to pack my things and get before nightfall.

Big Jim wasn't inside, but we had already said our goodbyes before he took the livery out that morning. He said he'd keep my side of the bed warm, but we both knew I wouldn't be back until the Wilderson baby was weaned. A lot could change in that kind of time. People could get sold, people could get killed, people could disappear in the middle of the night. I only promised that I would love him as long as I lived.

The cabin was neat except for a pile of bloody rags that sat by the door. Jim had probably used them to stop the bleeding on his arm where the whip had wrapped around his skin while he was trying to save my baby boy. The cabin wasn't much—a straw bed, a few chairs, and a table—but it was the place where we could speak our minds. After the old Master died, and Master Tom married, places like that had become harder and harder to find.

I put my other dress and my doll in a scarf and packed it in a wicker basket. Then I went out front to catch the delivery wagon as it made its way into town.

I sat on the back, and got off on the road outside the Wilderson place. The Wildersons had a bigger plantation than we did, and more babies this year than we did. But Missus Wilderson wouldn't tolerate a field hand nursing her babies, and she wanted someone "almost human"—like me. After I'd been there a while she told me I didn't talk like a nigger and if she closed her eyes she could pretend I was a person, someone worth talking to. She expected me to be flattered, and even though I thanked her in a quiet voice, I could see she was surprised by my tone.

Big arching trees hung over the Wildersons' lane. After the wagon dropped me off, I walked, exhaustion making my limbs shake. I had to stop once, and lean against a wide tree trunk to catch my breath. My mother used to go back to the fields the same day she had a baby, and my pa used to say that was what faded her away. Dizziness swept through me, just as it must have through her the day she collapsed on the field—the day after my baby brother was born—and the overseer beat her to death with his whip. The old Missus had fired him, and the old Master had jailed him for destroying property. But that never did bring my mama back.

"Hey, girl, they's expecting you up to the house."

The voice came from a big man standing just inside the trees. His skin was dark as tree bark and his muscles bulged out of his ripped and torn shirt. His eyes shone with intelligence and when he spoke, he smiled.

"How much farther is it?" My voice sounded breathless.

"Half mile maybe," he said.

I nodded, the thought of the extra distance defeating me. Maybe I could go a few more yards, but not a half mile. My body hadn't recovered enough.

He peered at me through the trees, then crossed the road and stopped beside me. He was a big man, bigger than Big Jim. "You don't look so good."

I nodded again, afraid to say anything.

"How long since you had that baby?"

"Three days." The words were no more than a whisper.

"And they sent you to walk? Here, honey, lean on me. I got strength enough for both of us."

He touched me and I jerked back.

"It's like that, is it?" He spoke softly, almost to himself. "Okay. I ain't gonna hurt you, honey. Just let me put my arm around you, and then you can lean against me. Okay?"

I swallowed, not wanting him to touch me, but knowing I wouldn't make it to the great house any other way. He slid his arm around my back, his skin hot against mine. He smelled of soap and honest sweat, and his touch was gentle.

"Come on," he said, and together we walked down the center of the road leading to the great house. The trees towered over us, and an occasional bird chirped. The Wilderson plantation was quiet. No one shouted over the breeze. No overseer's whip echoed in the distance. If I hadn't known better, I would have thought no one lived at the end of the road.

A bead of sweat trickled down my forehead, and the man tightened his grip. By the time we had reached the house, he was almost carrying me while keeping me upright.

"Lord a mercy, girl, where you been? The mistress is swearing and that baby's crying like it won't never shut up." A woman stood on the porch, hair tied back in a scarf, sun reflecting off her dark face. She had her arms crossed on her hips and her skirts swished as she walked.

She was in charge of the house. No one had to tell me that.

"She's three days from the baby," the man said, "and they left her down the road. She can barely walk and I think she's bleeding."

"Don't know how to take care of their people over there," the woman muttered as she walked down the stairs. She leaned over me and took me from the man. She was almost as strong as he was. Her hand brushed my breast as she reached around. "Lord, you're full up too. We'll get you to a bed, put that baby against you. He'll ease that pain in your chest some."

I looked at her sharply. Maybe she was referring to my swollen breasts. But I didn't think so. I wondered how many babies had been taken away from her.

The man hadn't let go of me. The woman looked at him. "I got her, Sam," she said. She pulled me close, but he still didn't let go. "Let her go, Sam. You ain't allowed in the house."

Sam released me. I stumbled against the woman, then she supported me.

"It's a crime," he said, "the way they treat people. When Sojourner comes—"

"Shush," the woman said. "We don't have talk like that at my house."

"This ain't your house." But he said no more. He tipped a make-believe hat at me. "When you're feeling better, you come sit with Sam. We'll have ourselves a talk."

I nodded, and the movement made me dizzy. When we reached the porch, the front door opened, and Missus Wilderson stood there, face blotchy and red. "They said you'd be here this morning. A sugar teat isn't doing my Charles any good."

Behind her, I could hear a baby wail. The sound made the pain in my chest grow stronger.

"She's sick," the woman holding me said.

"Something she'll pass to the baby?"

"Her babe was born a few days ago. She ain't recovered yet."

Missus Wilderson humphed and moved away from the door. "As long as she can feed my boy, I don't care what you do with her, Darcy."

Darcy didn't reply. She helped me in the front door. The house was cooler than the outdoors, and the hallway was lighter and airier than the one I was used to. She led me past the kitchen to a small room furnished with a cross and some figures made out of straw. I set my basket down, and she eased me onto a chair. The dizziness swept across me as she opened my bodice and handed me a wet rag. I ran it across my chest and my face. The cool cloth sent a shiver through me.

Then Darcy was beside me again, the squalling baby in her hands. I reached for him before I knew what I was doing. I didn't want to feed another woman's child. I wanted to feed my own. But if I closed my eyes, I didn't see this little boy's pale skin. All I felt was his soft baby fat. He smelled of newborn, and he clamped onto my breast with a greediness that hurt.

I rocked him, not opening my eyes, not wanting to see him, and I crooned a lullabye that Big Jim used to sing to our boys before they got taken away. But I couldn't pretend. I knew that someday this boy in my arms would grab a woman with skin darker than his, beat her senseless, knock her to the ground, and stick himself inside her. I knew he would hire an overseer who used a whip instead of kindness. I knew that no matter whose breast he nursed on, he would never see people with dark skin as human beings.

After a week of Darcy's food and care, I could walk on my own. The dizziness left me and the ache in my bones left with it. I missed the ache—it was my last attachment to my child. The bleeding stopped after about a day, and we didn't discuss it or what it might mean about my chances for having future children. Little Charles was growing fat, and he reached for me instead of his mother, much to her dismay.

I had no place in the household, except as a milk store for Charles. I had to stay near the house, so that I could feed him when he was hungry, but other than that, I could do anything I wanted.

It took me another week to find Sam. His words had bothered me because they echoed Nesta's. *When Sojourner comes ... When she gets here, all them white folks are going to learn the Truth.*

Twilight had fallen across the fields, making shadows long and dark. Charles was already asleep. I walked toward the field-hand cabins—no restrictions on me here. Apparently Master Tom hadn't told the Wildersons that I could infect their darkies with all kinds of evil knowledge.

Children scrabbled in the hard dirt, and adults sat on porches and talked. Sam sat outside his cabin, whittling, and listening to the conversation around him.

"Okay if I join you?" I asked.

He indicated a space on the wood stairs leading up to the door. I gathered my skirts under me and sat.

"I didn't spect to see you again," he said. "You one of them precious house girls your master always bragging up."

A shiver ran down my back and it was still light enough for Sam to catch it. "He don't treat his people right, do he?"

I bit my lip and looked across at the children. They were yelling and carrying on, playing a game I didn't understand.

"And he didn't want no baby around to remind him of that, did he?"

I started to stand up. Sam reached over and grabbed my arm. I pulled away from him.

"He hurt you right bad."

His words brought back that night: the smell of liquor on Master Tom's breath, the weight of his body on mine, the bruises I couldn't hide from Big Jim. He had wanted to kill Master Tom that night. I had stopped him.

Sam was watching me with the same intensity he had that day in the lane. "And you ain't never gonna let a man touch you again, are you?"

I was trembling but I didn't want Sam to see it. "Do you want to?"

"Lordy, girl, you a bunch of sticks and bones, and that baby broke some things when it busted out of ya. I had me a woman once. Don't need another." He waved a hand. "Sit. Tell me why you come searching me out."

I sat back down and laced my hands in my lap. My fingers were cold, despite the heat of the night. "When I came here, you spoke of something. You said, 'When Sojourner comes.' What did you mean by that?"

He let out air slowly, then glanced around to see if anyone was looking. Twilight had given way to darkness. The children were inside. Candles flickered through the open windows, and five cabins down an old man smoked a pipe on his porch.

"You ain't never heard of Sojourner?"

"Once I did. Nesta, the cook up to the Great House, told me when they took my baby away. She said when Sojourner gets here, white folks are going to learn the truth."

"The Truth, girl." He put an emphasis on truth so strong that I could hear the capital letter. "You was born into this life. I can tell from that fancy speech of yourn. Was your mama born into this life?"

I nodded. My family had come to the colony with the Master's family. The old Missus said we had a good and strong heritage.

"And you been a house woman your whole life?"

Again, I nodded.

"They raised you like family till the young master decided that the people can't be family."

"This isn't about me," I said. "I want to know about Sojourner."

"Girl, what I'm saying is you'd know if you was raised in the fields." He leaned back in his chair. The chair creaked. The muscles rippled through his dark skin. "When I was a boy, they'd sing a song when the overseer was gone. They'd sing about the promised land and how the savior would come and take them away. At night, my mama would lay me on my straw, and she'd say someday a leader would come to the land and take us all to a better place. You ain't never heard them stories?"

I shook my head. My mama was happy that the old Missus took me into the schoolroom. When Mama put me down at night, she would say, "You almost white, honey. Someday, you go free and you will live without no whip and no dogs."

"You do remember when that boy up to Virginia led a bunch of the people and killed the white folks?"

I didn't remember it because it happened the year of my birth. I had heard of it, though. Master Tom would talk to the overseer about it. The way they had to keep us separate so that we would never think of a rebellion. "I know of it," I said.

Sam stared straight ahead. Nothing moved in the darkness. "I was ten. The overseers came down and locked us all in our cabins. They took the men away and the women were left alone with the children for days. They was afraid the rebellion would spread down here and all the white folks would die. Anyone caught singing about the promised land got whipped. And anyone who talked about a savior got beat within an inch of his life."

"I don't remember that," I said, and felt inadequate because of it. I was glad the darkness hid my face. My mama talked about the bad times, but I never associated it with the rebellion. It hadn't mattered to me. It had happened before I was born.

"That didn't stop the stories. They just got whispered in bits and pieces, back and forth. We spected things to get worse. And we spected our savior to come. But no one ever did." Lights came on in the kitchen in the back of the house. I strained to hear the baby's cry, but the yard was quiet.

"Then a few years ago, a runaway come through the barn. He was torn and bloodied and tired, but he told a story, Lord, we wanted to hear. He said Sojourner came to his plantation and taught white folks Truth. And all the people went free."

I sat up straighter. "What happened?"

"He was too addled to tell us. We passed him along, and another came, just as bloodied, saying the same thing. Only he said Sojourner led them into battle, like the white folks' Bible talked about, and all the people went free."

"How come we haven't heard about it?"

Sam shook his head. "These battles are quiet ones. Ain't nobody getting caught, and ain't nobody gonna tell."

"Sounds like tales to me," I said. I stood up and brushed off my skirt. "White folks won't let niggers free, not without a fight. And if niggers put up a fight, then white folks kill them, and kill other niggers until the fight has gone out of us."

Sam was silent for a long moment. I thought, with my simple argument, I had knocked a hole in his belief, and I felt oddly disappointed. The story of Sojourner had an appeal to it that I wanted to feel. I didn't want to destroy his belief so easily.

"You call the people 'niggers,'" he said. "Just like the white folk. We all know we different. But we ain't niggers or pickaninnies or any of them pet terms they use. We's people just like they is. And we shouldn't make ourselves sound any other way."

He got up and walked around me. The steps sagged under his weight. He went into his cabin without saying good night.

My cheeks were hot. I hadn't meant to offend him, by insulting his beliefs or by using a word that I had heard since I was a child. I stood on his porch for a long time, thinking about the difference a word made. I had never thought of myself as a person. To me, people were always white.

The light in the kitchen grew, and a bad feeling ran through me. I lifted my skirt and crossed the now-empty yard. I was too awake to sleep, but something called me indoors.

I mounted the back porch steps and let myself in the back door. A hand slapped me across the mouth, and I stumbled backwards, holding up my arm to protect myself. Missus Wilderson stood there, her long hair flowing down her back, her nightgown askew. "You were brought here to feed my baby, not to go whoring."

I wiped my palm against my mouth, felt it come away bloody. "I wasn't—"

"Sam is a big man and probably just what you girls want, but I won't have my baby's milk tainted, you hear me? You stay in the house at night. You stay here where the baby can have you if he needs you."

I nodded, knowing that she would never listen to my denials. She turned, grabbed her lamp, and walked back through the darkened hallway, looking like Lady Macbeth from the Shakespeare stories the old Missus used to scare us with.

Darcy stepped out of the corner where she had been standing. She dipped a rag in the water basin and wiped my mouth. "She knows you wasn't doing nothing with Sam 'cept talking. She watched almost from the start. She just don't like him none. She'd have sold him long ago, but the Master says he's a good one in the fields, and won't let him go."

My lower lip hurt. I could feel it swelling. "Why did she hit me?"

"She's got a sense about her. When you showed up at the door, she said the final time was here, and there wasn't nothing she could do."

"Final time?"

"Lord, honey, white folks is as superstitious as we are. They got their strange beliefs too. I think all the white folks know they's sitting on a powder keg, and they just waiting for it to explode underneath them."

I took the cloth from Darcy's hand and wiped my own mouth. I had never thought of rebellion before. No one talked about it at home, at least no one had talked about it with me. If Sojourner had come there, would they have killed me with the white folks? Because I had lessons and could read and could talk like a white person, did that mean my skin had lightened? It didn't stop Master Tom from beating me senseless and planting a baby in me. Or did he only do that to some women? Those who could pass for his own kind?

"You don't like that?" she asked, moving her lamp closer so that she could look at me.

"They'll kill us," I said.

"Ah, honey." Darcy brushed a strand of hair from my forehead. "At least we'll die free."

I didn't leave the house for weeks. Little Charles grew heavier and more demanding. Missus Wilderson ignored me. Darcy made sure I was fed and had someone to talk with, and Sam waved whenever he saw me on the porch. I didn't wave back.

The humid spring turned into a hot summer. The aches left my body and Charles crawled into my heart. Sometimes, as I put him down to sleep, I called him mine. And in so many ways he was. He reached for me and cooed when he saw me. When he had angry fits, only I could stop them. He tolerated his mother, cried at his father, but loved me.

I found no solace in that.

Mid-July I was sitting in the porch swing, rocking Charles and humming him a lullabye. He didn't want to sleep. He reached for the butterfly circling around us, played with the buttons on my dress. His eyes would droop and then open again, as if he didn't want to miss anything. I told him now was the time for sleeping. When he grew up, sleeping would be something he would have no time for at all.

A noise stirred Charles out of his playfulness. He turned

his head toward the road, and so did I. A horse's hooves pounded against the dirt. An angry or panicked horse, one that had ridden at top speed all day. Darcy came onto the porch followed by the Master and Missus. Sam appeared from around back, and even though the Missus tried to send him away, he stayed.

The rider came around from under the canopy of trees. He leaned over his horse, mud-splattered and exhausted. His hair, plastered to the side of his head, was straight, and his skin under the dirt was white. His clothes had once been nice, but they were torn and showed signs of wear.

"Get them out of here," he said, waving a hand at Sam, Darcy, and me.

"How can we help you?" the Missus' tone was cold. She didn't take orders from anyone, especially from someone she didn't know.

"I came to warn you," he said. "But I won't do it with them here."

The Master nodded at Sam, Darcy, and me, but we didn't move. "Come inside," he said. "We'll find you something to drink and maybe a bite to eat. Give Sam your horse, and he'll take care of it."

The man clutched the reins tighter. "Just show me where," he said, "and I'll rub down the horse myself."

"Sam," the Master said, then caught the look on the man's face. Pure fear. I recognized it because I had seen it on so many dark faces all my life. "Never mind. I'll take him to the stables. I don't want you people here when I get back."

Charles was wide awake now, and leaning forward. The excitement entranced him. The Missus took him from me. "He's not going to sleep now," she said. But for the first time, her words held no blame. The situation had her as spooked as it had the rest of us.

Darcy took my arm and led me down the stairs. We followed Sam into the back. The Master and the stranger were on their way to the stable, the horse limping behind them.

"Something bad happened," Darcy said.

"He's scared of us," I said.

"They all scared of us." Sam reached in his pocket, took out a handkerchief, and rubbed the sweat off his face. "That's why they treat us the way they do."

"He's scared worse," Darcy said. "You seen him."

"Yeah." Sam tucked the handkerchief in his pocket. "That's why I want to hear what he says. He ain't going to tell it all to the Missus. He saying something right now."

The groom came out of the stable, along with two stableboys, looking as confused as we felt. Sam signaled us to stay where we were, and he hurried along the path, then went around behind the stable. Darcy shook her head.

"Boy gonna get himself a whipping if he not careful," she said.

I stood as quietly as I could. I didn't like the feeling that surrounded me. The stranger's presence had added a tension to the place, a tension that made all the other tensions visible.

The groom went to his cabin, and the stableboys sat outside, staring at the stable as if they could learn the secrets. Darcy said no more to me. After a few minutes, she touched my elbow. The Missus had come onto the pack porch and was staring at the stable. She no longer held Charles. A slight frown creased her face. She too knew she wasn't going to get the whole story.

And if she stood there long enough, she would see Sam.

I wiped my damp palms on my skirt and headed up the stairs. "Did you get Charles to sleep, ma'am?"

She looked at me as if I were intruding. "He's down. I don't think he's sleeping though."

"Long as he's quiet," I said. "I think it'll be a minute

before the men come back. Let me help you get out some lemonade, in case they want something cold."

Her glance was measuring. I brought my head down. My heart pounded. It seemed important to me that she didn't see Sam.

"I'll be gone before they get back. I promise."

She sighed then, and lifted her skirts. I followed her into the big cool kitchen. Her cousin had sent a shipment of lemons from Florida the week before, and although much of the fruit was bruised, some of it was good enough to use. We had had all of the lemonade that morning, and so I stood side by side with Missus Wilderson, squeezing lemons and listening for any sign of the men.

We had filled two pitchers by the time we heard footsteps on the stairs. I grabbed a towel and wiped off my hands, then disappeared out the front way, as the men came in the back.

"—didn't see me leave," the stranger was saying. "That's how they're getting away with this. No one is left."

I couldn't hear the Master's response. I went out the front door and circled around the house to find Sam and Darcy standing in the yard.

"There you are," Sam said. "Come to my cabin. We're far enough away there."

I glanced up to see if the Missus was watching, but she was nowhere in sight. Darcy and I followed Sam down the path to the one-room shack he called home.

The inside was neat and well kept. The straw mattress had a wooden frame beneath it, and the wooden furniture lining the walls was strong and well made. Not hand-me-downs issued by the family. Sam had made his own home.

I took a cane-backed chair in the corner, and Darcy sat beside me. Sam sat on the edge of the bed, where he could see through the windows and keep an eye on the door.

"It's happening," he said to Darcy. "Right now."

"That's just talk," she said.

"Not no more. He's been riding up from the south,

warning every Great House he sees. He ain't gonna stop until he hits every plantation between here and the capital."

"What happened?" I asked.

"He said the people were talking among themselves for days, then this stranger shows up, and suddenly the people don't take orders no more. Then, in the middle of the night, they come into the house just like they did in Virginia all them years ago, with pitchforks and knives and butcher the family. He'd been staying with one of the daughters—snuck in so's nobody would see, and he got out before the mess got too bad. He grabbed a horse and started to ride, to warn white folks it was coming."

"Now they've probably lynched all the people who done the killing," Darcy said, "and the rest of us will get punished."

"Maybe," Sam said. "Or maybe he's just the first wave in a battle we ain't begun to fight."

"Or maybe he's crazy," I said. "and none of this is true."

"Don't think so," Sam said. "He looks like a man who knows."

We were quiet after that. The small cabin grew oppressive. I went out onto the stairs and heard Charles wailing. He was hungry. The Missus came on the back porch, looking for me. When she saw where I was standing, her mouth set in a thin line.

"I guess you can come back in now," she said. "Charles needs you."

I nodded and crossed the yard. Missus Wilderson went back inside. As I climbed the stairs and stood on the porch, I heard voices coming from the kitchen.

"It doesn't make any sense," the Master said. "We give them a good home."

"A good home isn't all they want."

I pushed open the door. Missus Wilderson stood near it, biting her nails. Charles was in a basket on the table, face red and streaked with tears. I went to him and picked him up, not happy that she had let him cry without comforting him.

"I'll take him outside," I said.

She shook her head. "They're almost done. I don't want Charles outside."

I sighed and sat in a kitchen chair. I unbuttoned my blouse and put Charles to my chest. He clasped with his mouth and both hands. He hadn't been hungry, he had been starving.

Missus Wilderson watched for a minute, then went into the other room. Her look had left me cold. I had seen her use it with me before. Almost a jealousy, and half an envy, as if she wanted Charles at her breast instead of mine. But it was a sign of good breeding and wealth when a woman didn't have to feed her own children. Besides it would destroy her figure and give her marks.

I didn't mind the marks. I just wish they had come from my own child instead.

"I take good care of the people who work for me," the Master said. They must have been in the dining room. Only in the dining room could we hear the kitchen so well.

"They don't work for you," the stranger said. "You own them. I think that's what they object to."

"And I feed them, and house them, and clothe them. They're little more than savages. Only a few can be trained to do anything beyond the most menial task. I take care of them and they're grateful to me."

I brushed the thin hair on little Charles' scalp. Feeding his baby was a menial task? I could read and write and it was against the law for me to have those skills. I could speak better than Missus Wilderson and I was still owned by someone. I was as smart as they were, and still all of my children had been taken away from me. Maybe Sam was right. Maybe I had let their thinking invade my own.

"Grateful," I whispered to Charles. "We're not grateful. We're scared."

He closed his eyes and continued sucking. I cradled

him to me. I didn't want a revolution in which all the white folks would die. I loved some of them. I loved the little ones, like Charles, before they had time to turn into someone like Master Tom back at the plantation I was born at.

"I thank you for the warning," Master Wilderson said. "I will heed it as best I can."

"Protect your family," the stranger said. "Get rid of as many of those slaves as you can."

The voices receded from the dining room. Soon I couldn't hear them at all. I was tense, waiting for Missus Wilderson to come back. She didn't. Charles fell asleep, letting my nipple slip out of his mouth. I held him and rocked him just a little, clutching him to me.

After a few minutes, I heard a horse on the lane. The stranger was gone.

I took Charles to his daybed in the front parlor. The Master and Missus were standing on the porch looking at the dust cloud in the lane.

". . . give this kind of thing credence," he was saying. "It might give them ideas."

"But don't we have to protect ourselves?" she asked.

"This family has been on this piece of land for over a hundred years. If slaves were going to rebel, they would have done it long ago, when things were much more isolated. I think he got caught in an unusual incident, and it has spooked him so badly that he is afraid of any nigger he sees."

Missus Wilderson shrugged and moved away from her husband. She didn't believe him, but she had no choice except to abide by what he wanted. We weren't so different, she and I. She had a nice house and a legitimate place in society, but her husband still owned her. She couldn't do what she wanted to do.

She couldn't even nurse her child herself.

I made myself stop watching the interchange and took Charles to his bed. He didn't wake up as I put him down.

I covered him with a light sheet and kissed his forehead. He stirred, but his eyes remained closed.

"He's a beautiful baby." Missus Wilderson stood behind me. I made myself turn slowly, even though my heart was pounding a drumbeat against my chest. "Even though sometimes I think he's more yours than mine. Do you love my child?"

We had never had a moment like this before. She wasn't speaking to me out of anger or even fear. She was actually curious about how I felt. I was the one who felt the fear. I didn't know what she wanted of me.

I decided to tell her the truth.

"They took my baby away from me the day he was born," I said. "Once he left my body, I never got to see him or touch him again. Sometimes when I close my eyes, I pretend Charles is that baby. But he isn't. He's yours. He looks like you and he loves you and I could never ever do to another woman what's been done to me."

The words rushed out of me before I could stop them. She put a hand to her chest as if she were trying to guard her heart. "I never sold anyone's babies," she said. "I'm not like your owners."

"I'm not blaming you. I just wanted to reassure you that I would never hurt or steal your child."

She nodded, brushed her hair out of her face, and walked out of the room. I leaned against the daybed. My hands were shaking. I had never spoken that frankly with a white person before, not even with the old Missus.

I wondered if anything would change because of it.

The tensions remained after the stranger appeared. My Master and the Wildersons had a long conversation and other gentlemen from the area appeared to discuss the situation. From the bits and snatches I gathered, they decided to tighten security around their homes, to punish "uppity niggers," and to make sure more than three of us gathered got broken up.

Missus Wilderson didn't speak to me again, and I cared for Charles in almost complete silence. Sometimes I exchanged words with Darcy and sometimes I spoke to Sam, but mostly I kept to myself.

Early August brought with it hot nights and sweltering days. Just into the month, I carried a sheet to the back porch swing, hoping to catch a little midnight breeze. I lay across the wooden slats. Even though they were uncomfortable, they were better than the sweaty stickiness of my straw bed. Down by the cabins, I could hear restlessness and children crying as people moved about.

The moon was full, and cast a thin daylight across the path. The dogs started barking out near the road, then just as quickly stopped. The voices from the cabins stopped too. I sat up. It felt as if the entire yard was waiting.

People came out of their cabins and stood on the stairs as if they felt the same thing I did. In the Great House, no one got up except Darcy, who let herself out of the kitchen and stood by the door. She didn't seem to see me.

We were all looking in the direction of the dogs. Then I heard a gasp. I looked toward the sound. Sam was standing in his door, facing the opposite direction from everyone else. I followed his gaze and gasped myself.

A woman stood at the edge of the path. She was tall and angular, her hair cropped short. "Let's gather at the edge of the field," she said.

Sam went and got the others. Darcy and I walked toward the nearest field following the woman. As we got closer, we realized that she was old. Her skin was leathery and tough and her hair had turned white. Neither of us had ever seen her before.

She stood on a wooden box that Darcy brought over and watched as the people gathered around her. Mothers held their children close, and the men stood forward, eager for a fight.

"My name's Sojourner," she said, her voice just loud

enough for all of us to hear. "And I come to give you a message. The white folks ain't gonna give us freedom. It costs them too much. We got to take freedom. There's more of us than there is of them. It's time to make life ours not theirs."

She looked at her hands for a moment, then faced us again. In the moonlight, her face looked as if it had absorbed the night. "I'm going from place to place telling people it's time to be free. I want to see all my people stand on their own in my lifetime, and my lifetime is going away, quick."

"You telling us to fight?" Sam asked.

"I'm telling you to take control of your lives however you want to do it. And I want women to take control two places, with the white folks and with your men. We're all equal in God's eyes."

Simple words. As I repeat them back, they have lost the magic they held that night. She spoke with the power of a vision, and we listened as though the words of God himself came from her lips. She stepped down off the platform, and people tried to stop her, but she wouldn't talk. "I got too many places to stop," she said.

And she walked away.

The others stayed behind and talked, but I followed her to the road. She walked with her back straight, her head up, even though her movements were slow and tired. So the stranger had been right. Someone was leading my people home. A woman, with a single message, seeking to overthrow an injust system that had existed for generations.

Shouts and cries echoed behind me. I turned back to see people hacking at their own cabins and setting fire to the Great House. Through the smoke, I thought I saw the Missus' face. *Do you love my child?* she asked.

He was the only baby I got, and now they were setting his house on fire because he was born in the wrong place to the wrong family. Wasn't that as bad as what they had done to us all these years? Or did we follow their Bible:

an eye for an eye, a whip scar for a whip scar, a murder for a murder, and a baby for a baby?

A giddiness took me. I ran toward the house. I wanted to be free like the rest of them. I wanted to have my own babies and my own life. I wanted a house with more than one room and Big Jim beside me for all the rest of my days. I wanted to live like free people lived, making my own choices.

But I didn't want to do it at the expense of Charles and his mama.

Smoke was already inches thick as I burst through the front door. In the back, I heard glass smashing and people laughing. My eyes started to water. I charged up the stairs. Charles was crying, gasping wails that made my heart ache. I ran into his room and gathered him in my arms as the Missus came in.

"You're stealing my baby."

"I'm saving him." I wrapped him in his blankets and hid his face against my arms. "You got to get out now. They're going to kill you."

"I can't let you take my baby," she said.

"Then come with me. Get out now."

"Laurel?" The Master's voice echoed from the other room. For a moment, he sounded like Master Tom, and I wanted to go in and use a knife, hacking him to death. Beneath my surface lurked a sea of hatred.

"It's like the man said," she shouted. "They've gone crazy."

He came into the nursery, with a shotgun leveled at me. "Put the baby down," he said.

"You're not going to shoot me while I'm holding Charles," I said. "And you need me. I'm the only one who can get him away from here. You have to convince the people downstairs that you never meant them any harm. And I don't think you can do it."

He didn't move the gun, but I knew he wouldn't shoot. I turned and ran from the house, Charles pressed against me. The smoke had grown so thick that my breath caught in my lungs. Charles was gasping against me. The fire was eating the entire first floor. We ran past its heat and into the cooler night. I drank the fresh air like cold water. Charles coughed and spit up on me.

Sam was off to one side, leading them all on, and Darcy leaned against a tree, tears glinting off her cheeks. I ran down the road with half a dozen people I had never seen, not caring where I was going, careful to keep Charles' face hidden.

We ran for what seemed like miles until we found an abandoned barn. I crawled inside, followed by a few others. Charles was crying softly, in fear, and I bared my breast for him. He took the milk, but his eyes remained open. He knew something was wrong.

Outside, we could hear the sounds of destruction. A woman I had never seen before made a place beside me in the straw. "She never said kill 'em," the woman said. "She just said to take what's ours. We could have slipped away in the night and nobody would have known."

I didn't say anything. I watched Charles eat, and then I soothed him until he slept. The woman beside me slept and I watched the light change through the crack under the door.

I hadn't been thinking when I took Charles. I needed to go home, to Big Jim. When we took our freedom, we would search for our own children, our own past. But I knew, from the sounds all around me, that people had already scattered all over the countryside, and Big Jim was probably running, just like me.

We had said our goodbyes, just like we had done with our children. And even though I wasn't ever going to stop looking for them, I doubted I would ever find them.

My arms were growing tired from holding Charles. I wrapped him in his blanket and put him in a nest of straw. Then I went to the door and peeked out. Smoke rose over the trees like a threatening cloud.

When she gets here, all them white folks are going to learn the Truth.

What truth? I wondered. That we hated them for hold-ing us in place? That we hated the way they ripped up our lives and treated us like cattle? That we were human too? That was truth? That was something white folks had never been able to see? It seemed so simple. They had to have been blind to miss it.

Cries and yells echoed around me, and my body ached to join them. Smash a wall with an axe, destroy a man for taking a child. An eye for an eye.

A baby for a baby.

I looked back at Charles, sleeping peacefully. Within my reach, I had the best revenge of all.

I didn't take it. At least, not in the obvious way.

After the fires, we followed the old Underground Rail-road line and eventually ended up west, where the land goes on for miles and people are as scarce as coyotes. The trip wasn't easy, but it wasn't as rough as it could've been either. Charles and I survived.

Which was more than Big Jim did. I went back to my old home the morning after Sojourner appeared, and found his grave outside the house where I had been born. They'd buried him two weeks after I'd left. Master Tom had killed him for some infraction no one remembered. The Great House was torched, and the Master's family dead, just like the Wildersons, who had been too stupid to listen to me. I left with Sam and Darcy and the rest from the Wilderson house, and they were the ones who got me and Charles safe.

Now we live in a house with five rooms in a commu-nity made up of our people. I wasn't the only one who grabbed a white child, and by an unspoken pact, we never told them a word about their origins. Charles believes I'm his real mama and Sam his real papa. And he thinks that skin color changes like eye color. Some babies are born dark and others born light. I'm not going to tell him oth-erwise. I don't ever want him to see me as anything less than I am, nor do I want our roles to get reversed, and for him to become the slave to my master.

I've started to teach him to read. He's learning faster than Sam, but he's younger. And Sam asks too many questions.

We never learned what happened to Sojourner. We just know that most of the eastern and southern sides of the country disappeared in flames. All people may be equal in God's eyes, but every once in a while only wrath will make us equal on earth.

And I still dream about that moment in the barn, when I looked at Charles and saw only his white skin. Not his baby fat, not his beloved blue eyes, not the little hands that trusted me. Only a white boy who would grow into a white man, and white men had hurt me and left me to die. When I took him in my arms, the anger filled me—

And then I remembered why I ran into that house for him. Why I had risked a freedom I had always desired for one baby boy.

I had lied to Missus Wilderson.

He was a substitute, yes, for the children I would never ever see.

But that never stopped me from loving him.

AWARD-WINNING SF
FROM MIKE RESNICK

☐	51955-8	ALTERNATE KENNEDYS *Edited by Mike Resnick*	$4.99 Canada $5.99
☐	51192-1	ALTERNATE PRESIDENTS *Edited by Mike Resnick*	$4.99 Canada $5.99
☐	52346-6	ALTERNATE WARRIORS *Edited by Mike Resnick*	$4.99 Canada $5.99
☐	51246-4	BWANA/BULLY	$3.99 Canada $4.99
☐	55116-8	THE DARK LADY: A ROMANCE OF THE FAR FUTURE	$3.50 Canada $4.50
☐	50042-3	IVORY: A LEGEND OF PAST AND FUTURE	$4.95 Canada $5.95
☐	52257-6	SANTIAGO: A MYTH OF THE FAR FUTURE	$4.99 Canada $5.99
☐	51113-1	SECOND CONTACT	$3.95 Canada $4.95
☐	50985-4	STALKING THE UNICORN: A FABLE OF TONIGHT	$3.95 Canada $4.95

Buy them at your local bookstore or use this handy coupon:
Clip and mail this page with your order.

Publishers Book and Audio Mailing Service
P.O. Box 120159, Staten Island, NY 10312-0004

Please send me the book(s) I have checked above. I am enclosing $ _____
(Please add $1.25 for the first book, and $.25 for each additional book to cover postage and handling.
Send check or money order only—no CODs.)

Name _____
Address _____
City _____ State/Zip _____
Please allow six weeks for delivery. Prices subject to change without notice.